Mysterious Mr. Sabin

E. Phillips Oppenheim

Alpha Editions

This edition published in 2024

ISBN : 9789361473166

Design and Setting By
Alpha Editions
www.alphaedis.com
Email - info@alphaedis.com

Contents

CHAPTER I

A SUPPER PARTY AT THE "MILAN."

"To all such meetings as these!" cried Densham, lifting his champagne glass from under the soft halo of the rose-shaded electric lights. "Let us drink to them, Wolfenden—Mr. Felix!"

"To all such meetings!" echoed his *vis-à-vis*, also fingering the delicate stem of his glass. "An excellent toast!"

"To all such meetings as these!" murmured the third man, who made up the little party. "A capital toast indeed!"

They sat at a little round table in the brilliantly-lit supper-room of one of London's most fashionable restaurants. Around them were the usual throng of well dressed men, of women with bare shoulders and flashing diamonds, of dark-visaged waiters, deft, silent, swift-footed. The pleasant hum of conversation, louder and more unrestrained as the hour grew towards midnight, was varied by the popping of corks and many little trills of feminine laughter. Of discordant sounds there were none. The waiters' feet fell noiselessly upon the thick carpet, the clatter of plates was a thing unheard of. From the balcony outside came the low, sweet music of a German orchestra played by master hands.

As usual the place was filled. Several late-comers, who had neglected to order their table beforehand, had already, after a disconsolate tour of the room, been led to one of the smaller apartments, or had driven off again to where the lights from the larger but less smart Altoné flashed out upon the smooth, dark waters of the Thames. Only one table was as yet unoccupied, and that was within a yard or two of the three young men who were celebrating a chance meeting in Pall Mall so pleasantly. It was laid for two only, and a magnificent bunch of white roses had, a few minutes before, been brought in and laid in front of one of the places by the director of the rooms himself. A man's small visiting-card was leaning against a wineglass. The table was evidently reserved by some one of importance, for several late-comers had pointed to it, only to be met by a decided shake of the head on the part of the waiter to whom they had appealed. As time went on, this empty table became the object of some speculation to the three young men.

"Our neighbours," remarked Wolfenden, "are running it pretty fine. Can you see whose name is upon the card, Densham?"

The man addressed raised an eyeglass to his left eye and leaned forward. Then he shook his head, he was a little too far away.

"No! It is a short name. Seems to begin with S. Probably a son of Israel!"

"His taste in flowers is at any rate irreproachable," Wolfenden remarked. "I wish they would come. I am in a genial mood, and I do not like to think of any one having to hurry over such an excellent supper."

"The lady," Densham suggested, "is probably theatrical, and has to dress after the show. Half-past twelve is a barbarous hour to turn us out. I wonder——"

"Sh-sh!"

The slight exclamation and a meaning frown from Wolfenden checked his speech. He broke off in the middle of his sentence, and looked round. There was the soft swish of silk passing his chair, and the faint suggestion of a delicate and perfectly strange perfume. At last the table was being taken possession of. A girl, in a wonderful white dress, was standing there, leaning over to admire the great bunch of creamy-white blossoms, whilst a waiter respectfully held a chair for her. A few steps behind came her companion, an elderly man who walked with a slight limp, leaning heavily upon a stick. She turned to him and made some remark in French, pointing to the flowers. He smiled, and passing her, stood for a moment leaning slightly upon the back of his chair, waiting, with a courtesy which was obviously instinctive, until she should have seated herself. During the few seconds which elapsed before they were settled in their places he glanced around the room with a smile, slightly cynical, but still good-natured, parting his thin, well-shaped lips. Wolfenden and Densham, who were looking at him with frank curiosity, he glanced at carelessly. The third young man of the party, Felix, was bending low over his plate, and his face was hidden.

The buzz of conversation in their immediate vicinity had been temporarily suspended. Every one who had seen them enter had been interested in these late-comers, and many curious eyes had followed them to their seats. Briefly, the girl was beautiful and the man distinguished. When they had taken their places, however, the hum of conversation recommenced. Densham and Wolfenden leaned over to one another, and their questions were almost simultaneous.

"Who are they?"

"Who is she?"

Alas! neither of them knew; neither of them had the least idea. Felix, Wolfenden's guest, it seemed useless to ask. He had only just arrived in England, and he was a complete stranger to London. Besides, he did not seem to be interested. He was proceeding calmly with his supper, with his back directly turned upon the new-comers. Beyond one rapid, upward glance at their entrance he seemed almost to have avoided looking at them. Wolfenden thought of this afterwards.

"I see Harcutt in the corner," he said. "He will know who they are for certain. I shall go and ask him."

He crossed the room and chatted for a few minutes with a noisy little party in an adjacent recess. Presently he put his question. Alas! not one of them knew! Harcutt, a journalist of some note and a man who prided himself upon knowing absolutely everybody, was as helpless as the rest. To his humiliation he was obliged to confess it.

"I never saw either of them before in my life," he said. "I cannot imagine who they can be. They are certainly foreigners."

"Very likely," Wolfenden agreed quietly. "In fact, I never doubted it. An English girl of that age—she is very young by the bye—would never be so perfectly turned out."

"What a very horrid thing to say, Lord Wolfenden," exclaimed the woman on whose chair his hand was resting. "Don't you know that dressing is altogether a matter of one's maid? You may rely upon it that that girl has found a treasure!"

"Well, I don't know," Wolfenden said, smiling. "Young English girls always seem to me to look so dishevelled in evening dress. Now this girl is dressed with the art of a Frenchwoman of mature years, and yet with the simplicity of a child."

The woman laid down her lorgnettes and shrugged her shoulders.

"I agree with you," she said, "that she is probably not English. If she were she would not wear such diamonds at her age."

"By the bye," Harcutt remarked with sudden cheerfulness, "we shall be able to find out who the man is when we leave. The table was reserved, so the name will be on the list at the door."

His friends rose to leave and Harcutt, making his adieux, crossed the room with Wolfenden.

"We may as well have our coffee together," he said. "I ordered Turkish and I've been waiting for it ten minutes. We got here early. Hullo! where's your other guest?"

Densham was sitting alone. Wolfenden looked at him inquiringly.

"Your friend Felix has gone," he announced. "Suddenly remembered an engagement with his chief, and begged you to excuse him. Said he'd look you up to-morrow."

"Well, he's an odd fellow," Wolfenden remarked, motioning Harcutt to the vacant place. "His looks certainly belie his name."

"He's not exactly a cheerful companion for a supper party," Densham admitted, "but I like his face. How did you come across him, Wolfenden, and where does he hail from?"

"He's a junior attaché at the Russian Embassy," Wolfenden said, stirring his coffee. "Only just been appointed. Charlie Meynell gave him a line of introduction to me; said he was a decent sort, but mopish! I looked him up last week, met him in Pall Mall just as you came along, and asked you both to supper. What liqueurs, Harcutt?"

The conversation drifted into ordinary channels and flowed on steadily. At the same time it was maintained with a certain amount of difficulty. The advent of these two people at the next table had produced an extraordinary effect upon the three men. Harcutt was perhaps the least affected. He was a young man of fortune and natural gifts, who had embraced journalism as a career, and was really in love with his profession. Partly on account of his social position, which was unquestioned, and partly because his tastes tended in that direction, he had become the recognised scribe and chronicle of smart society. His pen was easy and fluent. He was an inimitable maker of short paragraphs. He prided himself upon knowing everybody and all about them. He could have told how much a year Densham, a rising young portrait painter, was making from his profession, and exactly what Wolfenden's allowance from his father was. A strange face was an annoyance to him; too, a humiliation. He had been piqued that he could not answer the eager questions of his own party as to these two people, and subsequently Wolfenden's inquiries. The thought that very soon at any rate their name would be known to him was, in a sense, a consolation. The rest would be easy. Until he knew all about them he meant to conceal so far as possible his own interest.

CHAPTER II

A DRAMA OF THE PAVEMENT

The pitch of conversation had risen higher, still mingled with the intermittent popping of corks and the striking of matches. Blue wreaths of cigarette smoke were curling upwards—a delicate feeling of "abandon" was making itself felt amongst the roomful of people. The music grew softer as the babel of talk grew in volume. The whole environment became tinged with a faint but genial voluptuousness. Densham was laughing over the foibles of some mutual acquaintance; Wolfenden leaned back in his chair, smoking a cigarette and sipping his Turkish coffee. His eyes scarcely left for a moment the girl who sat only a few yards away from him, trifling with a certain dainty indifference with the little dishes, which one after the other had been placed before her and removed. He had taken pains to withdraw himself from the discussion in which his friends were interested. He wanted to be quite free to watch her. To him she was certainly the most wonderful creature he had ever seen. In every one of her most trifling actions she seemed possessed of an original and curious grace, even the way she held her silver fork, toyed with her serviette, raised her glass to her lips and set it down again—all these little things she seemed to him to accomplish with a peculiar and wonderful daintiness. Of conversation between her companion and herself there was evidently very little, nor did she appear to expect it. He was enjoying his supper with the moderation and minute care for trifles which denote the epicure, and he only spoke to her between the courses. She, on the other hand, appeared to be eating scarcely anything. At last, however, the waiter set before her a dish in which she was evidently interested. Wolfenden recognised the pink frilled paper and smiled. She was human enough then to care for ices. She bent over it and shrugged her shoulders—turning to the waiter who was hovering near, she asked a question. He bowed and removed the plate. In a moment or two he reappeared with another. This time the paper and its contents were brown. She smiled as she helped herself—such a smile that Wolfenden wondered that the waiter did not lose his head, and hand her pepper and salt instead of gravely filling her glass. She took up her spoon and deliberately tasted the contents of her plate. Then she looked across the table, and spoke the first words in English which he had heard from her lips—

"Coffee ice. So much nicer than strawberry!"

The man nodded back.

"Ices after supper are an abomination," he said. "They spoil the flavour of your wine, and many other things. But after all, I suppose it is waste of time to tell you so! A woman never understands how to eat until she is fifty."

She laughed, and deliberately finished the ice. Just as she laid down the spoon, she raised her eyes quietly and encountered Wolfenden's. He looked away at once with an indifference which he felt to be badly assumed. Did she know, he wondered, that he had been watching her like an owl all the time? He felt hot and uncomfortable—a veritable schoolboy at the thought. He plunged into the conversation between Harcutt and Densham—a conversation which they had been sustaining with an effort. They too were still as interested in their neighbours, although their positions at the table made it difficult for either to observe them closely.

When three men are each thinking intently of something else, it is not easy to maintain an intelligent discussion. Wolfenden, to create a diversion, called for the bill. When he had paid it, and they were ready to depart, Densham looked up with a little burst of candour—

"She's wonderful!" he exclaimed softly.

"Marvellous!" Wolfenden echoed.

"I wonder who on earth they can possibly be," Harcutt said almost peevishly. Already he was being robbed of some part of his contemplated satisfaction. It was true that he would probably find the man's name on the table-list at the door, but he had a sort of presentiment that the girl's personality would elude him. The question of relationship between the man and the girl puzzled him. He propounded the problem and they discussed it with bated breath. There was no likeness at all! Was there any relationship? It was significant that although Harcutt was a scandalmonger and Wolfenden somewhat of a cynic, they discussed it with the most profound respect. Relationship after all of some sort there must be. What was it? It was Harcutt who alone suggested what to Wolfenden seemed an abominable possibility.

"Scarcely husband and wife, I should think," he said thoughtfully, "yet one never can tell!"

Involuntarily they all three glanced towards the man. He was well preserved and his little imperial and short grey moustache were trimmed with military precision, yet his hair was almost white, and his age could scarcely be less than sixty. In his way he was quite as interesting as the girl. His eyes, underneath his thick brows, were dark and clear, and his features were strong and delicately shaped. His hands were white and very shapely, the fingers were rather long, and he wore two singularly handsome rings, both set with strange stones. By the side of the table rested the stick upon which he had been leaning during his passage through the room. It was of smooth, dark wood polished like a malacca cane, and set at the top with a curious, green, opalescent stone, as large as a sparrow's egg. The eyes of the three men had each in turn been arrested by it. In the electric light which fell softly upon the upper part of it, the stone seemed to burn and glow with a peculiar, iridescent radiance. Evidently it was a precious possession, for once when a waiter had offered to remove it to a stand at the other end of the room, the man had stopped him sharply and drawn it a little closer towards him.

Wolfenden lit a fresh cigarette, and gazed thoughtfully into the little cloud of blue smoke.

"Husband and wife," he repeated slowly. "What an absurd idea! More likely father and daughter!"

"How about the roses?" Harcutt remarked. "A father does not as a rule show such excellent taste in flowers!"

They had finished supper. Suddenly the girl stretched out her left hand and took a glove from the table. Wolfenden smiled triumphantly.

"She has no wedding-ring," he exclaimed softly.

Then Harcutt, for the first time, made a remark for which he was never altogether forgiven—a remark which both the other men received in chilling silence.

"That may or may not be a matter for congratulation," he said, twirling his moustache. "One never knows!"

Wolfenden stood up, turning his back upon Harcutt and pointedly ignoring him.

"Let us go, Densham," he said. "We are almost the last."

As a matter of fact his movement was made at exactly the right time. They could scarcely have left the room at the same moment as these two people, in whom manifestly they had been taking so great an interest. But by the time they had sent for their coats and hats from the cloak-room, and Harcutt had coolly scrutinised the table-list, they found themselves all together in a little group at the head of the stairs.

Wolfenden, who was a few steps in front, drew back to allow them to pass. The man, leaning upon his stick, laid his hand upon the girl's sleeve. Then he looked up at the man, and addressed Wolfenden directly.

"You had better precede us, sir," he said; "my progress is unfortunately somewhat slow."

Wolfenden drew back courteously.

"We are in no hurry," he said. "Please go on."

The man thanked him, and with one hand upon the girl's shoulder and with the other on his stick commenced to descend. The girl had passed on without even glancing towards them. She had twisted a white lace mantilla around her head, and her features were scarcely visible—only as she passed, Wolfenden received a general impression of rustling white silk and lace and foaming tulle as she gathered her skirts together at the head of the stairs. It seemed to him, too, that the somewhat close atmosphere of the vestibule had become faintly sweet with the delicate fragrance of the white roses which hung by a loop of satin from her wrist.

The three men waited until they had reached the bend of the stairs before they began to descend. Harcutt then leaned forward.

"His name," he whispered, "is disenchanting. It is Mr. Sabin! Whoever heard of a Mr. Sabin? Yet he looks like a personage!"

At the doors there was some delay. It was raining fast and the departures were a little congested. The three young men still kept in the background. Densham affected to be busy lighting a cigarette, Wolfenden was slowly drawing on his gloves. His place was almost in a line with the girl's. He could see the diamonds flashing in her fair hair through the dainty tracery of the drooping white lace, and in a moment, through some slight change in her position, he could get a better view of her face than he had been able to obtain even in the supper-room. She was beautiful! There was no doubt about that! But there were many beautiful women in London, whom Wolfenden scarcely pretended to admire. This girl had something better even than supreme beauty. She was anything but a reproduction. She was a new type. She had originality. Her hair was dazzlingly fair; her eyebrows, delicately arched, were high and distinctly dark in colour. Her head was perfectly shaped—the features seemed to combine a delightful piquancy with a somewhat statuesque regularity. Wolfenden, wondering of what she in some manner reminded him, suddenly thought of some old French miniatures, which he had stopped to admire only a day or two before, in a little curio shop near Bond Street. There was a distinct dash of something foreign in her features and carriage. It might have been French, or Austrian—it was most certainly not Anglo-Saxon!

The crush became a little less, they all moved a step or two forward—and Wolfenden, glancing carelessly outside, found his attention immediately arrested. Just as he had been watching the girl, so was a man, who stood on the pavement side by side with the commissionaire, watching her companion. He was tall and thin; apparently dressed in evening clothes, for though his coat was buttoned up to his chin, he wore an opera hat. His hands were thrust into the loose pockets of his overcoat, and his face was mostly in the shadows. Once, however, he followed some motion of Mr. Sabin's and moved his head a little forward. Wolfenden started and looked at him fixedly. Was it fancy, or was there indeed something clenched in his right hand there, which gleamed like silver—or was it steel—in the momentary flash of a passing carriage-light? Wolfenden was puzzled. There was something, too, which seemed to him vaguely familiar in the man's figure and person. He was certainly waiting for somebody, and to judge from his expression his mission was no pleasant one. Wolfenden who, through the latter part of the evening, had felt a curious and unwonted sense of excitement stirring his blood, now felt it go tingling through all his veins. He had some subtle prescience that he was on the brink of an adventure. He glanced hurriedly at his two companions; neither of them had noticed this fresh development.

Just then the commissionaire, who knew Wolfenden by sight, turned round and saw him standing there. Stepping back on to the pavement, he called up the brougham, which was waiting a little way down the street.

"Your carriage, my lord," he said to Wolfenden, touching his cap.

Wolfenden, with ready presence of mind, shook his head.

"I am waiting for a friend," he said. "Tell my man to pass on a yard or two."

The man bowed, and the danger of leaving before these two people, in whom his interest now was becoming positively feverish, was averted. As if to enhance it, a singular thing now happened. The interest suddenly became reciprocal. At the sound of Wolfenden's voice the man with the club foot had distinctly started. He changed his position and, leaning forward, looked eagerly at him. His eyes remained for a moment or two fixed steadily upon him. There was no doubt about the fact, singular in itself though it was. Wolfenden noticed it himself, so did both Densham and Harcutt. But before any remark could pass between them a little *coupé* brougham had drawn up, and the man and the girl started forward.

Wolfenden followed close behind. The feeling which prompted him to do so was a curious one, but it seemed to him afterwards that he had even at that time a conviction that something unusual was about to happen. The girl stepped lightly across the carpeted way and entered the carriage. Her companion paused in the doorway to hand some silver to the commissionaire, then he too, leaning upon his stick, stepped across the pavement. His foot was already upon the carriage step, when suddenly what Wolfenden had been vaguely anticipating happened. A dark figure sprang from out of the shadows and seized him by the throat; something that glittered like a streak of silver in the electric light flashed upwards. The blow would certainly have fallen but for Wolfenden. He was the only person not wholly unprepared for something of the sort, and he was consequently not paralysed into inaction as were the others. He was so near, too, that a single step forward enabled him to seize the uplifted arm in a grasp of iron. The man who had been attacked was the next to recover himself. Raising his stick he struck at his assailant violently. The blow missed his head, but grazed his temple and fell upon his shoulder. The man, released from Wolfenden's grasp by his convulsive start, went staggering back into the roadway.

There was a rush then to secure him, but it was too late. Wolfenden, half expecting another attack, had not moved from the carriage door, and the commissionaire, although a powerful man, was not swift. Like a cat the man who had made the attack sprang across the roadway, and into the gardens which fringed the Embankment. The commissionaire and a loiterer followed him. Just then Wolfenden felt a soft touch on his shoulder. The girl had opened the carriage door, and was standing at his side.

"Is any one hurt?" she asked quickly.

"No one," he answered. "It is all over. The man has run away."

Mr. Sabin stooped down and brushed away some grey ash from the front of his coat. Then he took a match-box from his ticket-pocket, and re-lit the cigarette which had been crumpled in his fingers. His hand was perfectly steady. The whole affair had scarcely taken thirty seconds.

"It was probably some lunatic," he remarked, motioning to the girl to resume her place in the carriage. "I am exceedingly obliged to you, sir. Lord Wolfenden, I believe?" he added, raising his hat. "But for your intervention the matter might really have been serious. Permit me to offer you my card. I trust that some day I may have a better opportunity of expressing my thanks. At present you will excuse me if I hurry. I am not of your nation, but I share an antipathy with them—I hate a row!"

He stepped into the carriage with a farewell bow, and it drove off at once. Wolfenden remained looking after it, with his hat in his hand. From the Embankment below came the faint sound of hurrying footsteps.

CHAPTER III

THE WARNING OF FELIX

The three friends stood upon the pavement watching the little brougham until it disappeared round the corner in a flickering glitter of light. It would have been in accordance with precedent if after leaving the restaurant they had gone to some one of their clubs to smoke a cigar and drink whisky and apollinaris, while Harcutt retailed the latest society gossip, and Densham descanted on art, and Wolfenden contributed genial remarks upon things in general. But to-night all three were inclined to depart from precedent. Perhaps the surprising incident which they had just witnessed made anything like normal routine seem unattractive; whatever the reason may have been, the young men were of a sudden not in sympathy with one another. Harcutt murmured some conventional lie about having an engagement, supplemented it with some quite unconvincing statement about pressure of work, and concluded with an obviously disingenuous protest against the tyranny of the profession of journalism, then he sprang with alacrity into a hansom and said goodbye with a good deal less than his usual cordiality. Densham, too, hailed a cab, and leaning over the apron delivered himself of a farewell speech which sounded rather malignant. "You are a lucky beast, Wolfenden," he growled enviously, adding, with a note of venom in his voice, "but don't forget it takes more than the first game to win the rubber," and then he was whirled away, nodding his head and wearing an expression of wisdom deeply tinged with gloom.

Wolfenden was surprised, but not exactly sorry that the first vague expression of hostility had been made by the others.

"Both of them must be confoundedly hard hit," he murmured to himself; "I never knew Densham turn nasty before." And to his coachman he said aloud, "You may go home, Dawson. I am going to walk."

He turned on to the embankment, conscious of a curious sense of exhilaration. He was no *blasé* cynic; but the uniformly easy life tends to become just a trifle monotonous, and Lord Wolfenden's somewhat epicurean mind derived actual pleasure from the subtle luxury of a new sensation. What he had said of his friends he could have said with equal truth of himself: he was confoundedly hard hit. For the first time in his life he found the mere memory of a woman thrilling; his whole nature vibrated in response to the appeal she made to him, and he walked along buoyantly under the stars, revelling in the delight of being alive.

Suddenly he stopped abruptly. Huddled up in the corner of a seat was a man with a cloth cap pulled forward screening his face: at that moment Lord

Wolfenden was in a mood to be extravagantly generous to any poor applicant for alms, lavishly sympathetic to any tale of distress. But it was not ordinary curiosity that arrested his progress now. He knew almost at the first glance who it was that sat in this dejected attitude, although the opera hat was replaced by the soft cloth cap, and in other details the man's appearance was altered. It was indeed the Mr. Felix who had supped with him at the "Milan" and subsequently behaved in so astonishing a fashion.

He knew that he was recognised, and sat up, looking steadfastly at Wolfenden, although his lips trembled and his eyes gleamed wildly. Across his temples a bright red mark was scored.

Lord Wolfenden broke the silence.

"You're a nice sort of fellow to ask out to supper! What in the name of all that's wonderful were you trying to do?"

"I should have thought it was sufficiently obvious," the man replied bitterly. "I tried to kill him, and I failed. Well, why don't you call the police? I am quite ready. I shall not run again."

Wolfenden hesitated, and then sat down by the side of this surprising individual.

"The man you went for didn't seem to care, so I don't see why I should. But why do you want to kill him?"

"To keep a vow," the other answered; "how and why made I will not tell you."

"How did you escape?" Wolfenden asked abruptly.

"Probably because I didn't care whether I escaped or not," Felix replied, with a short, bitter laugh. "I stood behind some shrubs just inside the garden, and watched the hunt go by. Then I came out here and sat down."

"It all sounds very simple," said Wolfenden, a trifle sarcastically. "May I ask what you are going to do next?"

Felix's face so clearly intimated that he might not ask anything of the kind, or that if he did his curiosity would not be satisfied, that Wolfenden felt compelled to make some apology.

"Forgive me if I seem inquisitive, but I find the situation a little unusual. You were my guest, you see, and had it not been for my chance invitation you might not have met that man at all. Then again, had it not been for my interference he would have been dead now and you would have been in a fair way to be hanged."

Felix evinced no sign of gratitude for Wolfenden's intervention. Instead he said intensely,

"Oh, you fool! you fool!"

"Well, really," Wolfenden protested, "I don't see why——" But Felix interrupted him.

"Yes, you are a fool," he repeated, "because you saved his life. He is an old man now. I wonder how many there have been in the course of his long life who desired to kill him? But no one—not one solitary human being—has ever befriended him or come to his rescue in time of danger without living to be sorry for it. And so it will be with you. You will live to be sorry for what you have done to-night; you will live to think it would have been far better for him to fall by my hand than for yourself to suffer at his. And you will wish passionately that you had let him die. Before heaven, Wolfenden, I swear that that is true."

The man was so much in earnest, his passion was so quietly intense, that Wolfenden against his will was more than half convinced. He was silent. He suddenly felt cold, and the buoyant elation of mind in which he had started homewards vanished, leaving him anxious and heavy, perhaps just a little afraid.

"I did what any man would do for any one else," he said, almost apologetically. "It was instinctive. As a matter of fact, that particular man is a perfect stranger to me. I have never seen him before and it is quite possible that I shall never see him again."

Felix turned quickly towards him.

"If you believe in prayer," he said, "go down on your knees where you are and pray as you have never prayed for anything before that you may not see him again. There has never been a man or a woman yet who has not been the worse for knowing him. He is like the pestilence that walketh in the darkness, poisoning every one that is in the way of his horrible infection."

Wolfenden pulled himself together. There was no doubt about his companion's earnestness, but it was the earnestness of an unbalanced mind. Language so exaggerated as his was out of keeping with the times and the place.

"Tell me some more about him," he suggested. "Who is he?"

"I won't tell you," Felix answered, obstinately.

"Well, then, who is the lady?"

"I don't know. It is quite enough for me to know that she is his companion for the moment."

"You do not intend to be communicative, I can see," said Wolfenden, after a brief pause, "but I wish I could persuade you to tell me why you attempted his life to-night."

"There was the opportunity," said Felix, as if that in itself were sufficient explanation. Then he smiled enigmatically. "There are at least three distinct and separate reasons why I should take his life,—all of them good. Three, I mean, why I should do it. But I have not been his only victim. There are plenty of others who have a heavy reckoning against him, and he knows what it is to carry his life in his hand. But he bears a charmed existence. Did you see his stick?"

"Yes," said Wolfenden, "I did. It had a peculiar stone in the handle; in the electric light it looked like a huge green opal."

Felix assented moodily.

"That is it. He struck me with a stick. He would not part with it for anything. It was given him by some Indian fakir, and it is said that while he carries it he is proof against attack."

"Who says so?" Wolfenden inquired.

"Never mind," said Felix. "It's enough that it is said." He relapsed into silence, and when he next spoke his manner was different. His excited vehemence had gone and there was nothing in his voice or demeanour inconsistent with normal sanity. Yet his words were no less charged with deep intention. "I do not know much about you, Lord Wolfenden," he said; "but I beg you to take the advice I am offering you. No one ever gave you better in your life. Avoid that man as you would avoid the plague. Go away before he looks you up to thank you for what you did. Go abroad, anywhere; the farther the better; and stay away for ever, if that is the only means of escaping his friendship or even his acquaintance."

Lord Wolfenden shook his head.

"I'm a very ordinary, matter of fact Englishman," he said, "leading a very ordinary, matter of fact life, and you must forgive me if I consider such a sweeping condemnation a little extravagant and fantastic. I have no particular enemies on my conscience, I am implicated in no conspiracy, and I am, in short, an individual of very little importance. Consequently I have nothing to fear from anybody and am afraid of nobody. This man cannot have anything to gain by injuring me. I believe you said you did not know the lady?"

"The lady?" Felix repeated. "No, I do not know her, nor anything of her beyond the fact that she is with him for the time being. That is quite sufficient for me."

Wolfenden got up.

"Thanks," he said lazily. "I only asked you for facts. As for your suggestion— you will be well advised not to repeat it."

"Oh!" exclaimed Felix, scornfully, "how blind and pig-headed you English people are! I have told you something of the man's reputation. What can hers be, do you suppose, if she will sup alone with him in a public restaurant?"

"Good-night," said Wolfenden. "I will not listen to another word."

Felix rose to his feet and laid his hand upon Lord Wolfenden's arm.

"Lord Wolfenden," he said, "you are a very decent fellow: do try to believe that I am only speaking for your good. That girl——"

Wolfenden shook him off.

"If you allude to that young lady, either directly or indirectly," he said very calmly, "I shall throw you into the river."

Felix shrugged his shoulders.

"At least remember that I warned you," was all he ventured to say as Lord Wolfenden strode away.

Leaving the embankment Wolfenden walked quickly to Half Moon Street, where his chambers were. His servant let him in and took his coat. There was an anxious expression upon his usually passive face and he appeared to be rather at a loss for words in which to communicate his news. At last he got it out, accompanying the question with a nervous and deprecating cough.

"I beg your pardon, my lord, but were you expecting a young lady?"

"A what, Selby?" Wolfenden exclaimed, looking at him in amazement.

"A lady, my lord: a young lady."

"Of course not," said Wolfenden, with a frown. "What on earth do you mean?"

Selby gathered courage.

"A young lady called here about an hour ago, and asked for you. Johnson informed her that you might be home shortly, and she said she would wait.

Johnson, perhaps imprudently, admitted her, and she is in the study, my lord."

"A young lady in my study at this time of night!" Wolfenden exclaimed, incredulously. "Who is she, and what is she, and why has she come at all? Have you gone mad, Selby?"

"Then you were not expecting her?" the man said, anxiously. "She gave no name, but she assured Johnson that you did."

"You are a couple of idiots," Wolfenden said angrily. "Of course I wasn't expecting her. Surely both you and Johnson have been in my service long enough to know me better than that."

"I am exceedingly sorry, my lord," the man said abjectly. "But the young lady's appearance misled us both. If you will allow me to say so, my lord, I am quite sure that she is a lady. No doubt there is some mistake; but when you see her I think you will exonerate Johnson and me from——"

His master cut his protestations short.

"Wait where you are until I ring," he said. "It never entered my head that you could be such an incredible idiot."

He strode into the study, closing the door behind him, and Selby obediently waited for the bell. But a long time passed before the summons came.

CHAPTER IV

AT THE RUSSIAN AMBASSADOR'S

The brougham containing the man who had figured in the "Milan" table list as Mr. Sabin, and his companion, turned into the Strand and proceeded westwards. Close behind it came Harcutt's private cab—only a few yards away followed Densham's hansom. The procession continued in the same order, skirting Trafalgar Square and along Pall Mall.

Each in a different manner, the three men were perhaps equally interested in these people. Geoffrey Densham was attracted as an artist by the extreme and rare beauty of the girl. Wolfenden's interest was at once more sentimental and more personal. Harcutt's arose partly out of curiosity, partly from innate love of adventure. Both Densham and Harcutt were exceedingly interested as to their probable destination. From it they would be able to gather some idea as to the status and social position of Mr. Sabin and his companion. Both were perhaps a little surprised when the brougham, which had been making its way into the heart of fashionable London, turned into Belgrave Square and pulled up before a great, porticoed house, brilliantly lit, and with a crimson drugget and covered way stretched out across the pavement. Harcutt sprang out first, just in time to see the two pass through the opened doorway, the man leaning heavily upon his stick, the girl, with her daintily gloved fingers just resting upon his coat-sleeve, walking with that uncommon and graceful self-possession which had so attracted Densham during her passage through the supper-room at the "Milan" a short while ago.

Harcutt looked after them, watching them disappear with a frown upon his forehead.

"Rather a sell, isn't it?" said a quiet voice in his ear.

He turned abruptly round. Densham was standing upon the pavement by his side.

"Great Scott!" he exclaimed testily. "What are you doing here?"

Densham threw away his cigarette and laughed.

"I might return the question, I suppose," he remarked. "We both followed the young lady and her imaginary papa! We were both anxious to find out where they lived—and we are both sold!"

"Very badly sold," Harcutt admitted. "What do you propose to do now? We can't wait outside here for an hour or two!"

Densham hesitated.

"No, we can't do that," he said. "Have you any plan?"

Harcutt shook his head.

"Can't say that I have."

They were both silent for a moment. Densham was smiling softly to himself. Watching him, Harcutt became quite assured that he had decided what to do.

"Let us consider the matter together," he suggested, diplomatically. "We ought to be able to hit upon something."

Densham shook his head doubtfully.

"No," he said; "I don't think that we can run this thing in double harness. You see our interests are materially opposed."

Harcutt did not see it in the same light.

"Pooh! We can travel together by the same road," he protested. "The time to part company has not come yet. Wolfenden has got a bit ahead of us to-night. After all, though, you and I may pull level, if we help one another. You have a plan, I can see! What is it?"

Densham was silent for a moment.

"You know whose house this is?" he asked.

Harcutt nodded.

"Of course! It's the Russian Ambassador's!"

Densham drew a square card from his pocket, and held it out under the gas-light. From it, it appeared that the Princess Lobenski desired the honour of his company at any time that evening between twelve and two.

"A card for to-night, by Jove!" Harcutt exclaimed.

Densham nodded, and replaced it in his pocket.

"You see, Harcutt," he said, "I am bound to take an advantage over you! I only got this card by an accident, and I certainly do not know the Princess well enough to present you. I shall be compelled to leave you here! All that I can promise is, that if I discover anything interesting I will let you know about it to-morrow. Good-night!"

Harcutt watched him disappear through the open doors, and then walked a little way along the pavement, swearing softly to himself. His first idea was to wait about until they came out, and then follow them again. By that means he would at least be sure of their address. He would have gained something for his time and trouble. He lit a cigarette, and walked slowly to the corner of the street. Then he turned back and retraced his steps. As he neared the crimson strip of drugget, one of the servants drew respectfully aside, as though expecting him to enter. The man's action was like an inspiration to him. He glanced down the vista of covered roof. A crowd of people were making their way up the broad staircase, and amongst them Densham. After all, why not? He laughed softly to himself and hesitated no longer. He threw away his cigarette and walked boldly in. He was doing a thing for which he well knew that he deserved to be kicked. At the same time, he had made up his mind to go through with it, and he was not the man to fail through nervousness or want of *savoir faire*.

At the cloak-room the multitude of men inspired him with new confidence. There were some, a very fair sprinkling, whom he knew, and who greeted him indifferently, without appearing in any way to regard his presence as a thing out of the common. He walked up the staircase, one of a little group; but as they passed through the ante-room to where in the distance Prince and Princess Lobenski were standing to receive their guests, Harcutt adroitly disengaged himself—he affected to pause for a moment or two to speak to an acquaintance. When he was left alone, he turned sharp to the right and entered the main dancing-salon.

He was quite safe now, and his spirits began to rise. Yonder was Densham, looking very bored, dancing with a girl in yellow. So far at least he had gained no advantage. He looked everywhere in vain, however, for a man with a club foot and the girl in white and diamonds. They must be in one of the inner rooms. He began to make a little tour.

Two of the ante-chambers he explored without result. In the third, two men were standing near the entrance, talking. Harcutt almost held his breath as he came to an abrupt stop within a yard or two of them. One was the man for whom he had been looking, the other—Harcutt seemed to find his face perfectly familiar, but for the moment he could not identify him. He was tall, with white hair and moustaches. His coat was covered with foreign orders, and he wore English court dress. His hands were clasped behind his back; he was talking in a low, clear tone, stooping a little, and with eyes steadfastly fixed upon his companion. Mr. Sabin was leaning a little forward, with both hands resting upon his stick. Harcutt was struck at once with the singular immobility of his face. He did not appear either interested or amused or acquiescent. He was simply listening. A few words from the other man came to Harcutt's ears, as he lingered there on the other side of the curtain.

"If it were money—a question of monetary recompense—the secret service purse of my country opens easily, and it is well filled. If it were anything less simple, the proposal could but be made. I am taking the thing, you understand, at your own computation of its worth! I am taking it for granted that it carries with it the power you claim for it. Assuming these things, I am prepared to treat with you. I am going on leave very shortly, and I could myself conduct the negotiations."

Harcutt would have moved away, but he was absolutely powerless. Naturally, and from his journalistic instincts, he was one of the most curious of men. He had recognised the speaker. The interview was pregnant with possibilities. Who was this Mr. Sabin, that so great a man should talk with him so earnestly? He was looking up now, he was going to speak. What was he going to say? Harcutt held his breath. The idea of moving away never occurred to him now.

"Yet," Mr. Sabin said slowly, "your country should be a low bidder. The importance of such a thing to you must be less than to France, less than to her great ally. Your relations here are close and friendly. Nature and destiny seemed to have made you allies. As yet there has been no rift—no sign of a rift."

"You are right," the other man answered slowly; "and yet who can tell what lies before us? In less than a dozen years the face of all Europe may be changed. The policy of a great nation is, to all appearance, a steadfast thing. On the face of it, it continues the same, age after age. Yet if a change is to come, it comes from within. It develops slowly. It grows from within, outwards, very slowly, like a secret thing. Do you follow me?"

"I think—perhaps I do," Mr. Sabin admitted deliberately.

The Ambassador's voice dropped almost to a whisper, and but for its singularly penetrating quality Harcutt would have heard no more. As it was, he had almost to hold his breath, and all his nerves quivered with the tension of listening.

"Even the Press is deceived. The inspired organs purposely mislead. Outside to all the world there seems to be nothing brewing; yet, when the storm bursts, one sees that it has been long in gathering—that years of careful study and thought have been given to that hidden triumph of diplomacy. All has been locked in the breasts of a few. The thing is full-fledged when it is hatched upon the world. It has grown strong in darkness. You understand me?"

"Yes; I think that I understand you," Mr. Sabin said, his piercing eyes raised now from the ground and fixed upon the other man's face. "You have given me food for serious thought. I shall do nothing further till I have talked with you again."

Harcutt suddenly and swiftly withdrew. He had stayed as long as he dared. At any moment his presence might have been detected, and he would have been involved in a situation which even the nerve and effrontery acquired during the practice of his profession could not have rendered endurable. He found a seat in an adjoining room, and sat quite still, thinking. His brain was in a whirl. He had almost forgotten the special object of his quest. He felt like a conspirator. The fascination of the unknown was upon him. Their first instinct concerning these people had been a true one. They were indeed no ordinary people. He must follow them up—he must know more about them. Once more he thought over what he had heard. It was mysterious, but it was interesting. It might mean anything. The man with Mr. Sabin he had recognised the moment he spoke. It was Baron von Knigenstein, the German Ambassador. Those were strange words of his. He pondered them over again. The journalistic fever was upon him. He was no longer in love. He had overheard a few words of a discussion of tremendous import. If only he could get the key to it! If only he could follow this thing through, then farewell to society paragraphing and playing at journalism. His reputation would be made for ever!

He rose, and finding his way to the refreshment-room, drank off a glass of champagne. Then he walked back to the main salon. Standing with his back to the wall, and half-hidden by a tall palm tree, was Densham. He was alone. His arms were folded, and he was looking out upon the dancers with a gloomy frown. Harcutt stepped softly up to him.

"Well, how are you getting on, old chap?" he whispered in his ear.

Densham started, and looked at Harcutt in blank surprise.

"Why, how the—excuse me, how on earth did you get in?" he exclaimed.

Harcutt smiled in a mysterious manner.

"Oh! we journalists are trained to overcome small difficulties," he said airily. "It wasn't a very hard task. The *Morning* is a pretty good passport. Getting in was easy enough. Where is—she?"

Densham moved his head in the direction of the broad space at the head of the stairs, where the Ambassador and his wife had received their guests.

"She is under the special wing of the Princess. She is up at that end of the room somewhere with a lot of old frumps."

"Have you asked for an introduction?"

Densham nodded.

"Yes, I asked young Lobenski. It is no good. He does not know who she is; but she does not dance, and is not allowed to make acquaintances. That is what it comes to, anyway. It was not a personal matter at all. Lobenski did not even mention my name to his mother. He simply said a friend. The Princess replied that she was very sorry, but there was some difficulty. The young lady's guardian did not wish her to make acquaintances for the present."

"Her guardian! He's not her father, then?"

"No! It was either her guardian or her uncle! I am not sure which. By Jove! There they go! They're off."

They both hurried to the cloak-room for their coats, and reached the street in time to see the people in whom they were so interested coming down the stairs towards them. In the glare of the electric light, the girl's pale, upraised face shone like a piece of delicate statuary. To Densham, the artist, she was irresistible. He drew Harcutt right back amongst the shadows.

"She is the most beautiful woman I have ever seen in my life," he said deliberately. "Titian never conceived anything more exquisite. She is a woman to paint and to worship!"

"What are you going to do now?" Harcutt asked drily. "You can rave about her in your studio, if you like."

"I am going to find out where she lives, if I have to follow her home on foot! It will be something to know that."

"Two of us," Harcutt protested. "It is too obvious."

"I can't help that," Densham replied. "I do not sleep until I have found out."

Harcutt looked dubious.

"Look here," he said, "we need not both go! I will leave it to you on one condition."

"Well?"

"You must let me know to-morrow what you discover."

Densham hesitated.

"Agreed," he decided. "There they go! Good-night. I will call at your rooms, or send a note, to-morrow."

Densham jumped into his cab and drove away. Harcutt looked after them thoughtfully.

"The girl is very lovely," he said to himself, as he stood on the pavement waiting for his carriage; "but I do not think that she is for you, Densham, or for me! On the whole, I am more interested in the man!"

CHAPTER V

THE DILEMMA OF WOLFENDEN

Wolfenden was evidently absolutely unprepared to see the girl whom he found occupying his own particular easy chair in his study. The light was only a dim one, and as she did not move or turn round at his entrance he did not recognise her until he was standing on the hearthrug by her side. Then he started with a little exclamation.

"Miss Merton! Why, what on earth——"

He stopped in the middle of his question and looked intently at her. Her head was thrown back amongst the cushions of the chair, and she was fast asleep. Her hat was a little crushed and a little curl of fair hair had escaped and was hanging down over her forehead. There were undoubtedly tear stains upon her pretty face. Her plain, black jacket was half undone, and the gloves which she had taken off lay in her lap. Wolfenden's anger subsided at once. No wonder Selby had been perplexed. But Selby's perplexity was nothing to his own.

She woke up suddenly and saw him standing there, traces of his amazement still lingering on his face. She looked at him, half-frightened, half-wistfully. The colour came and went in her cheeks—her eyes grew soft with tears. He felt himself a brute. Surely it was not possible that she could be acting! He spoke to her more kindly than he had intended.

"What on earth has brought you up to town—and here—at this time of night? Is anything wrong at Deringham?"

She sat up in the chair and looked at him with quivering lips.

"N—no, nothing particular; only I have left."

"You have left!"

"Yes; I have been turned away," she added, piteously.

He looked at her blankly.

"Turned away! Why, what for? Do you mean to say that you have left for good?"

She nodded, and commenced to dry her eyes with a little lace handkerchief.

"Yes—your mother—Lady Deringham has been very horrid—as though the silly papers were of any use to me or any one else in the world! I have not copied them. I am not deceitful! It is all an excuse to get rid of me because of—of you."

She looked up at him and suddenly dropped her eyes. Wolfenden began to see some glimmerings of light. He was still, however, bewildered.

"Look here," he said kindly, "why you are here I cannot for the life of me imagine, but you had better just tell me all about it."

She rose up suddenly and caught her gloves from the table.

"I think I will go away," she said. "I was very stupid to come; please forget it and—— Goodbye."

He caught her by the wrist as she passed.

"Nonsense," he exclaimed, "you mustn't go like this."

She looked steadfastly away from him and tried to withdraw her arm.

"You are angry with me for coming," she said. "I am very, very sorry; I will go away. Please don't stop me."

He held her wrist firmly.

"Miss Merton!"

"Miss Merton!" She repeated his words reproachfully, lifting her eyes suddenly to his, that he might see the tears gathering there. Wolfenden began to feel exceedingly uncomfortable.

"Well, Blanche, then," he said slowly. "Is that better?"

She answered nothing, but looked at him again. Her hand remained in his. She suffered him to lead her back to the chair.

"It's all nonsense your going away, you know," he said a little awkwardly. "You can't wonder that I am surprised. Perhaps you don't know that it is a little late—after midnight, in fact. Where should you go to if you ran away like that? Do you know any one in London?"

"I—don't think so," she admitted.

"Well, do be reasonable then. First of all tell me all about it."

She nodded, and began at once, now and then lifting her eyes to his, mostly gazing fixedly at the gloves which she was smoothing carefully out upon her knee.

"I think," she said, "that Lord Deringham is not so well. What he has been writing has become more and more incoherent, and it has been very difficult to copy it at all. I have done my best but he has never seemed satisfied; and he has taken to watch me in an odd sort of way, just as though I was doing something wrong all the time. You know he fancies that the work he is putting together is of immense importance. Of course I don't know that it isn't. All I do know is that it sounds and reads like absolute rubbish, and it's awfully difficult to copy. He writes very quickly and uses all manner of abbreviations, and if I make a single mistake in typing it he gets horribly cross."

Wolfenden laughed softly.

"Poor little girl! Go on."

She smiled too, and continued with less constraint in her tone.

"I didn't really mind that so much, as of course I have been getting a lot of money for the work, and one can't have everything. But just lately he seems to have got the idea that I have been making two copies of this rubbish and keeping one back. He has kept on coming into the room unexpectedly, and has sat for hours watching me in a most unpleasant manner. I have not been allowed to leave the house, and all my letters have been looked over; it has been perfectly horrid."

"I am very sorry," Wolfenden said. "Of course you knew though that it was going to be rather difficult to please my father, didn't you? The doctors differ a little as to his precise mental condition, but we are all aware that he is at any rate a trifle peculiar."

She smiled a little bitterly.

"Oh! I am not complaining," she said. "I should have stood it somehow for the sake of the money; but I haven't told you everything yet. The worst part, so far as I am concerned, is to come."

"I am very sorry," he said; "please go on."

"This morning your father came very early into the study and found a sheet of carbon paper on my desk and two copies of one page of the work I was doing. As a matter of fact I had never used it before, but I wanted to try it for practice. There was no harm in it—I should have destroyed the second sheet in a minute or two, and in any case it was so badly done that it was absolutely worthless. But directly Lord Deringham saw it he went quite white, and I thought he was going to have a fit. I can't tell you all he said. He was brutal. The end of it was that my boxes were all turned out and my desk and everything belonging to me searched as though I were a house-maid suspected of theft, and all the time I was kept locked up. When they had finished, I was told to put my hat on and go. I—I had nowhere to go to, for Muriel—you remember I told you about my sister—went to America last week. I hadn't the least idea what to do—and so—I—you were the only person who had ever been kind to me," she concluded, suddenly leaning over towards him, a little sob in her throat, and her eyes swimming with tears.

There are certain situations in life when an honest man is at an obvious disadvantage. Wolfenden felt awkward and desperately ill at ease. He evaded the embrace which her movement and eyes had palpably invited, and compromised matters by taking her hands and holding them tightly in his. Even then he felt far from comfortable.

"But my mother," he exclaimed. "Lady Deringham surely took your part?"

She shook her head vigorously.

"Lady Deringham did nothing of the sort," she replied. "Do you remember last time when you were down you took me for a walk once or twice and you talked to me in the evenings, and—but perhaps you have forgotten. Have you?"

She was looking at him so eagerly that there was only one answer possible for him. He hastened to make it. There was a certain lack of enthusiasm in his avowal, however, which brought a look of reproach into her face. She sighed and looked away into the fire.

"Well," she continued, "Lady Deringham has never been the same since then to me. It didn't matter while you were there, but after you left it was very wretched. I wrote to you, but you never answered my letter."

He was very well aware of it. He had never asked her to write, and her note had seemed to him a trifle too ingenuous. He had never meant to answer it.

"I so seldom write letters," he said. "I thought, too, that it must have been your fancy. My mother is generally considered a very good-hearted woman."

She laughed bitterly.

"Oh, one does not fancy those things," she said. "Lady Deringham has been coldly civil to me ever since, and nothing more. This morning she seemed absolutely pleased to have an excuse for sending me away. She knows quite well, of course, that Lord Deringham is—not himself; but she took everything he said for gospel, and turned me out of the house. There, now you know everything. Perhaps after all it was idiotic to come to you. Well, I'm only a girl, and girls are idiots; I haven't a friend in the world, and if I were alone I should die of loneliness in a week. You won't send me away? You are not angry with me?"

She made a movement towards him, but he held her hands tightly. For the first time he began to see his way before him. A certain ingenuousness in her speech and in that little half-forgotten note—an ingenuousness, by the bye, of which he had some doubts—was his salvation. He would accept it as absolutely genuine. She was a child who had come to him, because he had been kind to her.

"Of course I am not angry with you," he said, quite emphatically. "I am very glad indeed that you came. It is only right that I should help you when my people seem to have treated you so wretchedly. Let me think for a moment."

She watched him very anxiously, and moved a little closer to him.

"Tell me," she murmured, "what are you thinking about?"

"I have it," he answered, standing suddenly up and touching the bell. "It is an excellent idea."

"What is it?" she asked quickly.

He did not appear to hear her question. Selby was standing upon the threshold. Wolfenden spoke to him.

"Selby, are your wife's rooms still vacant?"

Selby believed that they were.

"That's all right then. Put on your hat and coat at once. I want you to take this young lady round there."

"Very good, my lord."

"Her luggage has been lost and may not arrive until to-morrow. Be sure you tell Mrs. Selby to do all in her power to make things comfortable."

The girl had gone very pale. Wolfenden, watching her closely, was surprised at her expression.

"I think," he said, "that you will find Mrs. Selby a very decent sort of a person. If I may, I will come and see you to-morrow, and you shall tell me how I can help you. I am very glad indeed that you came to me."

She shot a single glance at him, partly of anger, partly reproach.

"You are very, very kind," she said slowly, "and very considerate," she added, after a moment's pause. "I shall not forget it."

She looked him then straight in the eyes. He was more glad than he would have liked to confess even to himself to hear Selby's knock at the door.

"You have nothing to thank me for yet at any rate," he said, taking her hand. "I shall be only too glad if you will let me be of service to you."

He led her out to the carriage and watched it drive away, with Selby on the box seat. Her last glance, as she leaned back amongst the cushions, was a tender one; her lips were quivering, and her little fingers more than returned his pressure. But Wolfenden walked back to his study with all the pleasurable feelings of a man who has extricated himself with tact from an awkward situation.

"The frankness," he remarked to himself, as he lit a pipe and stretched himself out for a final smoke, "was a trifle, just a trifle, overdone. She gave the whole show away with that last glance. I should like very much to know what it all means."

CHAPTER VI

A COMPACT OF THREE

Wolfenden, for an idler, was a young man of fairly precise habits. By ten o'clock next morning he had breakfasted, and before eleven he was riding in the Park. Perhaps he had some faint hope of seeing there something of the two people in whom he was now greatly interested. If so he was certainly disappointed. He looked with a new curiosity into the faces of the girls who galloped past him, and he was careful even to take particular notice of the few promenaders. But he did not see anything of Mr. Sabin or his companion.

At twelve o'clock he returned to his rooms and exchanged his riding-clothes for the ordinary garb of the West End. He even looked on his hall-table as he passed out again, to see if there were any note or card for him.

"He could scarcely look me up just yet, at any rate," he reflected, as he walked slowly along Piccadilly, "for he did not even ask me for my address. He took the whole thing so coolly that perhaps he does not mean even to call."

Nevertheless, he looked in the rack at his club to see if there was anything against his name, and tore into pieces the few unimportant notes he found there, with an impatience which they scarcely deserved. Of the few acquaintances whom he met there, he inquired casually whether they knew anything of a man named "Sabin." No one seemed to have heard the name before. He even consulted a directory in the hall, but without success. At one o'clock, in a fit of restlessness, he went out, and taking a hansom drove over to Westminster, to Harcutt's rooms. Harcutt was in, and with him Densham. At Wolfenden's entrance the three men looked at one another, and there was a simultaneous laugh.

"Here comes the hero," Densham remarked. "He will be able to tell us everything."

"I came to gather information, not to impart it," Wolfenden answered, selecting a cigarette, and taking an easy chair. "I know precisely as much as I knew last night."

"Mr. Sabin has not been to pour out his gratitude yet, then?" Densham asked.

Wolfenden shook his head.

"Not yet. On the whole, I am inclined to think that he will not come at all. He doubtless considers that he has done all that is necessary in the way of thanks. He did not even ask for my card, and giving me his was only a matter of form, for there was no address upon it."

"But he knew your name," Harcutt reminded him. "I noticed that."

"Yes. I suppose he could find me if he wished to," Wolfenden admitted. "If he had been very keen about it, though, I should think he would have said something more. His one idea seemed to be to get away before there was a row."

"I do not think," Harcutt said, "that you will find him overburdened with gratitude. He does not seem that sort of man."

"I do not want any gratitude from him," Wolfenden answered, deliberately. "So far as the man himself is concerned I should rather prefer never to see him again. By the bye, did either of you fellows follow them home last night?"

Harcutt and Densham exchanged quick glances. Wolfenden had asked his question quietly, but it was evidently what he had come to know.

"Yes," Harcutt said, "we both did. They are evidently people of some consequence. They went first to the house of the Russian Ambassador, Prince Lobenski."

Wolfenden swore to himself softly. He could have been there. He made a mental note to leave a card at the Embassy that afternoon.

"And afterwards?"

"Afterwards they drove to a house in Chilton Gardens, Kensington, where they remained."

"The presumption being, then——" Wolfenden began.

"That they live there," Harcutt put in. "In fact, I may say that we ascertained that definitely. The man's name is 'Sabin,' and the girl is reputed to be his niece. Now you know as much as we do. The relationship, however, is little more than a surmise."

"Did either of you go to the reception?" Wolfenden asked.

"We both did," Harcutt answered.

Wolfenden raised his eyebrows.

"You were there! Then why didn't you make their acquaintance?"

Densham laughed shortly.

"I asked for an introduction to the girl," he said, "and was politely declined. She was under the special charge of the Princess, and was presented to no one."

"And Mr. Sabin?" Wolfenden asked.

"He was talking all the time to Baron von Knigenstein, the German Ambassador. They did not stay long."

Wolfenden smiled.

"It seems to me," he said, "that you had an excellent opportunity and let it go."

Harcutt threw his cigarette into the fire with an impatient gesture.

"You may think so," he said. "All I can say is, that if you had been there yourself, you could have done no more. At any rate, we have no particular difficulty now in finding out who this mysterious Mr. Sabin and the girl are. We may assume that there is a relationship," he added, "or they would scarcely have been at the Embassy, where, as a rule, the guests make up in respectability what they lack in brilliancy."

"As to the relationship," Wolfenden said, "I am quite prepared to take that for granted. I, for one, never doubted it."

"That," Harcutt remarked, "is because you are young, and a little quixotic. When you have lived as long as I have you will doubt everything. You will take nothing for granted unless you desire to live for ever amongst the ruins of your shattered enthusiasms. If you are wise, you will always assume that your swans are geese until you have proved them to be swans."

"That is very cheap cynicism," Wolfenden remarked equably. "I am surprised at you, Harcutt. I thought that you were more in touch with the times. Don't you know that to-day nobody is cynical except schoolboys and dyspeptics? Pessimism went out with sack overcoats. Your remarks remind me of the morning odour of patchouli and stale smoke in a cheap Quartier Latin dancing-room. To be in the fashion of to-day, you must cultivate a gentle, almost arcadian enthusiasm, you must wear rose-coloured spectacles and pretend that you like them. Didn't you hear what Flaskett said last week? There is an epidemic of morality in the air. We are all going to be very good."

"Some of us," Densham remarked, "are going to be very uncomfortable, then."

"Great changes always bring small discomforts," Wolfenden rejoined. "But after all I didn't come here to talk nonsense. I came to ask you both something. I want to know whether you fellows are bent upon seeing this thing through?"

Densham and Harcutt exchanged glances. There was a moment's silence. Densham became spokesman.

"So far as finding out who they are and all about them," he said, "I shall not rest until I have done it."

"And you, Harcutt?"

Harcutt nodded gravely.

"I am with Densham," he said. "At the same time I may as well tell you that I am quite as much, if not more, interested in the man than in the girl. The girl is beautiful, and of course I admire her, as every one must. But that is all. The man appeals to my journalistic instincts. There is copy in him. I am convinced that he is a personage. You may, in fact, regard me, both of you, as an ally rather than as a rival."

"If you had your choice, then, of an hour's conversation with either of them——" Wolfenden began.

"I should choose the man without a second's hesitation," Harcutt declared. "The girl is lovely enough, I admit. I do not wonder at you fellows— Densham, who is a worshipper of beauty; you, Wolfenden, who are an idler—being struck with her! But as regards myself it is different. The man appeals to my professional instincts in very much the same way as the girl appeals to the artistic sense in Densham. He is a conundrum which I have set myself to solve."

Wolfenden rose to his feet.

"Look here, you fellows," he said, "I have a proposition to make. We are all three in the same boat. Shall we pull together or separately?"

Harcutt dropped his eyeglass and smiled quietly.

"Quixotic as usual, Wolf, old chap," he said. "We can't, our interests are opposed; at least yours and Densham's are. You will scarcely want to help one another under the circumstances."

Wolfenden drew on his gloves.

"I have not explained myself yet," he said. "The thing must have its limitations, of course, but for a step or two even Densham and I can walk together. Let us form an alliance so far as direct information is concerned. Afterwards it must be every man for himself, of course. I suppose we each have some idea as to how and where to set about making inquiries concerning these people. Very well. Let us each go our own way and share up the information to-night."

"I am quite willing," Densham said, "only let this be distinctly understood—we are allies only so far as the collection and sharing of information is concerned. Afterwards, and in other ways, it is each man for himself. If one of us succeeds in establishing a definite acquaintance with them, the thing ends. There is no need for either of us to do anything with regard to the others, which might militate against his own chances."

"I am agreeable to that," Harcutt said. "From Densham's very elaborate provisoes I think we may gather that he has a plan."

"I agree too," Wolfenden said, "and I specially endorse Densham's limit. It is an alliance so far as regards information only. Suppose we go and have some lunch together now."

"I never lunch out, and I have a better idea," said Harcutt. "Let us meet at the 'Milan' to-night for supper at the same time. We can then exchange information, supposing either of us has been fortunate enough to acquire any. What do you say, Wolfenden?"

"I am quite willing," Wolfenden said.

"And I," echoed Densham. "At half-past eleven, then," Harcutt concluded.

CHAPTER VII

WHO IS MR. SABIN?

Mrs. Thorpe-Satchell was not at home to ordinary callers. Nevertheless when a discreet servant brought her Mr. Francis Densham's card she gave orders for his admittance without hesitation.

That he was a privileged person it was easy to see. Mrs. Satchell received him with the most charming of smiles.

"My dear Francis," she exclaimed, "I do hope that you have lost that wretched headache! You looked perfectly miserable last night. I was so sorry for you."

Densham drew an easy chair to her side and accepted a cup of tea.

"I am quite well again," he said. "It was very bad indeed for a little time, but it did not last long. Still I felt that it made me so utterly stupid that I was half afraid you would have written me off your visitors' list altogether as a dull person. I was immensely relieved to be told that you were at home."

Mrs. Thorpe-Satchell laughed gaily. She was a bright, blonde little woman with an exquisite figure and piquante face. She had a husband whom no one knew, and gave excellent parties to which every one went. In her way she was something of a celebrity. She and Densham had known each other for many years.

"I am not sure," she said, "that you did not deserve it; but then, you see, you are too old a friend to be so summarily dealt with."

She raised her blue eyes to his and dropped them, smiling softly.

Densham looked steadily away into the fire, wondering how to broach the subject which had so suddenly taken the foremost place in his thoughts. He had not come to make even the idlest of love this afternoon. The time when he had been content to do so seemed very far away just now. Somehow this dainty little woman with her Watteau-like grace and delicate mannerisms had, for the present, at any rate, lost all her attractiveness for him, and he was able to meet the flash of her bright eyes and feel the touch of her soft fingers without any corresponding thrill.

"You are very good to me," he said, thoughtfully. "May I have some more tea?"

Now Densham was no strategist. He had come to ask a question, and he was dying to ask it. He knew very well that it would not do to hurry matters— that he must put it as casually as possible towards the close of his visit. But at the same time, the period of probation, during which he should have been more than usually entertaining, was scarcely a success, and his manner was restless and constrained. Every now and then there were long and unusual pauses, and he continuously and with obvious effort kept bringing back the conversation to the reception last night, in the hope that some remark from her might make the way easier for him. But nothing of the sort happened. The reception had not interested her in the slightest, and she had nothing to say about it, and his pre-occupation at last became manifest. She looked at him curiously after one of those awkward pauses to which she was quite unaccustomed, and his thoughts were evidently far away. As a matter of fact, he was at that moment actually framing the question which he had come to ask.

"My dear Francis," she said, quietly, "why don't you tell me what is the matter with you? You are not amusing. You have something on your mind. Is it anything you wish to ask of me?"

"Yes," he said, boldly, "I have come to ask you a favour."

She smiled at him encouragingly.

"Well, do ask it," she said, "and get rid of your woebegone face. You ought to know that if it is anything within my power I shall not hesitate."

"I want," he said, "to paint your portrait for next year's Academy."

This was a master stroke. To have Densham paint her picture was just at that moment the height of Mrs. Thorpe-Satchell's ambition. A flush of pleasure came into her cheeks, and her eyes were very bright.

"Do you really mean it?" she exclaimed, leaning over towards him. "Are you sure?"

"Of course I mean it," he answered. "If only I can do you justice, I think it ought to be the portrait of the year. I have been studying you for a long time in an indefinite sort of way, and I think that I have some good ideas."

Mrs. Thorpe-Satchell laughed softly. Densham, although not a great artist, was the most fashionable portrait painter of the minute, and he had the knack of giving a *chic* touch to his women—of investing them with a certain style without the sacrifice of similitude. He refused quite as many commissions as he accepted, and he could scarcely have flattered Mrs. Thorpe-Satchell more than by his request. She was delightfully amiable.

"You are a dear old thing," she said, beaming upon him. "What shall I wear? That yellow satin gown that you like, or say you like, so much?"

He discussed the question with her gravely. It was not until he rose to go that he actually broached the question which had been engrossing all his thoughts.

"By the bye," he said, "I wanted to ask you something. You know Harcutt?"

She nodded. Of course she knew Harcutt. Were her first suspicions correct! Had he some other reason for this visit of his?

"Well," Densham went on, "he is immensely interested in some people who were at that stupid reception last night. He tried to get an introduction but he couldn't find any one who knew them, and he doesn't know the Princess well enough to ask her. He thought that he saw you speaking to the man, so I promised that when I saw you I would ask about them."

"I spoke to a good many men," she said. "What is his name?"

"Sabin—Mr. Sabin; and there is a girl, his daughter, or niece, I suppose."

Was it Densham's fancy or had she indeed turned a shade paler. The little be-jewelled hand, which had been resting close to his, suddenly buried itself in the cushions. Densham, who was watching her closely, was conscious of a hardness about her mouth which he had never noticed before. She was silent some time before she answered him.

"I am sorry," she said, slowly, "but I can tell you scarcely anything about them. I only met him once in India many years ago, and I have not the slightest idea as to who he is or where he came from. I am quite sure that I should not have recollected him last night but for his deformity."

Densham tried very hard to hide his disappointment.

"So you met him in India," he remarked. "Do you know what he was doing there? He was not in the service at all, I suppose."

"I really do not know," she answered, "but I think not. I believe that he is, or was, very wealthy. I remember hearing a few things about him—nothing of much importance. But if Mr. Harcutt is your friend," she added, looking at him fixedly, "you can give him some excellent advice."

"Harcutt is a very decent fellow," Densham said, "and I know that he will be glad of it."

"Tell him to have nothing whatever to do with Mr. Sabin."

Densham looked at her keenly.

"Then you do know something about him," he exclaimed.

She moved her chair back a little to where the light no longer played upon her face, and she answered him without looking up.

"Very little. It was so long ago and my memory is not what it used to be. Never mind that. The advice is good anyhow. If," she continued, looking steadily up at Densham, "if it were not Mr. Harcutt who was interested in these people, if it were any one, Francis, for whose welfare I had a greater care, who was really my friend, I would make that advice, if I could, a thousand times stronger. I would implore him to have nothing whatever to do with this man or any of his creatures."

Densham laughed—not very easily. His disappointment was great, but his interest was stimulated.

"At any rate," he said, "the girl is harmless. She cannot have left school a year."

"A year with that man," she answered, bitterly, "is a liberal education in corruption. Don't misunderstand me. I have no personal grievance against him. We have never come together, thank God! But there were stories—I cannot remember them now—I do not wish to remember them, but the impression they made still remains. If a little of what people said about him is true he is a prince of wickedness."

"The girl herself——?"

"I know nothing of," she admitted.

Densham determined upon a bold stroke.

"Look here," he said, "do me this favour—you shall never regret it. You and the Princess are intimate, I know: order your carriage and go and see her this afternoon. Ask her what she knows about that girl. Get her to tell you everything. Then let me know. Don't ask me to explain just now—simply remember that we are old friends and that I ask you to do this thing for me."

She rang the bell.

"My victoria at once," she told the servant. Then she turned to Densham. "I will do exactly what you ask," she said. "You can come with me and wait while I see the Princess—if she is at home. You see I am doing for you what I would do for no one else in the world. Don't trouble about thanking me now. Do you mind waiting while I get my things on? I shall only be a minute or two."

Her minute or two was half an hour. Densham waited impatiently. He scarcely knew whether to be satisfied with the result of his mission or not. He had learnt a very little—he was probably going to learn a little more, but he was quite aware that he had not conducted the negotiations with any particular skill, and the bribe which he had offered was a heavy one. He was still uncertain about it when Mrs. Thorpe-Satchell reappeared. She had changed her indoor gown for a soft petunia-coloured costume trimmed with sable, and she held out her hands towards him with a delightful smile.

"Céleste is wretchedly awkward with gloves," she said, "so I have left them for you. Do you like my gown?"

"You look charming," he said, bending over his task, "and you know it."

"I always wear my smartest clothes when I am going to see my particular friends," she declared. "They quiz one so! Besides, I do not always have an escort! Come!"

She talked to him gaily on the stairs, as he handed her into the carriage, and all the way to their destination, yet he was conscious all the time of a subtle change in her demeanour towards him. She was a proud little woman, and she had received a shock. Densham was making use of her—Densham, of all men, was making use of her, of all women. He had been perfectly correct in those vague fears of his. She did not believe that he had come to her for his friend's sake. She never doubted but that it was he himself who was interested in this girl, and she looked upon his visit and his request to her as something very nearly approaching brutality. He must be interested in the girl, very deeply interested, or he would never have resorted to such means of gaining information about her. She was suddenly silent and turned a little pale as the carriage turned into the square. Her errand was not a pleasant one to her.

Densham was left alone in the carriage for nearly an hour. He was impatient, and yet her prolonged absence pleased him. She had found the Princess in, she would bring him the information he desired. He sat gazing idly into the faces of the passers-by with his thoughts very far away. How that girl's face had taken hold of his fancy; had excited in some strange way his whole artistic temperament! She was the exquisite embodiment of a new type of girlhood, from which was excluded all that was crude and unpleasing and unfinished. She seemed to him to combine in some mysterious manner all the dainty freshness of youth with the delicate grace and *savoir faire* of a Frenchwoman of the best period. He scarcely fancied himself in love with her; at any rate if it had been suggested to him he would have denied it. Her beauty had certainly taken a singular hold of him. His imagination was touched. He was immensely attracted, but as to anything serious—well, he would not have admitted it even to himself. Liberty meant so much to him, he had told himself over and over again that, for many years at least, his art must be his sole mistress. Besides, he was no boy to lose his heart, as certainly Wolfenden had done, to a girl with whom he had never even spoken. It was ridiculous, and yet——

A soft voice in his ear suddenly recalled him to the present. Mrs. Thorpe-Satchell was standing upon the pavement. The slight pallor had gone from her cheeks and the light had come back to her eyes. He looked at her, irresistibly attracted. She had never appeared more charming.

She stepped into the carriage, and the soft folds of her gown spread themselves out over the cushions. She drew them on one side to make room for him.

"Come," she said, "let us have one turn in the Park. It is quite early, although I am afraid that I have been a very long time."

He stepped in at once and they drove off. Mrs. Thorpe-Satchell laughingly repeated some story which the Princess had just told her. Evidently she was in high spirits. The strained look had gone from her face. Her gaiety was no longer forced.

"You want to know the result of my mission, I suppose," she remarked, pleasantly. "Well, I am afraid you will call it a failure. The moment I mentioned the man's name the Princess stopped me.

"'You mustn't talk to me about that man,' she said. 'Don't ask why, only you must not talk about him.'

"'I don't want to,' I assured her; 'but the girl.'"

"What did she say about the girl?" Densham asked.

"Well she did tell me something about her," Mrs. Thorpe-Satchell said, slowly, "but, unfortunately, it will not help your friend. She only told me when I had promised unconditionally and upon my honour to keep her information a profound secret. So I am sorry, Francis, but even to you———"

"Of course, you must not repeat it," Densham said, hastily. "I would not ask you for the world; but is there not a single scrap of information about the man or the girl, who he is, what he is, of what family or nationality the girl is—anything at all which I can take to Harcutt?"

Mrs. Thorpe-Satchell looked straight at him with a faint smile at the corners of her lips.

"Yes, there is one thing which you can tell Mr. Harcutt," she said.

Densham drew a little breath. At last, then!

"You can tell him this," Mrs. Thorpe-Satchell said, slowly and impressively, "that if it is the girl, as I suppose it is, in whom he is interested, that the very best thing he can do is to forget that he has ever seen her. I cannot tell you who she is or what, although I know. But we are old friends, Francis, and I know that my word will be sufficient for you. You can take this from me as the solemn truth. Your friend had better hope for the love of the Sphinx, or fix his heart upon the statue of Diana, as think of that girl."

Densham was looking straight ahead along the stream of vehicles. His eyes were set, but he saw nothing. He did not doubt her word for a moment. He knew that she had spoken the truth. The atmosphere seemed suddenly grey and sunless. He shivered a little—he was positively chilled. Just for a moment he saw the girl's face, heard the swirl of her skirts as she had passed their table and the sound of her voice as she had bent over the great cluster of white roses whose faint perfume reached even to where they were sitting. Then he half closed his eyes. He had come very near making a terrible mistake.

"Thank you," he said. "I will tell Harcutt."

CHAPTER VIII

A MEETING IN BOND STREET

Wolfenden returned to his rooms to lunch, intending to go round to see his last night's visitor immediately afterwards. He had scarcely taken off his coat, however, before Selby met him in the hall, a note in his hand.

"From the young lady, my lord," he announced. "My wife has just sent it round."

Wolfenden tore the envelope open and read it.

"Thursday morning.

"DEAR LORD WOLFENDEN,—Of course I made a mistake in coming to you last night. I am very sorry indeed—more sorry than you will ever know. A woman does not forget these things readily, and the lesson you have taught me it will not be difficult for me to remember all my life. I cannot consent to remain your debtor, and I am leaving here at once. I shall have gone long before you receive this note. Do not try to find me. I shall not want for friends if I choose to seek them. Apart from this, I do not want to see you again. I mean it, and I trust to your honour to respect my wishes. I think that I may at least ask you to grant me this for the sake of those days at Deringham, which it is now my fervent wish to utterly forget.—I am, yours sincerely,

"BLANCHE MERTON."

"The young lady, my lord," Selby remarked, "left early this morning. She expressed herself as altogether satisfied with the attention she had received, but she had decided to make other arrangements."

Wolfenden nodded, and walked into his dining-room with the note crushed up in his hand.

"For the sake of those days at Deringham," he repeated softly to himself. Was the girl a fool, or only an adventuress? It was true that there had been something like a very mild flirtation between them at Deringham, but it had been altogether harmless, and certainly more of her seeking than his. They had met in the grounds once or twice and walked together; he had talked to her a little after dinner, feeling a certain sympathy for her isolation, and perhaps a little admiration for her undoubted prettiness; yet all the time he had had a slightly uneasy feeling with regard to her. Her ingenuousness had become a matter of doubt to him. It was so now more than ever, yet he could not understand her going away like this and the tone of her note. So far as he was concerned, it was the most satisfactory thing that could have happened. It relieved him of a responsibility which he scarcely knew how to deal with. In the face of her dismissal from Deringham, any assistance which she might have accepted from him would naturally have been open to misapprehension. But that she should have gone away and have written to him in such a strain was directly contrary to his anticipations. Unless she was really hurt and disappointed by his reception of her, he could not see what she had to gain by it. He was puzzled a little, but his thoughts were too deeply engrossed elsewhere for him to take her disappearance very seriously. By the time he had finished lunch he had come to the conclusion that what had happened was for the best, and that he would take her at her word.

He left his rooms again about three o'clock, and at precisely the hour at which Densham had rung the bell of Mrs. Thorpe-Satchell's house in Mayfair he experienced a very great piece of good fortune.

Coming out of Scott's, where more from habit than necessity he had turned in to have his hat ironed, he came face to face, a few yards up Bond Street, with the two people whom, more than any one else in the world, he had desired to meet. They were walking together, the girl talking, the man listening with an air of half-amused deference. Suddenly she broke off and welcomed Wolfenden with a delightful smile of recognition. The man looked up quickly. Wolfenden was standing before them on the pavement, hat in hand, his pleasure at this unexpected meeting very plainly evidenced in his face. Mr. Sabin's greeting, if devoid of any special cordiality, was courteous and even genial. Wolfenden never quite knew whence he got the impression, which certainly came to him with all the strength and absoluteness of an original inspiration, that this encounter was not altogether pleasant to him.

"How strange that we should meet you!" the girl said. "Do you know that this is the first walk that I have ever had in London?"

She spoke rather softly and rather slowly. Her voice possessed a sibilant and musical intonation; there was perhaps the faintest suggestion of an accent. As she stood there smiling upon him in a deep blue gown, trimmed with a silvery fur, in the making of which no English dressmaker had been concerned, Wolfenden's subjection was absolute and complete. He was aware that his answer was a little flurried. He was less at his ease than he could have wished. Afterwards he thought of a hundred things he would have liked to have said, but the surprise of seeing them so suddenly had cost him a little of his usual self-possession. Mr. Sabin took up the conversation.

"My infirmity," he said, glancing downwards, "makes walking, especially on stone pavements, rather a painful undertaking. However, London is one of those cities which can only be seen on foot, and my niece has all the curiosity of her age."

She laughed out frankly. She wore no veil, and a tinge of colour had found its way into her cheeks, relieving that delicate but not unhealthy pallor, which to Densham had seemed so exquisite.

"I think shopping is delightful. Is it not?" she exclaimed.

Wolfenden was absolutely sure of it. He was, indeed, needlessly emphatic. Mr. Sabin smiled faintly.

"I am glad to have met you again, Lord Wolfenden," he said, "if only to thank you for your aid last night. I was anxious to get away before any fuss was made, or I would have expressed my gratitude at the time in a more seemly fashion."

"I hope," Wolfenden said, "that you will not think it necessary to say anything more about it. I did what any one in my place would have done without a moment's hesitation."

"I am not quite so sure of that," Mr. Sabin said. "But by the bye, can you tell me what became of the fellow? Did any one go after him?"

"There was some sort of pursuit, I believe," Wolfenden said slowly, "but he was not caught."

"I am glad to hear it," Mr. Sabin said.

Wolfenden looked at him in some surprise. He could not make up his mind whether it was his duty to disclose the name of the man who had made this strange attempt.

"Your assailant was, I suppose, a stranger to you?" he said slowly.

Mr. Sabin shook his head.

"By no means. I recognised him directly. So, I believe, did you."

Wolfenden was honestly amazed.

"He was your guest, I believe," Mr. Sabin continued, "until I entered the room. I saw him leave, and I was half-prepared for something of the sort."

"He was my guest, it is true, but none the less, he was a stranger to me," Wolfenden explained. "He brought a letter from my cousin, who seems to have considered him a decent sort of fellow."

"There is," Mr. Sabin said dryly, "nothing whatever the matter with him, except that he is mad."

"On the whole, I cannot say that I am surprised to hear it," Wolfenden remarked; "but I certainly think that, considering the form his madness takes, you ought to protect yourself in some way."

Mr. Sabin shrugged his shoulders contemptuously.

"He can never hurt me. I carry a talisman which is proof against any attempt that he can make; but none the less, I must confess that your aid last night was very welcome."

"I was very pleased to be of any service," Wolfenden said, "especially," he added, glancing toward Mr. Sabin's niece, "since it has given me the pleasure of your acquaintance."

A little thrill passed through him. Her delicately-curved lips were quivering as though with amusement, and her eyes had fallen; she had blushed slightly at that unwitting, ardent look of his. Mr. Sabin's cold voice recalled him to himself.

"I believe," he said, "that I overheard your name correctly. It is Wolfenden, is it not?"

Wolfenden assented.

"I am sorry that I haven't a card," he said. "That is my name."

Mr. Sabin looked at him curiously.

"Wolfenden is, I believe, the family name of the Deringhams? May I ask, are you any relation to Admiral Lord Deringham?"

Wolfenden was suddenly grave.

"Yes," he answered; "he is my father. Did you ever meet him?"

Mr. Sabin shook his head.

"No, I have heard of him abroad; also, I believe, of the Countess of Deringham, your mother. It is many years ago. I trust that I have not inadvertently——"

"Not at all," Wolfenden declared. "My father is still alive, although he is in very delicate health. I wonder, would you and your niece do me the honour of having some tea with me? It is Ladies' Day at the 'Geranium Club,' and I should be delighted to take you there if you would allow me."

Mr. Sabin shook his head.

Wolfenden had the satisfaction of seeing the girl look disappointed.

"We are very much obliged to you," Mr. Sabin said, "but I have an appointment which is already overdue. You must not mind, Helène, if we ride the rest of the way."

He turned and hailed a passing hansom, which drew up immediately at the kerb by their side. Mr. Sabin handed his niece in, and stood for a moment on the pavement with Wolfenden.

"I hope that we may meet again before long, Lord Wolfenden," he said. "In the meantime let me assure you once more of my sincere gratitude."

The girl leaned forward over the apron of the cab.

"And may I not add mine too?" she said. "I almost wish that we were not going to the 'Milan' again to-night. I am afraid that I shall be nervous."

She looked straight at Wolfenden. He was ridiculously happy.

"I can promise," he said, "that no harm shall come to Mr. Sabin to-night, at any rate. I shall be at the 'Milan' myself, and I will keep a very close look out."

"How reassuring!" she exclaimed, with a brilliant smile. "Lord Wolfenden is going to be at the 'Milan' to-night," she added, turning to Mr. Sabin. "Why don't you ask him to join us? I shall feel so much more comfortable."

There was a faint but distinct frown on Mr. Sabin's face—a distinct hesitation before he spoke. But Wolfenden would notice neither. He was looking over Mr. Sabin's shoulder, and his instructions were very clear.

"If you will have supper with us we shall be very pleased," Mr. Sabin said stiffly; "but no doubt you have already made your party. Supper is an institution which one seldom contemplates alone."

"I am quite free, and I shall be delighted," Wolfenden said without hesitation. "About eleven, I suppose?"

"A quarter past," Mr. Sabin said, stepping into the cab. "We may go to the theatre."

The hansom drove off, and Wolfenden stood on the pavement, hat in hand. What fortune! He could scarcely believe in it. Then, just as he turned to move on, something lying at his feet almost at the edge of the kerbstone attracted his attention. He looked at it more closely. It was a ribbon—a little delicate strip of deep blue ribbon. He knew quite well whence it must have come. It had fallen from her gown as she had stepped into the hansom. He looked up and down the street. It was full, but he saw no one whom he knew. The thing could be done in a minute. He stooped quickly down and picked it up crushing it in his gloved hand, and walking on at once with heightened colour and a general sense of having made a fool of himself. For a moment or two he was especially careful to look neither to the right or to the left; then a sense that some one from the other side of the road was watching him drew his eyes in that direction. A young man was standing upon the edge of the pavement, a peculiar smile parting his lips and a cigarette between his fingers. For a moment Wolfenden was furiously angry; then the eyes of the two men met across the street, and Wolfenden forgot his anger. He recognised him at once, notwithstanding his appearance in an afternoon toilette as carefully chosen as his own. It was Felix, Mr. Sabin's assailant.

CHAPTER IX

THE SHADOWS THAT GO BEFORE

Wolfenden forgot his anger at once. He hesitated for a moment, then he crossed the street and stood side by side with Felix upon the pavement.

"I am glad to see that you are looking a sane man again," Wolfenden said, after they had exchanged the usual greetings. "You might have been in a much more uncomfortable place, after your last night's escapade."

Felix shrugged his shoulders.

"I think," he said, "that if I had succeeded a little discomfort would only have amused me. It is not pleasant to fail."

Wolfenden stood squarely upon his feet, and laid his hand lightly upon the other's shoulder.

"Look here," he said, "it won't do for you to go following a man about London like this, watching for an opportunity to murder him. I don't like interfering in other people's business, but willingly or unwillingly I seem to have got mixed up in this, and I have a word or two to say about it. Unless you give me your promise, upon your honour, to make no further attempt upon that man's life, I shall go to the police, tell them what I know, and have you watched."

"You shall have," Felix said quietly, "my promise. A greater power than the threat of your English police has tied my hands; for the present I have abandoned my purpose."

"I am bound to believe you," Wolfenden said, "and you look as though you were speaking the truth; yet you must forgive my asking why, in that case, you are following the man about? You must have a motive."

Felix shook his head.

"As it happened," he said, "I am here by the merest accident. It may seem strange to you, but it is perfectly true. I have just come out of Waldorf's, above there, and I saw you all three upon the pavement."

"I am glad to hear it," Wolfenden said.

"More glad," Felix said, "than I was to see you with them. Can you not believe what I tell you? shall I give you proof? will you be convinced then? Every moment you spend with that man is an evil one for you. You may have thought me inclined to be melodramatic last night. Perhaps I was! All the same the man is a fiend. Will you not be warned? I tell you that he is a fiend."

"Perhaps he is," Wolfenden said indifferently. "I am not interested in him."

"But you are interested—in his companion."

Wolfenden frowned.

"I think," he said, "that we will leave the lady out of the conversation."

Felix sighed.

"You are a good fellow," he said; "but, forgive me, like all your countrymen, you carry chivalry just a thought too far—even to simplicity. You do not understand such people and their ways."

Wolfenden was getting angry, but he held himself in check.

"You know nothing against her," he said slowly.

"It is true," Felix answered. "I know nothing against her. It is not necessary. She is his creature. That is apparent. The shadow of his wickedness is enough."

Wolfenden checked himself in the middle of a hot reply. He was suddenly conscious of the absurdity of losing his temper in the open street with a man so obviously ill-balanced—possessed, too, of such strange and wild impulses.

"Let us talk," he said, "of something else, or say good-morning. Which way were you going?"

"To the Russian Embassy," Felix said, "I have some work to do this afternoon."

Wolfenden looked at him curiously.

"Our ways, then, are the same for a short distance," he said. "Let us walk together. Forgive me, but you are really, then, attached to the Embassy?"

Felix nodded, and glanced at his companion with a smile.

"I am not what you call a fraud altogether," he said. "I am junior secretary to Prince Lobenski. You, I think, are not a politician, are you?"

Wolfenden shook his head.

"I take no interest in politics," he said. "I shall probably have to sit in the House of Lords some day, but I shall be sorry indeed when the time comes."

Felix sighed, and was silent for a moment.

"You are perhaps fortunate," he said. "The ways of the politician are not exactly rose-strewn. You represent a class which in my country does not exist. There we are all either in the army, or interested in statecraft. Perhaps the secure position of your country does not require such ardent service?"

"You are—of what nationality, may I ask?" Wolfenden inquired.

Felix hesitated.

"Perhaps," he said, "you had better not know. The less you know of me the better. The time may come when it will be to your benefit to be ignorant."

Wolfenden took no pains to hide his incredulity.

"It is easy to see that you are a stranger in this country," he remarked. "We are not in Russia or in South America. I can assure you that we scarcely know the meaning of the word 'intrigue' here. We are the most matter-of-fact and perhaps the most commonplace nation in the world. You will find it out for yourself in time. Whilst you are with us you must perforce fall to our level."

"I, too, must become commonplace," Felix said, smiling. "Is that what you mean?"

"In a certain sense, yes," Wolfenden answered. "You will not be able to help it. It will be the natural result of your environment. In your own country, wherever that may be, I can imagine that you might be a person jealously watched by the police; your comings and goings made a note of; your intrigues—I take it for granted that you are concerned in some—the object of the most jealous and unceasing suspicion. Here there is nothing of that. You could not intrigue if you wanted to. There is nothing to intrigue about."

They were crossing a crowded thoroughfare, and Felix did not reply until they were safe on the opposite pavement. Then he took Wolfenden's arm, and, leaning over, almost whispered in his ear—

"You speak," he said, "what nine-tenths of your countrymen believe. Yet you are wrong. Wherever there are international questions which bring great powers such as yours into antagonism, or the reverse, with other great countries, the soil is laid ready for intrigue, and the seed is never long wanted. Yes; I know that, to all appearance, you are the smuggest and most respectable nation ever evolved in this world's history. Yet if you tell me that your's is a nation free from intrigue, I correct you; you are wrong, you do not know—that is all! That very man, whose life last night you so inopportunely saved, is at this moment deeply involved in an intrigue against your country."

"Mr. Sabin!" Wolfenden exclaimed.

"Yes, Mr. Sabin! Mind, I know this by chance only. I am not concerned one way or the other. My quarrel with him is a private one. I am robbed for the present of my vengeance by a power to which I am forced to yield implicit obedience. So, for the present, I have forgotten that he is my enemy. He is safe from me, yet if last night I had struck home, I should have ridded your country of a great and menacing danger. Perhaps—who can tell—he is a man who succeeds—I might even have saved England from conquest and ruin."

They had reached the top of Piccadilly, and downward towards the Park flowed the great afternoon stream of foot-people and carriages. Wolfenden, on whom his companion's words, charged as they were with an almost passionate earnestness, could scarcely fail to leave some impression, was silent for a moment.

"Do you really believe," he said, "that ours is a country which could possibly stand in any such danger? We are outside all Continental alliances! We are pledged to support neither the dual or the triple alliance. How could we possibly become embroiled?"

"I will tell you one thing which you may not readily believe," Felix said. "There is no country in the world so hated by all the great powers as England."

Wolfenden shrugged his shoulders.

"Russia," he remarked, "is perhaps jealous of our hold on Asia, but——"

"Russia," Felix interrupted, "of all the countries in the world, except perhaps Italy, is the most friendly disposed towards you."

Wolfenden laughed.

"Come," he said, "you forget Germany."

"Germany!" Felix exclaimed scornfully. "Believe it or not as you choose, but Germany detests you. I will tell you a thing which you can think of when you are an old man, and there are great changes and events for you to look back upon. A war between Germany and England is only a matter of time—of a few short years, perhaps even months. In the Cabinet at Berlin a war with you to-day would be more popular than a war with France."

"You take my breath away," Wolfenden exclaimed, laughing.

Felix was very much in earnest.

"In the little world of diplomacy," he said, "in the innermost councils these things are known. The outside public knows nothing of the awful responsibilities of those who govern. Two, at least, of your ministers have realised the position. You read this morning in the papers of more warships and strengthened fortifications—already there have been whispers of the conscription. It is not against Russia or against France that you are slowly arming yourselves, it is against Germany!"

"Germany would be mad to fight us," Wolfenden declared.

"Under certain conditions," Felix said slowly. "Don't be angry—Germany must beat you."

Wolfenden, looking across the street, saw Harcutt on the steps of his club, and beckoned to him.

"There is Harcutt," he exclaimed, pointing him out to Felix. "He is a journalist, you know, and in search of a sensation. Let us hear what he has to say about these things."

But Felix unlinked his arm from Wolfenden's hastily.

"You must excuse me," he said. "Harcutt would recognise me, and I do not wish to be pointed out everywhere as a would-be assassin. Remember what I have said, and avoid Sabin and his parasites as you would the devil."

Felix hurried away. Wolfenden remained for a moment standing in the middle of the pavement looking blankly along Piccadilly. Harcutt crossed over to him.

"You look," he remarked to Wolfenden, "like a man who needs a drink."

Wolfenden turned with him into the club.

"I believe that I do," he said. "I have had rather an eventful hour."

CHAPTER X

THE SECRETARY

Mr. Sabin, who had parted with Wolfenden with evident relief, leaned back in the cab and looked at his watch.

"That young man," he remarked, "has wasted ten minutes of my time. He will probably have to pay for it some day."

"By the bye," the girl asked, "who is he?"

"His name is Wolfenden—Lord Wolfenden."

"So I gathered; and who is Lord Wolfenden?"

"The only son of Admiral the Earl of Deringham. I don't know anything more than that about him myself."

"Admiral Deringham," the girl repeated, thoughtfully; "the name sounds familiar."

Mr. Sabin nodded.

"Very likely," he said. "He was in command of the Channel Squadron at the time of the *Magnificent* disaster. He was barely half a mile away and saw the whole thing. He came in, too, rightly or wrongly, for a share of the blame."

"Didn't he go mad, or something?" the girl asked.

"He had a fit," Mr. Sabin said calmly, "and left the service almost directly afterwards. He is living in strict seclusion in Norfolk, I believe. I should not like to say that he is mad. As a matter of fact, I do not believe that he is."

She looked at him curiously. There was a note of reserve in his tone.

"You are interested in him, are you not?" she asked.

"In a measure," he admitted. "He is supposed, mad or not, to be the greatest living authority on the coast defences of England and the state of her battleships. They shelved him at the Admiralty, but he wrote some vigorous letters to the papers and there are people pretty high up who believe in him. Others, of course, think that he is a crank."

"But why," she asked, languidly, "are you interested in such matters?"

Mr. Sabin knocked the ash off the cigarette he was smoking and was silent for a moment.

"One gets interested nowadays in—a great many things which scarcely seem to concern us," he remarked deliberately. "You, for instance, seem interested in this man's son. He cannot possibly be of any account to us."

She shrugged her shoulders.

"Did I say that I was interested in him?"

"You did not," Mr. Sabin answered, "but it was scarcely necessary; you stopped to speak to him of your own accord, and you asked him to supper, which was scarcely discreet."

"One gets so bored sometimes," she admitted frankly.

"You are only a woman," he said indulgently; "a year of waiting seems to you an eternity, however vast the stake. There will come a time when you will see things differently."

"I wonder!" she said softly, "I wonder!"

Mr. Sabin had unconsciously spoken the truth when he had pleaded an appointment to Lord Wolfenden. His servant drew him on one side directly they entered the house.

"There is a young lady here, sir, waiting for you in the study."

"Been here long?" Mr. Sabin asked.

"About two hours, sir. She has rung once or twice to ask about you."

Mr. Sabin turned away and opened the study door, carefully closing it behind him at once as he recognised his visitor. The air was blue with tobacco smoke, and the girl, who looked up at his entrance, held a cigarette between her fingers. Mr. Sabin was at least as surprised as Lord Wolfenden when he recognised his visitor, but his face was absolutely emotionless. He nodded not unkindly and stood looking at her, leaning upon his stick.

"Well, Blanche, what has gone wrong?" he asked.

"Pretty well everything," she answered. "I've been turned away."

"Detected?" he asked quickly.

"Suspected, at any rate. I wrote you that Lord Deringham was watching me sharply. Where he got the idea from I can't imagine, but he got it and he got it right, anyhow. He's followed me about like a cat, and it's all up."

"What does he know?"

"Nothing! He found a sheet of carbon on my desk, no more! I had to leave in an hour."

"And Lady Deringham?"

"She is like the rest—she thinks him mad. She has not the faintest idea that, mad or not, he has stumbled upon the truth. She was glad to have me go—for other reasons; but she has not the faintest doubt but that I have been unjustly dismissed."

"And he? How much does he know?"

"Exactly what I told you—nothing! His idea was just a confused one that I thought the stuff valuable—how you can make any sense of such trash I don't know—and that I was keeping a copy back for myself. He was worrying for an excuse to get rid of me, and he grabbed at it."

"Why was Lady Deringham glad to have you go?" Mr. Sabin asked.

"Because I amused myself with her son."

"Lord Wolfenden?"

"Yes!"

For the first time since he had entered the room Mr. Sabin's grim countenance relaxed. The corners of his lips slowly twisted themselves into a smile.

"Good girl," he said. "Is he any use now?"

"None," she answered with some emphasis. "None whatever. He is a fool."

The colour in her cheeks had deepened a little. A light shot from her eyes. Mr. Sabin's amusement deepened. He looked positively benign.

"You've tried him?" he suggested.

The girl nodded, and blew a little cloud of tobacco smoke from her mouth.

"Yes; I went there last night. He was very kind. He sent his servant out with me and got me nice, respectable rooms."

Mr. Sabin did what was for him an exceptional thing. He sat down and laughed to himself softly, but with a genuine and obvious enjoyment.

"Blanche," he said, "it was a lucky thing that I discovered you. No one else could have appreciated you properly."

She looked at him with a sudden hardness.

"You should appreciate me," she said, "for what I am you made me. I am of your handiwork: a man should appreciate the tool of his own fashioning."

"Nature," Mr. Sabin said smoothly, "had made the way easy for me. Mine were but finishing touches. But we have no time for this sort of thing. You have done well at Deringham and I shall not forget it. But your dismissal just now is exceedingly awkward. For the moment, indeed, I scarcely see my way. I wonder in what direction Lord Deringham will look for your successor?"

"Not anywhere within the sphere of your influence," she answered. "I do not think that I shall have a successor at all just yet. There was only a week's work to do. He will copy that himself."

"I am very much afraid," Mr. Sabin said, "that he will; yet we must have that copy."

"You will be very clever," she said slowly. "He has put watches all round the place, and the windows are barricaded. He sleeps with a revolver by his side, and there are several horrors in the shape of traps all round the house."

"No wonder," Mr. Sabin said, "that people think him mad."

The girl laughed shortly.

"He is mad," she said. "There is no possible doubt about that; you couldn't live with him a day and doubt it."

"Hereditary, no doubt," Mr. Sabin suggested quietly.

Blanche shrugged her shoulders and leaned back yawning.

"Anyhow," she said, "I've had enough of them all. It has been very tiresome work and I am sick of it. Give me some money. I want a spree. I am going to have a month's holiday."

Mr. Sabin sat down at his desk and drew out a cheque-book.

"There will be no difficulty about the money," he said, "but I cannot spare you for a month. Long before that I must have the rest of this madman's figures."

The girl's face darkened.

"Haven't I told you," she said, "that there is not the slightest chance of their taking me back? You might as well believe me. They wouldn't have me, and I wouldn't go."

"I do not expect anything of the sort," Mr. Sabin said. "There are other directions, though, in which I shall require your aid. I shall have to go to

Deringham myself, and as I know nothing whatever about the place you will be useful to me there. I believe that your home is somewhere near there."

"Well!"

"There is no reason, I suppose," Mr. Sabin continued, "why a portion of the vacation you were speaking of should not be spent there?"

"None!" the girl replied, "except that it would be deadly dull, and no holiday at all. I should want paying for it."

Mr. Sabin looked down at the cheque-book which lay open before him.

"I was intending," he said, "to offer you a cheque for fifty pounds. I will make it one hundred, and you will rejoin your family circle at Fakenham, I believe, in one week from to-day."

The girl made a wry face.

"The money's all right," she said; "but you ought to see my family circle! They are all cracked on farming, from the poor old dad who loses all his spare cash at it, down to little Letty my youngest sister, who can tell you everything about the last turnip crop. Do ride over and see us! You will find it so amusing!"

"I shall be charmed," Mr. Sabin said suavely, as he commenced filling in the body of the cheque. "Are all your sisters, may I ask, as delightful as you?"

She looked at him defiantly.

"Look here," she said, "none of that! Of course you wouldn't come, but in any case I won't have you. The girls are—well, not like me, I'm glad to say. I won't have the responsibility of introducing a Mephistocles into the domestic circle."

"I can assure you," Mr. Sabin said, "that I had not the faintest idea of coming. My visit to Norfolk will be anything but a pleasure trip, and I shall have no time to spare.

"I believe I have your address: 'Westacott Farm, Fakenham,' is it not? Now do what you like in the meantime, but a week from to-day there will be a letter from me there. Here is the cheque."

The girl rose and shook out her skirts.

"Aren't you going to take me anywhere?" she asked. "You might ask me to have supper with you to-night."

Mr. Sabin shook his head gently.

"I am sorry," he said, "but I have a young lady living with me."

"Oh!"

"She is my niece, and it takes more than my spare time to entertain her," he continued, without noticing the interjection. "You have plenty of friends. Go and look them up and enjoy yourself—for a week. I have no heart to go pleasure-making until my work is finished."

She drew on her gloves and walked to the door. Mr. Sabin came with her and opened it.

"I wish," she said, "that I could understand what in this world you are trying to evolve from those rubbishy papers."

He laughed.

"Some day," he said, "I will tell you. At present you would not understand. Be patient a little longer."

"It has been long enough," she exclaimed. "I have had seven months of it."

"And I," he answered, "seven years. Take care of yourself and remember, I shall want you in a week."

CHAPTER XI

THE FRUIT THAT IS OF GOLD

At precisely the hour agreed upon Harcutt and Densham met in one of the ante-rooms leading into the "Milan" restaurant. They surrendered their coats and hats to an attendant, and strolled about waiting for Wolfenden. A quarter of an hour passed. The stream of people from the theatres began to grow thinner. Still, Wolfenden did not come. Harcutt took out his watch.

"I propose that we do not wait any longer for Wolfenden," he said. "I saw him this afternoon, and he answered me very oddly when I reminded him about to-night. There is such a crowd here too, that they will not keep our table much longer."

"Let us go in, by all means," Densham agreed. "Wolfenden will easily find us if he wants to!"

Harcutt returned his watch to his pocket slowly, and without removing his eyes from Densham's face.

"You're not looking very fit, old chap," he remarked. "Is anything wrong?"

Densham shook his head and turned away.

"I am a little tired," he said. "We've been keeping late hours the last few nights. There's nothing the matter with me, though. Come, let us go in!"

Harcutt linked his arm in Densham's. The two men stood in the doorway.

"I have not asked you yet," Harcutt said, in a low tone. "What fortune?"

Densham laughed a little bitterly.

"I will tell you all that I know presently," he said.

"You have found out something, then?"

"I have found out," Densham answered, "all that I care to know! I have found out so much that I am leaving England within a week!"

Harcutt looked at him curiously.

"Poor old chap," he said softly. "I had no idea that you were so hard hit as all that, you know."

They passed through the crowded room to their table. Suddenly Harcutt stopped short and laid his hand upon Densham's arm.

"Great Scott!" he exclaimed. "Look at that! No wonder we had to wait for Wolfenden!"

Mr. Sabin and his niece were occupying the same table as on the previous night, only this time they were not alone. Wolfenden was sitting there between the two. At the moment of their entrance, he and the girl were laughing together. Mr. Sabin, with the air of one wholly detached from his companions, was calmly proceeding with his supper.

"I understand now," Harcutt whispered, "what Wolfenden meant this afternoon. When I reminded him about to-night, he laughed and said: 'Well, I shall see you, at any rate.' I thought it was odd at the time. I wonder how he managed it?"

Densham made no reply. The two men took their seats in silence. Wolfenden was sitting with his back half-turned to them, and he had not noticed their entrance. In a moment or two, however, he looked round, and seeing them, leaned over towards the girl and apparently asked her something. She nodded, and he immediately left his seat and joined them.

There was a little hesitation, almost awkwardness in their greetings. No one knew exactly what to say.

"You fellows are rather late, aren't you?" Wolfenden remarked.

"We were here punctually enough," Harcutt replied; "but we have been waiting for you nearly a quarter of an hour."

"I am sorry," Wolfenden said. "The fact is I ought to have left word when I came in, but I quite forgot it. I took it for granted that you would look into the room when you found that I was behind time."

"Well, it isn't of much consequence," Harcutt declared; "we are here now, at any rate, although it seems that after all we are not to have supper together."

Wolfenden glanced rapidly over his shoulder.

"You understand the position, of course," he said. "I need not ask you to excuse me."

Harcutt nodded.

"Oh, we'll excuse you, by all means; but on one condition—we want to know all about it. Where can we see you afterwards?"

"At my rooms," Wolfenden said, turning away and resuming his seat at the other table.

Densham had made no attempt whatever to join in the conversation. Once his eyes had met Wolfenden's, and it seemed to the latter that there was a certain expression there which needed some explanation. It was not anger— it certainly was not envy. Wolfenden was puzzled—he was even disturbed. Had Densham discovered anything further than he himself knew about this man and the girl? What did he mean by looking as though the key to this mysterious situation was in his hands, and as though he had nothing but pity for the only one of the trio who had met with any success? Wolfenden resumed his seat with an uncomfortable conviction that Densham knew more than he did about these people whose guest he had become, and that the knowledge had damped all his ardour. There was a cloud upon his face for a moment. The exuberance of his happiness had received a sudden check. Then the girl spoke to him, and the memory of Densham's unspoken warning passed away. He looked at her long and searchingly. Her face was as innocent and proud as the face of a child. She was unconscious even of his close scrutiny. The man might be anything; it might even be that every word that Felix had spoken was true. But of the girl he would believe no evil, he would not doubt her even for a moment.

"Your friend," remarked Mr. Sabin, helping himself to an ortolan, "is a journalist, is he not? His face seems familiar to me although I have forgotten his name, if ever I knew it."

"He is a journalist," Wolfenden answered. "Not one of the rank and file— rather a *dilettante*, but still a hard worker. He is devoted to his profession, though, and his name is Harcutt."

"Harcutt!" Mr. Sabin repeated, although he did not appear to recollect the name. "He is a political journalist, is he not?"

"Not that I am aware of," Wolfenden answered. "He is generally considered to be the great scribe of society. I believe that he is interested in foreign politics, though."

"Ah!"

Mr. Sabin's interjection was significant, and Wolfenden looked up quickly but fruitlessly. The man's face was impenetrable.

"The other fellow," Wolfenden said, turning to the girl, "is Densham, the painter. His picture in this year's Academy was a good deal talked about, and he does some excellent portraits."

She threw a glance at him over her gleaming white shoulder.

"He looks like an artist," she said. "I liked his picture—a French landscape, was it not? And his portrait of the Countess of Davenport was magnificent."

"If you would care to know him," Wolfenden said, "I should be very happy to present him to you."

Mr. Sabin looked up and shook his head quickly, but firmly.

"You must excuse us," he said. "My niece and I are not in England for very long, and we have reasons for avoiding new acquaintances as much as possible."

A shade passed across the girl's face. Wolfenden would have given much to have known into what worlds those clear, soft eyes, suddenly set in a far away gaze, were wandering—what those regrets were which had floated up so suddenly before her. Was she too as impenetrable as the man, or would he some day share with her what there was of sorrow or of mystery in her young life? His heart beat with unaccustomed quickness at the thought. Mr. Sabin's last remark, the uncertainty of his own position with regard to these people, filled him with sudden fear; it might be that he too was to be included in the sentence which had just been pronounced. He looked up from the table to find Mr. Sabin's cold, steely eyes fixed upon him, and acting upon a sudden impulse he spoke what was nearest to his heart.

"I hope," he said, "that the few acquaintances whom fate does bring you are not to suffer for the same reason."

Mr. Sabin smiled and poured himself out a glass of wine.

"You are very good," he said. "I presume that you refer to yourself. We shall always be glad that we met you, shall we not, Helène? But I doubt very much if, after to-night, we shall meet again in England at all."

To Wolfenden the light seemed suddenly to have gone out, and the soft, low music to have become a wailing dirge. He retained some command of his features only by a tremendous effort. Even then he felt that he had become pale, and that his voice betrayed something of the emotion that he felt.

"You are going away," he said slowly—"abroad!"

"Very soon indeed," Mr. Sabin answered. "At any rate, we leave London during the week. You must not look upon us, Lord Wolfenden, as ordinary pleasure-seekers. We are wanderers upon the face of the earth, not so much by choice as by destiny. I want you to try one of these cigarettes. They were given to me by the Khedive, and I think you will admit that he knows more about tobacco than he does about governing."

The girl had been gazing steadfastly at the grapes that lay untasted upon her plate, and Wolfenden glanced towards her twice in vain; now, however, she looked up, and a slight smile parted her lips as her eyes met his. How pale she was, and how suddenly serious!

"Do not take my uncle too literally, Lord Wolfenden," she said softly. "I hope that we shall meet again some time, if not often. I should be very sorry not to think so. We owe you so much."

There was an added warmth in those last few words, a subtle light in her eyes. Was she indeed a past mistress in all the arts of coquetry, or was there not some message for him in that lowered tone and softened glance? He sat spellbound for a moment. Her bosom was certainly rising and falling more quickly. The pearls at her throat quivered. Then Mr. Sabin's voice, cold and displeased, dissolved the situation.

"I think, Helène, if you are ready, we had better go," he said. "It is nearly half-past twelve, and we shall escape the crush if we leave at once."

She stood up silently, and Wolfenden, with slow fingers, raised her cloak from the back of the chair and covered her shoulders. She thanked him softly, and turning away, walked down the room followed by the two men. In the ante-room Mr. Sabin stopped.

"My watch," he remarked, "was fast. You will have time after all for a cigarette with your friends. Good-night."

Wolfenden had no alternative but to accept his dismissal. A little, white hand, flashing with jewels, but shapely and delicate, stole out from the dark fur of her cloak, and he held it within his for a second.

"I hope," he said, "that at any rate you will allow me to call, and say goodbye before you leave England?"

She looked at him with a faint smile upon her lips. Yet her eyes were very sad.

"You have heard what my inexorable guardian has said, Lord Wolfenden," she answered quietly. "I am afraid he is right. We are wanderers, he and I, with no settled home."

"I shall venture to hope," he said boldly, "that some day you will make one— in England."

A tinge of colour flashed into her cheeks. Her eyes danced with amusement at his audacity—then they suddenly dropped, and she caught up the folds of her gown.

"Ah, well," she said demurely, "that would be too great a happiness. Farewell! One never knows."

She yielded at last to Mr. Sabin's cold impatience, and turning away, followed him down the staircase. Wolfenden remained at the top until she had passed out of sight; he lingered even for a moment or two afterwards, inhaling the faint, subtle perfume shaken from her gown—a perfume which reminded him of an orchard of pink and white apple blossoms in Normandy. Then he turned back, and finding Harcutt and Densham lingering over their coffee, sat down beside them.

Harcutt looked at him through half-closed eyes—a little cloud of blue tobacco smoke hung over the table. Densham had eaten little, but smoked continually.

"Well?" he asked laconically.

"After all," Wolfenden said, "I have not very much to tell you fellows. Mr. Sabin did not call upon me; I met him by chance in Bond Street, and the girl asked me to supper, more I believe in jest than anything. However, of course I took advantage of it, and I have spent the evening since eleven o'clock with them. But as to gaining any definite information as to who or what they are, I must confess I've failed altogether. I know no more than I did yesterday."

"At any rate," Harcutt remarked, "you will soon learn all that you care to know. You have inserted the thin end of the wedge. You have established a visiting acquaintance."

Wolfenden flicked the end from his cigarette savagely.

"Nothing of the sort," he declared. "They have not given me their address, or asked me to call. On the contrary, I was given very clearly to understand by Mr. Sabin that they were only travellers and desired no acquaintances. I know them, that is all; what the next step is to be I have not the faintest idea."

Densham leaned over towards them. There was a strange light in his eyes—a peculiar, almost tremulous, earnestness in his tone.

"Why should there be any next step at all?" he said. "Let us all drop this ridiculous business. It has gone far enough. I have a presentiment—not altogether presentiment either, as it is based upon a certain knowledge. It is true that these are not ordinary people, and the girl is beautiful. But they are not of our lives! Let them pass out. Let us forget them."

Harcutt shook his head.

"The man is too interesting to be forgotten or ignored," he said. "I must know more about him, and before many days have passed."

Densham turned to the younger man.

"At least, Wolfenden," he said, "you will listen to reason. I tell you as a man of honour, and I think I may add as your friend, that you are only courting disappointment. The girl is not for you, or me, or any of us. If I dared tell you what I know, you would be the first to admit it yourself."

Wolfenden returned Densham's eager gaze steadfastly.

"I have gone," he said calmly, "too far to turn back. You fellows both know I am not a woman's man. I've never cared for a girl in all my life, or pretended to, seriously. Now that I do, it is not likely that I shall give her up without any definite reason. You must speak more plainly, Densham, or not at all."

Densham rose from his chair.

"I am very sorry," he said.

Wolfenden turned upon him, frowning.

"You need not be," he said. "You and Harcutt have both, I believe, heard some strange stories concerning the man; but as for the girl, no one shall dare to speak an unbecoming word of her."

"No one desired to," Densham answered quietly. "And yet there may be other and equally grave objections to any intercourse with her."

Wolfenden smiled confidently.

"Nothing in the world worth winning," he said, "is won without an effort, or without difficulty. The fruit that is of gold does not drop into your mouth."

The band had ceased to play and the lights went out. Around them was all the bustle of departure. The three men rose and left the room.

CHAPTER XII

WOLFENDEN'S LUCK

To leave London at all, under ordinary circumstances, was usually a hardship for Wolfenden, but to leave London at this particular moment of his life was little less than a calamity, yet a letter which he received a few mornings after the supper at the "Milan" left him scarcely any alternative. He read it over for the third time whilst his breakfast grew cold, and each time his duty seemed to become plainer.

"DERINGHAM HALL, NORFOLK.

"MY DEAR WOLFENDEN,—We have been rather looking for you to come down for a day or two, and I do hope that you will be able to manage it directly you receive this. I am sorry to say that your father is very far from well, and we have all been much upset lately. He still works for eight or nine hours a day, and his hallucinations as to the value of his papers increases with every page he writes. His latest peculiarity is a rooted conviction that there is some plot on hand to rob him of his manuscripts. You remember, perhaps, Miss Merton, the young person whom we engaged as typewriter. He sent her away the other day, without a moment's notice, simply because he saw her with a sheet of copying paper in her hand. I did not like the girl, but it is perfectly ridiculous to suspect her of anything of the sort. He insisted, however, that she should leave the house within an hour, and we were obliged to give in to him. Since then he has seemed to become even more fidgety. He has had cast-iron shutters fitted to the study windows, and two of the keepers are supposed to be on duty outside night and day, with loaded revolvers. People around here are all beginning to talk, and I am afraid that it is only natural that they should. He will see no one, and the library door is shut and bolted immediately he has entered it. Altogether it is a deplorable state of things, and what will be the end of it I cannot imagine. Sometimes it occurs to me that you might have more influence over him than I have. I hope that you will be able to come down, if only for a day or two, and see what effect your presence has. The shooting is not good this year, but Captain Willis was telling me yesterday that the golf links were in excellent condition, and there is the yacht, of course, if you care to use it. Your father seems to have quite forgotten that she is still in the neighbourhood, I am glad to say. Those inspection cruises were very bad things for him. He used to get so excited, and he was dreadfully angry if the photographs which I took were at all imperfectly developed. How is everybody? Have you seen Lady Susan lately? and is it true that Eleanor is engaged? I feel literally buried here, but I dare not suggest a move. London, for him at present, would be madness. I shall hope to get a wire from you to-morrow, and will send to Cromer to meet any train.—From your affectionate mother,

"Constance Manver Deringham."

There was not a word of reproach in the letter, but nevertheless Wolfenden felt a little conscience-stricken. He ought to have gone down to Deringham before; most certainly after the receipt of this summons he could not delay his visit any longer. He walked up and down the room impatiently. To leave London just now was detestable. It was true that he could not call upon them, and he had no idea where else to look for these people, who, for some mysterious reason, seemed to be doing all that they could to avoid his acquaintance. Yet chance had favoured him once—chance might stand his friend again. At any rate to feel himself in the same city with her was some consolation. For the last three days he had haunted Piccadilly and Bond Street. He had become a saunterer, and the shop windows had obtained from him an attention which he had never previously bestowed upon them. The thought that, at any turning, at any moment, they might meet, continually thrilled him. The idea of a journey which would place such a meeting utterly out of the question, was more than distasteful—it was hateful.

And yet he would have to go. He admitted that to himself as he ate his solitary breakfast, with the letter spread out before him. Since it was inevitable, he decided to lose no time. Better go at once and have it over. The sooner he got there the sooner he would be able to return. He rang the bell, and gave the necessary orders. At a quarter to twelve he was at King's Cross.

He took his ticket in a gloomy frame of mind, and bought the *Field* and a sporting novel at the bookstall. Then he turned towards the train, and walking idly down the platform, looking for Selby and his belongings, he experienced what was very nearly the greatest surprise of his life. So far, coincidence was certainly doing her best to befriend him. A girl was seated alone in the further corner of a first-class carriage. Something familiar in the poise of her head, or the gleam of her hair gathered up underneath an unusually smart travelling hat, attracted his attention. He came to a sudden standstill, breathless, incredulous. She was looking out of the opposite window, her head resting upon her fingers, but a sudden glimpse of her profile assured him that this was no delusion. It was Mr. Sabin's niece who sat there, a passenger by his own train, probably, as he reflected with a sudden illuminative flash of thought, to be removed from the risk of any more meetings with him.

Wolfenden, with a discretion at which he afterwards wondered, did not at once attract her attention. He hurried off to the smoking carriage before which his servant was standing, and had his own belongings promptly removed on to the platform. Then he paid a visit to the refreshment-room, and provided himself with an extensive luncheon basket, and finally, at the bookstall, he bought up every lady's paper and magazine he could lay his hands upon. There was only a minute now before the train was due to leave, and he walked along the platform as though looking for a seat, followed by his perplexed servant. When he arrived opposite to her carriage, he paused, only to find himself confronted by a severe-looking maid dressed in black, and the guard. For the first time he noticed the little strip, "engaged," pasted across the window.

"Plenty of room lower down, sir," the guard remarked. "This is an engaged carriage."

The maid whispered something to the guard, who nodded and locked the door. At the sound of the key, however, the girl looked round and saw Wolfenden. She lifted her eyebrows and smiled faintly. Then she came to the window and let it down.

"Whatever are you doing here?" she asked. "You——"

He interrupted her gently. The train was on the point of departure.

"I am going down into Norfolk," he said. "I had not the least idea of seeing you. I do not think that I was ever so surprised."

Then he hesitated for a moment.

"May I come in with you?" he asked.

She laughed at him. He had been so afraid of her possible refusal, that his question had been positively tremulous.

"I suppose so," she said slowly. "Is the train quite full, then?"

He looked at her quite keenly. She was laughing at him with her eyes—an odd little trick of hers. He was himself again at once, and answered mendaciously, but with emphasis—

"Not a seat anywhere. I shall be left behind if you don't take me in."

A word in the guard's ear was quite sufficient, but the maid looked at Wolfenden suspiciously. She leaned into the carriage.

"Would mademoiselle prefer that I, too, travelled with her?" she inquired in French.

The girl answered her in the same language.

"Certainly not, Céleste. You had better go and take your seat at once. We are just going!"

The maid reluctantly withdrew, with disapproval very plainly stamped upon her dark face. Wolfenden and his belongings were bundled in, and the whistle blew. The train moved slowly out of the station. They were off!

"I believe," she said, looking with a smile at the pile of magazines and papers littered all over the seat, "that you are an impostor. Or perhaps you have a peculiar taste in literature!"

She pointed towards the *Queen* and the *Gentlewoman*. He was in high spirits, and he made open confession.

"I saw you ten minutes ago," he declared, "and since then I have been endeavouring to make myself an acceptable travelling companion. But don't begin to study the fashions yet, please. Tell me how it is that after looking all over London for three days for you, I find you here."

"It is the unexpected," she remarked, "which always happens. But after all there is nothing mysterious about it. I am going down to a little house which my uncle has taken, somewhere near Cromer. You will think it odd, I suppose, considering his deformity, but he is devoted to golf, and some one has been telling him that Norfolk is the proper county to go to."

"And you?" he asked.

She shook her head disconsolately.

"I am afraid I am not English enough to care much for games," she admitted. "I like riding and archery, and I used to shoot a little, but to go into the country at this time of the year to play any game seems to me positively barbarous. London is quite dull enough—but the country—and the English country, too!—well, I have been engrossed in self-pity ever since my uncle announced his plans."

"I do not imagine," he said smiling, "that you care very much for England."

"I do not imagine," she admitted promptly, "that I do. I am a Frenchwoman, you see, and to me there is no city on earth like Paris, and no country like my own."

"The women of your nation," he remarked, "are always patriotic. I have never met a Frenchwoman who cared for England."

"We have reason to be patriotic," she said, "or rather, we had," she added, with a curious note of sadness in her tone. "But, come, I do not desire to talk about my country. I admitted you here to be an entertaining companion, and you have made me speak already of the subject which is to me the most mournful in the world. I do not wish to talk any more about France. Will you please think of another subject?"

"Mr. Sabin is not with you," he remarked.

"He intended to come. Something important kept him at the last moment. He will follow me, perhaps, by a later train to-day, if not to-morrow."

"It is certainly a coincidence," he said, "that you should be going to Cromer. My home is quite near there."

"And you are going there now?" she asked.

"I am delighted to say that I am."

"You did not mention it the other evening," she remarked. "You talked as though you had no intention at all of leaving London."

"Neither had I at that time," he said. "I had a letter from home this morning which decided me."

She smiled softly.

"Well, it is strange," she said. "On the whole, it is perhaps fortunate that you did not contemplate this journey when we had supper together the other night."

He caught at her meaning, and laughed.

"It is more than fortunate," he declared. "If I had known of it, and told Mr. Sabin, you would not have been travelling by this train alone."

"I certainly should not," she admitted demurely.

He saw his opportunity, and swiftly availed himself of it.

"Why does your uncle object to me so much?" he asked.

"Object to you!" she repeated. "On the contrary, I think that he rather approves of you. You saved his life, or something very much like it. He should be very grateful! I think that he is!"

"Yet," he persisted, "he does not seem to desire my acquaintance—for you, at any rate. You have just admitted, that if he had known that there was any chance of our being fellow passengers you would not have been here."

She did not answer him immediately. She was looking fixedly out of the window. Her face seemed to him more than ordinarily grave. When she turned her head, her eyes were thoughtful—a little sad.

"You are quite right," she said. "My uncle does not think it well for me to make any acquaintances in this country. We are not here for very long. No doubt he is right. He has at least reason on his side. Only it is a little dull for me, and it is not what I have been used to. Yet there are sacrifices always. I cannot tell you any more. You must please not ask me. You are here, and I am pleased that you are here! There! will not that content you?"

"It gives me," he answered earnestly, "more than contentment! It is happiness!"

"That is precisely the sort of thing," she said slowly to him, with laughter in her eyes, "which you are not to say! Please understand that!"

He accepted the rebuke lightly. He was far too happy in being with her to be troubled by vague limitations. The present was good enough for him, and he did his best to entertain her. He noticed with pleasure that she did not even glance at the pile of papers at her side. They talked without intermission. She was interested, even gay. Yet he could not but notice that every now and then, especially at any reference to the future, her tone grew graver and a shadow passed across her face. Once he said something which suggested the possibility of her living always in England. She had shaken her head at once, gently but firmly.

"No, I could never live in this country," she said, "even if my liking for it grew. It would be impossible!"

He was puzzled for a moment.

"You think that you could never care for it enough," he suggested; "yet you have scarcely had time to judge it fairly. London in the spring is gay enough, and the life at some of our country houses is very different to what it was a few years ago. Society is so much more tolerant and broader."

"It is scarcely a question," she said, "of my likes or dislikes. Next to Paris, I prefer London in the spring to any city in Europe, and a week I spent at Radnett was very delightful. But, nevertheless, I could never live here. It is not my destiny!"

The old curiosity was strong upon him. Radnett was the home of the Duchess of Radnett and Ilchester, who had the reputation of being the most exclusive hostess in Europe! He was bewildered.

"I would give a great deal," he said earnestly, "to know what you believe that destiny to be."

"We are bordering upon the forbidden subject," she reminded him, with a look which was almost reproachful. "You must please believe me when I tell you, that for me things have already been arranged otherwise. Come, I want you to tell me all about this country into which we are going. You must remember that to me it is all new!"

He suffered her to lead the conversation into other channels, with a vague feeling of disquiet. The mystery which hung around the girl and her uncle seemed only to grow denser as his desire to penetrate it grew. At present, at any rate, he was baffled. He dared ask no more questions.

The train glided into Peterborough station before either of them were well aware that they had entered in earnest upon the journey. Wolfenden looked out of the window with amazement.

"Why, we are nearly half way there!" he exclaimed. "How wretched!"

She smiled, and took up a magazine. Wolfenden's servant came respectfully to the window.

"Can I get you anything, my lord?" he inquired.

Wolfenden shook his head, and opening the door, stepped out on to the platform.

"Nothing, thanks, Selby," he said. "You had better get yourself some lunch. We don't get to Deringham until four o'clock."

The man raised his hat and turned away. In a moment, however, he was back again.

"You will pardon my mentioning it, my lord," he said, "but the young lady's maid has been travelling in my carriage, and a nice fidget she's been in all the way. She's been muttering to herself in French, and she seems terribly frightened about something or other. The moment the train stopped here, she rushed off to the telegraph office."

"She seems a little excitable," Wolfenden remarked. "All right, Selby, you'd better hurry up and get what you want to eat."

"Certainly, my lord; and perhaps your lordship knows that there is a flower-stall in the corner there."

Wolfenden nodded and hurried off. He returned to the carriage just as the train was moving off, with a handful of fresh, wet violets, whose perfume seemed instantly to fill the compartment. The girl held out her hands with a little exclamation of pleasure.

"What a delightful travelling companion you are," she declared. "I think these English violets are the sweetest flowers in the world."

She held them up to her lips. Wolfenden was looking at a paper bag in her lap.

"May I inquire what that is?" he asked.

"Buns!" she answered. "You must not think that because I am a girl I am never hungry. It is two o'clock, and I am positively famished. I sent my maid for them."

He smiled, and sweeping away the bundles of rugs and coats, produced the luncheon basket which he had secured at King's Cross, and opening it, spread out the contents.

"For two!" she exclaimed, "and what a delightful looking salad! Where on earth did that come from?"

"Oh, I am no magician," he exclaimed. "I ordered the basket at King's Cross, after I had seen you. Let me spread the cloth here. My dressing-case will make a capital table!"

They picnicked together gaily. It seemed to Wolfenden that chicken and tongue had never tasted so well before, or claret, at three shillings the bottle, so full and delicious. They cleared everything up, and then sat and talked over the cigarette which she had insisted upon. But although he tried more than once, he could not lead the conversation into any serious channel—she would not talk of her past, she distinctly avoided the future. Once, when he had made a deliberate effort to gain some knowledge as to her earlier surroundings, she reproved him with a silence so marked that he hastened to talk of something else.

"Your maid," he said, "is greatly distressed about something. She sent a telegram off at Peterborough. I hope that your uncle will not make himself unpleasant because of my travelling with you."

She smiled at him quite undisturbed.

"Poor Céleste," she said. "Your presence here has upset her terribly. Mr. Sabin has some rather strange notions about me, and I am quite sure that he would rather have sent me down in a special train than have had this happen. You need not look so serious about it."

"It is only on your account," he assured her.

"Then you need not look serious at all," she continued. "I am not under my uncle's jurisdiction. In fact, I am quite an independent person."

"I am delighted to hear it," he said heartily. "I should imagine that Mr. Sabin would not be at all a pleasant person to be on bad terms with."

She smiled thoughtfully.

"There are a good many people," she said, "who would agree with you. There are a great many people in the world who have cause to regret having offended him. Let us talk of something else. I believe that I can see the sea!"

They were indeed at Cromer. He found a carriage for her, and collected her belongings. He was almost amused at her absolute indolence in the midst of the bustle of arrival. She was evidently unused to doing the slightest thing for herself. He took the address which she gave to him, and repeated it to the driver. Then he asked the question which had been trembling many times upon his lips.

"May I come and see you?"

She had evidently been considering the matter, for she answered him at once and deliberately.

"I should like you to," she said; "but if for any reason it did not suit my uncle to have you come, it would not be pleasant for either of us. He is going to play golf on the Deringham links. You will be certain to see him there, and you must be guided by his manner towards you."

"And if he is still—as he was in London—must this be goodbye, then?" he asked earnestly.

She looked at him with a faint colour in her cheeks and a softer light in her proud, clear eyes.

"Well," she said, "goodbye would be the last word which could be spoken between us. But, *n'importe*, we shall see."

She flashed a suddenly brilliant smile upon him, and leaned back amongst the cushions. The carriage drove off, and Wolfenden, humming pleasantly to himself, stepped into the dogcart which was waiting for him.

CHAPTER XIII

A GREAT WORK

The Countess of Deringham might be excused for considering herself the most unfortunate woman in England. In a single week she had passed from the position of one of the most brilliant leaders of English society to be the keeper of a recluse, whose sanity was at least doubtful. Her husband, Admiral the Earl of Deringham, had been a man of iron nerve and constitution, with a splendid reputation, and undoubtedly a fine seaman. The horror of a single day had broken up his life. He had been the awe-stricken witness of a great naval catastrophe, in which many of his oldest friends and companions had gone to the bottom of the sea before his eyes, together with nearly a thousand British seamen. The responsibility for the disaster lay chiefly from those who had perished in it, yet some small share of the blame was fastened upon the onlookers, and he himself, as admiral in command, had not altogether escaped. From the moment when they had led him down from the bridge of his flagship, grey and fainting, he had been a changed man. He had never recovered from the shock. He retired from active service at once, under a singular and marvellously persistent delusion. Briefly he believed, or professed to believe, that half the British fleet had perished, and that the country was at the mercy of the first great Power who cared to send her warships up the Thames. It was a question whether he was really insane; on any ordinary topic his views were the views of a rational man, but the task which he proceeded to set himself was so absorbing that any other subject seemed scarcely to come within the horizon of his comprehension. He imagined himself selected by no less a person than the Secretary for War, to devote the rest of his life to the accomplishment of a certain undertaking! Practically his mission was to prove by figures, plans, and naval details (unknown to the general public), the complete helplessness of the empire. He bought a yacht and commenced a series of short cruises, lasting over two years, during the whole of which time his wife was his faithful and constant companion. They visited in turn each one of the fortified ports of the country, winding up with a general inspection of every battleship and cruiser within British waters. Then, with huge piles of amassed information before him, he settled down in Norfolk to the framing of his report, still under the impression that the whole country was anxiously awaiting it. His wife remained with him then, listening daily to the news of his progress, and careful never to utter a single word of discouragement or disbelief in the startling facts which he sometimes put before her. The best room in the house, the great library, was stripped perfectly bare and fitted up for his study, and a typist was engaged to copy out the result of his labours in fair form. Lately, the fatal results to England which would follow the public disclosure of her awful helplessness had weighed heavily upon him, and he was beginning to live in the fear of betrayal. The room in which he worked was fitted with iron shutters, and was guarded night and day. He saw no visitors, and was annoyed if any were permitted to enter the house. He met his wife only at dinner time, for which meal he dressed in great state, and at which no one else was ever allowed to be present. He suffered, when they were alone, no word to pass his lips, save with reference to the subject of his labours; it is certain he looked upon himself as the discoverer of terrible secrets. Any remark addressed to him upon other matters utterly failed to make any impression. If he heard it he did not reply. He would simply look puzzled, and, as speedily as possible withdraw. He was sixty years of age, of dignified and kindly appearance; a handsome man still, save that the fire of his blue eyes was quenched, and the firm lines of his commanding mouth had become tremulous. Wolfenden, on his arrival, was met in the hall by his mother, who carried him off at once to have tea in her own room. As he took a low chair opposite to her he was conscious at once of a distinct sense of self-reproach. Although still a handsome woman, the Countess of Deringham was only the wreck of her former brilliant self. Wolfenden, knowing what her life must be, under its altered circumstances, could scarcely wonder at it. The black hair was still only faintly streaked with grey, and her figure was as slim and upright as ever. But there were lines on her forehead and about her eyes, her cheeks were thinner, and even her hands were wasted. He looked at her in silent pity, and although a man of singularly undemonstrative habits, he took her hand in his and pressed it gently. Then he set himself to talk as cheerfully as possible.

"There is nothing much wrong physically with the Admiral, I hope?" he said, calling him by the name they still always gave him. "I saw him at the window as I came round. By the bye, what is that extraordinary looking affair like a sentry-box doing there?"

The Countess sighed.

"That is part of what I have to tell you," she said. "A sentry-box is exactly what it is, and if you had looked inside you would have seen Dunn or Heggs there keeping guard. In health your father seems as well as ever; mentally, I am afraid that he is worse. I fear that he is getting very bad indeed. That is why I have sent for you, Wolf!"

Wolfenden was seriously and genuinely concerned. Surely his mother had had enough to bear.

"I am very sorry," he said. "Your letter prepared me a little for this; you must tell me all about it."

"He has suddenly become the victim," the Countess said, "of a new and most extraordinary delusion. How it came to pass I cannot exactly tell, but this is what happened. He has a bed, you know, made up in an ante-room, leading from the library, and he sleeps there generally. Early this morning the whole house was awakened by the sound of two revolver shots. I hurried down in my dressing-gown, and found some of the servants already outside the library door, which was locked and barred on the inside. When he heard my voice he let me in. The room was in partial darkness and some disorder. He had a smoking revolver in his hand, and he was muttering to himself so fast that I could not understand a word he said. The chest which holds all his maps and papers had been dragged into the middle of the room, and the iron staple had been twisted, as though with a heavy blow. I saw that the lamp was flickering and a current of air was in the room, and when I looked towards the window I found that the shutters were open and one of the sashes had been lifted. All at once he became coherent.

"'Send for Morton and Philip Dunn!' he cried. 'Let the shrubbery and all the Home Park be searched. Let no one pass out of either of the gates. There have been thieves here!'

"I gave his orders to Morton. 'Where is Richardson?' I asked. Richardson was supposed to have been watching outside. Before he could answer Richardson came in through the window. His forehead was bleeding, as though from a blow.

"'What has happened, Richardson?' I asked. The man hesitated and looked at your father. Your father answered instead.

"'I woke up five minutes ago,' he cried, 'and found two men here. How they got past Richardson I don't know, but they were in the room, and they had dragged my chest out there, and had forced a crowbar through the lock! I was just in time; I hit one man in the arm and he fired back. Then they bolted right past Richardson. They must have nearly knocked you down. You must have been asleep, you idiot,' he cried, 'or you could have stopped them!'

"I turned to Richardson; he did not say a word, but he looked at me meaningly. The Admiral was examining his chest, so I drew Richardson on one side.

"'Is this true, Richardson?' I asked. The man shook his head.

"'No, your ladyship,' he said bluntly, 'it ain't; there's no two men been here at all! The master dragged the chest out himself; I heard him doing it, and I saw the light, so I left my box and stepped into the room to see what was wrong. Directly he saw me he yelled out and let fly at me with his revolver! It's a wonder I'm alive, for one of the bullets grazed my temple!'

"Then he went on to say that he would like to leave, that no wages were good enough to be shot at, and plainly hinted that he thought your father ought to be locked up. I talked him over, and then got the Admiral to go back to bed. We had the place searched as a matter of form, but of course there was no sign of anybody. He had imagined the whole thing! It is a mercy that he did not kill Richardson!"

"This is very serious," Wolfenden said gravely. "What about his revolver?"

"I managed to secure that," the Countess said. "It is locked up in my drawer, but I am afraid that he may ask for it at any moment."

"We can make that all right," Wolfenden said; "I know where there are some blank cartridges in the gun-room, and I will reload the revolver with them. By the bye, what does Blatherwick say about all this?"

"He is almost as worried as I am, poor little man," Lady Deringham said. "I am afraid every day that he will give it up and leave. We are paying him five hundred a year, but it must be miserable work for him. It is really almost amusing, though, to see how terrified he is at your father. He positively shakes when he speaks to him."

"What does he have to do?" Wolfenden asked.

"Oh, draw maps and make calculations and copy all sorts of things. You see it is wasted and purposeless work, that is what makes it so hard for the poor man."

"You are quite sure, I suppose," Wolfenden asked, after a moment's hesitation, "that it is all wasted work?"

"Absolutely," the Countess declared. "Mr. Blatherwick brings me, sometimes in despair, sheets upon which he has been engaged for days. They are all just a hopeless tangle of figures and wild calculations! Nobody could possibly make anything coherent out of them."

"I wonder," Wolfenden suggested thoughtfully, "whether it would be a good idea to get Denvers, the secretary, to write and ask him not to go on with the work for the present. He could easily make some excuse—say that it was attracting attention which they desired to avoid, or something of that sort! Denvers is a good fellow, and he and the Admiral were great friends once, weren't they?"

The Countess shook her head.

"I am afraid that would not do at all," she said. "Besides, out of pure good nature, of course, Denvers has already encouraged him. Only last week he wrote him a friendly letter hoping that he was getting on, and telling him how interested every one in the War Office was to hear about his work. He has known about it all the time, you see. Then, too, if the occupation were taken from your father, I am afraid he would break down altogether."

"Of course there is that to be feared," Wolfenden admitted. "I wonder what put this new delusion into his head? Does he suspect any one in particular?"

The Countess shook her head.

"I do not think so; of course it was Miss Merton who started it. He quite believes that she took copies of all the work she did here, but he was so pleased with himself at the idea of having found her out, that he has troubled very little about it. He seems to think that she had not reached the most important part of his work, and he is copying that himself now by hand."

"But outside the house has he no suspicions at all?"

"Not that I know of; not any definite suspicion. He was talking last night of Duchesne, the great spy and adventurer, in a rambling sort of way. 'Duchesne would be the man to get hold of my work if he knew of it,' he kept on saying. 'But none must know of it! The newspapers must be quiet! It is a terrible danger!' He talked like that for some time. No, I do not think that he suspects anybody. It is more a general uneasiness."

"Poor old chap!" Wolfenden said softly. "What does Dr. Whitlett think of him? Has he seen him lately? I wonder if there is any chance of his getting over it?"

"None at all," she answered. "Dr. Whitlett is quite frank; he will never recover what he has lost—he will probably lose more. But come, there is the dressing bell. You will see him for yourself at dinner. Whatever you do don't be late—he hates any one to be a minute behind time."

CHAPTER XIV

THE TEMPTING OF MR. BLATHERWICK

Wolfenden was careful to reach the hall before the dinner gong had sounded. His father greeted him warmly, and Wolfenden was surprised to see so little outward change in him. He was carefully dressed, well groomed in every respect, and he wore a delicate orchid in his button-hole.

During dinner he discussed the little round of London life and its various social events with perfect sanity, and permitted himself his usual good-natured grumble at Wolfenden for his dilatoriness in the choice of a profession.

He did not once refer to the subject of his own weakness until dessert had been served, when he passed the claret to Wolfenden without filling his own glass.

"You will excuse my not joining you," he said to his son, "but I have still three or four hours' writing to do, and such work as mine requires a very clear head—you can understand that, I daresay."

Wolfenden assented in silence. For the first time, perhaps, he fully realised the ethical pity of seeing a man so distinguished the victim of a hopeless and incurable mania. He watched him sitting at the head of his table, courteous, gentle, dignified; noted too the air of intellectual abstraction which followed upon his last speech, and in which he seemed to dwell for the rest of the time during which they sat together. Instinctively he knew what disillusionment must mean for him. Sooner anything than that. It must never be. Never! he repeated firmly to himself as he smoked a solitary cigar later on in the empty smoking-room. Whatever happens he must be saved from that. There was a knock at the door, and in response to his invitation to enter, Mr. Blatherwick came in. Wolfenden, who was in the humour to prefer any one's society to his own, greeted him pleasantly, and wheeled up an easy chair opposite to his own.

"Come to have a smoke, Blatherwick?" he said. "That's right. Try one of these cigars; the governor's are all right, but they are in such shocking condition."

Mr. Blatherwick accepted one with some hesitation, and puffed slowly at it with an air of great deliberation. He was a young man of mild demeanour and deportment, and clerical aspirations. He wore thick spectacles, and suffered from chronic biliousness.

"I am much obliged to you, Lord Wolfenden," he said. "I seldom smoke cigars—it is not good for my sight. An occasional cigarette is all I permit myself."

Wolfenden groaned inwardly, for his regalias were priceless and not to be replaced; but he said nothing.

"I have taken the liberty, Lord Wolfenden," Mr. Blatherwick continued, "of bringing for your inspection a letter I received this morning. It is, I presume, intended for a practical joke, and I need not say that I intend to treat it as such. At the same time as you were in the house, I imagined that no—er— harm would ensue if I ventured to ask for your opinion."

He handed an open letter to Wolfenden, who took it and read it through. It was dated "—— London," and bore the postmark of the previous day.

"MR. ARNOLD BLATHERWICK.

"DEAR SIR,—The writer of this letter is prepared to offer you one thousand pounds in return for a certain service which you are in a position to perform. The details of that service can only be explained to you in a personal interview, but broadly speaking it is as follows:—

"You are engaged as private secretary to the Earl of Deringham, lately an admiral in the British Navy. Your duties, it is presumed, are to copy and revise papers and calculations having reference to the coast defences and navy of Great Britain. The writer is himself engaged upon a somewhat similar task, but not having had the facilities accorded to Lord Deringham, is without one or two important particulars. The service required of you is the supplying of these, and for this you are offered one thousand pounds.

"As a man of honour you may possibly hesitate to at once embrace this offer. You need not! Lord Deringham's work is practically useless, for it is the work of a lunatic. You yourself, from your intimate association with him, must know that this statement is true. He will never be able to give coherent form to the mass of statistics and information which he has collected. Therefore you do him no harm in supplying these few particulars to one who will be able to make use of them. The sum you are offered is out of all proportion to their value—a few months' delay and they could easily be acquired by the writer without the expenditure of a single halfpenny. That, however, is not the point.

"I am rich and I have no time to spare. Hence this offer. I take it that you are a man of common sense, and I take it for granted, therefore, that you will not hesitate to accept this offer. Your acquiescence will be assumed if you lunch at the Grand Hotel, Cromer, between one and two, on Thursday following the receipt of this letter. You will then be put in full possession of all the information necessary to the carrying out of the proposals made to you. You are well known to the writer, who will take the liberty of joining you at your table."

The letter ended thus somewhat abruptly. Wolfenden, who had only glanced it through at first, now re-read it carefully. Then he handed it back to Blatherwick.

"It is a very curious communication," he said thoughtfully, "a very curious communication indeed. I do not know what to think of it."

Mr. Blatherwick laid down his cigar with an air of great relief. He would have liked to have thrown it away, but dared not.

"It must surely be intended for a practical joke, Lord Wolfenden," he said. "Either that, or my correspondent has been ludicrously misinformed."

"You do not consider, then, that my father's work is of any value at all?" Wolfenden asked.

Mr. Blatherwick coughed apologetically, and watched the extinction of the cigar by his side with obvious satisfaction.

"You would, I am sure, prefer," he said, "that I gave you a perfectly straightforward answer to that question. I—er—cannot conceive that the work upon which his lordship and I are engaged can be of the slightest interest or use to anybody. I can assure you, Lord Wolfenden, that my brain at times reels—positively reels—from the extraordinary nature of the manuscripts which your father has passed on to me to copy. It is not that they are merely technical, they are absolutely and entirely meaningless. You ask me for my opinion, Lord Wolfenden, and I conceive it to be my duty to answer you honestly. I am quite sure that his lordship is not in a fit state of mind to undertake any serious work."

"The person who wrote that letter," Wolfenden remarked, "thought otherwise."

"The person who wrote that letter," Mr. Blatherwick retorted quickly, "if indeed it was written in good faith, is scarcely likely to know so much about his lordship's condition of mind as I, who have spent the greater portion of every day for three months with him."

"Do you consider that my father is getting worse, Mr. Blatherwick?" Wolfenden asked.

"A week ago," Mr. Blatherwick said, "I should have replied that his lordship's state of mind was exactly the same as when I first came here. But there has been a change for the worse during the last week. It commenced with his sudden, and I am bound to say, unfounded suspicions of Miss Merton, whom I believe to be a most estimable and worthy young lady."

Mr. Blatherwick paused, and appeared to be troubled with a slight cough. The smile, which Wolfenden was not altogether able to conceal, seemed somewhat to increase his embarrassment.

"The extraordinary occurrence of last night, which her ladyship has probably detailed to you," Mr. Blatherwick continued, "was the next development of what, I fear, we can only regard as downright insanity. I regret having to speak so plainly, but I am afraid that any milder phrase would be inapplicable."

"I am very sorry to hear this," Wolfenden remarked gravely.

"Under the circumstances," Mr. Blatherwick said, picking up his cigar which was now extinct, and immediately laying it down again, "I trust that you and Lady Deringham will excuse my not giving the customary notice of my desire to leave. It is of course impossible for me to continue to draw a—er—a stipend such as I am in receipt of for services so ludicrously inadequate."

"Lady Deringham will be sorry to have you go," Wolfenden said. "Couldn't you put up with it a little longer?"

"I would much prefer to leave," Mr. Blatherwick said decidedly. "I am not physically strong, and I must confess that his lordship's attitude at times positively alarms me. I fear that there is no doubt that he committed an unprovoked assault last night upon that unfortunate keeper. There is—er—no telling whom he might select for his next victim. If quite convenient, Lord Wolfenden, I should like to leave to-morrow by an early train."

"Oh! you can't go so soon as that," Wolfenden said. "How about this letter?"

"You can take any steps you think proper with regard to it," Mr. Blatherwick answered nervously. "Personally, I have nothing to do with it. I thought of going to spend a week with an aunt of mine in Cornwall, and I should like to leave by the early train to-morrow."

Wolfenden could scarcely keep from laughing, although he was a little annoyed.

"Look here, Blatherwick," he said, "you must help me a little before you go, there's a good fellow. I don't doubt for a moment what you say about the poor old governor's condition of mind; but at the same time it's rather an odd thing, isn't it, that his own sudden fear of having his work stolen is followed up by the receipt of this letter to you? There is some one, at any rate, who places a very high value upon his manuscripts. I must say that I should like to know whom that letter came from."

"I can assure you," Mr. Blatherwick said, "that I have not the faintest idea."

"Of course you haven't," Wolfenden assented, a little impatiently. "But don't you see how easy it will be for us to find out? You must go to the Grand Hotel on Thursday for lunch, and meet this mysterious person."

"I would very much rather not," Mr. Blatherwick declared promptly. "I should feel exceedingly uncomfortable; I should not like it at all!"

"Look here," Wolfenden said persuasively "I must find out who wrote that letter, and can only do so with your help. You need only be there, I will come up directly I have marked the man who comes to your table. Your presence is all that is required; and I shall take it as a favour if you will allow me to make you a present of a fifty-pound note."

Mr. Blatherwick flushed a little and hesitated. He had brothers and sisters, whose bringing up was a terrible strain upon the slim purse of his father, a country clergyman, and a great deal could be done with fifty pounds. It was against his conscience as well as his inclinations to remain in a post where his duties were a farce, but this was different.

He sighed.

"You are very generous, Lord Wolfenden," he said. "I will stay until after Thursday."

"There's a good fellow," Wolfenden said, much relieved. "Have another cigar?"

Mr. Blatherwick rose hastily, and shook his head. "You must excuse me, if you please," he said. "I will not smoke any more. I think if you will not mind——"

Wolfenden turned to the window and held up his hand.

"Listen!" he said. "Is that a carriage at this time of night?"

A carriage it certainly was, passing by the window. In a moment they heard it draw up at the front door, and some one alighted.

"Odd time for callers," Wolfenden remarked.

Mr. Blatherwick did not reply. He, too, was listening. In a moment they heard the rustling of a woman's skirts outside, and the smoking-room door opened.

CHAPTER XV

THE COMING AND GOING OF MR. FRANKLIN WILMOT

Both men looked up as Lady Deringham entered the room, carefully closing the door behind her. She had a card in her hand, and an open letter.

"Wolfenden," she said. "I am so glad that you are here. It is most fortunate! Something very singular has happened. You will be able to tell me what to do."

Mr. Blatherwick rose quietly and left the room.

Wolfenden was all attention.

"Some one has just arrived," he remarked.

"A gentleman, a complete stranger," she assented. "This is his card. He seemed surprised that his name was not familiar to me. He was quite sure that you would know it."

Wolfenden took the card between his fingers and read it out.

"Mr. Franklin Wilmot."

He was thoughtful for a moment. The name was familiar enough, but he could not immediately remember in what connection. Suddenly it flashed into his mind.

"Of course!" he exclaimed. "He is a famous physician—a very great swell, goes to Court and all that!"

Lady Deringham nodded.

"He has introduced himself as a physician. He has brought this letter from Dr. Whitlett."

Wolfenden took the note from her hand. It was written on half a sheet of paper, and apparently in great haste:—

"DEAR LADY DERINGHAM,—My old friend, Franklin Wilmot, who has been staying at Cromer, has just called upon me. We have been having a chat, and he is extremely interested in Lord Deringham's case, so much so that I had arranged to come over with him this evening to see if you would care to have his opinion. Unfortunately, however, I have been summoned to attend a patient nearly ten miles away—a bad accident, I fear—and Wilmot is leaving for town to-morrow morning. I suggested, however, that he might call on his way back to Cromer, and if you would kindly let him see Lord Deringham, I should be glad, as his opinion would be of material assistance to me. Wilmot's reputation as the greatest living authority on cases of partial mania is doubtless known to you, and as he never, under any circumstances, visits patients outside London, it would be a great pity to lose this opportunity.

"In great haste and begging you to excuse this scrawl,

"I am, dear Lady Deringham,
"Yours sincerely,
"JOHN WHITLETT.

"P.S.—You will please not offer him any fee."

Wolfenden folded up the letter and returned it.

"Well, I suppose it's all right," he said. "It's an odd time, though, to call on an errand of this sort."

"So I thought," Lady Deringham agreed; "but Dr. Whitlett's explanation seems perfectly feasible, does it not? I said that I would consult you. You will come in and see him?"

Wolfenden followed his mother into the drawing-room. A tall, dark man was sitting in a corner, under a palm tree. In one hand he held a magazine, the pictures of which he seemed to be studying with the aid of an eyeglass, the other was raised to his mouth. He was in the act of indulging in a yawn when Wolfenden and his mother entered the room.

"This is my son, Lord Wolfenden," she said. "Dr. Franklin Wilmot."

The two men bowed.

"Lady Deringham has explained to you the reason of my untimely visit, I presume?" the latter remarked at once.

Wolfenden assented.

"Yes! I am afraid that it will be a little difficult to get my father to see you on such short notice."

"I was about to explain to Lady Deringham, before I understood that you were in the house," Dr. Wilmot said, "that although that would be an advantage, it is not absolutely necessary at present. I should of course have to examine your father before giving a definite opinion as to his case, but I can give you a very fair idea as to his condition without seeing him at all."

Wolfenden and his mother exchanged glances.

"You must forgive us," Wolfenden commenced hesitatingly, "but really I can scarcely understand."

"Of course not," their visitor interrupted brusquely. "My method is one which is doubtless altogether strange to you, but if you read the *Lancet* or the *Medical Journal*, you would have heard a good deal about it lately. I form my conclusions as to the mental condition of a patient almost altogether from a close inspection of their letters, or any work upon which they are, or have been, recently engaged. I do not say that it is possible to do this from a single letter, but when a man has a hobby, such as I understand Lord Deringham indulges in, and has devoted a great deal of time to real or imaginary work in connection with it, I am generally able, from a study of that work, to tell how far the brain is weakened, if at all, and in what manner it can be strengthened. This is only the crudest outline of my theory, but to be brief, I can give you my opinion as to Lord Deringham's mental condition, and my advice as to its maintenance, if you will place before me the latest work upon which he has been engaged. I hope I have made myself clear."

"Perfectly," Wolfenden answered. "It sounds very reasonable and very interesting, but I am afraid that there are a few practical difficulties in the way. In the first place, my father does not show his work or any portion of it to any one. On the other hand he takes the most extraordinary precautions to maintain absolute secrecy with regard to it."

"That," Dr. Wilmot remarked, "is rather a bad feature of the case. It is a difficulty which I should imagine you could get over, though. You could easily frame some excuse to get him away from his study for a short time and leave me there. Of course the affair is in your hands altogether, and I am presuming that you are anxious to have an opinion as to your father's state of health. I am not in the habit of seeking patients," he added, a little stiffly. "I was interested in my friend Whitlett's description of the case, and anxious to apply my theories to it, as it happens to differ in some respects from anything I have met with lately. Further, I may add," he continued, glancing at the clock, "if anything is to be done it must be done quickly. I have no time to spare."

"You had better," Wolfenden suggested, "stay here for the night in any case. We will send you to the station, or into Cromer, as early as you like in the morning."

"Absolutely impossible," Dr. Wilmot replied briefly. "I am staying with friends in Cromer, and I have a consultation in town early to-morrow morning. You must really make up your minds at once whether you wish for my opinion or not."

"I do not think," Lady Deringham said, "that we need hesitate for a moment about that!"

Wolfenden looked at him doubtfully. There seemed to be no possibility of anything but advantage in accepting this offer, and yet in a sense he was sorry that it had been made.

"In case you should attach any special importance to your father's manuscripts," Dr. Wilmot remarked, with a note of sarcasm in his tone, "I might add that it is not at all necessary for me to be alone in the study."

Wolfenden felt a little uncomfortable under the older man's keen gaze. Neither did he altogether like having his thoughts read so accurately.

"I suppose," he said, turning to his mother, "you could manage to get him away from the library for a short time?"

"I could at least try," she answered. "Shall I?"

"I think," he said, "that as Dr. Wilmot has been good enough to go out of his way to call here, we must make an effort."

Lady Deringham left the room.

Dr. Wilmot, whose expression of absolute impassiveness had not altered in the least during their discussion, turned towards Wolfenden.

"Have you yourself," he said, "never seen any of your father's manuscripts? Has he never explained the scheme of his work to you?"

Wolfenden shook his head.

"I know the central idea," he answered—"the weakness of our navy and coast defences, and that is about all I know. My father, even when he was an admiral on active service, took an absolutely pessimistic view of both. You may perhaps remember this. The Lords of the Admiralty used to consider him, I believe, the one great thorn in their sides."

Dr. Wilmot shook his head.

"I have never taken any interest in such matters," he said. "My profession has been completely absorbing during the last ten years."

Wolfenden nodded.

"I know," he remarked, "that I used to read the newspapers and wonder why on earth my father took such pains to try and frighten everybody. But he is altogether changed now. He even avoids the subject, although I am quite sure that it is his one engrossing thought. It is certain that no one has ever given such time and concentrated energy to it before. If only his work was the work of a sane man I could understand it being very valuable."

"Not the least doubt about it, I should say," Dr. Wilmot replied carelessly.

The door opened and Lady Deringham reappeared.

"I have succeeded," she said. "He is upstairs now. I will try and keep him there for half an hour. Wolfenden, will you take Dr. Wilmot into the study?"

Dr. Wilmot rose with quiet alacrity. Wolfenden led the way down the long passage which led to the study. He himself was scarcely prepared for such signs of unusual labours as confronted them both when they opened the door. The round table in the centre of the room was piled with books and a loose heap of papers. A special rack was hung with a collection of maps and charts. There were nautical instruments upon the table, and compasses, as well as writing materials, and a number of small models of men-of-war. Mr. Blatherwick, who was sitting at the other side of the room busy with some copying, looked up in amazement at the entrance of Wolfenden and a stranger upon what was always considered forbidden ground.

Wolfenden stepped forward at once to the table. A sheet of paper lay there on which the ink was scarcely yet dry. Many others were scattered about, almost undecipherable, with marginal notes and corrections in his father's handwriting. He pushed some of them towards his companion.

"You can help yourself," he said. "This seems to be his most recent work."

Dr. Wilmot seemed scarcely to hear him. He had turned the lamp up with quick fingers, and was leaning over those freshly written pages. Decidedly he was interested in the case. He stood quite still reading with breathless haste— the papers seemed almost to fly through his fingers. Wolfenden was a little puzzled. Mr. Blatherwick, who had been watching the proceedings with blank amazement, rose and came over towards them.

"You will excuse me, Lord Wolfenden," he said, "but if the admiral should come back and find a stranger with you looking over his work, he will——"

"It's all right, Blatherwick," Wolfenden interrupted, the more impatiently since he was far from comfortable himself. "This gentleman is a physician."

The secretary resumed his seat. Dr. Wilmot was reading with lightning-like speed sheet after sheet, making frequent notes in a pocket-book which he had laid on the table before him. He was so absorbed that he did not seem to hear the sound of wheels coming up the avenue.

Wolfenden walked to the window, and raising the curtain, looked out. He gave vent to a little exclamation of relief as he saw a familiar dogcart draw up at the hall door, and Dr. Whitlett's famous mare pulled steaming on to her haunches.

"It is Dr. Whitlett," he exclaimed. "He has followed you up pretty soon."

The sheet which the physician was reading fluttered through his fingers. There was a very curious look in his face. He walked up to the window and looked out.

"So it is," he remarked. "I should like to see him at once for half a minute—then I shall have finished. I wonder whether you would mind going yourself and asking him to step this way?"

Wolfenden turned immediately to leave the room. At the door he turned sharply round, attracted by a sudden noise and an exclamation from Blatherwick. Dr. Wilmot had disappeared! Mr. Blatherwick was gazing at the window in amazement!

"He's gone, sir! Clean out of the window—jumped it like a cat!"

Wolfenden sprang to the curtains. The night wind was blowing into the room through the open casement. Fainter and fainter down the long avenue came the sound of galloping horses. Dr. Franklin Wilmot had certainly gone!

Wolfenden turned from the window to find himself face to face with Dr. Whitlett.

"What on earth is the matter with your friend Wilmot?" he exclaimed. "He has just gone off through the window like a madman!"

"Wilmot!" the doctor exclaimed. "I never knew any one of that name in my life. The fellow's a rank impostor!"

CHAPTER XVI

GENIUS OR MADNESS?

For a moment Wolfenden was speechless. Then, with a presence of mind which afterwards he marvelled at, he asked no more questions, but stepped up to the writing-table.

"Blatherwick," he said hurriedly, "we seem to have made a bad mistake. Will you try and rearrange these papers exactly as the admiral left them, and do not let him know that any one has entered the room or seen them."

Mr. Blatherwick commenced his task with trembling fingers.

"I will do my best," he said nervously. "But I am not supposed to touch anything upon this table at all. If the admiral finds me here, he will be very angry."

"I will take the blame," Wolfenden said. "Do your best."

He took the country doctor by the arm and hurried him into the smoking-room.

"This is a most extraordinary affair, Dr. Whitlett," he said gravely. "I presume that this letter, then, is a forgery?"

The doctor took the note of introduction which Wilmot had brought, and adjusting his pince-nez, read it hastily through.

"A forgery from the beginning to end," he declared, turning it over and looking at it helplessly. "I have never known any one of the name in my life!"

"It is written on notepaper stamped with your address," Wolfenden remarked. "It is also, I suppose, a fair imitation of your handwriting, for Lady Deringham accepted it as such?"

The doctor nodded.

"I will tell you," he said, "all that I know of the affair. I started out to pay some calls this evening about six o'clock. As I turned into the main road I met a strange brougham and pair of horses being driven very slowly. There was a man who looked like a gentleman's servant sitting by the side of the coachman, and as I passed them the latter asked a question, and I am almost certain that I heard my name mentioned. I was naturally a little curious, and I kept looking back all along the road to see which way they turned after passing my house. As a matter of fact, although I pulled up and waited in the middle of the road, I saw no more of the carriage. When at last I drove on, I knew that one of two things must have happened. Either the carriage must have come to a standstill and remained stationary in the road, or it must have turned in at my gate. The hedge was down a little higher up the road, and I could see distinctly that they had not commenced to climb the hill. It seemed very odd to me, but I had an important call to make, so I drove on and got through as quickly as I could. On my way home I passed your north entrance, and, looking up the avenue, I saw the same brougham on its way up to the house. I had half a mind to run in then—I wish now that I had—but instead of doing so I drove quickly home. There I found that a gentleman had called a few minutes after I had left home, and finding me out had asked permission to leave a note. The girl had shown him into the study, and he had remained there about ten minutes. Afterwards he had let himself out and driven away. When I looked for the note for me there was none, but the writing materials had been used, and a sheet of notepaper was gone. I happened to remember that there was only one out. The whole thing seemed to me so singular that I ordered the dogcart out again and drove straight over here."

"For which," Wolfenden remarked, "we ought to feel remarkably grateful. So far the thing is plain enough! But what on earth did that man, whoever he was, expect to find in my father's study that he should make an elaborate attempt like this to enter it? He was no common thief!"

Dr. Whitlett shook his head. He had no elucidation to offer. The thing was absolutely mysterious.

"Your father himself," he said slowly, "sets a very high value upon the result of his researches!"

"And on the other hand," Wolfenden retorted promptly, "you, and my mother, Mr. Blatherwick, and even the girl who has been copying for him, have each assured me that his work is rubbish! You four comprise all who have seen any part of it, and I understand that you have come to the conclusion that, if not insane, he is at least suffering from some sort of mania. Now, how are we to reconcile this with the fact of an attempted robbery this evening, and the further fact that a heavy bribe has been secretly offered to Blatherwick to copy only a few pages of his later manuscripts?"

Dr. Whitlett started.

"Indeed!" he exclaimed. "When did you hear of this?"

"Only this afternoon," Wolfenden answered. "Blatherwick brought me the letter himself. What I cannot understand is, how these documents could ever become a marketable commodity. Yet we may look upon it now as an absolute fact, that there are persons—and no ordinary thieves either!— conspiring to obtain possession of them."

"Wolfenden!"

The two men started round. The Countess was standing in the doorway. She was pale as death, and her eyes were full of fear.

"Who was that man?" she cried. "What has happened?"

"He was an impostor, I am afraid," Wolfenden answered. "The letter from Dr. Whitlett was forged. He has bolted."

She looked towards the doctor.

"Thank God that you are here!" she cried. "I am frightened! There are some papers and models missing, and the admiral has found it out! I am afraid he is going to have a fit. Please come into the library. He must not be left alone!"

They both followed her down the passage and through the half-opened door. In the centre of the room Lord Deringham was standing, his pale cheeks scarlet with passion, his fists convulsively clenched. He turned sharply round to face them, and his eyes flashed with anger.

"Nothing shall make me believe that this room has not been entered, and my papers tampered with!" he stormed out. "Where is that reptile Blatherwick? I left my morning's work and two models on the desk there, less than half an hour ago; both the models are gone and one of the sheets! Either Blatherwick has stolen them, or the room has been entered during my absence! Where is that hound?"

"He is in his room," Lady Deringham answered. "He ran past me on the stairs trembling all over, and he has locked himself in and piled up the furniture against the door. You have frightened him to death!"

"It is scarcely possible——" Dr. Whitlett began.

"Don't lie, sir!" the admiral thundered out. "You are a pack of fools and old women! You are as ignorant as rabbits! You know no more than the kitchenmaids what has been growing and growing within these walls. I tell you that my work of the last few years, placed in certain hands, would alter the whole face of Europe—aye, of Christendom! There are men in this country to-day whose object is to rob me, and you, my own household, seem to be crying them welcome, bidding them come and help themselves, as though the labour of my life was worth no more than so many sheets of waste paper. You have let a stranger into this room to-day, and if he had not been disturbed, God knows what he might not have carried away with him!"

"We have been very foolish," Lady Deringham said pleadingly. "We will set a watch now day and night. We will run no more risks! I swear it! You can believe me, Horace!"

"Aye, but tell me the truth now," he cried. "Some one has been in this room and escaped through the window. I learnt as much as that from that blithering idiot, Blatherwick. I want to know who he was?"

She glanced towards the doctor. He nodded his head slightly. Then she went up to her husband and laid her hand upon his shoulders.

"Horace, you are right," she said. "It is no use trying to keep it from you. A man did impose upon us with a forged letter. He could not have been here more than five minutes, though. We found him out almost at once. It shall never happen again!"

The wisdom of telling him was at once apparent. His face positively shone with triumph! He became quite calm, and the fierce glare, which had alarmed them all so much, died out of his eyes. The confession was a triumph for him. He was gratified.

"I knew it," he declared, with positive good humour. "I have warned you of this all the time. Now perhaps you will believe me! Thank God that it was not Duchesne himself. I should not be surprised, though, if it were not one of his emissaries! If Duchesne comes," he muttered to himself, his face growing a shade paler, "God help us!"

"We will be more careful now," Lady Deringham said. "No one shall ever take us by surprise again. We will have special watchmen, and bars on all the windows."

"From this moment," the admiral said slowly, "I shall never leave this room until my work is ended, and handed over to Lord S——'s care. If I am robbed England is in danger! There must be no risks. I will have a sofa-bedstead down, and please understand that all my meals must be served here! Heggs and Morton must take it in turns to sleep in the room, and there must be a watchman outside. Now will you please all go away?" he added, with a little wave of his hand. "I have to reconstruct what has been stolen from me through your indiscretion. Send me in some coffee at eleven o'clock, and a box of cartridges you will find in my dressing-room."

They went away together. Wolfenden was grave and mystified. Nothing about his father's demeanour or language had suggested insanity. What if they were all wrong—if the work to which the best years of his life had gone was really of the immense importance he claimed for it? Other people thought so! The slight childishness, which was obvious in a great many of his actions, was a very different thing from insanity. Blatherwick might be deceived—Blanche was just as likely to have looked upon any technical work as rubbish. Whitlett was only a country practitioner—even his mother might have exaggerated his undoubted eccentricities. At any rate, one thing was certain. There were people outside who made a bold enough bid to secure the fruit of his father's labours. It was his duty to see that the attempt, if repeated, was still unsuccessful.

CHAPTER XVII

THE SCHEMING OF GIANTS

At very nearly the same moment as the man who had called himself Dr. Wilmot had leaped from the library window of Deringham Hall, Mr. Sabin sat alone in his sanctum waiting for a visitor. The room was quite a small one on the ground floor of the house, but was furnished with taste and evident originality in the Moorish fashion. Mr. Sabin himself was ensconced in an easy chair drawn close up to the fire, and a thin cloud of blue smoke was stealing up from a thick, Egyptian cigarette which was burning away between his fingers. His head was resting upon the delicate fingers of his left hand, his dark eyes were fixed upon the flaming coals. He was deep in thought.

"A single mistake now," he murmured softly, "and farewell to the labour of years. A single false step, and goodbye to all our dreams! To-night will decide it! In a few minutes I must say Yes or No to Knigenstein. I think—I am almost sure I shall say Yes! Bah!"

The frown on his forehead grew more marked. The cigarette burned on between his fingers, and a long grey ash fell to the floor. He was permitting himself the luxury of deep thought. All his life he had been a schemer; a builder of mighty plans, a great power in the destinies of great people. To-night he knew that he had reached the crisis of a career, in many respects marvellous. To-night he would take the first of those few final steps on to the desire of his life. It only rested with him to cast the die. He must make the decision and abide by it. His own life's ambition and the destinies of a mighty nation hung in the balance. Had he made up his mind which way to turn the scale? Scarcely even yet! There were so many things!

He sat up with a start. There was a knock at the door. He caught up the evening paper, and the cigarette smoke circled about his head. He stirred a cup of coffee by his side. The hard lines in his face had all relaxed. There was no longer any anxiety. He looked up and greeted pleasantly—with a certain deference, too—the visitor who was being ushered in. He had no appearance of having been engaged in anything more than a casual study of the *St. James's Gazette*.

"A gentleman, sir," the stolid-looking servant had announced briefly. No name had been mentioned. Mr. Sabin, when he rose and held out his hand, did not address his visitor directly. He was a tall, stout man, with an iron-grey moustache and the remains of a military bearing. When the servant had withdrawn and the two men were alone, he unbuttoned his overcoat. Underneath he wore a foreign uniform, ablaze with orders. Mr. Sabin glanced at them and smiled.

"You are going to Arlington Street," he remarked.

The other man nodded.

"When I leave here," he said.

Then there was a short silence. Each man seemed to be waiting for the other to open the negotiations. Eventually it was Mr. Sabin who did so.

"I have been carefully through the file of papers you sent me," he remarked.

"Yes!"

"There is no doubt but that, to a certain extent, the anti-English feeling of which you spoke exists! I have made other inquiries, and so far I am convinced!"

"So! The seed is sown! It has been sprinkled with a generous hand! Believe me, my friend, that for this country there are in store very great surprises. I speak as one who knows! I do know! So!"

Mr. Sabin was thoughtful. He looked into the fire and spoke musingly.

"Yet the ties of kindred and common origin are strong," he said. "It is hard to imagine an open rupture between the two great Saxon nations of the world!"

"The ties of kindred," said Mr. Sabin's visitor, "are not worth the snap of a finger! So!"

He snapped his fingers with a report as sharp as a pistol-shot. Mr. Sabin started in his chair.

"It is the ties of kindred," he continued, "which breed irritability, not kindliness! I tell you, my friend, that there is a great storm gathering. It is not for nothing that the great hosts of my country are ruled by a war lord! I tell you that we are arming to the teeth, silently, swiftly, and with a purpose. It may seem to you a small thing, but let me tell you this—we are a jealous nation! And we have cause for jealousy. In whatever part of the world we put down our foot, it is trodden on by our ubiquitous cousins! Wherever we turn to colonise, we are too late; England has already secured the finest territory, the most fruitful of the land. We must either take her leavings or go a-begging! Wherever we would develope, we are held back by the commercial and colonising genius—it amounts to that—of this wonderful nation. The world of to-day is getting cramped. There is no room for a growing England and a growing Germany! So! one must give way, and Germany is beginning to mutter that it shall not always be her sons who go to the wall. You say that France is our natural enemy. I deny it! France is our historical enemy—

nothing else! In military circles to-day a war with England would be wildly, hysterically popular; and sooner or later a war with England is as certain to come as the rising of the sun and the waning of the moon! I can tell you even now where the first blow will be struck! It is fixed! It is to come! So!"

"Not in Europe," Mr. Sabin said.

"Not in Europe or in Asia! The war-torch will be kindled in Africa!"

"The Transvaal!"

Mr. Sabin's visitor smiled.

"It is in Africa," he said, "that English monopoly has been most galling to my nation. We too feel the burden of over-population; we too have our young blood making itself felt throughout the land, eager, impetuous, thirsting for adventure and freedom. We need new countries where these may develop, and at once ease and strengthen our fatherland. I have seen it written in one of the great English reviews that my country has not the instinct for colonisation. It is false! We have the instinct and the desire, but not the opportunity. England is like a great octopus. She is ever on the alert, thrusting out her suckers, and drawing in for herself every new land where riches lay. No country has ever been so suitable for us as Africa, and behold—it is as I have said. Already England has grabbed the finest and most to be desired of the land—she has it now in her mind to take one step further and acquire the whole. But my country has no mind to suffer it! We have played second fiddle to a weaker Power long enough. We want Africa, my friend, and to my mind and the mind of my master, Africa is worth having at all costs—listen—even at the cost of war!"

Mr. Sabin was silent for a moment. There was a faint smile upon his lips. It was a situation such as he loved. He began to feel indeed that he was making history.

"You have convinced me," he said at last. "You have taught me how to look upon European politics with new eyes. But there remains one important question. Supposing I break off my negotiations in other quarters, are you willing to pay my price?"

The Ambassador waved his hand! It was a trifle!

"If what you give fulfils your own statements," he said, "you cannot ask a price which my master would not pay!"

Mr. Sabin moved a little in his chair. His eyes were bright. A faint tinge of colour was in his olive cheeks.

"Four years of my life," he said, "have been given to the perfecting of one branch only of my design; the other, which is barely completed, is the work of the only man in England competent to handle such a task. The combined result will be infallible. When I place in your hands a simple roll of papers and a small parcel, the future of this country is absolutely and entirely at your mercy. That is beyond question or doubt. To whomsoever I give my secret, I give over the destinies of England. But the price is a mighty one!"

"Name it," the Ambassador said quietly. "A million, two millions? Rank? What is it?"

"For myself," Mr. Sabin said, "nothing!"

The other man started. "Nothing!"

"Absolutely nothing!"

The Ambassador raised his hand to his forehead.

"You confuse me," he said.

"My conditions," Mr. Sabin said, "are these. The conquest of France and the restoration of the monarchy, in the persons of Prince Henri and his cousin, Princess Helène of Bourbon!"

"Ach!"

The little interjection shot from the Ambassador's lips with sharp, staccato emphasis! Then there was a silence—a brief, dramatic silence! The two men sat motionless, the eyes of each fastened upon the other. The Ambassador was breathing quickly, and his eyes sparkled with excitement. Mr. Sabin was pale and calm, yet there were traces of nervous exhilaration in his quivering lips and bright eyes.

"Yes, you were right; you were right indeed," the Ambassador said slowly. "It is a great price that you ask!"

Mr. Sabin laughed very softly.

"Think," he said. "Weigh the matter well! Mark first this fact. If what I give you has not the power I claim for it, our contract is at an end. I ask for nothing! I accept nothing. Therefore, you may assume that before you pay my price your own triumph is assured. Think! Reflect carefully! What will you owe to me! The humiliation of England, the acquisition of her colonies, the destruction of her commerce, and such a war indemnity as only the richest power on earth could pay. These things you gain. Then you are the one supreme Power in Europe. France is at your mercy! I will tell you why. The Royalist party have been gaining strength year by year, month by month, minute by minute! Proclaim your intentions boldly. The country will crumble up before you! It would be but a half-hearted resistance. France has not the temperament of a people who will remain for ever faithful to a democratic form of government. At heart she is aristocratic. The old nobility have a life in them which you cannot dream of. I know, for I have tested it. It has been weary waiting, but the time is ripe! France is ready for the cry of '*Vive le Roi! Vive la Monarchie!*' I who tell you these things have proved them. I have felt the pulse of my country, and I love her too well to mistake the symptoms!"

The Ambassador was listening with greedy ears—he was breathing hard through his teeth! It was easy to see that the glamour of the thing had laid hold of him. He foresaw for himself an immortal name, for his country a greatness beyond the wildest dreams of her most sanguine ministers. Bismarck himself had planned nothing like this! Yet he did not altogether lose his common sense.

"But Russia," he objected, "she would never sanction a German invasion of France."

Mr. Sabin smiled scornfully.

"You are a great politician, my dear Baron, and you say a thing like that! You amaze me! But of course the whole affair is new to you; you have not thought it out as I have done. Whatever happens in Europe, Russia will maintain the isolation for which geography and temperament have marked her out. She would not stir one finger to help France. Why should she? What could France give her in return? What would she gain by plunging into an exhausting war? To the core of his heart and the tips of his finger-nails the Muscovite is selfish! Then, again, consider this. You are not going to ruin France as you did before; you are going to establish a new dynasty, and not waste the land or exact a mighty tribute. Granted that sentiments of friendship exist between Russia and France, do you not think that Russia would not sooner see France a monarchy? Do you think that she would stretch out her little finger to aid a tottering republic and keep back a king from the throne of France? *Mon Dieu!* Never!"

Mr. Sabin's face was suddenly illuminated. A fire flashed in his dark eyes, and a note of fervent passion quivered lifelike in his vibrating voice. His manner had all the abandon of one pleading a great cause, nursed by a great heart. He was a patriot or a poet, surely not only a politician or a mere intriguing adventurer. For a moment he suffered his enthusiasm to escape him. Then the mask was as suddenly dropped. He was himself again, calm, convincing, impenetrable.

As the echoes of his last interjection died away there was a silence between the two men. It was the Ambassador at last who broke it. He was looking curiously at his companion.

"I must confess," he said slowly, "that you have fascinated me! You have done more, you have made me see dreams and possibilities which, set down upon paper, I should have mocked at. Mr. Sabin, I can no longer think of you as a person—you are a personage! We are here alone, and I am as secret as the grave; be so kind as to lift the veil of your incognito. I can no longer think of you as Mr. Sabin. Who are you?"

Mr. Sabin smiled a curious smile, and lit a cigarette from the open box before him.

"That," he said, pushing the box across the table, "you may know in good time if, in commercial parlance, we deal. Until that point is decided, I am Mr. Sabin. I do not even admit that it is an incognito."

"And yet," the Ambassador said, with a curious lightening of his face, as though recollection had suddenly been vouchsafed to him, "I fancy that if I were to call you——"

Mr. Sabin's protesting hand was stretched across the table.

"Excuse me," he interrupted, "let it remain between us as it is now! My incognito is a necessity for the present. Let it continue to be—Mr. Sabin! Now answer me. All has been said that can be said between us. What is your opinion?"

The Ambassador rose from his seat and stood upon the hearthrug with his back to the fire. There was a streak of colour upon his sallow cheeks, and his eyes shone brightly underneath his heavy brows. He had removed his spectacles and was swinging them lightly between his thumb and forefinger.

"I will be frank with you," he said. "My opinion is a favourable one. I shall apply for leave of absence to-morrow. In a week all that you have said shall be laid before my master. Such as my personal influence is, it will be exerted on behalf of the acceptance of your scheme. The greatest difficulty will be, of course, in persuading the Emperor of its practicability—in plain words, that what you say you have to offer will have the importance which you attribute to it."

"If you fail in that," Mr. Sabin said, also rising, "send for me! But bear this in mind, if my scheme should after all be ineffective, if it should fail in the slightest detail to accomplish all that I claim for it, what can you lose? The payment is conditional upon its success; the bargain is all in your favour. I should not offer such terms unless I held certain cards. Remember, if there are difficulties send for me!"

"I will do so," the Ambassador said as he buttoned his overcoat. "Now give me a limit of time for our decision."

"Fourteen days," Mr. Sabin said. "How I shall temporise with Lobenski so long I cannot tell. But I will give you fourteen days from to-day. It is ample!"

The two men exchanged farewells and parted. Mr. Sabin, with a cigarette between his teeth, and humming now and then a few bars from one of Verdi's operas, commenced to carefully select a bagful of golf clubs from a little pile which stood in one corner of the room. Already they bore signs of considerable use, and he handled them with the care of an expert, swinging each one gently, and hesitating for some time between a wooden or a metal putter, and longer still between the rival claims of a bulger and a flat-headed brassey. At last the bag was full; he resumed his seat and counted them out carefully.

"Ten," he said to himself softly. "Too many; it looks amateurish."

Some of the steel heads were a little dull; he took a piece of chamois leather from the pocket of the bag and began polishing them. As they grew brighter he whistled softly to himself. This time the opera tune seemed to have escaped him; he was whistling the "Marseillaise!"

CHAPTER XVIII

"HE HAS GONE TO THE EMPEROR!"

The Ambassador, when he left Mr. Sabin's house, stepped into a hired hansom and drove off towards Arlington Street. A young man who had watched him come out, from the other side of the way, walked swiftly to the corner of the street and stepped into a private brougham which was waiting there.

"To the Embassy," he said. "Drive fast!"

The carriage set him down in a few minutes at the house to which Densham and Harcutt had followed Mr. Sabin on the night of their first meeting with him. He walked swiftly into the hall.

"Is his Excellency within?" he asked a tall servant in plain dress who came forward to meet him.

"Yes, Monsieur Felix," the man answered; "he is dining very late to-night—in fact, he has not yet risen from the table."

"Who is with him?" Felix asked.

"It is a very small party. Madame la Princesse has just arrived from Paris, and his Excellency has been waiting for her."

He mentioned a few more names; there was no one of importance. Felix walked into the hall-porter's office and scribbled a few words on half a sheet of paper, which he placed in an envelope and carefully sealed.

"Let his Excellency have this privately and at once," he said to the man; "I will go into the waiting room."

The man withdrew with the note, and Felix crossed the hall and entered a small room nearly opposite. It was luxuriously furnished with easy chairs and divans; there were cigars, and cigarettes, and decanters upon a round table. Felix took note of none of these things, nor did he sit down. He stood with his hands behind him, looking steadily into the fire. His cheeks were almost livid, save for a single spot of burning colour high up on his cheek-bone. His fingers twitched nervously, his eyes were dry and restlessly bright. He was evidently in a state of great excitement. In less than two minutes the door opened, and a tall, distinguished-looking man, grey headed, but with a moustache still almost black, came softly into the room. His breast glittered with orders, and he was in full Court dress. He nodded kindly to the young man, who greeted him with respect.

"Is it anything important, Felix?" he asked; "you are looking tired."

"Yes, your Excellency, it is important," Felix answered; "it concerns the man Sabin."

The Ambassador nodded.

"Well," he said, "what of him? You have not been seeking to settle accounts with him, I trust, after our conversation, and your promise?"

Felix shook his head.

"No," he said. "I gave my word and I shall keep it! Perhaps you may some day regret that you interfered between us."

"I think not," the Prince replied. "Your services are valuable to me, my dear Felix; and in this country, more than any other, deeds of violence are treated with scant ceremony, and affairs of honour are not understood. No, I saved you from yourself for myself. It was an excellent thing for both of us."

"I trust," Felix repeated, "that your Excellency may always think so. But to be brief. The report from Cartienne is to hand."

The Ambassador nodded and listened expectantly.

"He confirms fully," Felix continued, "the value of the documents which are in question. How he obtained access to them he does not say, but his report is absolute. He considers that they justify fully the man Sabin's version of them."

The Prince smiled.

"My own judgment is verified," he said. "I believed in the man from the first. It is good. By the bye, have you seen anything of Mr. Sabin to-day?"

"I have come straight," Felix said, "from watching his house."

"Yes?"

"The Baron von Knigenstein has been there alone, incognito, for more than an hour. I watched him go in—and watched him out."

The Prince's genial smile vanished. His face grew suddenly as dark as thunder. The Muscovite crept out unawares. There was a fierce light in his eyes, and his face was like the face of a wolf; yet his voice when he spoke was low.

"So ho!" he said softly. "Mr. Sabin is doing a little flirting, is he? Ah!"

"I believe," the young man answered slowly, "that he has advanced still further than that. The Baron was there for an hour. He came out walking like a young man. He was in a state of great excitement."

The Prince sat down and stroked the side of his face thoughtfully.

"The great elephant!" he muttered. "Fancy such a creature calling himself a diplomatist! It is well, Felix," he added, "that I had finished my dinner, otherwise you would certainly have spoilt it. If they have met like this, there is no end to the possibilities of it. I must see Sabin immediately. It ought to be easy to make him understand that I am not to be trifled with. Find out where he is to-night, Felix; I must follow him."

Felix took up his hat.

"I will be back," he said, "in half an hour."

The Prince returned to his guests, and Felix drove off. When he returned his chief was waiting for him alone.

"Mr. Sabin," Felix announced, "left town half an hour ago."

"For abroad!" the Prince exclaimed, with flashing eyes. "He has gone to Germany!"

Felix shook his head.

"On the contrary," he said; "he has gone down into Norfolk to play golf."

"Into Norfolk to play golf!" the Prince repeated in a tone of scornful wonder. "Did you believe a story like that, Felix? Rubbish!"

Felix smiled slightly.

"It is quite true," he said. "Labanoff makes no mistakes, and he saw him come out of his house, take his ticket at King's Cross, and actually leave the station."

"Are you sure that it is not a blind?" the Prince asked incredulously.

Felix shook his head.

"It is quite true, your Excellency," he said. "If you knew the man as well as I do, you would not be surprised. He is indeed a very extraordinary person— he does these sort of things. Besides, he wants to keep out of the way."

The Prince's face darkened.

"He will find my way a little hard to get out of," he said fiercely. "Go and get some dinner, Felix, and then try and find out whether Knigenstein has any notion of leaving England. He will not trust a matter like this to correspondence. Stay—I know how to manage it. I will write and ask him to dine here next week. You shall take the invitation."

"He will be at Arlington Street," Felix remarked.

"Well, you can take it on to him there," the Prince directed. "Go first to his house and ask for his whereabouts. They will tell you Arlington Street. You will not know, of course, the contents of the letter you carry; your instructions were simply to deliver it and get an answer. Good! you will do that."

The Prince, while he talked, was writing the note.

Felix thrust it into his pocket and went out. In less than half an hour he was back. The Baron had returned to the German Embassy unexpectedly before going to Arlington Street, and Felix had caught him there. The Prince tore open the answer, and read it hastily through.

"THE GERMAN EMBASSY,
"*Wednesday evening.*

"Alas! my dear Prince, had I been able, nothing could have given me so much pleasure as to have joined your little party, but, unfortunately, this wretched climate, which we both so justly loathe, has upset my throat again, and I have too much regard for my life to hand myself over to the English doctors. Accordingly, all being well, I go to Berlin to-morrow night to consult our own justly-famed Dr. Steinlaus.

"Accept, my dear Prince, this expression of my most sincere regret, and believe me, yours most sincerely,

"KARL VON KNIGENSTEIN."

"The doctor whom he has gone to consult is no man of medicine," the Prince said thoughtfully. "He has gone to the Emperor."

CHAPTER XIX

WOLFENDEN'S LOVE-MAKING

"Lord Wolfenden?"

He laughed at her surprise, and took off his cap. He was breathless, for he had been scrambling up the steep side of the hill on which she was standing, looking steadfastly out to sea. Down in the valley from which he had come a small boy with a bag of golf clubs on his back was standing, making imaginary swings at the ball which lay before him.

"I saw you from below," he explained. "I couldn't help coming up. You don't mind?"

"No; I am glad to see you," she said simply. "You startled me, that is all. I did not hear you coming, and I had forgotten almost where I was. I was thinking."

He stood by her side, his cap still in his hand, facing the strong sea wind. Again he was conscious of that sense of extreme pleasure which had always marked his chance meetings with her. This time he felt perhaps that there was some definite reason for it. There was something in her expression, when she had turned so swiftly round, which seemed to tell him that her first words were not altogether meaningless. She was looking a little pale, and he fancied also a little sad. There was an inexpressible wistfulness about her soft, dark eyes; the light and charming gaiety of her manner, so un-English and so attractive to him, had given place to quite another mood. Whatever her thoughts might have been when he had first seen her there, her tall, slim figure outlined so clearly against the abrupt sky line, they were at all events scarcely pleasant ones. He felt that his sudden appearance had not been unwelcome to her, and he was unreasonably pleased.

"You are still all alone," he remarked. "Has Mr. Sabin not arrived?"

She shook her head.

"I am all alone, and I am fearfully and miserably dull. This place does not attract me at all: not at this time of the year. I have not heard from my uncle. He may be here at any moment."

There was no time like the present. He was suddenly bold. It was an opportunity which might never be vouchsafed to him again.

"May I come with you—a little way along the cliffs?" he asked.

She looked at him and hesitated. More than ever he was aware of some subtle change in her. It was as though her mental attitude towards him had adapted itself in some way to this new seriousness of demeanour. It was written in her features—his eyes read it eagerly. A certain aloofness, almost hauteur, about the lines of her mouth, creeping out even in her most careless tones, and plainly manifest in the carriage of her head, was absent. She seemed immeasurably nearer to him. She was softer and more womanly. Even her voice in its new and more delicate notes betrayed the change. Perhaps it was only a mood, yet he would take advantage of it.

"What about your golf?" she said, motioning down into the valley where his antagonist was waiting.

"Oh, I can easily arrange that," he declared cheerfully. "Fortunately I was playing the professional and he will not mind leaving off."

He waved to his caddie, and scribbled a few lines on the back of a card.

"Give that to McPherson," he said. "You can clean my clubs and put them in my locker. I shall not be playing again this morning."

The boy disappeared down the hill. They stood for a moment side by side.

"I have spoilt your game," she said. "I am sorry."

He laughed.

"I think you know," he said boldly, "that I would rather spend five minutes with you than a day at golf."

She moved on with a smile at the corners of her lips.

"What a downright person you are!" she said. "But honestly to-day I am not in the mood to be alone. I am possessed with an uneasy spirit of sadness. I am afraid of my thoughts."

"I am only sorry," he said, "that you should have any that are not happy ones. Don't you think perhaps that you are a little lonely? You seem to have so few friends."

"It is not that," she answered. "I have many and very dear friends, and it is only for a little time that I am separated from them. It is simply that I am not used to solitude, and I am becoming a creature of moods and presentiments. It is very foolish that I give way to them; but to-day I am miserable. You must stretch out that strong hand of yours, my friend, and pull me up."

"I will do my best," he said. "I am afraid I cannot claim that there is anything in the shape of affinity between us; for to-day I am particularly happy."

She met his eyes briefly, and looked away seawards with the ghost of a sorrowful smile upon her lips. Her words sounded like a warning.

"Do not be sure," she said. "It may not last."

"It will last," he said, "so long as you choose. For to-day you are the mistress of my moods!"

"Then I am very sorry for you," she said earnestly.

He laughed it off, but her words brought a certain depression with them. He went on to speak of something else.

"I have been thinking about you this morning," he said. "If your uncle is going to play golf here, it will be very dull for you. Would you care for my mother to come and see you? She would be delighted, I am sure, for it is dull for her too, and she is fond of young people. If you——"

He stopped short She was shaking her head slowly. The old despondency was back in her face. Her eyes were full of trouble. She laid her delicately gloved fingers upon his arm.

"My friend," she said, "it is very kind of you to think of it—but it is impossible. I cannot tell you why as I would wish. But at present I do not desire any acquaintances. I must not, in fact, think of it. It would give me great pleasure to know your mother. Only I must not. Believe me that it is impossible."

Wolfenden was a little hurt—a good deal mystified. It was a very odd thing. He was not in the least a snob, but he knew that the visit of the Countess of Deringham, whose name was still great in the social world, was not a thing to be refused without grave reasons by a girl in the position of Mr. Sabin's niece. The old question came back to him with an irresistible emphasis. Who were these people? He looked at her furtively. He was an observant man in the small details of a woman's toilette, and he knew that he had never met a girl better turned out than his present companion. The cut of her tailor-made gown was perfection, her gloves and boots could scarcely have come from anywhere but Paris. She carried herself too with a perfect ease and indefinable distinction which could only have come to her by descent. She was a perfect type of the woman of breeding—unrestrained, yet aristocratic to the tips of her finger-nails.

He sighed as he looked away from her.

"You are a very mysterious young woman," he said, with a forced air of gaiety.

"I am afraid that I am," she admitted regretfully. "I can assure you that I am very tired of it. But—it will not last for very much longer."

"You are really going away, then?" he asked quickly.

"Yes. We shall not be in England much longer."

"You are going for good?" he asked. "I mean, to remain away?"

"When we go," she said, "it is very doubtful if ever I shall set my foot on English soil again."

He drew a quick breath. It was his one chance, then. Her last words must be his excuse for such precipitation. They had scrambled down through an opening in the cliffs, and there was no one else in sight. Some instinct seemed to tell her what was coming. She tried to talk, but she could not. His hand had closed upon hers, and she had not the strength to draw it away. It was so very English this sudden wooing. No one had ever dared to touch her fingers before without first begging permission.

"Don't you know—Helène—that I love you? I want you to live in England—to be my wife. Don't say that I haven't a chance. I know that I ought not to have spoken yet, but you are going away so soon, and I am so afraid that I might not see you again alone. Don't stop me, please. I am not asking you now for your love. I know that it is too soon—to hope for that— altogether! I only want you to know, and to be allowed to hope."

"You must not. It is impossible."

The words were very low, and they came from her quivering with intense pain. He released her fingers. She leaned upon a huge boulder near and, resting her face upon her hand, gazed dreamily out to sea.

"I am very sorry," she said. "My uncle was right after all. It was not wise for us to meet. I ought to have no friends. It was not wise—it was very, very foolish."

Being a man, his first thoughts had been for himself. But at her words he forgot everything except that she too was unhappy.

"Do you mean," he said slowly, "that you cannot care for me, or that there are difficulties which seem to you to make it impossible?"

She looked up at him, and he scarcely knew her transfigured face, with the tears glistening upon her eyelashes.

"Do not tempt me to say what might make both of us more unhappy," she begged. "Be content to know that I cannot marry you."

"You have promised somebody else?"

"I shall probably marry," she said deliberately, "somebody else."

He ground his heel into the soft sands, and his eyes flashed.

"You are being coerced!" he cried.

She lifted her head proudly.

"There is no person breathing," she said quietly, "who would dare to attempt such a thing!"

Then he looked out with her towards the sea, and they watched the long, rippling waves break upon the brown sands, the faint and unexpected gleam of wintry sunshine lying upon the bosom of the sea, and the screaming seagulls, whose white wings shone like alabaster against the darker clouds. For him these things were no longer beautiful, nor did he see the sunlight, which with a sudden fitfulness had warmed the air. It was all very cold and grey. It was not possible for him to read the riddle yet—she had not said that she could not care for him. There was that hope!

"There is no one," he said slowly, "who could coerce you? You will not marry me, but you will probably marry somebody else. Is it, then, that you care for this other man, and not for me?"

She shook her head.

"Of the two," she said, with a faint attempt at her old manner, "I prefer you. Yet I shall marry him."

Wolfenden became aware of an unexpected sensation. He was getting angry.

"I have a right," he said, resting his hand upon her shoulder, and gaining courage from her evident weakness, "to know more. I have given you my love. At least you owe me in return your confidence. Let me have it. You shall see that even if I may not be your lover, I can at least be your faithful friend."

She touched his hand tenderly. It was scarcely kind of her—certainly not wise. She had taken off her glove, and the touch of her soft, delicate fingers thrilled him. The blood rushed through his veins like mad music. The longing to take her into his arms was almost uncontrollable. Her dark eyes looked upon him very kindly.

"My friend," she said, "I know that you would be faithful. You must not be angry with me. Nay, it is your pity I want. Some day you will know all. Then you will understand. Perhaps even you will be sorry for me, if I am not forgotten. I only wish that I could tell you more; only I may not. It makes me sad to deny you, but I must."

"I mean to know," he said doggedly—"I mean to know everything. You are sacrificing yourself. To talk of marrying a man whom you do not love is absurd. Who are you? If you do not tell me, I shall go to your guardian. I shall go to Mr. Sabin."

"Mr. Sabin is always at your service," said a suave voice almost at his elbow. "Never more so than at the present."

Wolfenden turned round with a start. It was indeed Mr. Sabin who stood there—Mr. Sabin, in unaccustomed guise, clad in a tweed suit and leaning upon an ordinary walking-stick.

"Come," he said good-humouredly, "don't look at me as though I were something uncanny. If you had not been so very absorbed you would have heard me call to you from the cliffs. I wanted to save myself the climb, but you were deaf, both of you. Am I the first man whose footsteps upon the sands have fallen lightly? Now, what is it you want to ask me, Lord Wolfenden?"

Wolfenden was in no way disturbed at the man's coming. On the contrary, he was glad of it. He answered boldly and without hesitation.

"I want to marry your niece, Mr. Sabin," he said.

"Very natural indeed," Mr. Sabin remarked easily. "If I were a young man of your age and evident taste I have not the least doubt but that I should want to marry her myself. I offer you my sincere sympathy. Unfortunately it is impossible."

"I want to know," Wolfenden said, "why it is impossible? I want a reason of some sort."

"You shall have one with pleasure," Mr. Sabin said. "My niece is already betrothed."

"To a man," Wolfenden exclaimed indignantly, "whom she admits that she does not care for!"

"Whom she has nevertheless," Mr. Sabin said firmly, and with a sudden flash of anger in his eyes, "agreed and promised of her own free will to marry. Look here, Lord Wolfenden, I do not desire to quarrel with you. You saved me from a very awkward accident a few nights ago, and I remain your debtor. Be reasonable! My niece has refused your offer. I confirm her refusal. Your proposal does us both much honour, but it is utterly out of the question. That is putting it plainly, is it not? Now, you must choose for yourself— whether you will drop the subject and remain our valued friend, or whether you compel me to ask you to leave us at once, and consider us henceforth as strangers."

The girl laid her hand upon his shoulder and looked at him pleadingly.

"For my sake," she said, "choose to remain our friend, and let this be forgotten."

"For your sake, I consent," he said. "But I give no promise that I will not at some future time reopen the subject."

"You will do so," Mr. Sabin said, "exactly when you desire to close your acquaintance with us. For the rest, you have chosen wisely. Now I am going to take you home, Helène. Afterwards, if Lord Wolfenden will give me a match, I shall be delighted to have a round of golf with him."

"I shall be very pleased," Wolfenden answered.

"I will see you at the Pavilion in half an hour," Mr. Sabin said. "In the meantime, you will please excuse us. I have a few words to say to my niece."

She held out both her hands, looking at him half kindly, half wistfully.

"Goodbye," she said. "I am so sorry!"

But he looked straight into her eyes, and he answered her bravely. He would not admit defeat.

"I hope that you are not," he said. "I shall never regret it."

CHAPTER XX

FROM A DIM WORLD

Wolfenden was in no particularly cheerful frame of mind when, a few moments after the half hour was up, Mr. Sabin appeared upon the pavilion tee, followed by a tall, dark young man carrying a bag of golf clubs. Mr. Sabin, on the other hand, was inclined to be sardonically cheerful.

"Your handicap," he remarked, "is two. Mine is one. Suppose we play level. We ought to make a good match."

Wolfenden looked at him in surprise.

"Did you say one?"

Mr. Sabin smiled.

"Yes; they give me one at Pau and Cannes. My foot interferes very little with my walking upon turf. All the same, I expect you will find me an easy victim here. Shall I drive? Just here, Dumayne," he added, pointing to a convenient spot upon the tee with the head of his driver. "Not too much sand."

"Where did you get your caddie?" Wolfenden asked. "He is not one of ours, is he?"

Mr. Sabin shook his head.

"I found him on some links in the South of France," he answered. "He is the only caddie I ever knew who could make a decent tee, so I take him about with me. He valets me as well. That will do nicely, Dumayne."

Mr. Sabin's expression suddenly changed. His body, as though by instinct, fell into position. He scarcely altered his stand an inch from the position he had first taken up. Wolfenden, who had expected a half-swing, was amazed at the wonderfully lithe, graceful movement with which he stooped down and the club flew round his shoulder. Clean and true the ball flew off the tee in a perfectly direct line—a capital drive only a little short of the two hundred yards. Master and servant watched it critically.

"A fairly well hit ball, I think, Dumayne," Mr. Sabin remarked.

"You got it quite clean away, sir," the man answered. "It hasn't run very well though; you will find it a little near the far bunker for a comfortable second."

"I shall carry it all right," Mr. Sabin said quietly.

Wolfenden also drove a long ball, but with a little slice. He had to play the odd, and caught the top of the bunker. The hole fell to Mr. Sabin in four.

They strolled off towards the second teeing ground.

"Are you staying down here for long?" Mr. Sabin asked.

Wolfenden hesitated.

"I am not sure," he said. "I am rather oddly situated at home. At any rate I shall probably be here as long as you."

"I am not sure about that," Mr. Sabin said. "I think that I am going to like these links, and if so I shall not hurry away. Forgive me if I am inquisitive, but your reference to home affairs is, I presume, in connection with your father's health. I was very sorry to hear that he is looked upon now as a confirmed invalid."

Wolfenden assented gravely. He did not wish to talk about his father to Mr. Sabin. On the other hand, Mr. Sabin was politely persistent.

"He does not, I presume, receive visitors," he said, as they left the tee after the third drive.

"Never," Wolfenden answered decisively. "He suffers a good deal in various ways, and apart from that he is very much absorbed in the collection of some statistics connected with a hobby of his. He does not see even his oldest friends."

Mr. Sabin was obviously interested.

"Many years ago," he said, "I met your father at Alexandria. He was then in command of the *Victoria*. He would perhaps scarcely recollect me now, but at the time he made me promise to visit him if ever I was in England. It must be—yes, it surely must be nearly fifteen years ago."

"I am afraid," Wolfenden remarked, watching the flight of his ball after a successful brassy shot, "that he would have forgotten all about it by now. His memory has suffered a good deal."

Mr. Sabin addressed his own ball, and from a bad lie sent it flying a hundred and fifty yards with a peculiar, jerking shot which Wolfenden watched with envy.

"You must have a wonderful eye," he remarked, "to hit a ball with a full swing lying like that. Nine men out of ten would have taken an iron."

Mr. Sabin shrugged his shoulders. He did not wish to talk golf.

"I was about to remark," he said, "that your father had then the reputation of, and impressed me as being, the best informed man with regard to English naval affairs with whom I ever conversed."

"He was considered an authority, I believe," Wolfenden admitted.

"What I particularly admired about him," Mr. Sabin continued, "was the absence of that cocksureness which sometimes, I am afraid, almost blinds the judgment of your great naval officers. I have heard him even discuss the possibility of an invasion of England with the utmost gravity. He admitted that it was far from improbable."

"My father's views," Wolfenden said, "have always been pessimistic as regards the actual strength of our navy and coast defences. I believe he used to make himself a great nuisance at the Admiralty."

"He has ceased now, I suppose," Mr. Sabin remarked, "to take much interest in the matter?"

"I can scarcely say that," Wolfenden answered. "His interest, however, has ceased to be official. I daresay you have heard that he was in command of the Channel Fleet at the time of the terrible disaster in the Solent. He retired almost immediately afterwards, and we fear that his health will never altogether recover from the shock."

There was a short intermission in the conversation. Wolfenden had sliced his ball badly from the sixth tee, and Mr. Sabin, having driven as usual with almost mathematical precision, their ways for a few minutes lay apart. They came together, however, on the putting-green, and had a short walk to the next tee.

"That was a very creditable half to you," Mr. Sabin remarked.

"My approach," Wolfenden admitted, "was a lucky one."

"It was a very fine shot," Mr. Sabin insisted. "The spin helped you, of course, but you were justified in allowing for that, especially as you seem to play most of your mashie shots with a cut. What were we talking about? Oh, I remember of course. It was about your father and the Solent catastrophe. Admiral Deringham was not concerned with the actual disaster in any way, was he?"

Wolfenden shook his hand.

"Thank God, no!" he said emphatically. "But Admiral Marston was his dearest friend, and he saw him go down with six hundred of his men. He was so close that they even shouted farewells to one another."

"It must have been a terrible shock," Mr. Sabin admitted. "No wonder he has suffered from it. Now you have spoken of it, I think I remember reading about his retirement. A sad thing for a man of action, as he always was. Does he remain in Norfolk all the year round?"

"He never leaves Deringham Hall," Wolfenden answered. "He used to make short yachting cruises until last year, but that is all over now. It is twelve months since he stepped outside his own gates."

Mr. Sabin remained deeply interested.

"Has he any occupation beyond this hobby of which you spoke?" he asked. "He rides and shoots a little, I suppose, like the rest of your country gentlemen."

Then for the first time Wolfenden began to wonder dimly whether Mr. Sabin had some purpose of his own in so closely pursuing the thread of this conversation. He looked at him keenly. At the moment his attention seemed altogether directed to the dangerous proximity of his ball and a tall sand bunker. Throughout his interest had seemed to be fairly divided between the game and the conversation which he had initiated. None the less Wolfenden was puzzled. He could scarcely believe that Mr. Sabin had any real, personal interest in his father, but on the other hand it was not easy to understand this persistent questioning as to his occupation and doings. The last inquiry, carelessly though it was asked, was a direct one. It seemed scarcely worth while to evade it.

"No; my father has special interests," he answered slowly. "He is engaged now upon some work connected with his profession."

"Indeed!"

Mr. Sabin's exclamation suggested a curiosity which it was not Wolfenden's purpose to gratify. He remained silent. The game proceeded without remark for a quarter of an hour. Wolfenden was now three down, and with all the stimulus of a strong opponent he set himself to recover lost ground. The ninth hole he won with a fine, long putt, which Mr. Sabin applauded heartily.

They drove from the next tee and walked together after their balls, which lay within a few yards of one another.

"I am very much interested," Mr. Sabin remarked, "in what you have been telling me about your father. It confirms rather a curious story about Lord Deringham which I heard in London a few weeks ago. I was told, I forget by whom, that your father had devoted years of his life to a wonderfully minute study of English coast defences and her naval strength. My informant went on to say that—forgive me, but this was said quite openly you know—that whilst on general matters your father's mental health was scarcely all that could be desired, his work in connection with these two subjects was of great value. It struck me as being a very singular and a very interesting case."

Wolfenden shook his head dubiously.

"Your informant was misled, I am afraid," he said. "My father takes his hobby very seriously, and of course we humour him. But as regards the value of his work I am afraid it is worthless."

"Have you tested it yourself?" Mr. Sabin asked.

"I have only seen a few pages," Wolfenden admitted, "but they were wholly unintelligible. My chief authority is his own secretary, who is giving up an excellent place simply because he is ashamed to take money for assisting in work which he declares to be utterly hopeless."

"He is a man," Mr. Sabin remarked, "whom you can trust, I suppose? His judgment is not likely to be at fault."

"There is not the faintest chance of it," Wolfenden declared. "He is a very simple, good-hearted little chap and tremendously conscientious. What your friend told you, by the bye, reminds me of rather a curious thing which happened yesterday."

Wolfenden paused. There did not seem, however, to be any reason for concealment, and his companion was evidently deeply interested.

"A man called upon us," Wolfenden continued, "with a letter purporting to be from our local doctor here. He gave his name as Franklin Wilmot, the celebrated physician, you know, and explained that he was interested in a new method of treating mental complaints. He was very plausible and he explained everything unusual about his visit most satisfactorily. He wanted a sight of the work on which my father was engaged, and after talking it over we introduced him into the study during my father's absence. From it he promised to give us a general opinion upon the case and its treatment. Whilst he was there our doctor drove up in hot haste. The letter was a forgery, the man an impostor."

Wolfenden, glancing towards Mr. Sabin as he finished his story, was surprised at the latter's imperfectly concealed interest. His lips were indrawn, his face seemed instinct with a certain passionate but finely controlled emotion. Only the slight hiss of his breath and the gleam of his black eyes betrayed him.

"What happened?" he asked. "Did you secure the fellow?"

Wolfenden played a long shot and waited whilst he watched the run of his ball. Then he turned towards his companion and shook his head.

"No! He was a great deal too clever for that. He sent me out to meet Whitlett, and when we got back he had shown us a clean pair of heels. He got away through the window."

"Did he take away any papers with him?" Mr. Sabin asked.

"He may have taken a loose sheet or two," Wolfenden said. "Nothing of any consequence, I think. He had no time. I don't think that that could have been his object altogether, or he would scarcely have suggested my remaining with him in the study."

Mr. Sabin drew a quick, little breath. He played an iron shot, and played it very badly.

"It was a most extraordinary occurrence," he remarked. "What was the man like? Did he seem like an ordinary thief?"

Wolfenden shook his head decidedly.

"Not in the least," he declared. "He was well dressed and his manners were excellent. He had all the appearance of a man of position. He completely imposed upon both my mother and myself."

"How long were you in the study before Dr. Whitlett arrived?" Mr. Sabin asked.

"Barely five minutes."

It was odd, but Mr. Sabin seemed positively relieved.

"And Mr. Blatherwick," he asked, "where was he all the time?"

"Who?" Wolfenden asked in surprise.

"Mr. Blatherwick—your father's secretary," Mr. Sabin repeated coolly; "I understood you to say that his name was Blatherwick."

"I don't remember mentioning his name at all," Wolfenden said, vaguely disturbed.

Mr. Sabin addressed his ball with care and played it deliberately on to the green. Then he returned to the subject.

"I think that you must have done," he said suavely, "or I should scarcely have known it. Was he in the room?"

"All the time," Wolfenden answered.

Mr. Sabin drew another little breath.

"He was there when the fellow bolted?"

Wolfenden nodded.

"Why did he not try to stop him?"

Wolfenden smiled.

"Physically," he remarked, "it would have been an impossibility. Blatherwick is a small man and an exceedingly nervous one. He is an honest little fellow, but I am afraid he would not have shone in an encounter of that sort."

Mr. Sabin was on the point of asking another question, but Wolfenden interrupted him. He scarcely knew why, but he wanted to get away from the subject. He was sorry that he had ever broached it.

"Come," he said, "we are talking too much. Let us play golf. I am sure I put you off that last stroke."

Mr. Sabin took the hint and was silent. They were on the eleventh green, and bordering it on the far side was an open road—the sea road, which followed the coast for a mile or two and then turned inland to Deringham. Wolfenden, preparing to putt, heard wheels close at hand, and as the stroke was a critical one for him he stood back from his ball till the vehicle had passed. Glancing carelessly up, he saw his own blue liveries and his mother leaning back in a barouche. With a word of apology to his opponent, he started forward to meet her.

The coachman, who had recognised him, pulled up his horses in the middle of the road. Wolfenden walked swiftly over to the carriage side. His mother's appearance had alarmed him. She was looking at him, and yet past him. Her cheeks were pale. Her eyes were set and distended. One of her hands seemed to be convulsively clutching the side of the carriage nearest to her. She had all the appearance of a woman who is suddenly face to face with some terrible vision. Wolfenden looked over his shoulder quickly. He could see nothing more alarming in the background than the figure of his opponent, who, with his back partly turned to them, was gazing out to sea. He stood at the edge of the green on slightly rising ground, and his figure was outlined with almost curious distinctness against the background of air and sky.

"Has anything fresh happened, mother?" Wolfenden asked, with concern. "I am afraid you are upset. Were you looking for me?"

She shook her head. It struck him that she was endeavouring to assume a composure which she assuredly did not possess.

"No; there is nothing fresh. Naturally I am not well. I am hoping that the drive will do me good. Are you enjoying your golf?"

"Very much," Wolfenden answered. "The course has really been capitally kept. We are having a close match."

"Who is your opponent?"

Wolfenden glanced behind him carelessly. Mr. Sabin had thrown several balls upon the green, and was practising long putts.

"Fellow named Sabin," he answered. "No one you would be likely to be interested in. He comes down from London, and he plays a remarkably fine game. Rather a saturnine-looking personage, isn't he?"

"He is a most unpleasant-looking man," Lady Deringham faltered, white now to the lips. "Where did you meet him? Here or in London?"

"In London," Wolfenden explained. "Rather a curious meeting it was too. A fellow attacked him coming out of a restaurant one night and I interfered— just in time. He has taken a little house down here."

"Is he alone?" Lady Deringham asked.

"He has a niece living with him," Wolfenden answered. "She is a very charming girl. I think that you would like her."

The last words he added with something of an effort, and an indifference which was palpably assumed. Lady Deringham, however, did not appear to notice them at all.

"Have no more to do with him than you can help, Wolfenden," she said, leaning a little over to him, and speaking in a half-fearful whisper. "I think his face is awful."

Wolfenden laughed.

"I am not likely to see a great deal of him," he declared. "In fact I can't say that he seems very cordially disposed towards me, considering that I saved him from rather a nasty accident. By the bye, he said something about having met the Admiral at Alexandria. You have never come across him, I suppose?"

The sun was warm and the wind had dropped, or Wolfenden could almost have declared that his mother's teeth were chattering. Her eyes were fixed again in a rigid stare which passed him by and travelled beyond. He looked over his shoulder. Mr. Sabin, apparently tired of practising, was standing directly facing them, leaning upon his putter. He was looking steadfastly at Lady Deringham, not in the least rudely, but with a faint show of curiosity and a smile which in no way improved his appearance slightly parting his lips. Meeting his gaze, Wolfenden looked away with an odd feeling of uneasiness.

"You are right," he said. "His face is really a handsome one in a way, but he certainly is not prepossessing-looking!"

Lady Deringham had recovered herself. She leaned back amongst the cushions.

"Didn't you ask me," she said, "whether I had ever met the man? I cannot remember—certainly I was at Alexandria with your father, so perhaps I did. You will be home to dinner?"

He nodded.

"Of course. How is the Admiral to-day?"

"Remarkably well. He asked for you just before I came out."

"I shall see him at dinner," Wolfenden said "Perhaps he will let me smoke a cigar with him afterwards."

He stood away from the carriage and lifted his cap with a smile. The coachman touched his horses and the barouche rolled on. Wolfenden walked slowly back to his companion.

"You will excuse my leaving you," he said. "I was afraid that my mother might have been looking for me."

"By all means," Mr. Sabin answered. "I hope that you did not hurry on my account. I am trying," he added, "to recollect if ever I met Lady Deringham. At my time of life one's reminiscences become so chaotic."

He looked keenly at Wolfenden, who answered him after a moment's hesitation.

"Lady Deringham was at Alexandria with my father, so it is just possible," he said.

CHAPTER XXI

HARCUTT'S INSPIRATION

Wolfenden lost his match upon the last hole; nevertheless it was a finely contested game, and when Mr. Sabin proposed a round on the following day, he accepted without hesitation. He did not like Mr. Sabin any the better—in fact he was beginning to acquire a deliberate distrust of him. Something of that fear with which other people regarded him had already communicated itself to Wolfenden. Without having the shadow of a definite suspicion with regard to the man or his character, he was inclined to resent that interest in the state of affairs at Deringham Hall which Mr. Sabin had undoubtedly manifested. At the same time he was Helène's guardian, and so long as he occupied that position Wolfenden was not inclined to give up his acquaintance.

They parted in the pavilion, Wolfenden lingering for a few minutes, half hoping that he might receive some sort of invitation to call at Mr. Sabin's temporary abode. Perhaps, under the circumstances, it was scarcely possible that any such invitation could be given, although had it been Wolfenden would certainly have accepted it. For he had no idea of at once relinquishing all hope as regards Helène. He was naturally sanguine, and he was very much in love. There was something mysterious about that other engagement of which he had been told. He had an idea that, but for Mr. Sabin's unexpected appearance, Helène would have offered him a larger share of her confidence. He was content to wait for it.

Wolfenden had ridden over from home, and left his horse in the hotel stables. As he passed the hall a familiar figure standing in the open doorway hailed him. He glanced quickly up, and stopped short. It was Harcutt who was standing there, in a Norfolk tweed suit and thick boots.

"Of all men in the world!" he exclaimed in blank surprise. "What, in the name of all that's wonderful, are you doing here?"

Harcutt answered with a certain doggedness, almost as though he resented Wolfenden's astonishment.

"I don't know why you should look at me as though I were a ghost," he said. "If it comes to that, I might ask you the same question. What are you doing here?"

"Oh! I'm at home," Wolfenden answered promptly. "I'm down to visit my people; it's only a mile or two from here to Deringham Hall."

Harcutt dropped his eyeglass and laughed shortly.

"You are wonderfully filial all of a sudden," he remarked. "Of course you had no other reason for coming!"

"None at all," Wolfenden answered firmly. "I came because I was sent for. It was a complete surprise to me to meet Mr. Sabin here—at least it would have been if I had not travelled down with his niece. Their coming was simply a stroke of luck for me."

Harcutt assumed a more amiable expression.

"I am glad to hear it," he said. "I thought that you were stealing a march on me, and there really was not any necessity, for our interests do not clash in the least. It was different between you and poor old Densham, but he's given it up of his own accord and he sailed for India yesterday."

"Poor old chap!" Wolfenden said softly. "He would not tell you, I suppose, even at the last, what it was that he had heard about—these people?"

"He would not tell me," Harcutt answered; "but he sent a message to you. He wished me to remind you that you had been friends for fifteen years, and he was not likely to deceive you. He was leaving the country, he said, because he had certain and definite information concerning the girl, which made it absolutely hopeless for either you or he to think of her. His advice to you was to do the same."

"I do not doubt Densham," Wolfenden said slowly; "but I doubt his information. It came from a woman who has been Densham's friend. Then, again, what may seem an insurmountable obstacle to him, may not be so to me. Nothing vague in the shape of warnings will deter me."

"Well," Harcutt said, "I have given you Densham's message and my responsibility concerning it is ended. As you know, my own interests lie in a different direction. Now I want a few minutes' conversation with you. The hotel rooms are a little too public. Are you in a hurry, or can you walk up and down the drive with me once or twice?"

"I can spare half an hour very well," Wolfenden said; "but I should prefer to do no more walking just yet. Come and sit down here—it isn't cold."

They chose a seat looking over the sea. Harcutt glanced carefully all around. There was no possibility of their being overheard, nor indeed was there any one in sight.

"I am developing fresh instincts," Harcutt said, as he crossed his legs and lit a cigarette. "I am here, I should like you to understand, purely in a professional capacity—and I want your help."

"But my dear fellow," Wolfenden said; "I don't understand. If, when you say professionally, you mean as a journalist, why, what on earth in this place can there be worth the chronicling? There is scarcely a single person known to society in the neighbourhood."

"Mr. Sabin is here!" Harcutt remarked quietly.

Wolfenden looked at him in surprise.

"That might have accounted for your presence here as a private individual," he said; "but professionally, how on earth can he interest you?"

"He interests me professionally very much indeed," Harcutt answered.

Wolfenden was getting puzzled.

"Mr. Sabin interests you professionally?" he repeated slowly. "Then you have learnt something. Mr. Sabin has an identity other than his own."

"I suspect him to be," Harcutt said slowly, "a most important and interesting personage. I have learnt a little concerning him. I am here to learn more; I am convinced that it is worth while."

"Have you learnt anything," Wolfenden asked, "concerning his niece?"

"Absolutely nothing," Harcutt answered decidedly. "I may as well repeat that my interest is in the man alone. I am not a sentimental person at all. His niece is perhaps the most beautiful woman I have ever seen in my life, but it is with no thought of her that I have taken up this investigation. Having assured you of that, I want to know if you will help me?"

"You must speak a little more plainly," Wolfenden said; "you are altogether too vague. What help do you want, and for what purpose?"

"Mr. Sabin," Harcutt said; "is engaged in great political schemes. He is in constant and anxious communication with the ambassadors of two great Powers. He affects secrecy in all his movements, and the name by which he is known is without doubt an assumed one. This much I have learnt for certain. My own ideas are too vague yet for me to formulate. I cannot say any more, except that I believe him to be deep in some design which is certainly not for the welfare of this country. It is my assurance of this which justifies me in exercising a certain espionage upon his movements—which justifies me also, Wolfenden, in asking for your assistance."

"My position," Wolfenden remarked, "becomes a little difficult. Whoever this man Sabin may be, nothing would induce me to believe ill of his niece. I could take no part in anything likely to do her harm. You will understand this better, Harcutt, when I tell you that, a few hours ago, I asked her to be my wife."

"You asked her—what?"

"To be my wife."

"And she?"

"Refused me!"

Harcutt looked at him for a moment in blank amazement.

"Who refused you—Mr. Sabin or his niece?"

"Both!"

"Did she—did Mr. Sabin know your position, did he understand that you are the future Earl of Deringham?"

"Without a doubt," Wolfenden answered drily; "in fact Mr. Sabin seems to be pretty well up in my genealogy. He had met my father once, he told me."

Harcutt, with the natural selfishness of a man engaged upon his favourite pursuit, quite forgot to sympathise with his friend. He thought only of the bearing of this strange happening upon his quest.

"This," he remarked, "disposes once and for all of the suggestion that these people are ordinary adventurers."

"If any one," Wolfenden said, "was ever idiotic enough to entertain the possibility of such a thing. I may add that from the first I have had almost to thrust my acquaintance upon them, especially so far as Mr. Sabin is concerned. He has never asked me to call upon them here, or in London; and this morning when he found me with his niece he was quietly but furiously angry."

"It is never worth while," Harcutt said, "to reject a possibility until you have tested and proved it. What you say, however, settles this one. They are not adventurers in any sense of the word. Now, will you answer me a few questions? It may be just as much to your advantage as to mine to go into this matter."

Wolfenden nodded.

"You can ask the questions, at any rate," he said; "I will answer them if I can."

"The young lady—did she refuse you from personal reasons? A man can always tell, you know. Hadn't you the impression, from her answer, that it was more the force of circumstances than any objection to you which prompted her negative? I've put it bluntly, but you know what I mean."

Wolfenden did not answer for nearly a minute. He was gazing steadily seaward, recalling with a swift effort of his imagination every word which had passed between them—he could even hear her voice, and see her face with the soft, dark eyes so close to his. It was a luxury of recollection.

"I will admit," he said, quietly, "that what you suggest has already occurred to me. If it had not, I should be much more unhappy than I am at this moment. To tell you the honest truth I was not content with her answer, or rather the manner of it. I should have had some hope of inducing her to, at any rate, modify it, but for Mr. Sabin's unexpected appearance. About him, at least, there was no hesitation; he said no, and he meant it."

"That is what I imagined might be the case," Harcutt said thoughtfully. "I don't want to have you think that I imagine any disrespect to the young lady, but don't you see that either she and Mr. Sabin must stand towards one another in an equivocal position, or else they must be in altogether a different station of life to their assumed one, when they dismiss the subject of an alliance with you so peremptorily."

Wolfenden flushed up to the temples, and his eyes were lit with fire.

"You may dismiss all idea of the former possibility," he said, with ominous quietness. "If you wish me to discuss this matter with you further you will be particularly careful to avoid the faintest allusion to it."

"I have never seriously entertained it," Harcutt assented cheerfully; "I, too, believe in the girl. She looks at once too proud and too innocent for any association of such thoughts with her. She has the bearing and the manners of a queen. Granted, then, that we dismiss the first possibility."

"Absolutely and for ever," Wolfenden said firmly. "I may add that Mr. Sabin met me with a distinct reason for his refusal—he informed me his niece was already betrothed."

"That may or may not be true," Harcutt said. "It does not affect the question which we are considering at present. We must come to the conclusion that these are people of considerable importance. That is what I honestly believe. Now what do you suppose brings Mr. Sabin to such an out of the way hole as this?"

"The golf, very likely," Wolfenden said. "He is a magnificent player."

Harcutt frowned.

"If I thought so," he said, "I should consider my journey here a wasted one. But I can't. He is in the midst of delicate and important negotiations—I know as much as that. He would not come down here at such a time to play golf. It is an absurd idea!"

"I really don't see how else you can explain it," Wolfenden remarked; "the greatest men have had their hobbies, you know. I need not remind you of Nero's fiddle, or Drake's bowls."

"Quite unnecessary," Harcutt declared briskly. "Frankly, I don't believe in Mr. Sabin's golf. There is somebody or something down here connected with his schemes; the golf is a subterfuge. He plays well because he does everything well."

"It will tax your ingenuity," Wolfenden said, "to connect his visit here with anything in the shape of political schemes."

"My ingenuity accepts the task, at any rate," Harcutt said. "I am going to find out all about it, and you must help me. It will be for both our interests."

"I am afraid," Wolfenden answered, "that you are on a wild goose chase. Still I am quite willing to help you if I can."

"Well, to begin then," Harcutt said; "you have been with him some time to-day. Did he ask you any questions about the locality? Did he show any curiosity in any of the residents?"

Wolfenden shook his head.

"Absolutely none," he answered. "The only conversation we had, in which he showed any interest at all, was concerning my own people. By the bye, that reminds me! I told him of an incident which occurred at Deringham Hall last night, and he was certainly interested and curious. I chanced to look at him at an unexpected moment, and his appearance astonished me. I have never seen him look so keen about anything before."

"Will you tell me the incident at once, please?" Harcutt begged eagerly. "It may contain the very clue for which I am hunting. Anything which interests Mr. Sabin interests me."

"There is no secrecy about the matter," Wolfenden said. "I will tell you all about it. You may perhaps have heard that my father has been in very poor health ever since the great Solent disaster. It unfortunately affected his brain to a certain extent, and he has been the victim of delusions ever since. The most serious of these is, that he has been commissioned by the Government to prepare, upon a gigantic scale, a plan and description of our coast defences and navy. He has a secretary and typist, and works ten hours a day; but from their report and my own observations I am afraid the only result is an absolutely unintelligible chaos. Still, of course, we have to take him seriously, and be thankful that it is no worse. Now the incident which I told Mr. Sabin was this. Last night a man called and introduced himself as Dr. Wilmot, the great mind specialist. He represented that he had been staying in the neighbourhood, and was on friendly terms with the local medico here, Dr.

Whitlett. My father's case had been mentioned between them, and he had become much interested in it. He had a theory of his own for the investigation of such cases which consisted, briefly of a careful scrutiny of any work done by the patient. He brought a letter from Dr. Whitlett and said that if we would procure him a sight of my father's most recent manuscripts he would give us an opinion on the case. We never had the slightest suspicion as to the truth of his statements, and I took him with me to the Admiral's study. However, while we were there, and he was rattling through the manuscripts, up comes Dr. Whitlett, the local man, in hot haste. The letter was a forgery, and the man an impostor. He escaped through the window, and got clean away. That is the story just as I told it to Mr. Sabin. What do you make of it?"

Harcutt stood up, and laid his hand upon the other's shoulder.

"Well, I've got my clue, that's all," he declared; "the thing's as plain as sunlight!"

Wolfenden rose also to his feet.

"I must be a fool," he said, "for I certainly can't see it."

Harcutt lowered his tone.

"Look here, Wolfenden," he said, "I have no doubt that you are right, and that your father's work is of no value; but you may be very sure of one thing—Mr. Sabin does not think so!"

"I don't see what Mr. Sabin has got to do with it," Wolfenden said.

Harcutt laughed.

"Well, I will tell you one thing," he said; "it is the contents of your father's study which has brought Mr. Sabin to Deringham!"

CHAPTER XXII

FROM THE BEGINNING

A woman stood, in the midst of a salt wilderness, gazing seaward. Around her was a long stretch of wet sand and of seaweed-stained rocks, rising from little pools of water left by the tide; and beyond, the flat, marshy country was broken only by that line of low cliffs, from which the little tufts of grass sprouted feebly. The waves which rolled almost to her feet were barely ripples, breaking with scarcely a visible effort upon the moist sand. Above, the sky was grey and threatening; only a few minutes before a cloud of white mist had drifted in from the sea and settled softly upon the land in the form of rain. The whole outlook was typical of intense desolation. The only sound breaking the silence, almost curiously devoid of all physical and animal noises, was the soft washing of the sand at her feet, and every now and then the jingling of silver harness, as the horses of her carriage, drawn up on the road above, tossed their heads and fidgeted. The carriage itself seemed grotesquely out of place. The coachman, with powdered hair and the dark blue Deringham livery, sat perfectly motionless, his head bent a little forward, and his eyes fixed upon his horses' ears. The footman, by their side, stood with folded arms, and expression as wooden as though he were waiting upon a Bond Street pavement. Both were weary, and both would have liked to vary the monotony by a little conversation; but only a few yards away the woman was standing whose curious taste had led her to visit such a spot.

Her arms were hanging listlessly by her side, her whole expression, although her face was upturned towards the sky, was one of intense dejection. Something about her attitude bespoke a keen and intimate sympathy with the desolation of her surroundings. The woman was unhappy; the light in her dark eyes was inimitably sad. Her cheeks were pale and a little wan. Yet Lady Deringham was very handsome—as handsome as a woman approaching middle age could hope to be. Her figure was still slim and elegant, the streaks of grey in her raven black hair were few and far between. She might have lived hand in hand with sorrow, but it had done very little to age her. Only a few years ago, in the crowded ball-room of a palace, a prince had declared her to be the handsomest woman of her age, and the prince had the reputation of knowing. It was easy to believe it.

How long the woman might have lingered there it is hard to say, for evidently the spot possessed a peculiar fascination for her, and she had given herself up to a rare fit of abstraction. But some sound—was it the low wailing of that seagull, or the more distant cry of a hawk, motionless in mid-air and scarcely visible against the cloudy sky, which caused her to turn her head inland? And then she saw that the solitude was no longer unbroken. A dark object had rounded the sandy little headland, and was coming steadily towards her. She looked at it with a momentary interest, her skirt raised in her hand, already a few steps back on her return to the waiting carriage. Was it a man? It was something human, at any rate, although its progression was slow and ungraceful, and marked with a peculiar but uniform action. She stood perfectly still, a motionless figure against the background of wan, cloud-shadowed sea and gathering twilight, her eyes riveted upon this strange thing, her lips slightly parted, her cheeks as pale as death. Gradually it came nearer and nearer. Her skirt dropped from her nerveless fingers, her eyes, a moment before dull, with an infinite and pitiful emptiness, were lit now with a new light. She was not alone, nor was she unprotected, yet the woman was suffering from a spasm of terror—one could scarcely imagine any sight revolting enough to call up that expression of acute and trembling fear, which had suddenly transformed her appearance. It was as though the level sands had yielded up their dead—the shipwrecked mariners of generations, and they all, with white, sad faces and wailing voices, were closing in around her. Yet it was hard to account for a terror so abject. There was certainly nothing in the figure, now close at hand, which seemed capable of inspiring it.

It was a man with a club foot—nothing more nor less. In fact it was Mr. Sabin! There was nothing about his appearance, save that ungainly movement caused by his deformity, in any way singular or threatening. He came steadily nearer, and the woman who awaited him trembled. Perhaps his expression was a trifle sardonic, owing chiefly to the extreme pallor of his skin, and the black flannel clothes with invisible stripe, which he had been wearing for golf. Yet when he lifted his soft felt hat from his head and bowed with an ease and effect palpably acquired in other countries, his appearance was far from unpleasant. He stood there bare-headed in the twilight, a strangely winning smile upon his dark face, and his head courteously bent.

"The most delightful of unexpected meetings," he murmured. "I am afraid that I have come upon you like an apparition, dear Lady Deringham! I must have startled you! Yes, I can see by your face that I did; I am so sorry. Doubtless you did not know until yesterday that I was in England."

Lady Deringham was slowly recovering herself. She was white still, even to the lips, and there was a strange, sick pain at her heart. Yet she answered him with something of her usual deliberateness, conscious perhaps that her servants, although their heads were studiously averted, had yet witnessed with surprise this unexpected meeting.

"You certainly startled me," she said; "I had imagined that this was the most desolate part of all unfrequented spots! It is here I come when I want to feel absolutely alone. I did not dream of meeting another fellow creature—least of all people in the world, perhaps, you!"

"I," he answered, smiling gently, "was perhaps the better prepared. A few minutes ago, from the cliffs yonder, I saw your carriage drawn up here, and I saw you alight. I wanted to speak with you, so I lost no time in scrambling down on to the sands. You have changed marvellously little, Lady Deringham!"

"And you," she said, "only in name. You are the Mr. Sabin with whom my son was playing golf yesterday morning?"

"I am Mr. Sabin," he answered. "Your son did me a good service a week or two back. He is a very fine young fellow; I congratulate you."

"And your niece," Lady Deringham asked; "who is she? My son spoke to me of her last night."

Mr. Sabin smiled faintly.

"Ah! Madame," he said, "there have been so many people lately who have been asking me that question, yet to you as to them I must return the same answer. She is my niece!"

"You call her?"

"She shares my name at present."

"Is she your daughter?"

He shook his head sadly.

"I have never been married," he said, with an indefinable mournfulness in his flexible tones. "I have had neither wife, nor child, nor friend. It is well for me that I have not!"

She looked down at his deformity, and woman-like she shivered.

"It is no better, then?" she murmured, with eyes turned seaward.

"It is absolutely incurable," he declared.

She changed the subject abruptly.

"The last I heard of you," she said, "was that you were in China. You were planning great things there. In ten years, I was told, Europe was to be at your mercy!"

"I left Pekin five years ago," he said. "China is a land of Cabals. She may yet be the greatest country in the world. I, for one, believe in her destiny, but it will be in the generations to come. I have no patience to labour for another to reap the harvest. Then, too, a craving for just one draught of civilisation brought me westward again. Mongolian habits are interesting but a little trying."

"And what," she asked, looking at him steadily, "has brought you to Deringham, of all places upon this earth?"

He smiled, and with his stick traced a quaint pattern in the sand.

"I have never told you anything that was not the truth," he said; "I will not begin now. I might have told you that I was here by chance, for change of air, or for the golf. Neither of these things would have been true. I am here because Deringham village is only a mile or two from Deringham Hall."

She drew a little closer to him. The jingling of harness, as her horses tossed their heads impatiently, reminded her of the close proximity of the servants.

"What do you want of me?" she asked hoarsely.

He looked at her in mild reproach, a good-humoured smile at the corner of his lips; yet after all was it good humour or some curious outward reflection of the working of his secret thoughts? When he spoke the reproach, at any rate, was manifest.

"Want of you! You talk as though I were a blackmailer, or something equally obnoxious. Is that quite fair, Constance?"

She evaded the reproach; perhaps she was not conscious of it. It was the truth she wanted.

"You had some end in coming here," she persisted. "What is it? I cannot conceive anything in the world you have to gain by coming to see me. We have left the world and society; we live buried. Whatever fresh schemes you may be planning, there is no way in which we could help you. You are richer, stronger, more powerful than we. I can think," she added, "of only one thing which may have brought you."

"And that?" he asked deliberately.

She looked at him with a certain tremulous wistfulness in her eyes, and with softening face.

"It may be," she said, "that as you grow older you have grown kinder; you may have thought of my great desire, and you were always generous, Victor, you may have come to grant it!"

The slightest possible change passed over his face as his Christian name slipped from her lips. The firm lines about his mouth certainly relaxed, his dark eyes gleamed for a moment with a kindlier light. Perhaps at that minute for both of them came a sudden lifting of the curtain, a lingering backward glance into the world of their youth, passionate, beautiful, seductive. There were memories there which still seemed set to music—memories which pierced even the armour of his equanimity. Her eyes filled with tears as she looked at him. With a quick gesture she laid her hand upon his.

"Believe me, Victor," she said, "I have always thought of you kindly; you have suffered terribly for my sake, and your silence was magnificent. I have never forgotten it."

His face clouded over, her impulsive words had been after all ill chosen, she had touched a sore point! There was something in these memories distasteful to him. They recalled the one time in his life when he had been worsted by another man. His cynicism returned.

"I am afraid," he said, "that the years, which have made so little change in your appearance, have made you a sentimentalist. I can assure you that these old memories seldom trouble me."

Then with a lightning-like intuition, almost akin to inspiration, he saw that he had made a mistake. His best hold upon the woman had been through that mixture of sentiment and pity, which something in their conversation had reawakened in her. He was destroying it ruthlessly and of his own accord. What folly!

"Bah! I am lying," he said softly; "why should I? Between you and me, Constance, there should be nothing but truth. We at least should be sincere one to the other. You are right, I have brought you something which should have been yours long ago."

She looked at him with wondering eyes.

"You are going to give me the letters?"

"I am going to give them to you," he said. "With the destruction of this little packet falls away the last link which held us together."

He had taken a little bundle of letters, tied with a faded ribbon, from his pocket and held them out to her. Even in that salt-odorous air the perfume of strange scents seemed to creep out from those closely written sheets as they fluttered in the breeze. Lady Deringham clasped the packet with both hands, and her eyes were very bright and very soft.

"It is not so, Victor," she murmured. "There is a new and a stronger link between us now, the link of my everlasting gratitude. Ah! you were always generous, always quixotic! Someday I felt sure that you would do this."

"When I left Europe," he said, "you would have had them, but there was no trusted messenger whom I could spare. Yet if I had never returned they were so bestowed that they would have come into your hands with perfect safety. Even now, Constance, will you think me very weak when I say that I part with them with regret? They have been with me through many dangers and many strange happenings."

"You are," she whispered, "the old Victor again! Thank God that I have had this one glimpse of you! I am ashamed to think how terrified I have been."

She held out her hand impulsively. He took it in his and, with a glance at her servants, let it fall almost immediately.

"Constance," he said, "I am going away now. I have accomplished what I came for. But first, would you care to do me a small service? It is only a trifle."

A thrill of the old mistrustful fear shook her heart. Half ashamed of herself she stifled it at once, and strove to answer him calmly.

"If there is anything within my power which I can do for you, Victor," she said, "it will make me very happy. You would not ask me, I know, unless— unless——"

"You need have no fear," he interrupted calmly; "it is a very little thing. Do you think that Lord Deringham would know me again after so many years?"

"My husband?"

"Yes!"

She looked at him in something like amazement. Before she could ask the question which was framing itself upon her lips, however, they were both aware of a distant sound, rapidly drawing nearer—the thunder of a horse's hoofs upon the soft sand. Looking up they both recognised the rider at the same instant.

"It is your son," Mr. Sabin said quickly; "you need not mind. Leave me to explain. Tell me when I can find you at home alone?"

"I am always alone," she answered. "But come to-morrow."

CHAPTER XXIII

MR. SABIN EXPLAINS

Mr. Sabin and his niece had finished their dinner, and were lingering a little over an unusually luxurious dessert. Wolfenden had sent some muscatel grapes and peaches from the forcing houses at Deringham Hall—such peaches as Covent Garden could scarcely match, and certainly not excel. Mr. Sabin looked across at Helène as they were placed upon the table, with a significant smile.

"An Englishman," he remarked, pouring himself out a glass of burgundy and drawing the cigarettes towards him, "never knows when he is beaten. As a national trait it is magnificent, in private life it is a little awkward."

Helène had been sitting through the meal, still and statuesque in her black dinner gown, a little more pale than usual, and very silent. At Mr. Sabin's remark she looked up quickly.

"Are you alluding to Lord Wolfenden?" she asked.

Mr. Sabin lit his cigarette, and nodded through the mist of blue smoke.

"To no less a person," he answered, with a shade of mockery in his tone. "I am beginning to find my guardianship no sinecure after all! Do you know, it never occurred to me, when we concluded our little arrangement, that I might have to exercise my authority against so ardent a suitor. You would have found his lordship hard to get rid of this morning, I am afraid, but for my opportune arrival."

"By no means," she answered. "Lord Wolfenden is a gentleman, and he was not more persistent than he had a right to be."

"Perhaps," Mr. Sabin remarked, "you would have been better pleased if I had not come?"

"I am quite sure of it," she admitted; "but then it is so like you to arrive just at a crisis! Do you know, I can't help fancying that there is something theatrical about your comings and goings! You appear—and one looks for a curtain and a tableau. Where could you have dropped from this morning?"

"From Cromer, in a donkey-cart," he answered smiling. "I got as far as Peterborough last night, and came on here by the first train. There was nothing very melodramatic about that, surely!"

"It does not sound so, certainly. Your playing golf with Lord Wolfenden afterwards was commonplace enough!"

"I found Lord Wolfenden very interesting," Mr. Sabin said thoughtfully. "He told me a good deal which was important for me to know. I am hoping that to-night he will tell me more."

"To-night! Is he coming here?"

Mr. Sabin assented calmly.

"Yes. I thought you would be surprised. But then you need not see him, you know. I met him riding upon the sands this afternoon—at rather an awkward moment, by the bye—and asked him to dine with us."

"He refused, of course?"

"Only the dinner; presumably he doubted our cook, for he asked to be allowed to come down afterwards. He will be here soon."

"Why did you ask him?"

Mr. Sabin looked keenly across the table. There was something in the girl's face which he scarcely understood.

"Well, not altogether for the sake of his company, I must confess," he replied. "He has been useful to me, and he is in the position to be a great deal more so."

The girl rose up. She came over and stood before him. Mr. Sabin knew at once that something unusual was going to happen.

"You want to make of him," she said, in a low, intense tone, "what you make of every one—a tool! Understand that I will not have it!"

"Helène!"

The single word, and the glance which flashed from his eyes, was expressive, but the girl did not falter.

"Oh! I am weary of it," she cried, with a little passionate outburst. "I am sick to death of it all! You will never succeed in what you are planning. One might sooner expect a miracle. I shall go back to Vienna. I am tired of masquerading. I have had more than enough of it."

Mr. Sabin's expression did not alter one iota; he spoke as soothingly as one would speak to a child.

"I am afraid," he said quietly, "that it must be dull for you. Perhaps I ought to have taken you more into my confidence; very well, I will do so now. Listen: you say that I shall never succeed. On the contrary, I am on the point of success; the waiting for both of us is nearly over."

The prospect startled, but did not seem altogether to enrapture her. She wanted to hear more.

"I received this dispatch from London this morning," he said. "Baron Knigenstein has left for Berlin to gain the Emperor's consent to an agreement which we have already ratified. The affair is as good as settled; it is a matter now of a few days only."

"Germany!" she exclaimed, incredulously, "I thought it was to be Russia."

"So," he answered, "did I. I have to make a certain rather humiliating confession. I, who have always considered myself keenly in touch with the times, especially since my interest in European matters revived, have remained wholly ignorant of one of the most extraordinary phases of modern politics. In years to come history will show us that it was inevitable, but I must confess that it has come upon me like a thunder clap. I, like all the world, have looked upon Germany and England as natural and inevitable allies. That is neither more nor less than a colossal blunder! As a matter of fact, they are natural enemies!"

She sank into a chair, and looked at him blankly.

"But it is impossible," she cried. "There are all the ties of relationship, and a common stock. They are sister countries."

"Don't you know," he said, "that it is the like which irritates and repels the like. It is this relationship which has been at the root of the great jealousy, which seems to have spread all through Germany. I need not go into all the causes of it with you now; sufficient it is to say that all the recent successes of England have been at Germany's expense. There has been a storm brewing for long; to-day, to-morrow, in a week, surely within a month, it will break."

"You may be right," she said; "but who of all the Frenchwomen I know would care to reckon themselves the debtors of Germany?"

"You will owe Germany nothing, for she will be paid and overpaid for all she does. Russia has made terms with the Republic of France. Politically, she has nothing to gain by a rupture; but with Germany it is different. She and France are ready at this moment to fly at one another's throats. The military popularity of such a war would be immense. The cry to arms would ring from the Mediterranean to the Rhine."

"Oh! I hope that it may not be war," she said. "I had hoped always that diplomacy, backed by a waiting army, would be sufficient. France at heart is true, I know. But after all, it sounds like a fairy tale. You are a wonderful man, but how can you hope to move nations? What can you offer Germany to exact so tremendous a price?"

"I can offer," Mr. Sabin said calmly, "what Germany desires more than anything else in the world—the key to England. It has taken me six years to perfect my schemes. As you know, I was in America part of the time I was supposed to be in China. It was there, in the laboratory of Allison, that I commenced the work. Step by step I have moved on—link by link I have forged the chain. I may say, without falsehood or exaggeration, that my work would be the work of another man's lifetime. With me it has been a labour of love. Your part, my dear Helène, will be a glorious one; think of it, and shake off your depression. This hole and corner life is not for long—the time for which we have worked is at hand."

She did not look up, there was no answering fire of enthusiasm in her dark eyes. The colour came into her cheeks and faded away. Mr. Sabin was vaguely disturbed.

"In what way," she said, without directly looking at him, "is Lord Wolfenden likely to be useful to you?"

Mr. Sabin did not reply for some time, in fact he did not reply at all. This new phase in the situation was suddenly revealed to him. When he spoke his tone was grave enough—grave with an undertone of contempt.

"Is it possible, Helène," he said, "that you have allowed yourself to think seriously of the love-making of this young man? I must confess that such a thing in connection with you would never have occurred to me in my wildest dreams!"

"I am the mistress of my own affections," she said coldly. "I am not pledged to you in any way. If I were to say that I intended to listen seriously to Lord Wolfenden—even if I were to say that I intended to marry him—well, there is no one who would dare to interfere! But, on the other hand, I have refused him. That should be enough for you. I am not going to discuss the matter at all; you would not understand it."

"I must admit," Mr. Sabin said, "that I probably should not. Of love, as you young people conceive it, I know nothing. But of that greater affection—the passionate love of a man for his race and his kind and his country—well, that has always seemed to me a thing worth living and working and dying for! I had fancied, Helène, that some spark of that same fire had warmed your blood, or you would not be here to-day."

"I think," she answered more gently, "that it has. I too, believe me, love my country and my people and my order. If I do not find these all-engrossing, you must remember that I am a woman, and I am young; I do not pretend to be capable only of impersonal and patriotic love."

"Ay, you are a woman, and the blood of some of your ancestors will make itself felt," he added, looking at her thoughtfully. "I ought to have considered the influence of sex and heredity. By the bye, have you heard from Henri lately?"

She shook her head.

"Not since he has been in France. We thought that whilst he was there it would be better for him not to write."

Mr. Sabin nodded.

"Most discreet," he remarked satirically. "I wonder what Henri would say if he knew?"

The girl's lip curled a little.

"If even," she said, "there was really something serious for him to know, Henri would survive it. His is not the temperament for sorrow. For twenty minutes he would be in a paroxysm. He would probably send out for poison, which he would be careful not to take; and play with a pistol, if he were sure that it was not loaded. By dinner time he would be calm, the opera would soothe him still more, and by the time it was over he would be quite ready to take Mademoiselle Somebody out to supper. With the first glass of champagne his sorrow would be drowned for ever. If any wound remained at all, it would be the wound to his vanity."

"You have considered, then, the possibility of upsetting my schemes and withdrawing your part?" Mr. Sabin said quietly. "You understand that your marriage with Henri would be an absolute necessity—that without it all would be chaos?"

"I do not say that I have considered any such possibility," she answered. "If I make up my mind to withdraw, I shall give you notice. But I will admit that I like Lord Wolfenden, and I detest Henri! Ah! I know of what you would remind me; you need not fear, I shall not forget! It will not be to-day, nor to-morrow, that I shall decide."

A servant entered the room and announced Lord Wolfenden. Mr. Sabin looked up.

"Where have you shown him?" he asked.

"Into the library, sir," the girl answered.

Mr. Sabin swore softly between his teeth, and sprang to his feet.

"Excuse me, Helène," he exclaimed, "I will bring Lord Wolfenden into the drawing-room. That girl is an idiot; she has shown him into the one room in the house which I would not have had him enter for anything in the world!"

CHAPTER XXIV

THE WAY OF THE WOMAN

Wolfenden had been shown, as he supposed, into an empty room by the servant of whom he had inquired for Mr. Sabin. But the door was scarcely closed before a familiar sound from a distant corner warned him that he was not alone. He stopped short and looked fixedly at the slight, feminine figure whose white fingers were flashing over the keyboard of a typewriter. There was something very familiar about the curve of her neck and the waving of her brown hair; her back was to him, and she did not turn round.

"Do leave me some cigarettes," she said, without lifting her head. "This is frightfully monotonous work. How much more of it is there for me to do?"

"I really don't know," Wolfenden answered hesitatingly. "Why, Blanche!"

She swung round in her chair and gazed at him in blank amazement; she was, at least, as much surprised as he was.

"Lord Wolfenden!" she exclaimed; "why, what are you doing here?"

"I might ask you," he said gravely, "the same question."

She stood up.

"You have not come to see me?"

He shook his head.

"I had not the least idea that you were here," he assured her.

Her face hardened.

"Of course not. I was an idiot to imagine that you would care enough to come, even if you had known."

"I do not know," he remarked, "why you should say that. On the contrary——"

She interrupted him.

"Oh! I know what you are going to say. I ran away from Mrs. Selby's nice rooms, and never thanked you for your kindness. I didn't even leave a message for you, did I? Well, never mind; you know why, I daresay."

Wolfenden thought that he did, but he evaded a direct answer.

"What I cannot understand," he said, "is why you are here."

"It is my new situation," she answered. "I was bound to look for one, you know. There is nothing strange about it. I advertised for a situation, and I got this one."

He was silent. There were things in connection with this which he scarcely understood. She watched him with a mocking smile parting her lips.

"It is a good deal harder to understand," she said, "why you are here. This is the very last house in the world in which I should have thought of seeing you."

"Why?" he asked quickly.

She shrugged her shoulders; her speech had been scarcely a discreet one.

"I should not have imagined," she said, "that Mr. Sabin would have come within the circle of your friends."

"I do not know why he should not," Wolfenden said. "I consider him a very interesting man."

She smiled upon him.

"Yes, he is interesting," she said; "only I should not have thought that your tastes were at all identical."

"You seem to know a good deal about him," Wolfenden remarked quietly.

For a moment an odd light gleamed in her eyes; she was very pale. Wolfenden moved towards her.

"Blanche," he said, "has anything gone wrong with you? You don't look well."

She withdrew her hands from her face.

"There is nothing wrong with me," she said. "Hush! he is coming."

She swung round in her seat, and the quick clicking of the instrument was resumed as her fingers flew over it. The door opened, and Mr. Sabin entered. He leaned on his stick, standing on the threshold, and glanced keenly at both of them.

"My dear Lord Wolfenden," he said apologetically, "this is the worst of having country servants. Fancy showing you in here. Come and join us in the other room; we are just going to have our coffee."

Wolfenden followed him with alacrity; they crossed the little hall and entered the dining-room. Helène was still sitting there sipping her coffee in an easy chair. She welcomed him with outstretched hand and a brilliantly soft smile.

Mr. Sabin, who was watching her closely, appreciated, perhaps for the first time, her rare womanly beauty, apart from its distinctly patrician qualities. There was a change, and he was not the man to be blind to it or to under-rate its significance. He felt that on the eve of victory he had another and an unexpected battle to fight; yet he held himself like a brave man and one used to reverses, for he showed no signs of dismay.

"I want you to try a glass of this claret, Lord Wolfenden," he said, "before you begin your coffee. I know that you are a judge, and I am rather proud of it. You are not going away, Helène?"

"I had no idea of going," she laughed. "This is really the only habitable room in the house, and I am not going to let Lord Wolfenden send me to shiver in what we call the drawing-room."

"I should be very sorry if you thought of such a thing," Wolfenden answered.

"If you will excuse me for a moment," Mr. Sabin said, "I will unpack some cigarettes. Helène, will you see that Lord Wolfenden has which liqueur he prefers?"

He limped away, and Helène watched him leave the room with some surprise. These were tactics which she did not understand. Was he already making up his mind that the game could be played without her? She was puzzled—a little uneasy.

She turned to find Wolfenden's admiring eyes fixed upon her; she looked at him with a smile, half-sad, half-humorous.

"Let me remember," she said, "I am to see that you have—what was it? Oh! liqueurs. We haven't much choice; you will find Kummel and Chartreuse on the sideboard, and Benedictine, which my uncle hates, by the bye, at your elbow."

"No liqueurs, thanks," he said. "I wonder, did you expect me to-night? I don't think that I ought to have come, ought I?"

"Well, you certainly show," she answered with a smile, "a remarkable disregard for all precedents and conventions. You ought to be already on your way to foreign parts with your guns and servants. It is Englishmen, is it not, who go always to the Rocky Mountains to shoot bears when their love affairs go wrong?"

He was watching her closely, and he saw that she was less at her ease than she would have had him believe. He saw, too, or fancied that he saw, a softening in her face, a kindliness gleaming out of her lustrous eyes which suggested new things to him.

"The Rocky Mountains," he said slowly, "mean despair. A man does not go so far whilst he has hope."

She did not answer him; he gathered courage from her silence.

"Perhaps," he said, "I might now have been on my way there but for a somewhat sanguine disposition—a very strong determination, and," he added more softly, "a very intense love."

"It takes," she remarked, "a very great deal to discourage an Englishman."

"Speaking for myself," he answered, "I defy discouragement; I am proof against it. I love you so dearly, Helène, that I simply decline to give you up; I warn you that I am not a lover to be shaken off."

His voice was very tender; his words sounded to her simple but strong. He was so sure of himself and his love. Truly, she thought, for an Englishman this was no indifferent wooer; his confidence thrilled her; she felt her heart beat quickly under its sheath of drooping black lace and roses.

"I am giving you," she said quietly, "no hope. Remember that; but I do not want you to go away."

The hope which her tongue so steadfastly refused to speak he gathered from her eyes, her face, from that indefinable softening which seems to pervade at the moment of yielding a woman's very personality. He was wonderfully happy, although he had the wit to keep it to himself.

"You need not fear," he whispered, "I shall not go away."

Outside they heard the sound of Mr. Sabin's stick. She leaned over towards him.

"I want you," she said, "to—kiss me."

His heart gave a great leap, but he controlled himself. Intuitively he knew how much was permitted to him; he seemed to have even some faint perception of the cause for her strange request. He bent over and took her face for a moment between his hands; her lips touched his—she had kissed him!

He stood away from her, breathless with the excitement of the moment. The perfume of her hair, the soft touch of her lips, the gentle movement with which she had thrust him away, these things were like the drinking of strong wine to him. Her own cheeks were scarlet; outside the sound of Mr. Sabin's stick grew more and more distinct; she smoothed her hair and laughed softly up at him.

"At least," she murmured, "there is that to remember always."

CHAPTER XXV

A HANDFUL OF ASHES

The Countess of Deringham was sitting alone in her smaller drawing-room, gazing steadfastly at a certain spot in the blazing fire before her. A little pile of grey ashes was all that remained of the sealed packet which she had placed within the bars only a few seconds ago. She watched it slowly grow shapeless—piece after piece went fluttering up the broad chimney. A gentle yet melancholy smile was parting her lips. A chapter of her life was floating away there with the little trembling strips lighter than the air, already hopelessly destroyed. Their disintegration brought with it a sense of freedom which she had lacked for many years. Yet it was only the folly of a girl, the story of a little foolish love-making, which those grey, ashen fragments, clinging so tenaciously to the iron bars, could have unfolded. Lady Deringham was not a woman who had ever for a single moment had cause to reproach herself with any real lack of duty to the brave young Englishman whom she had married so many years ago. It was of those days she was thinking as she sat there waiting for the caller, whose generosity had set her free.

At precisely four o'clock there was the sound of wheels in the drive, the slow movement of feet in the hall, and a servant announced a visitor.

"Mr. Sabin."

Lady Deringham smiled and greeted him graciously. Mr. Sabin leaned upon his wonderful stick for a moment, and then bent low over Lady Deringham's hand. She pointed to an easy chair close to her own, and he sank into it with some appearance of weariness. He was looking a little old and tired, and he carried himself without any of his usual buoyancy.

"Only a few minutes ago," she said, "I burnt my letters. I was thinking of those days in Paris when the man announced you! How old it makes one feel."

He looked at her critically.

"I am beginning to arrive at the conclusion," he said, "that the poets and the novelists are wrong. It is the man who suffers! Look at my grey hairs!"

"It is only the art of my maid," she said smiling, "which conceals mine. Do not let us talk of the past at all; to think that we lived so long ago is positively appalling!"

He shook his head gently.

"Not so appalling," he answered, "as the thought of how long we still have to live! One regrets one's youth as a matter of course, but the prospect of old age is more terrible still! Lucky those men and those women who live and then die. It is that interregnum—the level, monotonous plain of advancing old age, when one takes the waters at Carlsbad and looks askance at the *entrées*—that is what one has to dread. To watch our own degeneration, the dropping away of our energies, the decline of our taste—why, the tortures of the Inquisition were trifles to it!"

She shuddered a little.

"You paint old age in dreary colours," she said.

"I paint it as it must seem to men who have kept the kernel of life between their teeth," he answered carelessly. "To the others—well, one cares little about them. Most men are like cows, they are contented so long as they are fed. To that class I daresay old age may seem something of a rest. But neither you nor I are akin to them."

"You talk as you always talked," she said. "Mr. Sabin is very like——"

He stopped her.

"Mr. Sabin, if you please," he exclaimed. "I am particularly anxious to preserve my incognito just now. Ever since we met yesterday I have been regretting that I did not mention it to you—I do not wish it to be known that I am in England."

"Mr. Sabin it shall be, then," she answered; "only if I were you I would have chosen a more musical name."

"I wonder—have you by chance spoken of me to your son?" he asked.

"It is only by chance that I have not," she admitted. "I have scarcely seen him alone to-day, and he was out last evening. Do you wish to remain Mr. Sabin to him also?"

"To him particularly," Mr. Sabin declared; "young men are seldom discreet."

Lady Deringham smiled.

"Wolfenden is not a gossip," she remarked; "in fact I believe he is generally considered too reserved."

"For the present, nevertheless," he said, "let me remain Mr. Sabin to him also. I do not ask you this without a purpose."

Lady Deringham bowed her head. This man had a right to ask her more than such slight favours.

"You are still," she said, "a man of mystery and incognitos. You are still, I suppose, a plotter of great schemes. In the old days you used to terrify me almost; are you still as daring?"

"Alas! no," he answered. "Time is rapidly drawing me towards the great borderland, and when my foot is once planted there I shall carry out my theories and make my bow to the world with the best grace a man may whose life has been one long chorus of disappointments. No! I have retired from the great stage; mine is now only a passive occupation. One returns always, you know, and in a mild way I have returned to the literary ambitions of my youth. It is in connection, by the bye, with this that I arrive at the favour which you so kindly promised to grant me."

"If you knew, Victor," she said, "how grateful I feel towards you, you would not hesitate to ask me anything within my power to grant."

Mr. Sabin toyed with his stick and gazed steadfastly into the fire. He was pensive for several minutes; then, with the air of a man who suddenly detaches himself from a not unpleasant train of thought, he looked up with a smile.

"I am not going to tax you very severely," he said. "I am writing a critical paper on the armaments of the world for a European review. I had letters of introduction to Mr. C., and he gave me a great deal of valuable information. There were one or two points, however, on which he was scarcely clear, and in the course of conversation he mentioned your husband's name as being the greatest living authority upon those points. He offered to give me a letter to him, but I thought it would perhaps scarcely be wise. I fancied, too, you might be inclined, for reasons which we need not enlarge upon, to help me."

For a simple request Lady Deringham's manner of receiving it was certainly strange; she was suddenly white almost to the lips. A look of positive fear was in her eyes. The frank cordiality, the absolute kindliness with which she had welcomed her visitor was gone. She looked at him with new eyes; the old mistrust was born again. Once more he was the man to be feared and dreaded above all other men; yet she would not give way altogether. He was watching her narrowly, and she made a brave effort to regain her composure.

"But do you not know," she said hesitatingly, "that my husband is a great invalid? It is a very painful subject for all of us, but we fear that his mind is not what it used to be. He has never been the same man since that awful night in the Solent. His work is more of a hobby with him; it would not be at all reliable for reference."

"Not all of it, certainly," he assented. "Mr. C. explained that to me. What I want is an opportunity to discriminate. Some would be very useful to me— the majority, of course, worse than useless. The particular information which I want concerns the structural defects in some of the new battleships. It would save an immense amount of time to get this succinctly."

She looked away from him, still agitated.

"There are difficulties," she murmured; "serious ones. My husband has an extraordinary idea as to the value of his own researches, and he is always haunted by a fear lest some one should break in and steal his papers. He would not suffer me to glance at them; and the room is too closely guarded for me to take you there without his knowledge. He is never away himself, and one of the keepers is stationed outside."

"The wit of a woman," Mr. Sabin said softly, "is all-conquering."

"Providing always," Lady Deringham said, "that the woman is willing. I do not understand what it all means. Do you know this? Perhaps you do. There have been efforts made by strangers to break into my husband's room. Only a few days ago a stranger came here with a forged letter of introduction, and obtained access to the Admiral's library. He did not come to steal. He came to study my husband's work; he came, in fact, for the very purpose which you avow. Only yesterday my son began to take the same interest in the same thing. The whole of this morning he spent with his father, under the pretence of helping him; really he was studying and examining for himself. He has not told me what it is, but he has a reason for this; he, too, has some suspicions. Now you come, and your mission is the same. What does it all mean? I will write to Mr. C. myself; he will come down and advise me."

"I would not do that if I were you," Mr. Sabin said quietly. "Mr. C. would not thank you to be dragged down here on such an idle errand."

"Ay, but would it be an idle errand?" she said slowly. "Victor, be frank with me. I should hate to refuse anything you asked me. Tell me what it means. Is my husband's work of any real value, and if so to whom, and for what purpose?"

Mr. Sabin was gently distressed.

"My dear Lady Deringham," he said, "I have told you the exact truth. I want to get some statistics for my paper. Mr. C. himself recommended me to try and get them from your husband; that is absolutely all. As for this attempted robbery of which you were telling me, believe me when I assure you that I know nothing whatever about it. Your son's interest is, after all, only natural. The study of the papers on which your husband has been engaged is the only reasonable test of his sanity. Frankly, I cannot believe that any one in Lord

Deringham's mental state could produce any work likely to be of the slightest permanent value."

The Countess sighed.

"I suppose that I must believe you, Victor," she said; "yet, notwithstanding all that you say, I do not know how to help you—my husband scarcely ever leaves the room. He works there with a revolver by his side. If he were to find a stranger near his work I believe that he would shoot him without hesitation."

"At night time——"

"At night time he usually sleeps there in an ante-room, and outside there is a man always watching."

Mr. Sabin looked thoughtful.

"It is only necessary," he said, "for me to be in the room for about ten minutes, and I do not need to carry anything away; my memory will serve me for all that I require. By some means or other I must have that ten minutes."

"You will risk your life," Lady Deringham said, "for I cannot suggest any plan; I would help you if I could, but I am powerless."

"I must have that ten minutes," Mr. Sabin said slowly.

"Must!" Lady Deringham raised her eyebrows. There was a subtle change in the tone of the man, a note of authority, perhaps even the shadow of a threat; he noted the effect and followed it up.

"I mean what I say, Constance," he declared. "I am not asking you a great thing; you have your full share of woman's wit, and you can arrange this if you like."

"But, Victor, be reasonable," she protested; "suggest a way yourself if you think it so easy. I tell you that he never leaves the room!"

"He must be made to leave it."

"By force?"

"If necessary," Mr. Sabin answered coolly.

Lady Deringham raised her hand to her forehead and sat thinking. The man's growing earnestness bewildered her. What was to be done—what could she say? After all he was not changed; the old fear of him was creeping through her veins, yet she made her effort.

"You want those papers for something more than a magazine article!" she declared. "There is something behind all this! Victor, I cannot help you; I am powerless. I will take no part in anything which I cannot understand."

He stood up, leaning a little upon his stick, the dull, green stone of which flashed brightly in the firelight.

"You will help me," he said slowly. "You will let me into that room at night, and you will see that your husband is not there, or that he does not interfere. And as to that magazine article, you are right! What if it were a lie! I do not fly at small game. Now do you understand?"

She rose to her feet and drew herself up before him proudly. She towered above him, handsome, dignified, angry.

"Victor," she said firmly, "I refuse; you can go away at once! I will have no more to say or to do with you! You have given me up my letters, it is true, yet for that you have no special claim upon my gratitude. A man of honour would have destroyed them long ago."

He looked up at her, and the ghost of an unholy smile flickered upon his lips.

"Did I tell you that I had given them all back to you?" he said. "Ah! that was a mistake; all save one, I should have said! One I kept, in case—— Well, your sex are proverbially ungrateful, you know. It is the one on the yellow paper written from Mentone! You remember it? I always liked it better than any of the others."

Her white hands flashed out in the firelight. It seemed almost as though she must have struck him. He had lied to her! She was not really free; he was still the master and she his slave! She stood as though turned to stone.

"I think," he said, "that you will listen now to a little plan which has just occurred to me, will you not?"

She looked away from him with a shudder.

"What is it?" she asked hoarsely.

CHAPTER XXVI

MR. BLATHERWICK AS ST. ANTHONY

"I am afraid," Harcutt said, "that either the letter was a hoax, or the writer has thought better of the matter. It is half an hour past the time, and poor Mr. Blatherwick is still alone."

Wolfenden glanced towards the distant table where his father's secretary was already finishing his modest meal.

"Poor old Blatherwick!" he remarked; "I know he's awfully relieved. He's too nervous for this sort of thing; I believe he would have lost his head altogether if his mysterious correspondent had turned up."

"I suppose," Harcutt said, "that we may take it for granted that he is not in the room."

"Every soul here," Wolfenden answered, "is known to me either personally or by sight. The man with the dark moustache sitting by himself is a London solicitor who built himself a bungalow here four years ago, and comes down every other week for golf. The two men in the corner are land speculators from Norwich; and their neighbour is Captain Stoneham, who rides over from the barracks twice a week, also for golf."

"It is rather a sell for us," Harcutt remarked. "On the whole I am not sorry that I have to go back to town to-night. Great Scott! what a pretty girl!"

"Lean back, you idiot!" Wolfenden exclaimed softly; "don't move if you can help it!"

Harcutt grasped the situation and obeyed at once. The portion of the dining-room in which they were sitting was little more than a recess, divided off from the main apartment by heavy curtains and seldom used except in the summer when visitors were plentiful. Mr. Blatherwick's table was really within a few feet of theirs, but they themselves were hidden from it by a corner of the folding doors. They had chosen the position with care and apparently with success.

The girl who had entered the room stood for a moment looking round as though about to select a table. Harcutt's exclamation was not without justification, for she was certainly pretty. She was neatly dressed in a grey walking suit, and a velvet Tam-o-shanter hat with a smart feather. Suddenly she saw Mr. Blatherwick and advanced towards him with outstretched hand and a charming smile.

"Why, my dear Mr. Blatherwick, what on earth are you doing here?" she exclaimed. "Have you left Lord Deringham?"

Mr. Blatherwick rose to his feet confused, and blushing to his spectacles; he greeted the young lady, however, with evident pleasure.

"No; that is, not yet," he answered; "I am leaving this week. I did not know— I had no idea that you were in the vicinity! I am very pleased to see you."

She looked at the empty place at his table.

"I was going to have some luncheon," she said; "I have walked so much further than I intended and I am ravenously hungry. May I sit at your table?"

"With much pleasure," Mr. Blatherwick assented. "I was expecting a—a— friend, but he is evidently not coming."

"I will take his place then, if I may," she said, seating herself in the chair which the waiter was holding for her, and raising her veil. "Will you order something for me? I am too hungry to mind what it is."

Mr. Blatherwick gave a hesitating order, and the waiter departed. Miss Merton drew off her gloves and was perfectly at her ease.

"Now do tell me about the friend whom you were going to meet," she said, smiling gaily at him, "I hope—you really must not tell me, Mr. Blatherwick, that it was a lady!"

Mr. Blatherwick coloured to the roots of his hair at the mere suggestion, and hastened to disclaim it.

"My—my dear Miss Merton!" he exclaimed, "I can assure you that it was not! I—I should not think of such a thing."

She nodded, and began to break up her roll and eat it.

"I am very glad to hear it, Mr. Blatherwick," she said; "I warn you that I was prepared to be very jealous. You used to tell me, you know, that I was the only girl with whom you cared to talk."

"It is—quite true, quite true, Miss Merton," he answered eagerly, dropping his voice a little and glancing uneasily over his shoulder. "I—I have missed you very much indeed; it has been very dull."

Mr. Blatherwick sighed; he was rewarded by a very kind glance from a pair of very blue eyes. He fingered the wine list, and began to wonder whether she would care for champagne.

"Now tell me," she said, "all the news. How are they all at Deringham Hall—the dear old Admiral and the Countess, and that remarkably silly young man, Lord Wolfenden?"

Wolfenden received a kick under the table, and Harcutt's face positively beamed with delight. Mr. Blatherwick, however, had almost forgotten their proximity. He had made up his mind to order champagne.

"The Ad—Ad—Admiral is well in health, but worse mentally," he answered. "I am leaving for that very reason. I do not conceive that in fairness to myself I should continue to waste my time in work which can bring forth no fruit. I trust, Miss Merton, that you agree with me."

"Perfectly," she answered gravely.

"The Countess," he continued, "is well, but much worried. There have been strange hap—hap—happenings at the Hall since you left. Lord Wolfenden is there. By the bye, Miss Merton," he added, dropping his voice, "I do not—not—think that you used to consider Lord Wolfenden so very silly when you were at Deringham."

"It was very dull sometimes—when you were busy, Mr. Blatherwick," she answered, beginning her lunch. "I will confess to you that I did try to amuse myself a little with Lord Wolfenden. But he was altogether too rustic—too stupid! I like a man with brains!"

Harcutt produced a handkerchief and stuffed it to his mouth; his face was slowly becoming purple with suppressed laughter. Mr. Blatherwick ordered the champagne.

"I—I was very jealous of him," he admitted almost in a whisper.

The blue eyes were raised again very eloquently to his.

"You had no cause," she said gently; "and Mr. Blatherwick, haven't you forgotten something?"

Mr. Blatherwick had sipped his glass of champagne, and answered without a stutter.

"I have not," he said, "forgotten you!"

"You used to call me by my Christian name!"

"I should be delighted to call you Miss—Blanche for ever," he said boldly. "May I?"

She laughed softly.

"Well, I don't quite know about that," she said; "you may for this morning, at least. It is so pleasant to see you again. How is the work getting on?"

He groaned.

"Don't ask me, please; it is awful! I am truly glad that I am leaving—for many reasons!"

"Have you finished copying those awful details of the defective armour plates?" she asked, suddenly dropping her voice so that it barely reached the other side of the table.

"Only last night," he answered; "it was very hard work, and so ridiculous! It went into the box with the rest of the finished work this morning."

"Did the Admiral engage a new typewriter?" she inquired.

He shook his head.

"No; he says that he has nearly finished."

"I am so glad," she said. "You have had no temptation to flirt then with anybody else, have you?"

"To flirt—with anybody else! Oh! Miss—I mean Blanche. Do you think that I could do that?"

His little round face shone with sincerity and the heat of the unaccustomed wine. His eyes were watering a little, and his spectacles were dull. The girl looked at him in amusement.

"I am afraid," she said, with a sigh, "that you used to flirt with me."

"I can assure you, B—B—Blanche," he declared earnestly, "that I never said a word to you which I—I did not hon—hon—honestly mean. Blanche, I should like to ask you something."

"Not now," she interrupted hastily. "Do you know, I fancy that we must be getting too confidential. That odious man with the eyeglass keeps staring at us. Tell me what you are going to do when you leave here. You can ask me—what you were going to, afterwards."

Mr. Blatherwick grew eloquent and Blanche was sympathetic. It was quite half an hour before they rose and prepared to depart.

"I know you won't mind," Blanche said to him confidentially, "if I ask you to leave the hotel first; the people I am with are a little particular, and it would scarcely do, you see, for us to go out together."

"Certainly," he replied. "Would you l—like me to leave you here—would it be better?"

"You might walk to the door with me, please," she said. "I am afraid you must be very disappointed that your friend did not come. Are you not?"

Mr. Blatherwick's reply was almost incoherent in its excess of protestation. They walked down the room together. Harcutt and Wolfenden look at one another.

"Well," the former exclaimed, drinking up his liqueur, "it is a sell!"

"Yes," Wolfenden agreed thoughtfully, with his eyes fixed upon the two departing figures, "it is a sell!"

CHAPTER XXVII

BY CHANCE OR DESIGN

Wolfenden sent his phaeton to the station with Harcutt, who had been summoned back to town upon important business. Afterwards he slipped back to the hall to wait for its return, and came face to face with Mr. Blatherwick, who was starting homewards.

"I was looking for you," Wolfenden said; "your luncheon party turned out a little differently to anything we had expected."

"I am happy," Mr. Blatherwick said, "to be able to believe that the letter was after all a hoax. There was no one in the room, as you would doubtless observe, likely to be in any way concerned in the matter."

Wolfenden knocked the ash off his cigarette without replying.

"You seem," he remarked, "to be on fairly intimate terms with Miss Merton."

"We were fellow workers for several months," Mr. Blatherwick reminded him; "naturally, we saw a good deal of one another."

"She is," Wolfenden continued, "a very charming girl."

"I consider her, in every way," Mr. Blatherwick said with enthusiasm, "a most delightful young lady. I—I am very much attached to her."

Wolfenden laid his hand on the secretary's shoulder.

"Blatherwick," he said, "you're a good fellow, and I like you. Don't be offended at what I am going to say. You must not trust Miss Merton; she is not quite what she appears to you."

Mr. Blatherwick took a step backward, and flushed red with anger.

"I do not understand you, Lord Wolfenden," he said. "What do you know of Miss Merton?"

"Not very much," Wolfenden said quietly; "quite enough, though, to justify me in warning you seriously against her. She is a very clever young person, but I am afraid a very unscrupulous one."

Mr. Blatherwick was grave, almost dignified.

"Lord Wolfenden," he said, "you are the son of my employer, but I take the liberty of telling you that you are a l—l——"

"Steady, Blatherwick," Wolfenden interrupted; "you must not call me names."

"You are not speaking the truth," Mr. Blatherwick continued, curbing himself with an effort. "I will not listen to, or—or permit in my presence any aspersion against that young lady!"

Wolfenden shook his head gently.

"Mr. Blatherwick," he said, "don't be a fool! You ought to know that I am not the sort of man to make evil remarks about a lady behind her back, unless I knew what I was talking about. I cannot at this moment prove it, but I am morally convinced that Miss Merton came here to-day at the instigation of the person who wrote to you, and that she only refrained from making you some offer because she knew quite well that we were within hearing."

"I will not listen to another word, Lord Wolfenden," Mr. Blatherwick declared vigorously. "If you are honest, you are cruelly misjudging that young lady; if not you must know yourself the proper epithet to be applied to the person who defames an innocent girl behind her back! I wish you good afternoon, sir. I shall leave Deringham Hall to-morrow."

He strode away, and Wolfenden watched him with a faint, regretful smile upon his lips. Then he turned round suddenly; a little trill of soft musical laughter came floating out from a recess in the darkest corner of the hall. Miss Merton was leaning back amongst the cushions of a lounge, her eyes gleaming with amusement. She beckoned Wolfenden to her.

"Quite melodramatic, wasn't it?" she exclaimed, moving her skirts for him to sit by her side. "Dear little man! Do you know he wants to marry me?"

"What a clever girl you are," Wolfenden remarked; "really you'd make an admirable wife for him."

She pouted a little.

"Thank you very much," she said. "I am not contemplating making any one an admirable wife; matrimony does not attract me at all."

"I don't know what pleasure you can find in making a fool of a decent little chap like that," he said; "it's too bad of you, Blanche."

"One must amuse oneself, and he is so odd and so very much in earnest."

"Of course," Wolfenden continued, "I know that you had another object."

"Had I?"

"You came here to try and tempt the poor little fellow with a thousand pounds!"

"I have never," she interposed calmly, "possessed a thousand shillings in my life."

"Not on your own account, of course: you came on behalf of your employer, Mr. Sabin, or some one behind him! What is this devilry, Blanche?"

She looked at him out of wide-open eyes, but she made no answer.

"So far as I can see," he remarked, "I must confess that foolery seems a better term. I cannot imagine anything in my father's work worth the concoction of any elaborate scheme to steal. But never mind that; there is a scheme, and you are in it. Now I will make a proposition to you. It is a matter of money, I suppose; will you name your terms to come over to my side?"

A look crept into her eyes which puzzled him.

"Over to your side," she repeated thoughtfully. "Do you mind telling me exactly what you mean by that?"

As though by accident the delicate white hand from which she had just withdrawn her glove touched his, and remained there as though inviting his clasp. She looked quickly up at him and drooped her eyes. Wolfenden took her hand, patted it kindly, and replaced it in her lap.

"Look here, Blanche," he said, "I won't affect to misunderstand you; but haven't you learnt by this time that adventures are not in my way?—less now than at any time perhaps."

She was watching his face and read its expression with lightning-like truth.

"Bah!" she said, "there is no man who would be so brutal as you unless——"

"Unless what?"

"He were in love with another girl!"

"Perhaps I am, Blanche!"

"I know that you are."

He looked at her quickly.

"But you do not know with whom?"

She had not guessed, but she knew now.

"I think so," she said; "it is with the beautiful niece of Mr. Sabin! You have admirable taste."

"Never mind about that," he said; "let us come to my offer. I will give you a hundred a year for life, settle it upon you, if you will tell me everything."

"A hundred a year," she repeated. "Is that much money?"

"Well, it will cost more than two thousand pound," he said; "still, I would like you to have it, and you shall if you will be quite frank with me."

She hesitated.

"I should like," she said, "to think it over till to-morrow morning; it will be better, for supposing I decide to accept, I shall know a good deal more of this than I know now."

"Very well," he said, "only I should strongly advise you to accept."

"One hundred a year," she repeated thoughtfully. "Perhaps you will have changed your mind by to-morrow."

"There is no fear of it," he assured her quietly.

"Write it down," she said. "I think that I shall agree."

"Don't you trust me, Blanche?"

"It is a business transaction," she said coolly; "you have made it one yourself."

He tore a sheet from his pocket-book and scribbled a few lines upon it.

"Will that do?" he asked her.

She read it through and folded it carefully up.

"It will do very nicely," she said with a quiet smile. "And now I must go back as quickly as I can."

They walked to the hall door; Lord Wolfenden's carriage had come back from the station and was waiting for him.

"How are you going?" he asked.

She shook her head.

"I must hire something, I suppose," she said. "What beautiful horses! Do you see, Hector remembers me quite well; I used to take bread to him in the stable when I was at Deringham Hall. Good old man!"

She patted the horse's neck. Wolfenden did not like it, but he had no alternative.

"Won't you allow me to give you a lift?" he said, with a marked absence of cordiality in his tone; "or if you would prefer it, I can easily order a carriage from the hotel."

"Oh! I would much rather go with you, if you really don't mind," she said. "May I really?"

"I shall be very pleased," he answered untruthfully. "I ought perhaps to tell you that the horses are very fresh and don't go well together: they have a nasty habit of running away down hill."

She smiled cheerfully, and lifting her skirts placed a dainty little foot upon the step.

"I detest quiet horses," she said, "and I have been used to being run away with all my life. I rather like it."

Wolfenden resigned himself to the inevitable. He took the reins, and they rattled off towards Deringham. About half-way there, they saw a little black figure away on the cliff path to the right.

"It is Mr. Blatherwick," Wolfenden said, pointing with his whip. "Poor little chap! I wish you'd leave him alone, Blanche!"

"On one condition," she said, smiling up at him, "I will!"

"It is granted already," he declared.

"That you let me drive for just a mile!"

He handed her the reins at once, and changed seats. From the moment she took them, he could see that she was an accomplished whip. He leaned back and lit a cigarette.

"Blatherwick's salvation," he remarked, "has been easily purchased."

She smiled rather curiously, but did not reply. A hired carriage was coming towards them, and her eyes were fixed upon it. In a moment they swept past, and Wolfenden was conscious of a most unpleasant sensation. It was Helène, whose dark eyes were glancing from the girl to him in cold surprise; and Mr. Sabin, who was leaning back by her side wrapped in a huge fur coat. Blanche looked down at him innocently.

"Fancy meeting them," she remarked, touching Hector with the whip. "It does not matter, does it? You look dreadfully cross!"

Wolfenden muttered some indefinite reply and threw his cigarette savagely into the road. After all he was not so sure that Mr. Blatherwick's salvation had been cheaply won!

CHAPTER XXVIII

A MIDNIGHT VISITOR

"Wolf! Wolf!"

Wolfenden, to whom sleep before the early morning hours was a thing absolutely impossible, was lounging in his easy chair meditating on the events of the day over a final cigarette. He had come to his room at midnight in rather a dejected frame of mind; the day's happenings had scarcely gone in his favour. Helène had looked upon him coldly—almost with suspicion. In the morning he would be able to explain everything, but in the meantime Blanche was upon the spot, and he had an uneasy feeling that the girl was his enemy. He had begun to doubt whether that drive, so natural a thing, as it really happened, was not carefully planned on her part, with a full knowledge of the fact that they would meet Mr. Sabin and his niece. It was all the more irritating because during the last few days he had been gradually growing into the belief that so far as his suit with Helène was concerned, the girl herself was not altogether indifferent to him. She had refused him definitely enough, so far as mere words went, but there were lights in her soft, dark eyes, and something indefinable, but apparent in her manner, which had forbidden him to abandon all hope. Yet it was hard to believe that she was in any way subject to the will of her guardian, Mr. Sabin. In small things she took no pains to study him; she was evidently not in the least under his dominion. On the contrary, there was in his manner towards her a certain deference, as though it were she whose will was the ruling one between them. As a matter of fact, her appearance and whole bearing seemed to indicate one accustomed to command. Her family or connections she had never spoken of to him, yet he had not the slightest doubt but that she was of gentle birth. Even if it should turn out that this was not the case, Wolfenden was democratic enough to think that it made no difference. She was good enough to be his wife. Her appearance and manners were almost typically aristocratic— whatever there might be in her present surroundings or in her past which savoured of mystery, he would at least have staked his soul upon her honesty. He realised very fully, as he sat there smoking in the early hours of the morning, that this was no passing fancy of his; she was his first love—for good or for evil she would be his last. Failure, he said to himself, was a word which he would not admit in his vocabulary. She was moving towards him already, some day she should be his! Through the mists of blue tobacco smoke which hovered around him he seemed, with a very slight and very pleasant effort of his imagination, to see some faint visions of her in that more softening mood, the vaguest recollection of which set his heart beating fast and sent the blood moving through his veins to music. How delicately handsome she was, how exquisite the lines of her girlish, yet graceful and queenly figure. With her clear, creamy skin, soft as alabaster below the red gold of her hair, the somewhat haughty poise of her small, shapely head, she brought him vivid recollections of that old aristocracy of France, as one reads of them now only in the pages of romance or history. She had the grand air—even the great Queen could not have walked to the scaffold with a more magnificent contempt of the rabble, whose victim she was. Some more personal thought came to him; he half closed his eyes and leaned back in his chair steeped in pleasant thoughts; and then it all came to a swift, abrupt end, these reveries and pleasant castle-building. He was back in the present, suddenly recalled in a most extraordinary manner, to realisation of the hour and place. Surely he could not have been mistaken! That was a low knocking at his locked door outside; there was no doubt about it. There it was again! He heard his own name, softly but unmistakably spoken in a trembling voice. He glanced at his watch, it was between two and three o'clock; then he walked quickly to the door and opened it without hesitation. It was his father who stood there fully dressed, with pale face and angrily burning eyes. In his hand he carried a revolver. Wolfenden noticed that the fingers which clasped it were shaking, as though with cold.

"Father," Wolfenden exclaimed, "what on earth is the matter?"

He dropped his voice in obedience to that sudden gesture for silence. The Admiral answered him in a hoarse whisper.

"A great deal is the matter! I am being deceived and betrayed in my own house! Listen!"

They stood together on the dimly lit landing; holding his breath and listening intently, Wolfenden was at once aware of faint, distant sounds. They came from the ground floor almost immediately below them. His father laid his hand heavily upon Wolfenden's shoulder.

"Some one is in the library," he said. "I heard the door open distinctly. When I tried to get out I found that the door of my room was locked; there is treachery here!"

"How did you get out?" Wolfenden asked.

"Through the bath-room and down the back stairs; that door was locked too, but I found a key that fitted it. Come with me. Be careful! Make no noise!"

They were on their way downstairs now. As they turned the angle of the broad oak stairway, Wolfenden caught a glimpse of his father's face, and shuddered; it was very white, and his eyes were bloodshot and wild, his forefinger was already upon the trigger of his revolver.

"Let me have that," Wolfenden whispered, touching it; "my hand is steadier than yours."

But the Admiral shook his head; he made no answer in words, but the butt end of the revolver became almost welded into the palm of his hand. Wolfenden began to feel that they were on the threshold of a tragedy. They had reached the ground floor now; straight in front of them was the library door. The sound of muffled movements within the room was distinctly audible. The Admiral's breath came fast.

"Tread lightly, Wolf," he muttered. "Don't let them hear us! Let us catch them red-handed!"

But the last dozen yards of the way was over white flags tesselated, and polished like marble. Wolfenden's shoes creaked; the Admiral's tip-toe walk was no light one. There was a sudden cessation of all sounds; they had been heard! The Admiral, with a low cry of rage, leaped forwards. Wolfenden followed close behind.

Even as they crossed the threshold the room was plunged into sudden darkness; they had but a momentary and partial glimpse of the interior. Wolfenden saw a dark, slim figure bending forward with his finger still pressed to the ball of the lamp. The table was strewn with papers, something—somebody—was fluttering behind the screen yonder. There was barely a second of light; then with a sharp click the lamp went out, and the figure of the man was lost in obscurity. Almost simultaneously there came a flash of level fire and the loud report of the Admiral's revolver. There was no groan, so Wolfenden concluded that the man, whoever he might be, had not been hit. The sound of the report was followed by a few seconds' breathless silence. There was no movement of any sort in the room; only a faint breeze stealing in through the wide-open windows caused a gentle rustling of the papers with which the table was strewn, and the curtains swayed gently backwards and forwards. The Admiral, with his senses all on the alert, stood motionless, the revolver tense in his hand, his fiercely eager eyes straining to pierce the darkness. By his side, Wolfenden, equally agitated now, though from a different reason, stood holding his breath, his head thrust forward, his eyes striving to penetrate the veil of gloom which lay like a thick barrier between him and the screen. His fear had suddenly taken to itself a very real and terrible form. There had been a moment, before the extinction of the lamp had plunged the room into darkness, when he had seen, or fancied that he had seen, a woman's skirts fluttering there. Up to the present his father's attention had been wholly riveted upon the other end of the room; yet he was filled with a nervous dread lest at any moment that revolver might change its direction. His ears were strained to the uttermost to catch the slightest sign of any movement.

At last the silence was broken; there was a faint movement near the window, and then again, without a second's hesitation, there was that level line of fire and loud report from the Admiral's revolver. There was no groan, no sign of any one having been hit. The Admiral began to move slowly in the direction of the window; Wolfenden remained where he was, listening intently. He was right, there was a smothered movement from behind the screen. Some one was moving from there towards the door, some one with light footsteps and a trailing skirt. He drew back into the doorway; he meant to let her pass whoever it might be, but he meant to know who it was. He could hear her hurried breathing; a faint, familiar perfume, shaken out by the movement of her skirts, puzzled him; it's very familiarity bewildered him. She knew that he was there; she must know it, for she had paused. The position was terribly critical. A few yards away the Admiral was groping about, revolver in hand, mumbling to himself a string of terrible threats. The casting of a shadow would call forth that death-dealing fire. Wolfenden thrust out his hand cautiously; it fell upon a woman's arm. She did not cry out, although her rapid breathing sank almost to a moan. For a moment he was staggered—the room seemed to be going round with him; he had to bite his lips to stifle the exclamation which very nearly escaped him. Then he stood away from the door with a little shudder, and guided her through it. He heard her footsteps die away along the corridor with a peculiar sense of relief. Then he thrust his hand into the pocket of his dinner coat and drew out a box of matches.

"I am going to strike a light," he whispered in his father's ear.

"Quick, then," was the reply, "I don't think the fellow has got away yet; he must be hiding behind some of the furniture."

There was the scratching of a match upon a silver box, a feeble flame gradually developing into a sure illumination. Wolfenden carefully lit the lamp and raised it high over his head. The room was empty! There was no doubt about it! They two were alone. But the window was wide open and a chair in front of it had been thrown over. The Admiral strode to the casement and called out angrily—

"Heggs! are you there? Is no one on duty?"

There was no answer; the tall sentry-box was empty.

Wolfenden came over to his father's side and brought the lamp with him, and together they leaned out. At first they could see nothing; then Wolfenden threw off the shade from the lamp and the light fell in a broad track upon a dark, motionless figure stretched out upon the turf. Wolfenden stooped down hastily.

"My God!" he exclaimed, "it is Heggs! Father, won't you sound the gong? We shall have to arouse the house."

There was no need. Already the library was half full of hastily dressed servants, awakened by the sound of the Admiral's revolver. Pale and terrified, but never more self-composed, Lady Deringham stepped out to them in a long, white dressing-gown.

"What has happened?" she cried. "Who is it, Wolfenden—has your father shot any one?"

But Wolfenden shook his head, as he stood for a moment upright, and looked into his mother's face.

"There is a man hurt," he said; "it is Heggs, I think, but he is not shot. The evil is not of our doing!"

CHAPTER XXIX

"IT WAS MR. SABIN"

It was still an hour or two before dawn. No trace whatever of the marauders had been discovered either outside the house or within. With difficulty the Earl had been persuaded to relinquish his smoking revolver, and had retired to his room. The doors had all been locked, and two of the most trustworthy servants left in charge of the library. Wolfenden had himself accompanied his father upstairs and after a few words with him had returned to his own apartment. With his mother he had scarcely exchanged a single sentence. Once their eyes had met and he had immediately looked away. Nevertheless he was not altogether unprepared for that gentle knocking at his door which came about half an hour after the house was once more silent.

He rose at once from his chair—it seemed scarcely a night for sleep—and opened it cautiously. It was Lady Deringham who stood there, white and trembling. He held out his hand and she leaned heavily on it during her passage into the room.

He wheeled his own easy chair before the fire and helped her into it. She seemed altogether incapable of speech. She was trembling violently, and her face was perfectly bloodless. Wolfenden dropped on his knees by her side and began chafing her hands. The touch of his fingers seemed to revive her. She was not already judged then. She lifted her eyes and looked at him sorrowfully.

"What do you think of me, Wolfenden?" she asked.

"I have not thought about it at all," he answered. "I am only wondering. You have come to explain everything?"

She shuddered. Explain everything! That was a task indeed. When the heart is young and life is a full and generous thing; in the days of romance, when adventures and love-making come as a natural heritage and form part of the order of things, then the words which the woman had to say would have come lightly enough from her lips, less perhaps as a confession than as a half apologetic narration. But in the days when youth lies far behind, when its glamour has faded away and nothing but the bare incidents remain, unbeautified by the full colouring and exuberance of the springtime of life, the most trifling indiscretions then stand out like idiotic crimes. Lady Deringham had been a proud woman—a proud woman all her life. She had borne in society the reputation of an almost ultra-exclusiveness; in her home life she had been something of an autocrat. Perhaps this was the most miserable moment of her life. Her son was looking at her with cold, inquiring eyes. She was on her defence before him. She bowed her head and spoke:

"Tell me what you thought, Wolfenden."

"Forgive me," he said, "I could only think that there was robbery, and that you, for some sufficient reason, I am sure, were aiding. I could not think anything else, could I?"

"You thought what was true, Wolfenden," she whispered. "I was helping another man to rob your father! It was only a very trifling theft—a handful of notes from his work for a magazine article. But it was theft, and I was an accomplice!"

There was a short silence. Her eyes, seeking steadfastly to read his face, could make nothing of it.

"I will not ask you why," he said slowly. "You must have had very good reasons. But I want to tell you one thing. I am beginning to have grave doubts as to whether my father's state is really so bad as Dr. Whitlett thinks— whether, in short, his work is not after all really of some considerable value. There are several considerations which incline me to take this view."

The suggestion visibly disturbed Lady Deringham. She moved in her chair uneasily.

"You have heard what Mr. Blatherwick says," she objected. "I am sure that he is absolutely trustworthy."

"There is no doubt about Blatherwick's honesty," he admitted, "but the Admiral himself says that he dare trust no one, and that for weeks he has given him no paper of importance to work upon simply for that reason. It has been growing upon me that we may have been mistaken all along, that very likely Miss Merton was paid to steal his work, and that it may possess for certain people, and for certain purposes, a real technical importance. How else can we account for the deliberate efforts which have been made to obtain possession of it?"

"You have spent some time examining it yourself," she said in a low tone; "what was your own opinion?"

"I found some sheets," he answered, "and I read them very carefully; they were connected with the various landing-places upon the Suffolk coast. An immense amount of detail was very clearly given. The currents, bays, and fortifications were all set out; even the roads and railways into the interior were dealt with. I compared them afterwards with a map of Suffolk. They were, so far as one could judge, correct. Of course this was only a page or two at random, but I must say it made an impression upon me."

There was another silence, this time longer than before. Lady Deringham was thinking. Once more, then, the man had lied to her! He was on some secret business of his own. She shuddered slightly. She had no curiosity as to its nature. Only she remembered what many people had told her, that where he went disaster followed. A piece of coal fell into the grate hissing from the fire. He stooped to pick it up, and catching a glimpse of her face became instantly graver. He remembered that as yet he had heard nothing of what she had come to tell him. Her presence in the library was altogether unexplained.

"You were very good," she said slowly; "you stayed what might have been a tragedy. You knew that I was there, you helped me to escape; yet you must have known that I was in league with the man who was trying to steal those papers."

"There was no mistake, then! You were doing that. You!"

"It is true," she answered. "It was I who let him in, who unlocked your father's desk. I was his accomplice!"

"Who was the man?"

She did not tell him at once.

"He was once," she said, "my lover!"

"Before——"

"Before I met your father! We were never really engaged. But he loved me, and I thought I cared for him. I wrote him letters—the foolish letters of an impulsive girl. These he has kept. I treated him badly, I know that! But I too have suffered. It has been the desire of my life to have those letters. Last night he called here. Before my face he burnt all but one! That he kept. The price of his returning it to me was my help—last night."

"For what purpose?" Wolfenden asked. "What use did he propose to make of the Admiral's papers if he succeeded in stealing them?"

She shook her head mournfully.

"I cannot tell. He answered me at first that he simply needed some statistics to complete a magazine article, and that Mr. C. himself had sent him here. If what you tell me of their importance is true, I have no doubt that he lied."

"Why could he not go to the Admiral himself?"

Lady Deringham's face was as pale as death, and she spoke with downcast head, her eyes fixed upon her clenched hands.

"At Cairo," she said, "not long after my marriage, we all met. I was indiscreet, and your father was hot-headed and jealous. They quarrelled and fought, your father wounded him; he fired in the air. You understand now that he could not go direct to the Admiral."

"I cannot understand," he admitted, "why you listened to his proposal."

"Wolfenden, I wanted that letter," she said, her voice dying away in something like a moan. "It is not that I have anything more than folly to reproach myself with, but it was written—it was the only one—after my marriage. Just at first I was not very happy with your father. We had had a quarrel, I forget what about, and I sat down and wrote words which I have many a time bitterly repented ever having put on paper. I have never forgotten them—I never shall! I have seen them often in my happiest moments, and they have seemed to me to be written with letters of fire."

"You have it back now? You have destroyed it?"

She shook her head wearily.

"No, I was to have had it when he had succeeded; I had not let him in five minutes when you disturbed us."

"Tell me the man's name."

"Why?"

"I will get you the letter."

"He would not give it you. You could not make him."

Wolfenden's eyes flashed with a sudden fire.

"You are mistaken," he said. "The man who holds for blackmail over a woman's head, a letter written twenty years ago, is a scoundrel! I will get that letter from him. Tell me his name!"

Lady Deringham shuddered.

"Wolfenden, it would bring trouble! He is dangerous. Don't ask me. At least I have kept my word to him. It was not my fault that we were disturbed. He will not molest me now."

"Mother, I will know his name!"

"I cannot tell it you!"

"Then I will find it out; it will not be difficult. I will put the whole matter in the hands of the police. I shall send to Scotland Yard for a detective. There are marks underneath the window. I picked up a man's glove upon the library floor. A clever fellow will find enough to work upon. I will find this blackguard for myself, and the law shall deal with him as he deserves."

"Wolfenden, have mercy! May I not know best? Are my wishes, my prayers, nothing to you?"

"A great deal, mother, yet I consider myself also a judge as to the wisest course to pursue. The plan which I have suggested may clear up many things. It may bring to light the real object of this man. It may solve the mystery of that impostor, Wilmot. I am tired of all this uncertainty. We will have some daylight. I shall telegraph to-morrow morning to Scotland Yard."

"Wolfenden, I beseech you!"

"So also do I beseech you, mother, to tell me that man's name. Great heavens!"

Wolfenden sprang suddenly from his chair with startled face. An idea, slow of coming, but absolutely convincing from its first conception, had suddenly flashed home to him. How could he have been so blind? He stood looking at his mother in fixed suspense. The light of his knowledge was in his face, and she saw it. She had been dreading this all the while.

"It was Mr. Sabin!—the man who calls himself Sabin!"

A little moan of despair crept out from her lips. She covered her face with her hands and sobbed.

CHAPTER XXX

THE GATHERING OF THE WAR-STORM

Mr. Sabin, entering his breakfast-room as usual at ten o'clock on the following morning, found, besides the usual pile of newspapers and letters, a telegram, which had arrived too late for delivery on the previous evening. He opened it in leisurely fashion whilst he sipped his coffee. It was handed in at the Charing Cross Post Office, and was signed simply "K.":—

"Just returned. When can you call and conclude arrangements? Am anxious to see you. Read to-night's paper.—K."

The telegram slipped from Mr. Sabin's fingers. He tore open the *St. James's Gazette,* and a little exclamation escaped from his lips as he saw the thick black type which headed the principal columns:—

"EXTRAORDINARY TELEGRAM OF THE GERMAN EMPEROR TO MOENIG!

GERMAN SYMPATHY WITH THE REBELS!

WARSHIPS ORDERED TO DELAMERE BAY!

GREAT EXCITEMENT ON THE STOCK EXCHANGE!"

Mr. Sabin's breakfast remained untasted. He read every word in the four columns, and then turned to the other newspapers. They were all ablaze with the news. England's most renowned ally had turned suddenly against her. Without the slightest warning the fire-brand of war had been kindled, and waved threateningly in our very faces. The occasion was hopelessly insignificant. A handful of English adventurers, engaged in a somewhat rash but plucky expedition in a distant part of the world, had met with a sharp reverse. In itself the affair was nothing; yet it bade fair to become a matter of international history. Ill-advised though they may have been, the Englishmen carried with them a charter granted by the British Government. There was no secret about it—the fact was perfectly understood in every Cabinet of Europe. Yet the German Emperor had himself written a telegram congratulating the State which had repelled the threatened attack. It was scarcely an invasion—it was little more than a demonstration on the part of an ill-treated section of the population! The fact that German interests were in no way concerned—that any outside interference was simply a piece of gratuitous impertinence—only intensified the significance of the incident. A deliberate insult had been offered to England; and the man who sat there with the paper clenched in his hand, whilst his keen eyes devoured the long columns of wonder and indignation, knew that his had been the hand which had hastened the long-pent-up storm. He drew a little breath when he had finished, and turned to his breakfast.

"Is Miss Sabin up yet?" he asked the servant, who waited upon him.

The man was not certain, but withdrew to inquire. He reappeared almost directly. Miss Sabin had been up for more than an hour. She had just returned from a walk, and had ordered breakfast to be served in her room.

"Tell her," Mr. Sabin directed, "that I should be exceedingly obliged if she would take her coffee with me. I have some interesting news."

The man was absent for several minutes. Before he returned Hélène came in. Mr. Sabin greeted her with his usual courtesy and even more than his usual cordiality.

"You are missing the best part of the morning with your Continental habits," she exclaimed brightly. "I have been out on the cliffs since half-past eight. The air is delightful."

She threw off her hat, and going to the sideboard, helped herself to a cup of coffee. There was a becoming flush upon her cheeks—her hair was a little tossed by the wind. Mr. Sabin watched her curiously.

"You have not, I suppose, seen a morning paper—or rather last night's paper?" he remarked.

She shook her head.

"A newspaper! You know that I never look at an English one," she answered. "You wanted to see me, Reynolds said. Is there any news?"

"There is great news," he answered. "There is such news that by sunset to-day war will probably be declared between England and Germany!"

The flush died out of her cheeks. She faced him pallid to the lips.

"It is not possible!" she exclaimed.

"So the whole world would have declared a week ago! As a matter of fact it is not so sudden as we imagine! The storm has been long brewing! It is we who have been blind. A little black spot of irritation has spread and deepened into a war-cloud."

"This will affect us?" she asked.

"For us," he answered, "it is a triumph. It is the end of our schemes, the climax of our desires. When Knigenstein came to me I knew that he was in earnest, but I never dreamed that the torch was so nearly kindled. I see now why he was so eager to make terms with me."

"And you," she said, "you have their bond?"

For a moment he looked thoughtful.

"Not yet. I have their promise—the promise of the Emperor himself. But as yet my share of the bargain is incomplete. There must be no more delay. It must be finished now—at once. That telegram would never have been sent from Berlin but for their covenant with me. It would have been better, perhaps, had they waited a little time. But one cannot tell! The opportunity was too good to let slip."

"How long will it be," she asked, "before your work is complete?"

His face clouded over. In the greater triumph he had almost forgotten the minor difficulties of the present. He was a diplomatist and a schemer of European fame. He had planned great things, and had accomplished them. Success had been on his side so long that he might almost have been excused for declining to reckon failure amongst the possibilities. The difficulty which was before him now was as trifling as the uprooting of a hazel switch after the conquest of a forest of oaks. But none the less for the moment he was perplexed. It was hard, in the face of this need for urgent haste, to decide upon the next step.

"My work," he said slowly, "must be accomplished at once. There is very little wanted. Yet that little, I must confess, troubles me."

"You have not succeeded, then, in obtaining what you want from Lord Deringham?"

"No."

"Will he not help you at all?"

"Never."

"How, then, do you mean to get at these papers of his?"

"At present," he replied, "I scarcely know. In an hour or two I may be able to tell you. It is possible that it might take me twenty-four hours; certainly no longer than that."

She walked to the window, and stood there with her hands clasped behind her back. Mr. Sabin had lit a cigarette and was smoking it thoughtfully.

Presently she spoke to him.

"You will get them," she said; "yes, I believe that. In the end you will succeed, as you have succeeded in everything."

There was a lack of enthusiasm in her tone. He looked up quietly, and flicked the ash from the end of his cigarette.

"You are right," he said. "I shall succeed. My only regret is that I have made a slight miscalculation. It will take longer than I imagined. Knigenstein will be in a fever, and I am afraid that he will worry me. At the same time he is himself to blame. He has been needlessly precipitate."

She turned away from the window and stood before him. She had a look in her face which he had seen there but once before, and the memory of which had ever since troubled him.

"I want you," she said, "to understand this. I will not have any direct harm worked upon the Deringhams. If you can get what they have and what is necessary to us by craft—well, very good. If not, it must go! I will not have force used. You should remember that Lord Wolfenden saved your life! I will have nothing to do with any scheme which brings harm upon them!"

He looked at her steadily. A small spot of colour was burning high up on his pallid cheeks. The white, slender fingers, toying carelessly with one of the breakfast appointments, were shaking. He was very near being passionately angry.

"Do you mean," he said, speaking slowly and enunciating every word with careful distinctness, "do you mean that you would sacrifice or even endanger the greatest cause which has ever been conceived in the heart of the patriot, to the whole skin of a household of English people? I wonder whether you realise the position as it stands at this moment. I am bound in justice to you to believe that you do not. Do you realise that Germany has closed with our offer, and will act at our behest; that only a few trifling sheets of paper stand between us and the fullest, the most glorious success? Is it a time, do you think, for scruples or for maudlin sentiment? If I were to fail in my obligations towards Knigenstein I should not only be dishonoured and disgraced, but our cause would be lost for ever. The work of many years would crumble into ashes. My own life would not be worth an hour's purchase. Helène, you are mad! You are either mad, or worse!"

She faced him quite unmoved. It was more than ever apparent that she was not amongst those who feared him.

"I am perfectly sane," she said, "and I am very much in earnest. Ours shall be a strategic victory, or we will not triumph at all. I believe that you are planning some desperate means of securing those papers. I repeat that I will not have it!"

He looked at her with curling lips.

"Perhaps," he said, "it is I who have gone mad! At least I can scarcely believe that I am not dreaming. Is it really you, Helène of Bourbon, the descendant of kings, a daughter of the rulers of France, who falters and turns pale at the idea of a little blood, shed for her country's sake? I am very much afraid," he added with biting sarcasm, "that I have not understood you. You bear the name of a great queen, but you have the heart of a serving-maid! It is Lord Wolfenden for whom you fear!"

She was not less firm, but her composure was affected. The rich colour streamed into her cheeks. She remained silent.

"For a betrothed young lady," he said slowly, "you will forgive me if I say that your anxiety is scarcely discreet. What you require, I suppose, is a safe conduct for your lover. I wonder how Henri would——"

She flashed a glance and an interjection upon him which checked the words upon his lips. The gesture was almost a royal one. He was silenced.

"How dare you, sir?" she exclaimed. "You are taking insufferable liberties. I do not permit you to interfere in my private concerns. Understand that even if your words were true, if I choose to have a lover it is my affair, not yours. As for Henri, what has he to complain of? Read the papers and ask yourself that! They chronicle his doings freely enough! He is singularly discreet, is he not?—singularly faithful!"

She threw at him a glance of contempt and turned as though to leave the room. Mr. Sabin, recognising the fact that the situation was becoming dangerous, permitted himself no longer the luxury of displaying his anger. He was quite himself again, calm, judicial, incisive.

"Don't go away, please," he said. "I am sorry that you have read those reports—more than sorry that you should have attached any particular credence to them. As you know, the newspapers always exaggerate; in many of the stories which they tell I do not believe that there is a single word of truth. But I will admit that Henri has not been altogether discreet. Yet he is young, and there are many excuses to be made for him. Apart from that, the whole question of his behaviour is beside the question. Your marriage with him was never intended to be one of affection. He is well enough in his way, but there is not the stuff in him to make a man worthy of your love. Your alliance with him is simply a necessary link in the chain of our great undertaking. Between you you will represent the two royal families of France.

That is what is necessary. You must marry him, but afterwards—well, you will be a queen!"

Again he had erred. She looked at him with bent brows and kindling eyes.

"Oh! you are hideously cynical!" she exclaimed. "I may be ambitious, but it is for my country's sake. If I reign, the Court of France shall be of a new type; we will at least show the world that to be a Frenchwoman is not necessarily to abjure morals."

He shrugged his shoulders.

"That," he said, "will be as you choose. You will make your Court what you please. Personally, I believe that you are right. Such sentiments as you have expressed, properly conveyed to them, would make yours abjectly half the bourgeois of France! Be as ambitious as you please, but at least be sensible. Do not think any more of this young Englishman, not at any rate at present. Nothing but harm can come of it. He is not like the men of our own country, who know how to take a lady's dismissal gracefully."

"He is, at least, a man!"

"Helène, why should we discuss him? He shall come to no harm at my hands. Be wise, and forget him. He can be nothing whatever to you. You know that. You are pledged to greater things."

She moved back to her place by the window. Her eyes were suddenly soft, her face was sorrowful. She did not speak, and he feared her silence more than her indignation. When a knock at the door came he was grateful for the interruption—grateful, that is, until he saw who it was upon the threshold. Then he started to his feet with a little exclamation.

"Lord Wolfenden! You are an early visitor."

Wolfenden smiled grimly, and advanced into the room.

"I was anxious," he said, "to run no risk of finding you out. My mission is not altogether a pleasant one!"

CHAPTER XXXI

"I MAKE NO PROMISE"

A single glance from Mr. Sabin into Wolfenden's face was sufficient. Under his breath he swore a small, quiet oath. Wolfenden's appearance was unlooked for, and almost fatal, yet that did not prevent him from greeting his visitor with his usual ineffusive but well bred courtesy.

"I am finishing a late breakfast," he remarked. "Can I offer you anything—a glass of claret or Benedictine?"

Wolfenden scarcely heard him, and answered altogether at random. He had suddenly become aware that Helène was in the room; she was coming towards him from the window recess, with a brilliant smile upon her lips.

"How very kind of you to look us up so early!" she exclaimed.

Mr. Sabin smiled grimly as he poured himself out a liqueur and lit a cigarette. He was perfectly well aware that Wolfenden's visit was not one of courtesy; a single glance into his face had told him all that he cared to know. It was fortunate that Helène had been in the room. Every moment's respite he gained was precious.

"Have you come to ask me to go for a drive in that wonderful vehicle?" she said lightly, pointing out of the window to where his dogcart was waiting. "I should want a step-ladder to mount it!"

Wolfenden answered her gravely.

"I should feel very honoured at being allowed to take you for a drive at any time," he said, "only I think that I would rather bring a more comfortable carriage."

She shrugged her shoulders, and looked at him significantly.

"The one you were driving yesterday?"

He bit his lip and frowned with vexation, yet on the whole, perhaps, he did not regret her allusion. It was proof that she had not taken the affair too seriously.

"The one I was driving yesterday would be a great deal more comfortable," he said; "to-day I only thought of getting here quickly. I have a little business with Mr. Sabin."

"Is that a hint for me to go?" she asked. "You are not agreeable this morning! What possible business can you have with my uncle which does not include me? I am not inclined to go away; I shall stay and listen."

Mr. Sabin smiled faintly; the girl was showing her sense now at any rate. Wolfenden was obviously embarrassed. Helène remained blandly unconscious of anything serious.

"I suppose," she said, "that you want to talk golf again! Golf! Why one hears nothing else but golf down here. Don't you ever shoot or ride for a change?"

Wolfenden was suddenly assailed by an horrible suspicion. He could scarcely believe that her unconsciousness was altogether natural. At the bare suspicion of her being in league with this man he stiffened. He answered without looking at her, conscious though he was that her dark eyes were seeking his invitingly, and that her lips were curving into a smile.

"I am not thinking of playing golf to-day," he said. "Unfortunately I have less pleasant things to consider. If you could give me five minutes, Mr. Sabin," he added, "I should be very glad."

She rose immediately with all the appearance of being genuinely offended; there was a little flush in her cheeks and she walked straight to the door. Wolfenden held it open for her.

"I am exceedingly sorry to have been in the way for a moment," she said; "pray proceed with your business at once."

Wolfenden did not answer her. As she passed through the doorway she glanced up at him; he was not even looking at her. His eyes were fixed upon Mr. Sabin. The fingers which rested upon the door knob seemed twitching with impatience to close it. She stood quite still for a moment; the colour left her cheeks, and her eyes grew soft. She was not angry any longer. Instinctively some idea of the truth flashed in upon her; she passed out thoughtfully. Wolfenden closed the door and turned to Mr. Sabin.

"You can easily imagine the nature of my business," he said coldly. "I have come to have an explanation with you."

Mr. Sabin lit a fresh cigarette and smiled on Wolfenden thoughtfully.

"Certainly," he said; "an explanation! Exactly!"

"Well," said Wolfenden, "suppose you commence, then."

Mr. Sabin looked puzzled.

"Had you not better be a little more explicit?" he suggested gently.

"I will be," Wolfenden replied, "as explicit as you choose. My mother has given me her whole confidence. I have come to ask how you dare to enter Deringham Hall as a common burglar attempting to commit a theft; and to demand that you instantly return to me a letter, on which you have attempted to levy blackmail. Is that explicit enough?"

Mr. Sabin's face did not darken, nor did he seem in any way angry or discomposed. He puffed at his cigarette for a moment or two, and then looked blandly across at his visitor.

"You are talking rubbish," he said in his usual calm, even tones, "but you are scarcely to blame. It is altogether my own fault. It is quite true that I was in your house last night, but it was at your mother's invitation, and I should very much have preferred coming openly at the usual time, to sneaking in according to her directions through a window. It was only a very small favour I asked, but Lady Deringham persuaded me that your father's mental health and antipathy to strangers was such that he would never give me the information I desired, voluntarily, and it was entirely at her suggestion that I adopted the means I did. I am very sorry indeed that I allowed myself to be over-persuaded and placed in an undoubtedly false position. Women are always nervous and imaginative, and I am convinced that if I had gone openly to your father and laid my case before him he would have helped me."

"He would have done nothing of the sort!" Wolfenden declared. "Nothing would induce him to show even a portion of his work to a stranger."

Mr. Sabin shrugged his shoulders gently, and continued without heeding the interruption.

"As to my blackmailing Lady Deringham, you have spoken plainly to me, and you must forgive me for answering you in the same fashion. It is a lie! I had letters of hers, which I voluntarily destroyed in her presence; they were only a little foolish, or I should have destroyed them long ago. I had the misfortune to be once a favoured suitor for your mother's hand; and I think I may venture to say—I am sure she will not contradict me—that I was hardly treated. The only letter I ever had from her likely to do her the least harm I destroyed fifteen years ago, when I first embarked upon what has been to a certain extent a career of adventure. I told her that it was not in the packet which we burnt together yesterday. If she understood from that that it was still in my possession, and that I was retaining it for any purpose whatever, she was grievously mistaken in my words. That is all I have to say."

He had said it very well indeed. Wolfenden, listening intently to every word, with his eyes rigidly fixed upon the man's countenance, could not detect a single false note anywhere. He was puzzled. Perhaps his mother had been nervously excited, and had mistaken some sentence of his for a covert threat.

Yet he thought of her earnestness, her terrible earnestness, and a sense of positive bewilderment crept over him.

"We will leave my mother out of the question then," he said. "We will deal with this matter between ourselves. I should like to know exactly what part of my father's work you are so anxious to avail yourself of, and for what purpose?"

Mr. Sabin drew a letter from his pocket, and handed it over to Wolfenden. It was from the office of one of the first European Reviews, and briefly contained a request that Mr. Sabin would favour them with an article on the comparative naval strengths of European Powers, with particular reference to the armament and coast defences of Great Britain. Wolfenden read it carefully and passed it back. The letter was genuine, there was no doubt about that.

"It seemed to me," Mr. Sabin continued, "the most natural thing in the world to consult your father upon certain matters concerning which he is, or has been, a celebrated authority. In fact I decided to do so at the instigation of one of the Lords of your Admiralty, to whom he is personally well known. I had no idea of acting except in the most open manner, and I called at Deringham Hall yesterday afternoon, and sent in my card in a perfectly orthodox way, as you may have heard. Your mother took quite an unexpected view of the whole affair, owing partly to your father's unfortunate state of health and partly to some extraordinary attempts which, I am given to understand, have been made to rob him of his work. She was very anxious to help me, but insisted that it must be secretly. Last night's business was, I admit, a ghastly mistake—only it was not my mistake! I yielded to Lady Deringham's proposals under strong protest. As a man, I think I may say of some intelligence, I am ashamed of the whole affair; at the same time I am guilty only of an indiscretion which was sanctioned and instigated by your mother. I really do not see how I can take any blame to myself in the matter."

"You could scarcely attribute to Lady Deringham," Wolfenden remarked, "the injury to the watchman."

"I can take but little blame to myself," Mr. Sabin answered promptly. "The man was drunk; he had been, I imagine, made drunk, and I merely pushed him out of the way. He fell heavily, but the fault was not mine. Look at my physique, and remember that I was unarmed, and ask yourself what mischief I could possibly have done to the fellow."

Wolfenden reflected.

"You appear to be anxious," he said, "to convince me that your desire to gain access to a portion of my father's papers is a harmless one. I should like to ask you why you have in your employ a young lady who was dismissed from Deringham Hall under circumstances of strong suspicion?"

Mr. Sabin raised his eyebrows.

"It is the first time I have heard of anything suspicious connected with Miss Merton," he said. "She came into my service with excellent testimonials, and I engaged her at Willing's bureau. The fact that she had been employed at Deringham Hall was merely a coincidence."

"Was it also a coincidence," Wolfenden continued, "that in reply to a letter attempting to bribe my father's secretary, Mr. Blatherwick, it was she, Miss Merton, who kept an appointment with him?"

"That," Mr. Sabin answered, "I know nothing of. If you wish to question Miss Merton you are quite at liberty to do so; I will send for her."

Wolfenden shook his head.

"Miss Merton was far too clever to commit herself," he said; "she knew from the first that she was being watched, and behaved accordingly. If she was not there as your agent, her position becomes more extraordinary still."

"I can assure you," Mr. Sabin said, with an air of weariness, "that I am not the man of mystery you seem to think me. I should never dream of employing such roundabout means for gaining possession of a few statistics."

Wolfenden was silent. His case was altogether one of surmises; he could prove nothing.

"Perhaps," he said, "I have been precipitate. It would appear so. But if I am unduly suspicious, you have yourself only to blame! You admit that your name is an assumed one. You refuse my suit to your niece without any reasonable cause. You are evidently, to be frank, a person of much more importance than you lay claim to be. Now be open with me. If there is any reason, although I cannot conceive an honest one, for concealing your identity, why, I will respect your confidence absolutely. You may rely upon that. Tell me who you are, and who your niece is, and why you are travelling about in this mysterious way."

Mr. Sabin smiled good-humouredly.

"Well," he said, "you must forgive me if I plead guilty to the false identity— and preserve it. For certain reasons it would not suit me to take even you into my confidence. Besides which, if you will forgive my saying so, there does not seem to be the least necessity for it. We are leaving here during the week, and shall in all probability go abroad almost at once; so we are not likely to meet again. Let us part pleasantly, and abandon a somewhat profitless discussion."

For a moment Wolfenden was staggered. They were leaving England! Going away! That meant that he would see no more of Helène. His indignation against the man, kindled almost into passionate anger by his mother's story, was forgotten, overshadowed by a keen thrill of personal disappointment. If they were really leaving England, he might bid farewell to any chance of winning her; and there were certain words of hers, certain gestures, which had combined to fan that little flame of hope, which nothing as yet had ever been able to extinguish. He looked into Mr. Sabin's quiet face, and he was conscious of a sense of helplessness. The man was too strong and too wily for him; it was an unequal contest.

"We will abandon the discussion then, if you will," Wolfenden said slowly. "I will talk with Lady Deringham again. She is in an extremely nervous state; it is possible of course that she may have misunderstood you."

Mr. Sabin sighed with an air of gentle relief. Ah! if the men of other countries were only as easy to delude as these Englishmen! What a triumphant career might yet be his!

"I am very glad," he said, "that you do me the honour to take, what I can assure you, is the correct view of the situation. I hope that you will not hurry away; may I not offer you a cigarette?"

Wolfenden sat down for the first time.

"Are you in earnest," he asked, "when you speak of leaving England so soon?"

"Assuredly! You will do me the justice to admit that I have never pretended to like your country, have I? I hope to leave it for several years, if not for ever, within the course of a few weeks."

"And your niece, Mr. Sabin?"

"She accompanies me, of course; she likes this country even less than I do. Perhaps, under the circumstances, our departure is the best thing that could happen; it is at any rate opportune."

"I cannot agree with you," Wolfenden said; "for me it is most inopportune. I need scarcely say that I have not abandoned my desire to make your niece my wife."

"I should have thought," Mr. Sabin said, with a fine note of satire in his tone, "that you would have put far away from you all idea of any connection with such suspicious personages."

"I have never had," Wolfenden said calmly, "any suspicion at all concerning your niece."

"She would be, I am sure, much flattered," Mr. Sabin declared. "At the same time I can scarcely see on what grounds you continue to hope for an impossibility. My niece's refusal seemed to me explicit enough, especially when coupled with my own positive prohibition."

"Your niece," Wolfenden said, "is doubtless of age. I should not trouble about your consent if I could gain hers, and I may as well tell you at once, that I by no means despair of doing so."

Mr. Sabin bit his lip, and his dark eyes flashed out with a sudden fire.

"I should be glad to know, sir," he said, "on what grounds you consider my voice in the affair to be ineffective?"

"Partly," Wolfenden answered, "for the reason which I have already given you—because your niece is of age; and partly also because you persist in giving me no definite reason for your refusal."

"I have told you distinctly," Mr. Sabin said, "that my niece is betrothed and will be married within six months."

"To whom? where is he? why is he not here? Your niece wears no engagement ring. I will answer for it, that if she is as you say betrothed, it is not of her own free will."

"You talk," Mr. Sabin said with dangerous calm, "like a fool. It is not customary amongst the class to which my niece belongs to wear always an engagement ring. As for her affections, she has had, I am glad to say, a sufficient self-control to keep them to herself. Your presumption is simply the result of your entire ignorance. I appeal to you for the last time, Lord Wolfenden, to behave like a man of common sense, and abandon hopes which can only end in disappointment."

"I have no intention of doing anything of the sort," Wolfenden said doggedly; "we Englishmen are a pig-headed race, as you were once polite enough to observe. Your niece is the only woman whom I have wished to marry, and I shall marry her, if I can."

"I shall make it my especial concern," Mr. Sabin said firmly, "to see that all intercourse between you ends at once."

Wolfenden rose to his feet.

"It is obviously useless," he said, "to continue this conversation. I have told you my intentions. I shall pursue them to the best of my ability. Good-morning."

Mr. Sabin held out his hand.

"I have just a word more to say to you," he declared. "It is about your father."

"I do not desire to discuss my father, or any other matter with you," Wolfenden said quietly. "As to my father's work, I am determined to solve the mystery connected with it once and for all. I have wired for Mr. C. to come down, and, if necessary, take possession of the papers. You can get what information you require from him yourself."

Mr. Sabin rose up slowly; his long, white fingers were clasped around the head of that curious stick of his. There was a peculiar glint in his eyes, and his cheeks were pale with passion.

"I am very much obliged to you for telling me that," he said; "it is valuable information for me. I will certainly apply to Mr. C."

He had been drawing nearer and nearer to Wolfenden. Suddenly he stopped, and, with a swift movement, raised the stick on which he had been leaning, over his head. It whirled round in a semi-circle. Wolfenden, fascinated by that line of gleaming green light, hesitated for a moment, then he sprang backwards, but he was too late. The head of the stick came down on his head, his upraised arm did little to break the force of the blow. He sank to the ground with a smothered groan.

CHAPTER XXXII

THE SECRET OF MR. SABIN'S NIECE

At the sound of his cry, Helène, who had been crossing the hall, threw open the door just as Mr. Sabin's fingers were upon the key. Seeing that he was powerless to keep from her the knowledge of what had happened, he did not oppose her entrance. She glided into the centre of the room with a stifled cry of terror. Together, she and Mr. Sabin bent over Wolfenden's motionless figure. Mr. Sabin unfastened the waistcoat and felt his heart. She did not speak until he had held his hand there for several seconds, then she asked a question.

"Have you killed him?"

Mr. Sabin shook his head and smiled gently.

"Too tough a skull by far," he said. "Can you get a basin and a towel without any one seeing you?"

She nodded, and fetched them from her own room. The water was fresh and cold, and the towel was of fine linen daintily hemmed, and fragrant with the perfume of violets. Yet neither of these things, nor the soft warmth of her breathing upon his cheek, seemed to revive him in the least. He lay quite still in the same heavy stupor. Mr. Sabin stood upright and looked at him thoughtfully. His face had grown almost haggard.

"We had better send for a doctor," she whispered fiercely. "I shall fetch one myself if you do not!"

Mr. Sabin gently dissented.

"I know quite as much as any doctor," he said; "the man is not dead, or dying, or likely to die. I wonder if we could move him on to that sofa!"

Together they managed it somehow. Mr. Sabin, in the course of his movements to and fro about the room, was attracted by the sight of the dogcart still waiting outside. He frowned, and stood for a moment looking thoughtfully at it. Then he went outside.

"Are you waiting for Lord Wolfenden?" he asked the groom.

The man looked up in surprise.

"Yes, sir. I set him down here nearly an hour ago. I had no orders to go home."

"Lord Wolfenden has evidently forgotten all about you," Mr. Sabin said. "He left by the back way for the golf course, and I am going to join him there directly. He is not coming back here at all. You had better go home, I should think."

The man touched his hat.

"Very good, sir."

There was a little trampling up of the gravel, and Wolfenden's dogcart rapidly disappeared in the distance. Mr. Sabin, with set face and a hard glitter in his eyes went back into the morning room. Helène was still on her knees by Wolfenden's prostrate figure when he entered. She spoke to him without looking up.

"He is a little better, I think; he opened his eyes just now."

"He is not seriously hurt," Mr. Sabin said; "there may be some slight concussion, nothing more. The question is, first, what to do with him, and secondly, how to make the best use of the time which must elapse before he will be well enough to go home."

She looked at him now in horror. He was always like this, unappalled by anything which might happen, eager only to turn every trick of fortune to his own ends. Surely his nerves were of steel and his heart of iron.

"I think," she said, "that I should first make sure that he is likely to recover at all."

Mr. Sabin answered mechanically, his thoughts seemed far away.

"His recovery is a thing already assured," he said. "His skull was too hard to crack; he will be laid up for an hour or two. What I have to decide is how to use that hour or two to the best possible advantage."

She looked away from him and shuddered. This passionate absorption of all his energies into one channel had made a fiend of the man. Her slowly growing purpose took to itself root and branch, as she knelt by the side of the young Englishman, who only a few moments ago had seemed the very embodiment of all manly vigour.

Mr. Sabin stood up. He had arrived at a determination.

"Helène," he said, "I am going away for an hour, perhaps two. Will you take care of him until I return?"

"Yes."

"You will promise not to leave him, or to send for a doctor?"

"I will promise, unless he seems to grow worse."

"He will not get worse, he will be conscious in less than an hour. Keep him with you as long as you can, he will be safer here. Remember that!"

"I will remember," she said.

He left the room, and soon she heard the sound of carriage wheels rolling down the avenue. His departure was an intense relief to her. She watched the carriage, furiously driven, disappear along the road. Then she returned to Wolfenden's side. For nearly an hour she remained there, bathing his head, forcing now and then a little brandy between his teeth, and watching his breathing become more regular and the ghastly whiteness leaving his face. And all the while she was thoughtful. Once or twice her hands touched his hair tenderly, almost caressingly. There was a certain wistfulness in her regard of him. She bent close over his face; he was still apparently as unconscious as ever. She hesitated for a moment; the red colour burned in one bright spot on her cheeks. She stooped down and kissed him on the forehead, whispering something under her breath. Almost before she could draw back, he opened his eyes. She was overwhelmed with confusion, but seeing that he had no clear knowledge of what had happened, she rapidly recovered herself. He looked around him and then up into her face.

"What has happened?" he asked. "Where am I?"

"You are at the Lodge," she said quietly. "You called to see Mr. Sabin this morning, you know, and I am afraid you must have quarrelled."

"Ah! it was that beastly stick," he said slowly. "He struck at me suddenly. Where is he now?"

She did not answer him at once. It was certainly better not to say that she had seen him driven rapidly away only a short time ago, with his horses' heads turned to Deringham Hall.

"He will be back soon," she said. "Do not think about him, please. I cannot tell you how sorry I am."

He was recovering himself rapidly. Something in her eyes was sending the blood warmly through his veins; he felt better every instant.

"I do not want to think about him," he murmured, "I do not want to think about any one else but you."

She looked down at him with a half pathetic, half humorous twitching of her lips.

"You must please not make love to me, or I shall have to leave you," she said. "The idea of thinking about such a thing in your condition! You don't want to send me away, do you?"

"On the contrary," he answered, "I want to keep you always with me."

"That," she said briefly, "is impossible."

"Nothing," he declared, "is impossible, if only we make up our minds to it. I have made up mine!"

"You are very masterful! Are all Englishmen as confident as you?"

"I know nothing about other men," he declared. "But I love you, Helène, and I am not sure that you do not care a little for me."

She drew her hand away from his tightening clasp.

"I am going," she said; "it is your own fault—you have driven me away."

Her draperies rustled as she moved towards the door, but she did not go far.

"I do not feel so well," he said quietly; "I believe that I am going to faint."

She was on her knees by his side again in a moment. For a fainting man, the clasp of his fingers around hers was wonderfully strong.

"I feel better now," he announced calmly. "I shall be all right if you stay quietly here, and don't move about."

She looked at him doubtfully.

"I do not believe," she said, "that you felt ill at all; you are taking advantage of me!"

"I can assure you that I am not," he answered; "when you are here I feel a different man."

"I am quite willing to stay if you will behave yourself," she said.

"Will you please define good behaviour?" he begged.

"In the present instance," she laughed, "it consists in not saying silly things."

"A thing which is true cannot be silly," he protested. "It is true that I am never happy without you. That is why I shall never give you up."

She looked down at him with bright eyes, and a frown which did not come easily.

"If you persist in making love to me," she said, "I am going away. It is not permitted, understand that!"

He sighed.

"I am afraid," he answered softly, "that I shall always be indulging in the luxury of the forbidden. For I love you, and I shall never weary of telling you so."

"Then I must see," she declared, making a subtle but unsuccessful attempt to disengage her hand, "that you have fewer opportunities."

"If you mean that," he said, "I must certainly make the most of this one. Helène, you could care for me, I know, and I could make you happy. You say 'No' to me because there is some vague entanglement—I will not call it an engagement—with some one else. You do not care for him, I am sure. Don't marry him! It will be for your sorrow. So many women's lives are spoilt like that. Dearest," he added, gaining courage from her averted face, "I can make you happy, I am sure of it! I do not know who you are or who your people are, but they shall be my people—nothing matters, except that I love you. I don't know what to say to you, Helène. There is something shadowy in your mind which seems to you to come between us. I don't know what it is, or I would dispel it. Tell me, dear, won't you give me a chance?"

She yielded her other hand to his impatient fingers, and looked down at him wistfully. Yet there was something in her gaze which he could not fathom. Of one thing he was very sure, there was a little tenderness shining out of her dark, brilliant eyes, a little regret, a little indecision. On the whole he was hopeful.

"Dear," she said softly, "perhaps I do care for you a little. Perhaps—well, some time in the future—what you are thinking of might be possible; I cannot say. Something, apart from you, has happened, which has changed my life. You must let me go for a little while. But I will promise you this. The entanglement of which you spoke shall be broken off. I will have no more to do with that man!"

He sat upright.

"Helène," he said, "you are making me very happy, but there is one thing which I must ask you, and which you must forgive me for asking. This entanglement of which you speak has nothing to do with Mr. Sabin?"

"Nothing whatever," she answered promptly. "How I should like to tell you everything! But I have made a solemn promise, and I must keep it. My lips are sealed. But one thing I should like you to understand, in case you have ever had any doubt about it. Mr. Sabin is really my uncle, my mother's brother. He is engaged in a great enterprise in which I am a necessary figure. He has suddenly become very much afraid of you."

"Afraid of me!" Wolfenden repeated.

She nodded.

"I ought to tell you, perhaps, that my marriage with some one else is necessary to insure the full success of his plans. So you see he has set himself to keep us apart."

"The more you tell me, the more bewildered I get," Wolfenden declared. "What made him attack me just now without any warning? Surely he did not wish to kill me?"

Her hand within his seemed to grow colder.

"You were imprudent," she said.

"Imprudent! In what way?"

"You told him that you had sent for Mr. C. to come and go through your father's papers."

"What of it?"

"I cannot tell you any more!"

Wolfenden rose to his feet; he was still giddy, but he was able to stand.

"All that he told me here was a tissue of lies then! Helène, I will not leave you with such a man. You cannot continue to live with him."

"I do not intend to," she answered; "I want to get away. What has happened to-day is more than I can pardon, even from him. Yet you must not judge him too harshly. In his way he is a great man, and he is planning great things which are not wholly for his advantage. But he is unscrupulous! So long as the end is great, he believes himself justified in stooping to any means."

Wolfenden shuddered.

"You must not live another day with him," he exclaimed; "you will come to Deringham Hall. My mother will be only too glad to come and fetch you. It is not very cheerful there just now, but anything is better than leaving you with this man."

She looked at him curiously. Her eyes were soft with something which suggested pity, but resembled tears.

"No," she said, "that would not do at all. You must not think because I have been living with Mr. Sabin that I have no other relations or friends. I have a very great many of both, only it was arranged that I should leave them for a while. I can go back at any time; I am altogether my own mistress."

"Then go back at once," he begged her feverishly. "I could not bear to think of you living here with this man another hour. Have your things put together now and tell your maid. Let me take you to the station. I want to see you leave this infernal house, and this atmosphere of cheating and lies, when I do!"

Her lips parted into the ghost of a smile.

"I have not found so much to regret in my stay here," she said softly.

He held out his arms, but she eluded him gently.

"I hope," he said, "nay, I know that you will never regret it. Never! Tell me what you are going to do now?"

"I shall leave here this afternoon," she said, "and go straight to some friends in London. Then I shall make new plans, or rather set myself to the remaking of old ones. When I am ready, I will write to you. But remember again—I make no promise!"

He held out his hands.

"But you will write to me?"

She hesitated.

"No, I shall not write to you. I am not going to give you my address even; you must be patient for a little while."

"You will not go away? You will not at least leave England without seeing me?"

"Not unless I am compelled," she promised, "and then, if I go, I will come back again, or let you know where I am. You need not fear; I am not going to slip away and be lost! You shall see me again."

Wolfenden was dissatisfied.

"I hate letting you go," he said. "I hate all this mystery. When one comes to think of it, I do not even know your name! It is ridiculous! Why cannot I take you to London, and we can be married to-morrow. Then I should have the right to protect you against this blackguard."

She laughed softly. Her lips were parted in dainty curves, and her eyes were lit with merriment.

"How delightful you are," she exclaimed. "And to think that the women of my country call you Englishmen slow wooers!"

"Won't you prove the contrary?" he begged.

She shook her head.

"It is already proved. But if you are sure you feel well enough to walk, please go now. I want to catch the afternoon train to London."

He held out his hands and tried once more to draw her to him. But she stepped backwards laughing.

"You must please be patient," she said, "and remember that to-day I am betrothed to—somebody else! Goodbye!"

CHAPTER XXXIII

MR. SABIN TRIUMPHS

Wolfenden, for perhaps the first time in his life, chose the inland road home. He was still feeling faint and giddy, and the fresh air only partially revived him. He walked slowly, and rested more than once. It took him almost half an hour to reach the cross roads. Here he sat on a stile for a few minutes, until he began to feel himself again. Just as he was preparing to resume his walk, he was aware of a carriage being driven rapidly towards him, along the private road from Deringham Hall.

He stood quite still and watched it. The roads were heavy after much rain, and the mud was leaping up into the sunshine from the flying wheels, bespattering the carriage, and reaching even the man who sat upon the box. The horses had broken into a gallop, the driver was leaning forward whip in hand. He knew at once whose carriage it was: it was the little brougham which Mr. Sabin had brought down from London. He had been up to the hall, then! Wolfenden's face grew stern. He stood well out in the middle of the road. The horses would have to be checked a little at the sharp turn before him. They would probably shy a little, seeing him stand there in the centre of the road; he would be able to bring them to a standstill. So he remained there motionless. Nearer and nearer they came. Wolfenden set his teeth hard and forgot his dizziness.

They were almost upon him now. To his surprise the driver was making no effort to check his galloping horses. It seemed impossible that they could round that narrow corner at the pace they were going. A froth of white foam was on their bits, and their eyes were bloodshot. They were almost upon Wolfenden before he realised what was happening. They made no attempt to turn the corner which he was guarding, but flashed straight past him along the Cromer road. Wolfenden shouted and waved his arms, but the coachman did not even glance in his direction. He caught a glimpse of Mr. Sabin's face as he leaned back amongst the cushions, dark, satyr-like, forbidding. The thin lips seemed to part into a triumphant smile as he saw Wolfenden standing there. It was all over in a moment. The carriage, with its whirling wheels, was already a speck in the distance.

Wolfenden looked at his watch. It was five-and-twenty minutes to one. Mr. Sabin's purpose was obvious. He was trying to catch the one o'clock express to London. To pursue that carriage was absolutely hopeless. Wolfenden set his face towards Deringham Hall and ran steadily along the road. He was filled with vague fears. The memory of Mr. Sabin's smile haunted him. He had succeeded. By what means? Perhaps by violence! Wolfenden forgot his own aching head. He was filled only with an intense anxiety to reach his destination. If Mr. Sabin had so much as raised his hand, he should pay for it. He understood now why that blow had been given. It was to keep him out of the way. As he ran on, his teeth clenched, and his breath coming fast, he grew hot with passionate anger. He had been Mr. Sabin's dupe! Curse the man.

He turned the final corner in the drive, climbed the steps and entered the hall. The servants were standing about as usual. There was no sign of anything having happened. They looked at him curiously, but that might well be, owing to his dishevelled condition.

"Where is the Admiral, Groves?" he asked breathlessly.

"His lordship is in the billiard-room," the man answered.

Wolfenden stopped short in his passage across the hall, and looked at the man in amazement.

"Where?"

"In the billiard-room, my lord," the man repeated. "He was inquiring for you only a moment ago."

Wolfenden turned sharp to the left and entered the billiard-room. His father was standing there with his coat off and a cue in his hand. Directly he turned round Wolfenden was aware of a peculiar change in his face and expression. The hard lines had vanished, every trace of anxiety seemed to have left him. His eyes were soft and as clear as a child's. He turned to Wolfenden with a bland smile, and immediately began to chalk his cue.

"Come and play me a game, Wolf," he cried out cheerfully. "You'll have to give me a few, I'm so out of practice. We'll make it a hundred, and you shall give me twenty. Which will you have, spot, or plain?"

Wolfenden gulped down his amazement with an effort.

"I'll take plain," he said. "It's a long time, isn't it, since we played?"

His father faced him for a minute and seemed perplexed.

"Not so very long, surely. Wasn't it yesterday, or the day before?"

Wolfenden wondered for a moment whether that blow had affected his brain. It was years since he had seen the billiard-room at Deringham Hall opened.

"I don't exactly remember," he faltered. "Perhaps I was mistaken. Time goes so quickly."

"I wonder," the Admiral said, making a cannon and stepping briskly round the table, "how it goes at all with you young men who do nothing. Great mistake to have no profession, Wolf! I wish I could make you see it."

"I quite agree with you," Wolfenden said. "You must not look upon me as quite an idler, though. I am a full-fledged barrister, you know, although I do not practise, and I have serious thoughts of Parliament."

The Admiral shook his head.

"Poor career, my boy, poor career for a gentleman's son. Take my advice and keep out of Parliament. I am going to pot the red. I don't like the red ball, Wolf! It keeps looking at me like—like that man! Ah!"

He flung his cue with a rattle upon the floor of inlaid wood, and started back.

"Look, Wolf!" he cried. "He's grinning at me! Come here, boy! Tell me the truth! Have I been tricked? He told me that he was Mr. C. and I gave him everything! Look at his face how it changes! He isn't like C. now! He is like— who is it he is like? C.'s face is not so pale as that, and he does not limp. I seem to remember him too! Can't you help me? Can't you see him, boy?"

He had been moving backwards slowly. He was leaning now against the wall, his face blanched and perfectly bloodless, his eyes wild and his pupils dilated. Wolfenden laid his cue down and came over to his side.

"No, I can't see him, father," he said gently. "I think it must be fancy; you have been working too hard."

"You are blind, boy, blind," the Admiral muttered. "Where was it I saw him last? There were sands—and a burning sun—his shot went wide, but I aimed low and I hit him. He carried himself bravely. He was an aristocrat, and he never forgot it. But why does he call himself Mr. C.? What has he to do with my work?"

Wolfenden choked down a lump in his throat. He began to surmise what had happened.

"Let us go into the other room, father," he said gently. "It is too cold for billiards."

The Admiral held out his arm. He seemed suddenly weak and old. His eyes were dull and he was muttering to himself. Wolfenden led him gently from the room and upstairs to his own apartment. There he made an excuse for leaving him for a moment, and hurried down into the library. Mr. Blatherwick was writing there alone.

"Blatherwick," Wolfenden exclaimed, "what has happened this morning? Who has been here?"

Mr. Blatherwick blushed scarlet.

"Miss Merton called, and a gentleman with her, from the Home Office, I b-b-believe."

"Who let him into the library?" Wolfenden asked sternly.

Mr. Blatherwick fingered his collar, as though he found it too tight for him, and appeared generally uncomfortable.

"At Miss Merton's request, Lord Wolfenden," he said nervously, "I allowed him to come in. I understood that he had been sent for by her ladyship. I trust that I did not do wrong."

"You are an ass, Blatherwick," Wolfenden exclaimed angrily. "You seem to enjoy lending yourself to be the tool of swindlers and thieves. My father has lost his reason entirely now, and it is your fault. You had better leave here at once! You are altogether too credulous for this world."

Wolfenden strode away towards his mother's room, but a cry from upstairs directed his steps. Lady Deringham and he met outside his father's door, and entered the room together. They came face to face with the Admiral.

"Out of my way!" he cried furiously. "Come with me, Wolf! We must follow him. I must have my papers back, or kill him! I have been dreaming. He told me that he was C. I gave him all he asked for! We must have them back. Merciful heavens! if he publishes them, we are ruined ... where did he come from?... They told me that he was dead.... Has he crawled back out of hell? I shot him once! He has never forgotten it! This is his vengeance! Oh, God!"

He sank down into a chair. The perspiration stood out in great beads upon his white forehead. He was shaking from head to foot. Suddenly his head drooped in the act of further speech, the words died away upon his lips. He was unconscious. The Countess knelt by his side and Wolfenden stood over her.

"Do you know anything of what has happened?" Wolfenden asked.

"Very little," she whispered; "somehow, he—Mr. Sabin—got into the library, and the shock sent him—like this. Here is the doctor."

Dr. Whitlett was ushered in. They all three looked down upon the Admiral, and the doctor asked a few rapid questions. There was certainly a great change in his face. A strong line or two had disappeared, the countenance was milder and younger. It was like the face of a child. Wolfenden was afraid to see the eyes open, he seemed already in imagination to picture to himself their vacant, unseeing light. Dr. Whitlett shook his head sadly.

"I am afraid," he said gravely, "that when Lord Deringham recovers he will remember nothing! He has had a severe shock, and there is every indication that his mind has given way."

Wolfenden drew his teeth together savagely. This, then, was the result of Mr. Sabin's visit.

CHAPTER XXXIV

BLANCHE MERTON'S LITTLE PLOT

At about four o'clock in the afternoon, as Helène was preparing to leave the Lodge, a telegram was brought in to her from Mr. Sabin.

"I have succeeded and am now *en route* for London. You had better follow when convenient, but do not be later than to-morrow."

She tore it into small pieces and hummed a tune.

"It is enough," she murmured. "I am not ambitious any longer. I am going to London, it is true, my dear uncle, but not to Kensington! You can play Richelieu to Henri and my cousin, if it pleases you. I wonder———"

Her face grew softer and more thoughtful. Suddenly she laughed outright to herself. She went and sat down on the couch, where Wolfenden had been lying.

"It would have been simpler," she said to herself. "How like a man to think of such a daring thing. I wish—I almost wish—I had consented. What a delightful sensation it would have made. Cécile will laugh when I tell her of this. To her I have always seemed ambitious, and ambitious only ... and now I have found out that I have a heart only to give it away. *Hélas!*"

There was a knock at the door. A servant entered.

"Miss Merton would be glad to know if you could spare her a moment before you left, Miss," the man announced.

Helène glanced at the clock.

"I am going very shortly," she said; "she had better come in now."

The man withdrew, but returned almost immediately, ushering in Miss Merton. For the first time Helène noticed how pretty the girl was. Her trim, dainty little figure was shown off to its utmost advantage by the neat tailor gown she was wearing, and there was a bright glow of colour in her cheeks. Helène, who had no liking for her uncle's typewriter, and who had scarcely yet spoken to her, remained standing, waiting to hear what she had to say.

"I wanted to see Mr. Sabin," she began. "Can you tell me when he will be back?"

"He has gone to London," Helène replied. "He will not be returning here at all."

The girl's surprise was evidently genuine.

"But he said nothing about it a few hours ago," she exclaimed. "You are in his confidence, I know. This morning he gave me something to do. I was to get Mr. Blatherwick away from the Hall, and keep him with me as long as I could. You do not know Mr. Blatherwick? then you cannot sympathise with me. Since ten o'clock I have been with him. At last I could keep him no longer. He has gone back to the Hall."

"Mr. Sabin will probably write to you," Helène said. "This house is taken for another fortnight, and you can of course remain here, if you choose. You will certainly hear from him within the next day or two."

Miss Merton shrugged her shoulders.

"Well, I shall take a holiday," she declared. "I've finished typing all the copy I had. Haven't you dropped something there?"

She stooped suddenly forward, and picked up a locket from the floor.

"Is this yours?" she asked. "Why——"

She held the locket tightly in her hand. Her eyes seemed rivetted upon it. It was very small and fashioned of plain gold, with a coronet and letter on the face. Miss Merton looked at it in amazement.

"Why, this belongs to Wolf—to Lord Wolfenden," she exclaimed.

Helène looked at her in cold surprise.

"It is very possible," she said. "He was here a short time ago."

Miss Merton clenched the locket in her hand, as though she feared for its safety.

"Here! In this room?"

"Certainly! He called to see Mr. Sabin and remained for some time."

Miss Merton was a little paler. She did not look quite so pretty now.

"Did you see him?" she asked.

Helène raised her eyebrows.

"I scarcely understand," she said, "what business it is of yours. Since you ask me, however, I have no objection to telling you that I did see Lord Wolfenden. He remained some time here with me after Mr. Sabin left."

"Perhaps," Miss Merton suggested, with acidity, "that was why I was sent out of the way."

Helène looked at her through half-closed eyes.

"I am afraid," she said, "that you are a very impertinent young woman. Be so good as to put that locket upon the table and leave the room."

The girl did neither. On the contrary, she slipped the locket into the bosom of her gown.

"I will take care of this," she remarked.

Helène laid her hand upon the bell.

"I am afraid," she said, "that you must be unwell. I am going to ring the bell. Perhaps you will be good enough to place the locket on that table and leave the room."

Miss Merton drew herself up angrily.

"I have a better claim upon the locket than any one," she said. "I am seeing Lord Wolfenden constantly. I will give it to him."

"Thank you, you need not trouble," Helène answered. "I shall send a servant with it to Deringham Hall. Will you be good enough to give it to me?"

Miss Merton drew a step backwards and shook her head.

"I think," she said, "that I am more concerned in it than you are, for I gave it to him."

"You gave it to him?"

Miss Merton nodded.

"Yes! If you don't believe me, look here."

She drew the locket from her bosom and, holding it out, touched a spring. There was a small miniature inside; Helène, leaning over, recognised it at once. It was a likeness of the girl herself. She felt the colour leave her cheeks, but she did not flinch.

"I was not aware," she said, "that you were on such friendly terms with Lord Wolfenden."

The girl smiled oddly.

"Lord Wolfenden," she said, "has been very kind to me."

"Perhaps," Helène continued, "I ought not to ask, but I must confess that you have surprised me. Is Lord Wolfenden—your lover?"

Miss Merton shut up the locket with a click and returned it to her bosom. There was no longer any question as to her retaining it. She looked at Helène thoughtfully.

"Has he been making love to you?" she asked abruptly.

Helène raised her eyes and looked at her. The other girl felt suddenly very insignificant.

"You must not ask me impertinent questions," she said calmly. "Of course you need not tell me anything unless you choose. It is for you to please yourself."

The girl was white with anger. She had not a tithe of Helène's self-control, and she felt that she was not making the best of her opportunities.

"Lord Wolfenden," she said slowly, "did promise to marry me once. I was his father's secretary, and I was turned away on his account."

"Indeed!"

There was a silence between the two women. Miss Merton was watching Helène closely, but she was disappointed. Her face was set in cold, proud lines, but she showed no signs of trouble.

"Under these circumstances," Helène said, "the locket certainly belongs to you. If you will allow me, I will ring now for my maid. I am leaving here this evening."

"I should like," Miss Merton said, "to tell you about Lord Wolfenden and myself."

Helène smiled languidly.

"You will excuse me, I am sure," she said. "It is scarcely a matter which interests me."

Miss Merton flushed angrily. She was at a disadvantage and she knew it.

"I thought that you were very much interested in Lord Wolfenden," she said spitefully.

"I have found him much pleasanter than the majority of Englishmen."

"But you don't care to hear about him—from me!" Miss Merton exclaimed.

Helène smiled.

"I have no desire to be rude," she said, "but since you put it in that way I will admit that you are right."

The girl bit her lip. She felt that she had only partially succeeded. This girl was more than her match. She suddenly changed her tactics.

"Oh! you are cruel," she exclaimed. "You want to take him from me; I know you do! He promised—to marry me—before you came. He must marry me! I dare not go home!"

"I can assure you," Helène said quietly, "that I have not the faintest desire to take Lord Wolfenden from you—or from any one else! I do not like this conversation at all, and I do not intend to continue it. Perhaps if you have nothing more to say you will go to your room, or if you wish to go away I will order a carriage for you. Please make up your mind quickly."

Miss Merton sprang up and walked towards the door. Her pretty face was distorted with anger.

"I do not want your carriage," she said. "I am leaving the house, but I will walk."

"Just as you choose, if you only go," Helène murmured.

She was already at the door, but she turned back.

"I can't help it!" she exclaimed. "I've got to ask you a question. Has Lord Wolfenden asked you to marry him?"

Helène was disgusted, but she was not hard-hearted. The girl was evidently distressed—it never occurred to her that she might not be in earnest. She herself could not understand such a lack of self-respect. A single gleam of pity mingled with her contempt.

"I am not at liberty to answer your question," she said coldly, "as it concerns Lord Wolfenden as well as myself. But I have no objection to telling you this. I am the Princess Helène of Bourbon, and I am betrothed to my cousin, Prince Henri of Ortrens! So you see that I am not likely to marry Lord Wolfenden! Now, please, go away at once!"

Miss Merton obeyed. She left the room literally speechless. Helène rang the bell.

"If that young person—Miss Merton I think her name is—attempts to see me again before I leave, be sure that she is not admitted," she told the servant.

The man bowed and left the room. Helène was left alone. She sank into an easy chair by the fire and leaned her head upon her hand. Her self-control was easy and magnificent, but now that she was alone her face had softened. The proud, little mouth was quivering. A feeling of uneasiness, of utter depression stole over her. Tears stood for a moment in her eyes but she brushed them fiercely away.

"How could he have dared?" she murmured. "I wish that I were a man! After all, then, it must be—ambition!"

CHAPTER XXXV

A LITTLE GAME OF CARDS

Mr. Sabin, whose carriage had set him down at the Cromer railway station with barely two minutes to spare, took his seat in an empty first-class smoking carriage of the London train and deliberately lit a fine cigar. He was filled with that sense of triumphant self-satisfaction which falls to the lot of a man who, after much arduous labour successfully accomplished, sees very near at hand the great desire of his life. Two days' more quiet work, and his task was done. All that he had pledged himself to give, he would have ready for the offering. The finishing touches were but a matter of detail. It had been a great undertaking—more difficult at times than he had ever reckoned for. He told himself with some complacency that no other man breathing could have brought it to so satisfactory a conclusion. His had been a life of great endeavours; this one, however, was the crowning triumph of his career.

He watched the people take their seats in the train with idle eyes; he was not interested in any of them. He scarcely saw their faces; they were not of his world nor he of theirs. But suddenly he received a rude shock. He sat upright and wiped away the moisture from the window in order that he might see more clearly. A young man in a long ulster was buying newspapers from a boy only a yard or two away. Something about the figure and manner of standing seemed to Mr. Sabin vaguely familiar. He waited until his head was turned, and the eyes of the two men met—then the last vestige of doubt disappeared. It was Felix! Mr. Sabin leaned back in his corner with darkening face. He had noticed to his dismay that the encounter, surprising though it had been to him, had been accepted by Felix as a matter of course—he was obviously prepared for it. He had met Mr. Sabin's anxious and incredulous gaze with a faint, peculiar smile. His probable presence in the train had evidently been confidently reckoned upon. Felix had been watching him secretly, and knowing what he did know of that young man, Mr. Sabin was seriously disturbed. He did not hesitate for a moment, however, to face the position. He determined at once upon a bold course of action. Letting down the window he put out his head.

"Are you going to town?" he asked Felix, as though seeing him then was the most natural thing in the world.

The young man nodded.

"Yes, it's getting pretty dreary down here, isn't it? You're off back, I see."

Mr. Sabin assented.

"Yes," he said, "I've had about enough of it. Besides, I'm overdue at Pau, and I'm anxious to get there. Are you coming in here?"

Felix hesitated. At first the suggestion had astonished him; almost immediately it became a temptation. It would be distinctly piquant to travel with this man. On the other hand it was distinctly unwise; it was running an altogether unnecessary risk. Mr. Sabin read his thoughts with the utmost ease.

"I should rather like to have a little chat with you," he said quietly; "you are not afraid, are you? I am quite unarmed, and as you see Nature has not made me for a fighting man."

Felix hesitated no longer. He motioned to the porter who was carrying his dressing-case and golf clubs, and had them conveyed into Mr. Sabin's carriage. He himself took the opposite seat.

"I had no idea," Mr. Sabin remarked, "that you were in the neighbourhood."

Felix smiled.

"You have been so engrossed in your—golf," he remarked. "It is a fascinating game, is it not?"

"Very," Mr. Sabin assented. "You yourself are a devotee, I see."

"I am a beginner," Felix answered, "and a very clumsy beginner too. I take my clubs with me, however, whenever I go to the coast at this time of year; they save one from being considered a madman."

"It is singular," Mr. Sabin remarked, "that you should have chosen to visit Cromer just now. It is really a most interesting meeting. I do not think that I have had the pleasure of seeing you since that evening at the 'Milan,' when your behaviour towards me—forgive my alluding to it—was scarcely considerate."

Mr. Sabin was quite friendly and unembarrassed. He seemed to treat the affair as a joke. Felix looked glumly out of the window.

"Your luck stood you in good stead—as usual," he said. "I meant to kill you that night. You see I don't mind confessing it! I had sworn to make the attempt the first time we met face to face."

"Considering that we are quite alone," Mr. Sabin remarked, looking around the carriage, "and that from physical considerations my life under such conditions is entirely at your mercy, I should like some assurance that you have no intention of repeating the attempt. It would add very materially to my comfort."

The young man smiled without immediately answering. Then he was suddenly grave; he appeared to be reflecting. Almost imperceptibly Mr. Sabin's hand stole towards the window. He was making a mental calculation as to what height above the carriage window the communication cord might be. Felix, watching his fingers, smiled again.

"You need have no fear," he said; "the cause of personal enmity between you and me is dead. You have nothing more to fear from me at any time."

Mr. Sabin's hand slid down again to his side.

"I am charmed to hear it," he declared. "You are, I presume, in earnest?"

"Most certainly. It is as I say; the cause for personal enmity between us is removed. Save for a strong personal dislike, which under the circumstances I trust that you will pardon me"—Mr. Sabin bowed—"I have no feeling towards you whatever!"

Mr. Sabin drew a somewhat exaggerated sigh of relief. "I live," he said, "with one more fear removed. But I must confess," he added, "to a certain amount of curiosity. We have a somewhat tedious journey before us, and several hours at our disposal; would it be asking you too much——"

Felix waved his hand.

"Not at all," he said. "A few words will explain everything. I have other matters to speak of with you, but they can wait. As you remark, we have plenty of time before us. Three weeks ago I received a telegram from Brussels. It was from—forgive me, if I do not utter her name in your presence; it seems somehow like sacrilege."

Mr. Sabin bowed; a little red spot was burning through the pallor of his sunken cheeks.

"I was there," Felix continued, "in a matter of twenty-four hours. She was ill—believed herself to be dying. We spoke together of a little event many years old; yet which I venture to think, neither you, nor she, nor I have ever forgotten."

Mr. Sabin pulled down the blind by his side; it was only a stray gleam of wintry sunshine, which had stolen through the grey clouds, but it seemed to dazzle him.

"It had come to her knowledge that you and I were together in London— that you were once more essaying to play a part in civilised and great affairs. And lest our meeting should bring harm about, she told me—something of which I have always been in ignorance."

"Ah!"

Mr. Sabin moved uneasily in his seat. He drew his club-foot a little further back; Felix seemed to be looking at it absently.

"She showed me," he continued, "a little pistol; she explained to me that a woman's aim is a most uncertain thing. Besides, you were some distance away, and your spring aside helped you. Then, too, so far as I could see from the mechanism of the thing—it was an old and clumsy affair—it carried low. At any rate the shot, which was doubtless meant for your heart, found a haven in your foot. From her lips I learned for the first time that she, the sweetest and most timid of her sex, had dared to become her own avenger. Life is a sad enough thing, and pleasure is rare, yet I tasted pleasure of the keenest and subtlest kind when she told me that story. I feel even now some slight return of it when I look at your—shall we call deformity, and consider how different a person——"

Mr. Sabin half rose to his feet; his face was white and set, save where a single spot of colour was flaring high up near his cheek-bone. His eyes were bloodshot; for a moment he seemed about to strike the other man. Felix broke off in his sentence, and watched him warily.

"Come," he said, "it is not like you to lose control of yourself in that manner. It is a simple matter. You wronged a woman, and she avenged herself magnificently. As for me, I can see that my interference was quite uncalled for; I even venture to offer you my apologies for the fright I must have given you at the 'Milan.' The account had already been straightened by abler hands. I can assure you that I am no longer your enemy. In fact, when I look at you"—his eyes seemed to fall almost to the ground—"when I look at you, I permit myself some slight sensation of pity for your unfortunate affliction. But it was magnificent! Shall we change the subject now?"

Mr. Sabin sat quite still in his corner; his eyes seemed fixed upon a distant hill, bordering the flat country through which they were passing. Felix's stinging words and mocking smile had no meaning for him. In fact he did not see his companion any longer, nor was he conscious of his presence. The narrow confines of the railway carriage had fallen away. He was in a lofty room, in a chamber of a palace, a privileged guest, the lover of the woman whose dark, passionate eyes and soft, white arms were gleaming there before his eyes. It was but one of many such scenes. He shuddered very slightly, as he went back further still. He had been faithful to one god, and one god only—the god of self! Was it a sign of coming trouble, that for the first time for many years he had abandoned himself to the impotent morbidness of abstract thought? He shook himself free from it with an effort; what lunacy! To-day he was on the eve of a mighty success—his feet were planted firmly upon the threshold! The end of all his ambitions stood fairly in view, and the path to it was wide and easy. Only a little time, and his must be one of the first names in Europe! The thought thrilled him, the little flood of impersonal recollections ebbed away; he was himself again, keen, alert, vigorous! Suddenly he met the eyes of his companion fixed steadfastly upon him, and his face darkened. There was something ominous about this man's appearance; his very presence seemed like a foreboding of disaster.

"I am much obliged to you for your little romance," he said. "There is one point, however, which needs some explanation. If your interest is really, as you suggest, at an end, what are you doing down here? I presume that your appearance is not altogether a coincidence."

"Certainly not," Felix answered. "Let me correct you, however, on one trifling point. I said, you must remember—my personal interest."

"I do not," Mr. Sabin remarked, "exactly see the distinction; in fact, I do not follow you at all!"

"I am so stupid," Felix declared apologetically. "I ought to have explained myself more clearly. It is even possible that you, who know everything, may yet be ignorant of my present position."

"I certainly have no knowledge of it," Mr. Sabin admitted.

Felix was gently astonished.

"Really! I took it for granted, of course, that you knew. Well, I am employed—not in any important post, of course—at the Russian Embassy. His Excellency has been very kind to me."

Mr. Sabin for once felt his nerve grow weak; those evil forebodings of his had very swiftly become verified. This man was his enemy. Yet he recovered himself almost as quickly. What had he to fear? His was still the winning hand.

"I am pleased to hear," he said, "that you have found such creditable employment. I hope you will make every effort to retain it; you have thrown away many chances."

Felix at first smiled; then he leaned back amongst the cushions and laughed outright. When he had ceased, he wiped the tears from his eyes. He sat up again and looked with admiration at the still, pale figure opposite to him.

"You are inimitable," he said—"wonderful! If you live long enough, you will certainly become very famous. What will it be, I wonder—Emperor, Dictator, President of a Republic, the Minister of an Emperor? The latter I should imagine; you were always such an aristocrat. I would not have missed this journey for the world. I am longing to know what you will say to Prince Lobenski at King's Cross."

Mr. Sabin looked at him keenly.

"So you are only a lacquey after all, then?" he remarked—"a common spy!"

"Very much at your service," Felix answered, with a low bow. "A spy, if you like, engaged for the last two weeks in very closely watching your movements, and solving the mystery of your sudden devotion to a heathenish game!"

"There, at any rate," Mr. Sabin said calmly, "you are quite wrong. If you had watched my play I flatter myself that you would have realised that my golf at any rate was no pretence."

"I never imagined," Felix rejoined, "that you would be anything but proficient at any game in which you cared to interest yourself; but I never imagined either that you came to Cromer to play golf—especially just now."

"Modern diplomacy," Mr. Sabin said, after a brief pause, "has undergone, as you may be aware, a remarkable transformation. Secrecy is now quite out of date; it is the custom amongst the masters to play with the cards upon the table."

"There is a good deal in what you say," Felix answered thoughtfully. "Come, we will play the game, then! It is my lead. Very well! I have been down here watching you continually, with the object of discovering the source of this wonderful power by means of which you are prepared to offer up this country, bound hand and foot, to whichever Power you decide to make terms with. Sounds like a fairy tale, doesn't it? But you obviously believe in it yourself, and Lobenski believes in you."

"Good!" Mr. Sabin declared. "That power of which I have spoken I now possess! It was nearly complete a month ago; an hour's work now will make it a living and invulnerable fact."

"You obtained," Felix said, "your final success this afternoon, when you robbed the mad Admiral."

Mr. Sabin shook his head gently.

"I have not robbed any one," he said; "I never use force."

Felix looked at him reproachfully.

"I have heard much that is evil about you," he said, "but I have never heard before that you were known to—to—dear me, it is a very unpleasant thing to say!"

"Well, sir?"

"To cheat at cards!"

Mr. Sabin drew a short, little breath.

"What I have said is true to the letter," he repeated "The Admiral gave me the trifling information I asked for, with his own hands."

Felix remained incredulous.

"Then you must add the power of hypnotism," he declared, "to your other accomplishments."

Mr. Sabin laughed scornfully, nevertheless he did not seem to be altogether at his ease. The little scene in the library at Deringham Hall was not a pleasant recollection for him.

"The matter after all," he said coldly, "is unimportant; it is merely a detail. I will admit that you have done your spy's work well. Now, what will buy your memory, and your departure from this train, at the next station?"

Felix smiled.

"You are becoming more sensible," he said; "very fair question to ask. My price is the faithful fulfilment of your contract with my chief."

"I have made no contract with him."

"You have opened negotiations; he is ready to come to terms with you. You have only to name your price."

"I have no price," Mr. Sabin said quietly, "that he could pay."

"What Knigenstein can give," Felix said, "he can give double. The Secret Service funds of Russia are the largest in the world; you can have practically a blank cheque upon them."

"I repeat," Mr. Sabin said, "I have no price that Prince Lobenski could pay. You talk as though I were a blackmailer, or a common thief. You have always misunderstood me. Come! I will remember that the cards are upon the table; I will be wholly frank with you. It is Knigenstein with whom I mean to treat, and not your chief. He has agreed to my terms—Russia never could."

Felix was silent for a moment.

"You are holding," he said, "your trump card in your hand. Whatever in this world Germany could give you, Russia could improve upon."

"She could do so," Mr. Sabin said, "only at the expense of her honour. Come! here is that trump card. I will throw it upon the table; now you see that my hands are empty. My price is the invasion of France, and the restoration of the Monarchy."

Felix looked at him as a man looks upon a lunatic.

"You are playing with me," he cried.

"I was never more in earnest in my life," Mr. Sabin said.

"Do you mean to tell me that you—in cold blood—are working for so visionary, so impossible an end?"

"It is neither visionary," Mr. Sabin said, "nor impossible. I do not believe that any man, save myself, properly appreciates the strength of the Royalist party in France. Every day, every minute brings it fresh adherents. It is as certain that some day a king will reign once more at Versailles, as that the sun will set before many hours are past. The French people are too bourgeois at heart to love a republic. The desire for its abolition is growing up in their hearts day by day. You understand me now when I say that I cannot treat with your country? The honour of Russia is bound up with her friendship to France. Germany, on the other hand, has ready her battle cry. She and France have been quivering on the verge of war for many a year. My whole hand is upon the table now, Felix. Look at the cards, and tell me whether we can treat!"

Felix was silent. He looked at his opponent with unwilling admiration; the man after all, then, was great. For the moment he could think of nothing whatever to say.

"Now, listen to me," Mr. Sabin continued earnestly. "I made a great mistake when I ever mentioned the matter to Prince Lobenski. I cannot treat with him, but on the other hand, I do not want to be hampered by his importunities for the next few days. You have done your duty, and you have done it well. It is not your fault that you cannot succeed. Leave the train at the next station—disappear for a week, and I will give you a fortune. You are young—the world is before you. You can seek distinction in whatever way you will. I have a cheque-book in my pocket, and a fountain pen. I will give you an order on the Crédit Lyonnaise for £20,000."

Felix laughed softly; his face was full of admiration. He looked at his watch, and began to gather together his belongings.

"Write out the cheque," he said; "I agree. We shall be at the junction in about ten minutes."

CHAPTER XXXVI

THE MODERN RICHELIEU

"So I have found you at last!"

Mr. Sabin looked up with a distinct start from the table where he sat writing. When he saw who his visitor was, he set down his pen and rose to receive her at once. He permitted himself to indulge in a little gesture of relief; her noiseless entrance had filled him with a sudden fear.

"My dear Helène," he said, placing a chair for her, "if I had had the least idea that you wished to see me, I would have let you know my whereabouts. I am sorry that you should have had any difficulty; you should have written."

She shrugged her shoulders slightly.

"What does it all mean?" she asked. "Why are you masquerading in cheap lodgings, and why do they say at Kensington that you have gone abroad? Have things gone wrong?"

He turned and faced her directly. She saw then that pale and haggard though he was, his was not the countenance of a man tasting the bitterness of failure.

"Very much the contrary," he said; "we are on the brink of success. All that remains to be done is the fitting together of my American work with the last of these papers. It will take me about another twenty-four hours."

She handed across to him a morning newspaper, which she had been carrying in her muff. A certain paragraph was marked.

"We regret to state that Admiral, the Earl of Deringham, was seized yesterday morning with a fit, whilst alone in his study. Dr. Bond, of Harley Street, was summoned at once to a consultation, but we understand that the case is a critical one, and the gravest fears are entertained. Lord Deringham was the greatest living authority upon the subject of our fleet and coast defences, and we are informed that at the time of his seizure he was completing a very important work in connection with this subject."

Mr. Sabin read the paragraph slowly, and then handed the paper back to Helène.

"Deringham was a very distinguished man," he remarked, "but he was stark mad, and has been for years. They have been able to keep it quiet, only because he was harmless."

"You remember what I told you about these people," Helène said sternly; "I told you distinctly that I would not have them harmed in any way. You were at Deringham Hall on the morning of his seizure. You went straight there from the Lodge."

"That is quite true," he admitted; "but I had nothing to do with his illness."

"I wish I could feel quite certain of that," Helène answered. "You are a very determined man, and you went there to get papers from him by any means. You proved that you were altogether reckless as to how you got them, by your treatment of Lord Wolfenden. You succeeded! No one living knows by what means!"

He interrupted her with an impatient gesture.

"There is nothing in this worth discussion," he declared. "Lord Deringham is nothing to you—you never even saw him in your life, and if you really have any misgivings about it, I can assure you that I got what I wanted from him without violence. It is not a matter for you to concern yourself in, nor is it a matter worth considering at all, especially at such a time as the present."

She sat quite still, her head resting upon her gloved hand. He did not altogether like her appearance.

"I want you to understand," he continued slowly, "that success, absolute success is ours. I have the personal pledge of the German Emperor, signed by his own hand. To-morrow at noon the compact is concluded. In a few weeks, at the most, the thunderbolt will have fallen. These arrogant Islanders will be facing a great invasion, whose success is already made absolutely sure. And then——"

He paused: his face kindled with a passionate enthusiasm, his eyes were lit with fire. There was something great in the man's rapt expression.

"Then, the only true, the only sweet battle-cry in the French tongue, will ring through the woods of Brittany, ay, even to the walls of Paris. *Vive la France! Vive la Monarchie!*"

"France has suffered so much," she murmured; "do not you who love her so tremble when you think of her rivers running once more red with blood?"

"If there be war at all," he answered, "it will be brief. Year by year the loyalists have gained power and influence. I have notes here from secret agents in every town, almost in every village; the great heart of Paris is with us. Henri will only have to show himself, and the voice of the people will shout him king! And you——"

"For me," she interrupted, "nothing! I withdraw! I will not marry Henri, he must stand his chance alone! His is the elder branch—he is the direct heir to the throne!"

Mr. Sabin drew in a long breath between his teeth. He was nerving himself for a great effort. This fear had been the one small, black cloud in the sky of his happiness.

"Helène," he said, "if I believed that you meant—that you could possibly mean—what you have this moment said, I would tear my compact in two, throw this box amongst the flames, and make my bow to my life's work. But you do not mean it. You will change your mind."

"But indeed I shall not!"

"Of necessity you must; the alliance between you and Henri is absolutely compulsory. You unite the two great branches of our royal family. The sound of your name, coupled with his, will recall to the ears of France all that was most glorious in her splendid history. And apart from that, Henri needs such a woman as you for his queen. He has many excellent qualities, but he is weak, a trifle too easy, a trifle thoughtless."

"He is a dissipated *roué*," she said in a low tone, with curling lip.

Mr. Sabin, who had been walking restlessly up and down the room, came and stood over her, leaning upon his wonderful stick.

"Helène," he said gravely, "for your own sake, and for your country's sake, I charge you to consider well what you are doing. What does it matter to you if Henri is even as bad as you say, which, mark you, I deny. He is the King of France! Personally, you can be strangers if you please, but marry him you must. You need not be his wife, but you must be his queen! Almost you make me ask myself whether I am talking to Helène of Bourbon, a Princess Royal of France, or to a love-sick English country girl, pining for a sweetheart, whose highest ambition it is to bear children, and whose destiny is to become a drudge. May God forbid it! May God forbid, that after all these years of darkness you should play me false now when the dawn is already lightening the sky. Sink your sex! Forget it! Remember that you are more than a woman—you are royal, and your country has the first claim upon your heart. The dignity which exalts demands also sacrifices! Think of your great ancestors, who died with this prayer upon their lips—that one day their children's children should win again the throne which they had lost. Their eyes may be upon you at this moment. Give me a single reason for this change in you—one single valid reason, and I will say no more."

She was silent; the colour was coming and going in her cheeks. She was deeply moved; the honest passion in his tone had thrilled her.

"I would not dare to suggest, even in a whisper, to myself," he went on, his dark eyes fixed upon her, and his voice lowered, "that Helène of Bourbon,

Princess of Brittany, could set a greater price upon the love of a man—and that man an Englishman—than upon her country's salvation. I would not even suffer so dishonouring a thought to creep into my brain. Yet I will remember that you are a girl—a woman—that is to say, a creature of strange moods; and I remind you that the marriage of a queen entails only the giving of a hand, her heart remains always at her disposal, and never yet has a queen of France been without her lover!"

She looked up at him with burning cheeks.

"You have spoken bitterly to me," she said, "but from your point of view I have deserved it. Perhaps I have been weak; after all, men are not so very different. They are all ignoble. You are right when you call us women creatures of moods. To-day I should prefer the convent to marriage with any man. But listen! If you can persuade me that my marriage with Henri is necessary for his acceptance by the people of France, if I am assured of that, I will yield."

Mr. Sabin drew a long breath of relief, Blanche had succeeded, then. Even in that moment he found time to realise that, without her aid, he would have run a terrible risk of failure. He sat down and spoke calmly, but impressively.

"From my point of view," he said, "and I have considered the subject exhaustively, I believe that it is absolutely necessary. You and Henri represent the two great Houses, who might, with almost equal right, claim the throne. The result of your union must be perfect unanimity. Now, suppose that Henri stands alone; don't you see that your cousin, Louis of Bourbon, is almost as near in the direct line? He is young and impetuous, without ballast, but I believe ambitious. He would be almost sure to assert himself. At any rate, his very existence would certainly lead to factions, and the splitting up of nobles into parties. This is the greatest evil we could possibly have to face. There must be no dissensions whatever during the first generation of the re-established monarchy. The country would not be strong enough to bear it. With you married to Henri, the two great Houses of Bourbon and Ortrens are allied. Against their representative there would be no one strong enough to lift a hand. Have I made it clear?"

"Yes," the girl answered, "you have made it very clear. Will you let me consider for a few moments?"

She sat there with her back half-turned to him, gazing into the fire. He moved back in the chair and went on with his writing. She heard the lightning rush of his pen, as he covered sheet after sheet of paper without even glancing towards her; he had no more to say, he knew very well that his work was done. The influence of his words were strong upon her; in her heart they had awakened some echo of those old ambitions which had once been very real and live things. She set herself the task of fanning them once more with the fire of enthusiasm. For she had no longer any doubts as to her duty. Wolfenden's words—the first spoken words of love which had ever been addressed to her—had carried with them at the time a peculiar and a very sweet conviction. She had lost faith, too, in Mr. Sabin and his methods. She had begun to wonder whether he was not after all a visionary, whether there was really the faintest chance of the people of her country ever being stirred into a return to their old faith and allegiance. Wolfenden's appearance had been for him singularly opportune, and she had almost decided a few mornings ago, that, after all, there was not any real bar between them. She was a princess, but of a fallen House; he was a nobleman of the most powerful country in the world. She had permitted herself to care for him a little; she was astonished to find how swiftly that sensation had grown into something which had promised to become very real and precious to her— and then, this insolent girl had come to her—her photograph was in his locket. He was like Henri, and all the others! She despised herself for the heartache of which she was sadly conscious. Her cheeks burned with shame, and her heart was hot with rage, when she thought of the kiss she had given him—perhaps he had even placed her upon a level with the typewriting girl, had dared to consider her, too, as a possible plaything for his idle moments. She set her teeth, and her eyes flashed.

Mr. Sabin, as his pen flew over the paper, felt a touch upon his arm.

"I am quite convinced," she said. "When the time comes I shall be ready."

He looked up with a faint, but gratified smile.

"I had no fear of you," he said. "Frankly, in Henri alone I should have been destitute of confidence. I should not have laboured as I have done, but for you! In your hands, largely, the destinies of your country will remain."

"I shall do my duty," she answered quietly.

"I always knew it! And now," he said, looking back towards his papers, "how about the present? I do not want you here. Your presence would certainly excite comment, and I am virtually in hiding for the next twenty-four hours."

"The Duchess of Montegarde arrived in London yesterday," she replied. "I am going to her."

"You could not do a wiser thing," he declared. "Send your address to Avon House; to-morrow night or Saturday night I shall come for you. All will be settled then; we shall have plenty to do, but after the labour of the last seven years it will not seem like work. It will be the beginning of the harvest."

She looked at him thoughtfully.

"And your reward," she said, "what is that to be?"

He smiled.

"I will not pretend," he answered, "that I have worked for the love of my country and my order alone. I also am ambitious, although my ambition is more patriotic than personal. I mean to be first Minister of France!"

"You will deserve it," she said. "You are a very wonderful man."

She walked out into the street, and entered the cab which she had ordered to wait for her.

"Fourteen, Grosvenor Square," she told the man, "but call at the first telegraph office."

He set her down in a few minutes. She entered a small post-office and stood for a moment before one of the compartments. Then she drew a form towards her, and wrote out a telegram—

"To Lord Wolfenden,
"Deringham Hall,
"Norfolk.

"I cannot send for you as I promised. Farewell—HELÈNE."

CHAPTER XXXVII

FOR A GREAT STAKE

"GERMANY'S INSULT TO ENGLAND!

ENGLAND'S REPLY.

MOBILISATION IMMINENT.

ARMING OF THE FLEET.

WAR ALMOST CERTAIN!"

Wolfenden, who had bought no paper on his way up from Norfolk, gazed with something approaching amazement at the huge placards everywhere displayed along the Strand, thrust into his cab by adventurous newsboys, flaunting upon every lamp-post. He alighted near Trafalgar Square, and purchased a *Globe*. The actual facts were meagre enough, but significant when considered in the light of a few days ago. A vacancy had occurred upon the throne of one of England's far off dependencies. The British nominee had been insulted in his palace by the German consul—a rival, denounced as rebel by the authorities, had been carried off in safety on to a German gunboat, and accorded royal honours. The thing was trivial as it stood, but its importance had been enhanced a thousandfold by later news. The German Emperor had sent a telegram, approving his consul's action and forbidding him to recognise the new sovereign. There was no possibility of misinterpreting such an action; it was an overt and deliberate insult, the second within a week. Wolfenden read the news upon the pavements of Pall Mall, jostled from right to left by hurrying passers by, conscious too, all the while, of that subtle sense of excitement which was in the air and was visibly reflected in the faces of the crowd. He turned into his club, and here he found even a deeper note of the prevailing fever. Men were gathered around the tape in little clusters, listening to the click click of the instrument, and reading aloud the little items of news as they appeared. There was a burst of applause when the Prime Minister's dignified and peremptory demand for an explanation eked out about four o'clock in the afternoon—an hour later it was rumoured that the German Ambassador had received his papers. The Stock Exchange remained firm—there was enthusiasm, but no panic. Wolfenden began to wish that he, too, were a soldier, as he passed from one to another of the eager groups of young men about his own age, eagerly discussing the chances of the coming campaign. He walked out into the streets presently, and made his way boldly down to the house which had been pointed out to him as the town abode of Mr. Sabin and his niece. He found it shut up and apparently empty. The servant, who after some time answered his numerous ringings, was, either from design or chance, more than usually stupid. He could not tell where Mr. Sabin was or when he would return—he seemed to have no information whatever as regards the young lady. Wolfenden turned away in despair and walked slowly back towards Pall Mall. At the bottom of Piccadilly he stopped for a moment to let a little stream of carriages pass by; he was about to cross the road when a large barouche, with a pair of restive horses, again blocked the way. Attracted by an unknown coronet upon the panel, and the quiet magnificence of the servants' liveries, he glanced curiously at the occupants as the carriage passed him. It was one of the surprises of his life. The woman nearest to him he knew well by sight; she was the Duchess de Montegarde, one of the richest and most famous of Frenchwomen—a woman often quoted as exactly typical of the old French nobility, and who had furthermore gained for herself a personal reputation for delicate and aristocratic exclusiveness, not altogether shared by her compeers in English society. By her side—in the seat of honour—was Helène, and opposite to them was a young man with a dark, fiercely twisted moustache and distinctly foreign appearance. They passed slowly, and Wolfenden remained upon the edge of the pavement with his eyes fixed upon them.

He was conscious at once of something about her which seemed strange to him—some new development. She leaned back in her seat, barely pretending to listen to the young man's conversation, her lips a little curled, her own face the very prototype of aristocratic languor! All the lines of race were in her delicately chiselled features; the mere idea of regarding her as the niece of the unknown Mr. Sabin seemed just then almost ridiculous. The carriage went by without her seeing him—she appeared to have no interest whatever in the passers-by. But Wolfenden remained there without moving until a touch on the arm recalled him to himself.

He turned abruptly round, and to his amazement found himself shaking hands vigorously with Densham!

"Where on earth did you spring from, old chap?" he asked. "Dick said that you had gone abroad."

Densham smiled a little sadly.

"I was on my way," he said, "when I heard the war rumours. There seemed to be something in it, so I came back as fast as express trains and steamers would bring me. I only landed in England this morning. I am applying for the post of correspondent to the *London News*."

Wolfenden sighed.

"I would give the world," he said, "for some such excitement as that!"

Densham drew his hand through Wolfenden's arm.

"I saw whom you were watching just now," he said. "She is as beautiful as ever!"

Wolfenden turned suddenly round.

"Densham," he said, "you know who she is—tell me."

"Do you mean to say that you have not found out?"

"I do! I know her better, but still only as Mr. Sabin's niece!"

Densham was silent for several moments. He felt Wolfenden's fingers gripping his arm nervously.

"Well, I do not see that I should be betraying any confidence now," he said. "The promise I gave was only binding for a short time, and now that she is to be seen openly with the Duchess de Montegarde, I suppose the embargo is removed. The young lady is the Princess Helène Frances de Bourbon, and the young man is her betrothed husband, the Prince of Ortrens!"

Piccadilly became suddenly a vague and shadowy thoroughfare to Wolfenden. He was not quite sure whether his footsteps even reached the pavement. Densham hastened him into the club and, installing him into an easy chair, called for brandies and soda.

"Poor old Wolf!" he said softly. "I'm afraid you're like I was—very hard hit. Here, drink this! I'm beastly sorry I told you, but I certainly thought that you would have had some idea."

"I have been a thick-headed idiot!" Wolfenden exclaimed. "There have been heaps of things from which I might have guessed something near the truth, at any rate. What a fool she must have thought me!"

The two men were silent. Outside in the street there was a rush for a special edition, and a half cheer rang in the room. A waiter entered with a handful of copies which were instantly seized upon. Wolfenden secured one and read the headings.

"MOBILIZATION DECLARED.

ALL LEAVE CANCELLED.

CABINET COUNCIL STILL SITTING."

"Densham, do you realise that we are really in for war?"

Densham nodded.

"I don't think there can be any doubt about it myself. What a thunderbolt! By the bye, where is your friend, Mr. Sabin?"

Wolfenden shook his head.

"I do not know; I came to London partially to see him. I have an account to settle when we do meet; at present he has disappeared. Densham!"

"Well!"

"If Miss Sabin has become the Princess Helène of Bourbon, who is Mr. Sabin?"

"I am not sure," Densham answered, "I have been looking into the genealogy of the family, and if he is really her uncle, there is only one man whom he can be—the Duke de Souspennier!"

"Souspennier! Wasn't he banished from France for something or other— intriguing for the restoration of the Monarchy, I think it was?"

Densham nodded.

"Yes, he disappeared at the time of the Commune, and since then he is supposed to have been in Asia somewhere. He has quite a history, I believe, and at different times has been involved in several European complications. I shouldn't be at all surprised if he isn't our man. Mr. Sabin has rather the look of a man who has travelled in the East, and he is certainly an aristocrat."

Wolfenden was suddenly thoughtful.

"Harcutt would be very much interested in this," he declared. "What's up outside?"

There had been a crash in the street, and the sound of a horse plunging; the two men walked to the windows. The *débris* of a hansom was lying in the road, with one wheel hopelessly smashed, a few yards off. A man, covered with mud, rose slowly up from the wreck. Densham and Wolfenden simultaneously recognised him.

"It is Felix," Wolfenden exclaimed. "Come on!"

They both hurried out into the street. The driver of the hansom, who also was covered with mud, stood talking to Felix while staunching the blood from a wound in his forehead.

"I'm very sorry, sir," he was saying, "I hope you'll remember as it was your orders to risk an accident, sooner than lose sight of t'other gent. Mine's a good 'oss, but what is he against a pair and a light brougham? and Piccadilly ain't the place for a chase of this sort! It'll cost me three pun ten, sir, to say nothing of the wheel——"

Felix motioned him impatiently to be silent, and thrust a note into his hand.

"If the damage comes to more than that," he said, "ask for me at the Russian Embassy, and I will pay it. Here is my card."

Felix was preparing to enter another cab, but Wolfenden laid his hand upon his shoulder.

"Won't you come into my club here, and have a wash?" he suggested. "I am afraid that you have cut your cheek."

Felix raised his handkerchief to his face, and found it covered with blood.

"Thank you, Lord Wolfenden," he said, "I should be glad to; you seem destined always to play the part of the Good Samaritan to me!"

They both went with him into the lavatory.

"Do you know," he asked Wolfenden, when he had sponged his face, "whom I was following?"

Wolfenden shook his head.

"Mr. Sabin?" he suggested.

"Not Mr. Sabin himself," Felix answered, "but almost the same thing. It was Foo Cha, his Chinese servant who has just arrived in England. Have you any idea where Mr. Sabin is?"

They both shook their heads.

"I do not know," Wolfenden said, "but I am very anxious to find out. I have an account to settle with him!"

"And I," Felix murmured in a low tone, "have a very much longer one against him. To-night, if I am not too late, there will be a balance struck between us! I have lost Foo Cha, but others, better skilled than I am, are in search of his master. They will succeed, too! They always succeed. What have you against him, Lord Wolfenden?"

Wolfenden hesitated; yet why not tell the man the truth? He had nothing to gain by concealment.

"He forced himself into my father's house in Norfolk and obtained, either by force or craft, some valuable papers. My father was in delicate health, and we fear that the shock will cost him his reason."

"Do you want to know what they were?" Felix said. "I can tell you! Do you want to know what he required them for? I can tell you that too! He has concocted a marvellous scheme, and if he is left to himself for another hour or two, he will succeed. But I have no fear; I have set working a mightier machinery than even he can grapple with!"

They had walked together into the smoke-room; Felix seemed somewhat shaken and was glad to rest for a few minutes.

"Has he outstepped the law, been guilty of any crime?" Wolfenden asked; "he is daring enough!"

Felix laughed shortly. He was lighting a cigarette, but his hand trembled so that he could scarcely hold the match.

"A further reaching arm than the law," he said, dropping his voice, "more powerful than governments. Even by this time his whereabouts is known. If we are only in time; that is the only fear."

"Cannot you tell us," Wolfenden asked, "something of this wonderful scheme of his—why was he so anxious to get those papers and drawings from my father—to what purpose can he possibly put them?"

Felix hesitated.

"Well," he said, "why not? You have a right to know. Understand that I myself have only the barest outline of it; I will tell you this, however. Mr. Sabin is the Duc de Souspennier, a Frenchman of fabulous wealth, who has played many strange parts in European history. Amongst other of his accomplishments, he is a mechanical and strategical genius. He has studied under Addison in America, one subject only, for three years—the destruction of warships and fortifications by electrical contrivances unknown to the general world. Then he came to England, and collected a vast amount of information concerning your navy and coast defences in many different ways—finally he sent a girl to play the part of typist to your father, whom he knew to be the greatest living authority upon all naval matters connected with your country. Every line he wrote was copied and sent to Mr. Sabin, until by some means your father's suspicions were aroused, and the girl was dismissed. The last portion of your father's work consisted of a set of drawings, of no fewer than twenty-seven of England's finest vessels, every one of which has a large proportion of defective armour plating, which would render the vessels utterly useless in case of war. These drawings show the exact position of the defective plates, and it was to secure these illustrations that Mr. Sabin paid that daring visit to your father on Tuesday morning. Now, what he professes broadly is that he has elaborated a scheme, by means of which, combined with the aid of his inventions, a few torpedo boats can silence every fort in the Thames, and leave London at the mercy of any invaders. At the same time his plans include the absolutely safe landing of troops on the east and south coast, at certain selected spots. This scheme, together with some very alarming secret information affecting the great majority of your battleships, will, he asserts with absolute confidence, place your country at the mercy of any Power to whom he chooses to sell it. He offered it to Russia first, and then to Germany. Germany has accepted his terms and will declare war upon England the moment she has his whole scheme and inventions in her possession."

Wolfenden and Densham looked at one another, partly incredulous, partly aghast. It was like a page from the Arabian Nights. Surely such a thing as this was not possible. Yet even that short silence was broken by the cry of the newsboys out in the street—

"GERMANY ARMING!

REPORTED DECLARATION OF WAR!"

CHAPTER XXXVIII

THE MEN WHO SAVED ENGLAND

Mr. Sabin leaned back in his chair with a long, deep sigh of content. The labour of years was concluded at last. With that final little sketch his work was done. A pile of manuscripts and charts lay before him; everything was in order. He took a bill of lading from his letter-case, and pinned it carefully to the rest. Then he glanced at his watch, and, taking a cigarette-case from his pocket, began to smoke.

There was a knock at the door, and Mr. Sabin, who had recognised the approaching footsteps, glanced up carelessly.

"What is it, Foo Cha? I told you that I would ring when I wanted you."

The Chinaman glided to his side.

"Master," he said softly, "I have fears. There is something not good in the air."

Mr. Sabin turned sharply around.

"What do you mean?" he asked.

Foo Cha was apologetic but serious.

"Master, I was followed from the house of the German by a man, who drove fast after me in a two-wheeled cab. He lost me on the way, but there are others. I have been into the street, and I am sure of it. The house is being watched on all sides."

Mr. Sabin drew a quiet, little breath. For a moment his haggard face seemed almost ghastly. He recovered himself, however, with an effort.

"We are not in China, Foo Cha," he said. "I have done nothing against the law of this country; no man can enter here if we resist. If we are really being watched, it must be by persons in the pay of the Russian. But they can do nothing; it is too late; Knigenstein will be here in half an hour. The thing will be settled then, once and for ever."

Foo Cha was troubled still.

"Me afraid," he admitted frankly. "Strange men this end and that end of street. Me no like it. Ah!"

The front door bell rang softly; it was a timid, hesitating ring, as though some one had but feebly touched the knob. Foo Cha and his master looked at one another in silence. There was something almost ominous in that gentle peal.

"You must see who it is, Foo Cha," Mr. Sabin said. "It may be Knigenstein come early; if so, show him in at once. To everybody else the house is empty."

Foo Cha bowed silently and withdrew. He struck a match in the dark passage, and lit the hanging gas-lamp. Then he opened the door cautiously.

One man alone was standing there. Foo Cha looked at him in despair; it was certainly not Knigenstein, nor was there any sign of his carriage in the street. The stranger was a man of middle height, squarely built and stout. He wore a long black overcoat, and he stood with his hands in his pockets.

"What you want?" Foo Cha asked. "What you want with me?"

The man did not answer at once, but he stepped inside into the passage. Foo Cha tried to shut the door in his face, but it was like pushing against a mountain.

"Where is your master?" he asked.

"Master? He not here," Foo Cha answered, with glib and untruthful earnestness. "Indeed he is not here—quite true. He come to-morrow; I preparing house for him. What do you want? Go away, or me call policeman."

The intruder smiled indulgently into the Chinaman's earnest, upturned face.

"Foo Cha," he said, "that is enough. Take this card to your master, Mr. Sabin."

Foo Cha was ready to begin another torrent of expostulations, but in the gas-light he met the new-comer's steadfast gaze, and he was silent. The stranger was dressed in the garb of a superior working man, but his speech and manner indicated a very different station. Foo Cha took the card and left him in the passage. He made his way softly into the sitting-room, and as he entered he turned the key in the lock behind him; there, at any rate, was a moment or two of respite.

"Master," he said, "there is a man there whom we cannot stop. When me tell him you no here, he laugh at me. He will see you; he no go way. He laugh again when I try shut the door. He give me card; I no understand what on it."

Mr. Sabin stretched out his hand and took the card from the Chinaman's fingers. There seemed to be one or two words upon it, traced in a delicate, sloping handwriting. Mr. Sabin had snatched at the little piece of pasteboard with some impatience, but the moment he had read those few words a remarkable change came over him. He started as though he had received an electric shock; the pupils of his eyes seemed hideously dilated; the usual pallor of his face was merged in a ghastly whiteness. And then, after the first shock, came a look of deep and utter despair; his hand fell to his side, a half-muttered imprecation escaped from his trembling lips, yet he laid the card gently, even with reverence, upon the desk before him.

"You can show him in, Foo Cha," he directed, in a low tone; "show him in at once."

Foo Cha glided out disappointed. Something had gone terribly wrong, he was sure of that. He went slowly downstairs, his eyes fixed upon the dark figure standing motionless in the dimly-lit hall. He drew a sharp breath, which sounded through his yellow, protuberant teeth like a hiss. A single stroke of that long knife—it would be so easy. Then he remembered the respect with which Mr. Sabin had treated that card, and he sighed. Perhaps it would be a mistake; it might make evil worse. He beckoned to the stranger, and conducted him upstairs.

Mr. Sabin received his visitor standing. He was still very pale, but his face had resumed its wonted impassiveness. In the dim lamp-lit room he could see very little of his visitor, only a thick-set man with dark eyes and a closely-cropped black beard. He was roughly dressed, yet held himself well. The two men eyed one another steadily for several moments, before any speech passed between them.

"You are surprised," the stranger said; "I do not wonder at it. Perhaps—you have been much engrossed, it is said—you had even forgotten."

Mr. Sabin's lips curled in a bitter smile.

"One does not forget those things," he said. "To business. Let me know what is required of me."

"It has been reported," the stranger said, "that you have conceived and brought to great perfection a comprehensive and infallible scheme for the conquest of this country. Further, that you are on the point of handing it over to the Emperor of Germany, for the use of that country. I think I may conclude that the report is correct?" he added, with a glance at the table. "We are not often misinformed."

"The report," Mr. Sabin assented, "is perfectly correct."

"We have taken counsel upon the matter," the stranger continued, "and I am here to acquaint you with our decision. The papers are to be burnt, and the appliances to be destroyed forthwith. No portion of them is to be shown to the German Government or any person representing that country, nor to any other Power. Further, you are to leave England within two months."

Mr. Sabin stood quite still, his hands resting lightly upon the desk in front of him. His eyes, fixed on vacancy, were looking far out of that shabby little room, back along the avenues of time, thronged with the fragments of his broken dreams. He realised once more the full glory of his daring and ambitious scheme. He saw his country revelling again in her old splendour, stretching out her limbs and taking once more the foremost place among her sister nations. He saw the pageantry and rich colouring of Imperialism, firing the imagination of her children, drawing all hearts back to their allegiance, breaking through the hard crust of materialism which had spread like an evil dream through the land. He saw himself great and revered, the patriot, the Richelieu of his days, the adored of the people, the friend and restorer of his king. Once more he was a figure in European history, the consort of Emperors, the man whose slightest word could shake the money markets of the world. He saw all these things, as though for the last time, with strange, unreal vividness; once more their full glory warmed his blood and dazzled his eyes. Then a flash of memory, an effort of realisation chilled him; his feet were upon the earth again, his head was heavy. That thick-set, motionless figure before him seemed like the incarnation of his despair.

"I shall appeal," he said hoarsely; "England is no friend of ours."

The man shrugged his shoulders.

"England is tolerant at least," he said; "and she has sheltered us."

"I shall appeal," Mr. Sabin repeated.

The man shook his head.

"It is the order of the High Council," he said; "there is no appeal."

"It is my life's work," Mr. Sabin faltered.

"Your life's work," the man said slowly, "should be with us."

"God knows why I ever——"

The man stretched out a white hand, which gleamed through the semi-darkness. Mr. Sabin stopped short.

"You very nearly," he said solemnly, "pronounced your own death-sentence. If you had finished what you were about to say, I could never have saved you. Be wise, friend. This is a disappointment to you; well, is not our life one long torturing disappointment? What of us, indeed? We are like the waves which beat ceaselessly against the sea-shore, what we gain one day we lose the next. It is fate, it is life! Once more, friend, remember! Farewell!"

Mr. Sabin was left alone, a martyr to his thoughts. Already it was past the hour for Knigenstein's visit. Should he remain and brave the storm, or should he catch the boat-train from Charing Cross and hasten to hide himself in one of the most remote quarters of the civilised world? In any case it was a dreary outlook for him. Not only had this dearly cherished scheme of his come crashing about his head, but he had very seriously compromised himself with a great country. The Emperor's gracious letter was in his pocket—he smiled grimly to himself as he thought for a moment of the consternation of Berlin, and of Knigenstein's disgrace. And then the luxury of choice was suddenly denied him; he was brought back to the present, and a sense of its paramount embarrassments by a pealing ring at the bell, and the trampling of horse's feet in the street. He had no time to rescind his previous instructions to Foo Cha before Knigenstein himself, wrapped in a great sealskin coat, and muffled up to the chin with a silk handkerchief, was shown into the room.

The Ambassador's usually phlegmatic face bore traces of some anxiety. Behind his spectacles his eyes glittered nervously; he grasped Mr. Sabin's hand with unwonted cordiality, and was evidently much relieved to have found him.

"My dear Souspennier," he said, "this is a great occasion. I am a little late, but, as you can imagine, I am overwhelmed with work of the utmost importance. You have finished now, I hope. You are ready for me?"

"I am as ready for you," Mr. Sabin said grimly, "as I ever shall be!"

"What do you mean?" Knigenstein asked sharply. "Don't tell me that anything has gone amiss! I am a ruined man, unless you carry out your covenant to the letter. I have pledged my word upon your honour."

"Then I am afraid," Mr. Sabin said, "that we are both of us in a very tight place! I am bound hand and foot. There," he cried, pointing to the grate, half choked with a pile of quivering grey ashes, "lies the work of seven years of my life—seven years of intrigue, of calculation, of unceasing toil. By this time all my American inventions, which would have paralysed Europe, are blown sky high! That is the position, Knigenstein; we are undone!"

Knigenstein was shaking like a child; he laid his hand upon Mr. Sabin's arm, and gripped it fiercely.

"Souspennier," he said, "if you are speaking the truth I am ruined, and disgraced for ever. The Emperor will never forgive me! I shall be dismissed and banished. I have pledged my word for yours; you cannot mean to play me false like this. If there is any personal favour or reward, which the Emperor can grant, it is yours—I will answer for it. I will answer for it, too, that war shall be declared against France within six months of the conclusion of peace with England. Come, say that you have been jesting. Good God! man, you are torturing me. Why, have you seen the papers to-night? The Emperor has been hasty, I own, but he has already struck the first blow. War is as good as declared. I am waiting for my papers every hour!"

"I cannot help it," Mr. Sabin said doggedly. "The thing is at an end. To give up all the fruits of my work—the labour of the best years of my life—is as bitter to me as your dilemma is to you! But it is inevitable! Be a man, Knigenstein, put the best face on it you can."

The utter impotence of all that he could say was suddenly revealed to Knigenstein in Mr. Sabin's set face and hopeless words. His tone of entreaty changed to one of anger; the veins on his forehead stood out like knotted string, his mouth twitched as he spoke, he could not control himself.

"You have made up your mind," he cried. "Very well! Russia has bought you, very well! If Lobenski has bribed you with all the gold in Christendom you shall never enjoy it! You shall not live a year! I swear it! You have insulted and wronged our country, our fatherland! Listen! A word shall be breathed in the ears of a handful of our officers. Where you go, they shall go; if you leave England you will be struck on the cheek in the first public place at which you show yourself. If one falls, there are others—hundreds, thousands, an army! Oh! you shall not escape, my friend. But if ever you dared to set foot in Germany——"

"I can assure you," Mr. Sabin interrupted, "that I shall take particular care never to visit your delightful country. Elsewhere, I think I can take care of myself. But listen, Knigenstein, all your talk about Russia and playing you false is absurd. If I had wished to deal with Lobenski, I could have done so, instead of with you. I have not even seen him. A greater hand than his has stopped me, a greater even than the hand of your Emperor!"

Knigenstein looked at him as one looks at a madman.

"There is no greater hand on earth," he said, "than the hand of his Imperial Majesty, the Emperor of Germany."

Mr. Sabin smiled.

"You are a German," he said, "and you know little of these things, yet you call yourself a diplomatist, and I suppose you have some knowledge of what this means."

He lifted the lamp from the table and walked to the wall opposite to the door. Knigenstein followed him closely. Before them, high up as the fingers of a man could reach, was a small, irregular red patch—something between a cross and a star. Mr. Sabin held the lamp high over his head and pointed to the mark.

"Do you know what that means?" he asked.

The man by his side groaned.

"Yes," he answered, with a gesture of abject despair, "I know!"

Mr. Sabin walked back to the table and set down the lamp.

"You know now," he said coolly, "who has intervened."

"If I had had any idea," Knigenstein said, "that you were one of them I should not have treated with you."

"It was many years ago," Mr. Sabin said with a sigh. "My father was half a Russian, you know. It served my purpose whilst I was envoy at Teheran; since then I had lost sight of them; I thought that they too had lost sight of me. I was mistaken—only an hour ago I was visited by a chief official. They knew everything, they forbade everything. As a matter of fact they have saved England!"

"And ruined us," Knigenstein groaned. "I must go and telegraph. But Souspennier, one word."

Mr. Sabin looked up.

"You are a brave man and a patriot; you want to see your country free. Well, why not free it still? You and I are philosophers, we know that life after all is an uncertain thing. Hold to your bargain with us. It will be to your death, I do not deny that. But I will pledge the honour of my country, I will give you the holy word of the Emperor, that we will faithfully carry out our part of the contract, and the whole glory shall be yours. You will be immortalised; you will win fame that shall be deathless. Your name will be enshrined in the heart of your country's history."

Mr. Sabin shook his head slowly.

"My dear Knigenstein," he said "pray don't misunderstand me. I do not cast the slightest reflection upon your Emperor or your honour. But if ever there was a country which required watching, it is yours. I could not carry your pledges with me into oblivion, and there is no one to whom I could leave the legacy. That being the case, I think that I prefer to live."

Knigenstein buttoned up his coat and sighed.

"I am a ruined man, Souspennier," he said, "but I bear you no malice. Let me leave you a little word of warning, though. The Nihilists are not the only people in the world who have the courage and the wit to avenge themselves. Farewell!"

Mr. Sabin broke into a queer little laugh as he listened to his guest's departing footsteps. Then he lit a cigarette, and called to Foo Cha for some coffee.

CHAPTER XXXIX

THE HEART OF THE PRINCESS

When Wolfenden opened his paper on Saturday morning, London had already drawn a great breath, partly of relief partly of surprise, for the black head-lines which topped the columns of the papers, the placards in the streets, and the cry of the newsboys, all declared a most remarkable change in the political situation.

"THE GERMAN EMPEROR EXPLAINS!

THERE WILL BE NO WAR!

GERMAN CONSUL ORDERED HOME!

NO RUPTURE!"

Wolfenden, in common with most of his fellow-countrymen, could scarcely believe his eyes; yet there it was in plain black and white. The dogs of war had been called back. Germany was climbing down—not with dignity; she had gone too far for that—but with a scuffle. Wolfenden read the paper through before he even thought of his letters Then he began to open them slowly. The first was from his mother. The Admiral was distinctly better; the doctors were more hopeful. He turned to the next one; it was in a delicate, foreign handwriting, and exhaled a faint perfume which seemed vaguely familiar to him. He opened it and his heart stood still.

> "14, GROSVENOR SQUARE,
> "LONDON, W

"Will you come and see me to-day about four o'clock? —HELÈNE."

He looked at his watch—four o'clock seemed a very long way off. He decided that he would go out and find Felix; but almost immediately the door was opened and that very person was shown in.

Felix was radiant; he appeared to have grown years younger. He was immaculately dressed, and he wore an exquisite orchid in his button-hole.

Wolfenden greeted him warmly.

"Have you seen the paper?" he asked. "Do you know the news?"

Felix laughed.

"Of course! You may not believe it, but it is true that I am the person who has saved your country! And I am quits at last with Herbert de la Meux, Duc de Souspennier!"

"Meaning, I suppose, the person whom we have been accustomed to call—Mr. Sabin?" Wolfenden remarked.

"Exactly!"

Wolfenden pushed an easy chair towards his visitor and produced some cigarettes.

"I must say," he continued, "that I should exceedingly like to know how the thing was done."

Felix smiled.

"That, my dear friend," he said, "you will never know. No one will ever know the cause of Germany's suddenly belligerent attitude, and her equally speedy climb-down! There are many pages of diplomatic history which the world will never read, and this is one of them. Come and lunch with me, Lord Wolfenden. My vow is paid and without bloodshed. I am a free man, and my promotion is assured. To-day is the happiest of my life!"

Wolfenden smiled and looked at the letter on the table before him; might it not also be the happiest day of his own life!

And it was! Punctually at four o'clock he presented himself at Grosvenor Square and was ushered into one of the smaller reception rooms. Helène came to him at once, a smile half-shy, half-apologetic upon her lips. He was conscious from the moment of her entrance of a change in her deportment towards him. She held in her hand a small locket.

"I wanted to ask you, Lord Wolfenden," she said, drawing her fingers slowly away from his lingering clasp, "does this locket belong to you?"

He glanced at it and shook his head at once.

"I never saw it before in my life," he declared. "I do not wear a watch chain, and I don't possess anything of that sort."

She threw it contemptuously away from her into the grate.

"A woman lied to me about it," she said slowly. "I am ashamed of myself that I should have listened to her, even for a second. I chanced to look at it last night, and it suddenly occurred to me where I had seen it. It was on a man's watch-chain, but not on yours."

"Surely," he said, "it belongs to Mr. Sabin?"

She nodded and held out both her hands.

"Will you forgive me?" she begged softly, "and—and—I think—I promised to send for you!"

They had been together for nearly an hour when the door opened abruptly, and the young man whom Wolfenden had seen with Helène in the barouche entered the room. He stared in amazement at her, and rudely at Wolfenden. Helène rose and turned to him with a smile.

"Henri," she said, "let me present to you the English gentleman whom I am going to marry. Prince Henri of Ortrens—Lord Wolfenden."

The young man barely returned Wolfenden's salute. He turned with flashing eyes to Helène and muttered a few hasty words in French—

"A kingdom and my betrothed in one day! It is too much! We will see!"

He left the room hurriedly. Helène laughed.

"He has gone to find the Duchess," she said, "and there will be a scene! Let us go out in the Park."

They walked about under the trees; suddenly they came face to face with Mr. Sabin. He was looking a little worn, but he was as carefully dressed as usual, and he welcomed them with a smile and an utter absence of any embarrassment.

"So soon!" he remarked pleasantly. "You Englishmen are as prompt in love as you are in war, Lord Wolfenden! It is an admirable trait."

Helène laid her hand upon his arm. Yes, it was no fancy; his hair was greyer, and heavy lines furrowed his brow.

"Uncle," she said, "believe me that I am sorry for you, though for myself—I am glad!"

He looked at her kindly, yet with a faint contempt.

"The Bourbon blood runs very slowly in your veins, child," he said. "After all I begin to doubt whether you would have made a queen! As for myself—well, I am resigned. I am going to Pau, to play golf!"

"For how long, I wonder," she said smiling, "will you be able to content yourself there?"

"For a month or two," he answered; "until I have lost the taste of defeat. Then I have plans—but never mind; I will tell you later on. You will all hear of me again! So far as you two are concerned at any rate," he added, "I have no need to reproach myself. My failure seems to have brought you happiness."

He passed on, and they both watched his slim figure lost in the throng of passers-by.

"He is a great man," she murmured. "He knows how to bear defeat."

"He is a great man," Wolfenden answered; "but none the less I am not sorry to see the last of Mr. Sabin!"

CHAPTER XL

THE WAY TO PAU

The way to Pau which Mr. Sabin chose may possibly have been the most circuitous, but it was certainly the safest. Although not a muscle of his face had moved, although he had not by any physical movement or speech betrayed his knowledge of the fact, he was perfectly well aware that his little statement as to his future movements was overheard and carefully noted by the tall, immaculately dressed young man who by some strange chance seemed to have been at his elbow since he had left his rooms an hour ago. "Into the lion's mouth, indeed," he muttered to himself grimly as he hailed a hansom at the corner and was driven homewards. The limes of Berlin were very beautiful, but it was not with any immediate idea of sauntering beneath them that a few hours later he was driven to Euston and stepped into an engaged carriage on the Liverpool express. There, with a travelling cap drawn down to his eyes and a rug pulled up to his throat, he sat in the far corner of his compartment apparently enjoying an evening paper—as a matter of fact anxiously watching the platform. He had taken care to allow himself only a slender margin of time. In two minutes the train glided out of the station.

He drew a little sigh of relief—he, who very seldom permitted himself the luxury of even the slightest revelation of his feelings. At least he had a start. Then he unlocked a travelling case, and, drawing out an atlas, sat with it upon his knee for some time. When he closed it there was a frown upon his face.

"America," he exclaimed softly to himself. "What a lack of imagination even the sound of the place seems to denote! It is the most ignominious retreat I have ever made."

"You made the common mistake," a quiet voice at his elbow remarked, "of many of the world's greatest diplomatists. You underrated your adversaries."

Mr. Sabin distinctly started, and clutching at his rug, leaned back in his corner. A young man in a tweed travelling suit was standing by the opposite window. Behind him Mr. Sabin noticed for the first time a narrow mahogany door. Mr. Sabin drew a short breath, and was himself again. Underneath the rug his fingers stole into his overcoat pocket and clasped something cold and firm.

"One at least," he said grimly, "I perceive that I have held too lightly. Will you pardon a novice at necromancy if he asks you how you found your way here?"

Felix smiled.

"A little forethought," he remarked, "a little luck and a sovereign tip to an accommodating inspector. The carriage in which you are travelling is, as you will doubtless perceive before you reach your journey's end, a species of saloon. This little door"—touching the one through which he had issued—"leads on to a lavatory, and on the other side is a non-smoking carriage. I found that you had engaged a carriage on this train, by posing as your servant. I selected this one as being particularly suited to an old gentleman of nervous disposition, and arranged also that the non-smoking portion should be reserved for me."

Mr. Sabin nodded. "And how," he asked, "did you know that I meant to go to America?"

Felix shrugged his shoulders and took a seat.

"Well," he said, "I concluded that you would be looking for a change of air somewhere, and I really could not see what part of the world you had left open to yourself. America is the only country strong enough to keep you! Besides, I reckoned a little upon that curiosity with regard to undeveloped countries which I have observed to be one of your traits. So far as I am aware, you have never resided long in America."

"Neither have I even visited Kamtchatka or Greenland," Mr. Sabin remarked.

"I understand you," Felix remarked, nodding his head. "America is certainly one of the last places one would have dreamed of looking for you. You will find it, I am afraid, politically unborn; your own little methods, at any rate, would scarcely achieve popularity there. Further, its sympathies, of course, are with democratic France. I can imagine that you and the President of the United States would represent opposite poles of thought. Yet there were two considerations which weighed with me."

"This is very interesting," Mr. Sabin remarked. "May I know what they were? To be permitted a glimpse into the inward workings of a brain like yours is indeed a privilege!"

Felix bowed with a gratified smile upon his lips. The satire of Mr. Sabin's dry tone was apparently lost upon him.

"You are most perfectly welcome," he declared. "In the first place I said to myself that Kamtchatka and Greenland, although equally interesting to you, would be quite unable to afford themselves the luxury of offering you an asylum. You must seek the shelter of a great and powerful country, and one which you had never offended, and save America, there is none such in the world. Secondly, you are a Sybarite, and you do not without very serious reasons place yourself outside the pale of civilisation. Thirdly, America is the only country save those which are barred to you where you could play golf!"

"You are really a remarkable young man," Sabin declared, softly stroking his little grey imperial. "You have read me like a book! I am humiliated that the course of my reasoning should have been so transparent. To prove the correctness of your conclusions, see the little volume which I had brought to read on my way to Liverpool."

He handed it out to Felix. It was entitled, "The Golf Courses of the World," and a leaf was turned down at the chapter headed, "United States."

"I wish," he remarked, "that you were a golfer! I should like to have asked your opinion about that plan of the Myopia golf links. To me it seems cramped, and the bunkers are artificial."

Felix looked at him admiringly.

"You are a wonderful man," he said. "You do not bear me any ill-will then?"

"None in the least," Mr. Sabin said quietly. "I never bear personal grudges. So far as I am concerned, I never have a personal enemy. It is fate itself which vanquished me. You were simply an instrument. You do not figure in my thoughts as a person against whom I bear any ill-will. I am glad, though, that you did not cash my cheque for £20,000!"

Felix smiled. "You went to see, then?" he asked.

"I took the liberty," Mr. Sabin answered, "of stopping payment of it."

"It will never be presented," Felix said "I tore it into pieces directly I left you."

Mr. Sabin nodded.

"Quixotic," he murmured.

The express was rushing on through the night. Mr. Sabin thrust his hand into his bag and took out a handful of cigars. He offered one to Felix, who accepted, and lit it with the air of a man enjoying the reasonable civility of a chance fellow passenger.

"You had, I presume," Mr. Sabin remarked, "some object in coming to see the last of me? I do not wish to seem unduly inquisitive, but I feel a little natural interest, or shall we say curiosity as to the reason for this courtesy on your part?"

"You are quite correct," Felix answered. "I am here with a purpose. I am the bearer of a message to you."

"May I ask, a friendly message, or otherwise?"

His fingers were tightening upon the little hard substance in his pocket, but he was already beginning to doubt whether after all Felix had come as an enemy.

"Friendly," was the prompt answer. "I bring you an offer."

"From Lobenski?"

"From his august master! The Czar himself has plans for you!"

"His serene Majesty," Mr. Sabin murmured, "has always been most kind."

"Since you left the country of the Shah," Felix continued, "Russian influence in Central Asia has been gradually upon the wane. All manner of means have been employed to conceal this, but the unfortunate fact remains. You were the only man who ever thoroughly grasped the situation and attained any real influence over the master of western Asia! Your removal from Teheran was the result of an intrigue on the part of the English. It was the greatest misfortune which ever befel Russia!"

"And your offer?" Mr. Sabin asked.

"Is that you return to Teheran not as the secret agent, but as the accredited ambassador of Russia, with an absolutely free hand and unlimited powers."

"Such an offer," Mr. Sabin remarked, "ten years ago would have made Russia mistress of all Asia."

"The Czar," Felix said, "is beginning to appreciate that. But what was possible then is possible now!"

Mr. Sabin shook his head. "I am ten years older," he said, "and the Shah who was my friend is dead."

"The new Shah," Felix said, "has a passion for intrigue, and the sands around Teheran are magnificent for golf."

Mr. Sabin shook his head.

"Too hard," he said, "and too monotonous. I am peculiar perhaps in that respect, but I detest artificial bunkers. Now there is a little valley," he continued thoughtfully, "about seven miles north of Teheran, where something might be done! I wonder——"

"You accept," Felix asked quietly.

Mr. Sabin shook his head.

"No, I decline."

It was a shock to Felix, but he hid his disappointment.

"Absolutely?"

"And finally."

"Why?"

"I am ten years too old!"

"That is resentment!"

Mr. Sabin denied it.

"No! Why should I not be frank with you, my friend? What I would have done for Russia ten years ago, I would not do to-day! She has made friends with the French Republic. She has done more than recognise the existence of that iniquitous institution—she has pressed her friendship upon the president—she has spoken the word of alliance. Henceforth my feeling for Russia has changed. I have no object to gain in her development. I am richer than the richest of her nobles, and there is no title in Europe for which I would exchange my own. You see Russia has absolutely nothing to offer me. On the other hand, what would benefit Russia in Asia would ruin England, and England has given me and many of my kind a shelter, and has even held aloof from France. Of the two countries I would much prefer to aid England. If I had been the means of destroying her Asiatic empire ten years ago it would have been to me to-day a source of lasting regret. There, my friend, I have paid you the compliment of perfect frankness."

"If," Felix said slowly, "the price of your success at Teheran should be the breach of our covenants with France—what then? Remember that it is the country whose friendship is pleasing to us, not the government. You cannot seriously doubt but that an autocrat, such as the Czar, would prefer to extend his hand to an Emperor of France than to soil his fingers with the clasp of a tradesman!"

Mr. Sabin shook his head softly. "I have told you why I decline," he said, "but in my heart there are many other reasons. For one, I am no longer a young man. This last failure of mine has aged me. I have no heart for fresh adventures."

Felix sighed.

"My mission to you comes," he said, "at an unfortunate time. For the present, then, I accept defeat."

"The fault," Mr. Sabin murmured, "is in no way with you. My refusal was a thing predestined. The Czar himself could not move me."

The train was slowing a little. Felix looked out of the window.

"We are nearing Crewe," he said. "I shall alight then and return to London. You are for America, then?"

"Beyond doubt," Mr. Sabin declared.

Felix drew from his pocket a letter.

"If you will deliver this for me," he said, "you will do me a kindness, and you will make a pleasant acquaintance."

Mr. Sabin glanced at the imprescription. It was addressed to—

"Mrs. J. B. Peterson,
"Lenox,
"Mass., U.S.A."

"I will do so with pleasure," he remarked, slipping it into his dressing-case.

"And remember this," Felix remarked, glancing out at the platform along which they were gliding. "You are a marked man. Disguise is useless for you. Be ever on your guard. You and I have been enemies, but after all you are too great a man to fall by the hand of a German assassin. Farewell!"

"I will thank you for your caution and remember it," Mr. Sabin answered. "Farewell!"

Felix raised his hat, and Mr. Sabin returned the salute. The whistle sounded. Felix stepped out on to the platform.

"You will not forget the letter?" he asked

"I will deliver it in person without fail," Mr. Sabin answered.

CHAPTER XLI

MR. AND MRS. WATSON OF NEW YORK

It was their third day out, and Mr. Sabin was enjoying the voyage very much indeed. The *Calipha* was a small boat sailing to Boston instead of New York, and contemptuously termed by the ocean-going public an old tub. She carried, consequently, only seven passengers besides Mr. Sabin, and it had taken him but a very short time to decide that of those seven passengers not one was interested in him or his affairs. He had got clear away, for the present at any rate, from all the complications and dangers which had followed upon the failure of his great scheme. Of course by this time the news of his departure and destination was known to every one whom his movements concerned. That was almost a matter of course, and realising even the impossibility of successful concealment, Mr. Sabin had made no attempt at any. He had given the name of Sabin to the steward, and had secured the deck's cabin for his own use. He chatted every day with the captain, who treated him with respect, and in reply to a question from one of the stewards who was a Frenchman, he admitted that he was the Duc de Souspennier, and that he was travelling incognito only as a whim. He was distinctly popular with every one of the seven passengers, who were a little doubtful how to address him, but whom he succeeded always in putting entirely at their ease. He entered, too, freely into the little routine of steamer life. He played shuffleboard for an hour or more every morning, and was absolutely invincible at the game; he brought his golf clubs on deck one evening after dinner, and explained the manner of their use to an admiring little circle of the seven passengers, the captain, and doctor. He rigorously supported the pool each day, and he even took a hand at a mild game of poker one wet afternoon, when timidly invited to do so by Mr. Hiram Shedge, an oil merchant of Boston. He had in no way the deportment or manner of a man who had just passed through a great crisis, nor would any one have gathered from his conversation or demeanour that he was the head of one of the greatest houses in Europe and a millionaire. The first time a shadow crossed his face was late one afternoon, when, coming on deck a little behind the others after lunch, he found them all leaning over the starboard bow, gazing intently at some object a little distance off, and at the same time became aware that the engines had been put to half-speed.

He was strolling towards the little group, when the captain, seeing him, beckoned him on to the bridge.

"Here's something that will interest you, Mr. Sabin," he called out. "Won't you step this way?"

Mr. Sabin mounted the iron steps carefully but with his eyes turned seawards; a large yacht of elegant shape and painted white from stern to bows was lying-to about half a mile off flying signals.

Mr. Sabin reached the bridge and stood by the captain's side.

"A pleasure yacht," he remarked. "What does she want?"

"I shall know in a moment," the captain answered with his glass to his eye. "She flew a distress signal at first for us to stand by, so I suppose she's in trouble. Ah! there it goes. 'Mainshaft broken,' she says."

"She doesn't lie like it," Mr. Sabin remarked quietly.

The captain looked at him with a smile.

"You know a bit about yachting too," he said, "and, to tell you the truth, that's just what I was thinking."

"Holmes."

"Yes, sir."

"Ask her what she wants us to do."

The signalman touched his hat, and the little row of flags ran fluttering up in the breeze.

"She signals herself the *Mayflower*, private yacht, owner Mr. James Watson of New York," he remarked. "She's a beautiful boat."

Mr. Sabin, who had brought his own glasses, looked at her long and steadily.

"She's not an American built boat, at any rate," he remarked.

An answering signal came fluttering back. The captain opened his book and read it.

"She's going on under canvas," he said, "but she wants us to take her owner and his wife on board."

"Are you compelled to do so?" Mr. Sabin asked.

The captain laughed.

"Not exactly! I'm not expected to pick up passengers in mid ocean."

"Then I shouldn't do it," Mr. Sabin said. "If they are in a hurry the *Alaska* is due up to-day, isn't she? and she'll be in New York in three days, and the *Baltimore* must be close behind her. I should let them know that."

"Well," the captain answered, "I don't want fresh passengers bothering just now."

The flags were run up, and the replies came back as promptly. The captain shut up his glass with a bang.

"No getting out of them," he remarked to Mr. Sabin. "They reply that the lady is nervous and will not wait; they are coming on board at once—for fear I should go on, I suppose. They add that Mr. Watson is the largest American holder of Cunard stock and a director of the American Board, so have them we must—that's pretty certain. I must see the purser."

He descended, and Mr. Sabin, following him, joined the little group of passengers. They all stood together watching the long rowing boat which was coming swiftly towards them through the smooth sea. Mr. Sabin explained to them the messages which had passed, and together they admired the disabled yacht.

Mr. Sabin touched the first mate on the arm as he passed.

"Did you ever see a vessel like that, Johnson?" he remarked.

The man shook his head.

"Their engineer is a fool, sir!" he declared scornfully. "Nothing but my own eyes would make me believe there's anything serious the matter with her shaft."

"I agree with you," Mr. Sabin said quietly.

The boat was now within hailing distance. Mr. Sabin leaned down over the side and scanned its occupants closely. There was nothing in the least suspicious about them. The man who sat in the stern steering was a typical American, with thin sallow face and bright eyes. The woman wore a thick veil, but she was evidently young, and when she stood up displayed a figure and clothes distinctly Parisian. The two came up the ladder as though perfectly used to boarding a vessel in mid ocean, and the lady's nervousness was at least not apparent. The captain advanced to meet them, and gallantly assisted the lady on to the deck.

"This is Captain Ackinson, I presume," the man remarked with extended hand. "We are exceedingly obliged to you, sir, for taking us off. This is my wife, Mrs. James B. Watson."

Mrs. Watson raised her veil, and disclosed a dark, piquant face with wonderfully bright eyes.

"It's real nice of you, Captain," she said frankly. "You don't know how good it is to feel the deck of a real ocean-going steamer beneath your feet after that little sailing boat of my husband's. This is the very last time I attempt to cross the Atlantic except on one of your steamers."

"We are very glad to be of any assistance," the captain answered, more heartily than a few minutes before he would have believed possible. "Full speed ahead, John!"

There was a churning of water and dull throb of machinery restarting. The little rowing boat, already well away on its return journey, rocked on the long waves. Mr. Watson turned to shout some final instructions. Then the captain beckoned to the purser.

"Mr. Wilson will show you your state rooms," he remarked. "Fortunately we have plenty of room. Steward, take the baggage down."

The lady went below, but Mr. Watson remained on deck talking to the captain. Mr. Sabin strolled up to them.

"Your yacht rides remarkably well, if her shaft is really broken," he remarked.

Mr. Watson nodded.

"She's a beautifully built boat," he remarked with enthusiasm. "If the weather is favourable her canvas will bring her into Boston Harbour two days after us."

"I suppose," the captain asked, looking at her through his glass, "you satisfied yourself that her shaft was really broken?"

"I did not, sir," Mr. Watson answered. "My engineer reported it so, and, as I know nothing of machinery myself, I was content to take his word. He holds very fine diplomas, and I presume he knows what he is talking about. But anyway Mrs. Watson would never have stayed upon that boat one moment longer than she was compelled. She's a wonderfully nervous woman is Mrs. Watson."

"That's a somewhat unusual trait for your countrywoman, is it not?" Mr. Sabin asked.

Mr. J. B. Watson looked steadily at his questioner.

"My wife, sir," he said, "has lived for many years on the Continent. She would scarcely consider herself an American."

"I beg your pardon," Mr. Sabin remarked courteously. "One can see at least that she has acquired the polish of the only habitable country in the world.

But if I had taken the liberty of guessing at her nationality, I should have taken her to be a German."

Mr. Watson raised his eyebrows, and somehow managed to drop the match he was raising to his cigar.

"You astonish me very much, sir," he remarked. "I always looked upon the fair, rotund woman as the typical German face."

Mr. Sabin shook his head gently.

"There are many types," he said "and nationality, you know, does not always go by complexion or size. For instance, you are very like many American gentlemen whom I have had the pleasure of meeting, but at the same time I should not have taken you for an American."

The captain laughed.

"I can't agree with you, Mr. Sabin," he said. "Mr. Watson appears to me to be, if he will pardon my saying so, the very type of the modern American man."

"I'm much obliged to you, Captain," Mr. Watson said cheerfully. "I'm a Boston man, that's sure, and I believe, sir, I'm proud of it. I want to know for what nationality you would have taken me if you had not been informed?"

"I should have looked for you also," Mr. Sabin said deliberately, "in the streets of Berlin."

CHAPTER XLII

A WEAK CONSPIRATOR

At dinner-time Mrs. Watson appeared in a very dainty toilette of black and white, and was installed at the captain's right hand. She was introduced at once to Mr. Sabin, and proceeded to make herself a very agreeable companion.

"Why, I call this perfectly delightful!" was almost her first exclamation, after a swift glance at Mr. Sabin's quiet but irreproachable dinner attire. "You can't imagine how pleased I am to find myself once more in civilised society. I was never so dull in my life as on that poky little yacht."

"Poky little yacht, indeed!" Mr. Watson interrupted, with a note of annoyance in his tone. "The *Mayflower* anyway cost me pretty well two hundred thousand dollars, and she's nearly the largest pleasure yacht afloat."

"I don't care if she cost you a million dollars," Mrs. Watson answered pettishly. "I never want to sail on her again. I prefer this infinitely."

She laughed at Captain Ackinson, and her husband continued his dinner in silence. Mr. Sabin made a mental note of two things—first, that Mr. Watson did not treat his wife with that consideration which is supposed to be distinctive of American husbands, and secondly, that he drank a good deal of wine without becoming even a shade more amiable. His wife somewhat pointedly drank water, and turning her right shoulder upon her husband, devoted herself to the entertainment of her two companions. At the conclusion of the meal the captain was her abject slave, and Mr. Sabin was quite willing to admit that Mrs. J. B. Watson, whatever her nationality might be, was a very charming woman.

After dinner Mr. Sabin went to his lower state room for an overcoat, and whilst feeling for some cigars, heard voices in the adjoining room, which had been empty up to now.

"Won't you come and walk with me, James?" he heard Mrs. Watson say. "It is such a nice evening, and I want to go on deck."

"You can go without me, then," was the gruff answer. "I'm going to have a cigar in the smoke-room."

"You can smoke," she reminded him, "on deck."

"Thanks," he replied, "but I don't care to give my Laranagas to the winds. You would come here, and you must do the best you can. You can't expect to have me dangling after you all the time."

There was a silence, and then the sound of Mr. Watson's heavy tread, as he left the state room, followed in a moment or two by the light footsteps and soft rustle of silk skirts, which indicated the departure also of his wife.

Mr. Sabin carefully enveloped himself in an ulster, and stood for a moment or two wondering whether that conversation was meant to be overheard or not. He rang the bell for the steward.

The man appeared almost immediately. Mr. Sabin had known how to ensure prompt service.

"Was it my fancy, John? or did I hear voices in the state room opposite?" Mr. Sabin asked.

"Mr. and Mrs. Watson have taken it, sir," the man answered.

Mr. Sabin appeared annoyed.

"You know that some of my clothes are hung up there," he remarked, "and I have been using it as a dressing-room. There are heaps of state-rooms vacant. Surely you could have found them another?"

"I did my best, sir," the man answered, "but they seemed to take a particular fancy to that one. I couldn't get them off it nohow."

"Did they know," Mr. Sabin asked carelessly, "that the room opposite was occupied?"

"Yes, sir," the man answered. "I told them that you were in number twelve, and that you used this as a dressing-room, but they wouldn't shift. It was very foolish of them, too, for they wanted two, one each; and they could just as well have had them together."

"Just as well," Mr. Sabin remarked quietly. "Thank you, John. Don't let them know I have spoken to you about it."

"Certainly not, sir."

Mr. Sabin walked upon deck. As he passed the smoke-room he saw Mr. Watson stretched upon a sofa with a cigar in his mouth. Mr. Sabin smiled to himself, and passed on.

The evening promenade on deck after dinner was quite a social event on board the *Calipha*. As a rule the captain and Mr. Sabin strolled together, none of the other passengers, notwithstanding Mr. Sabin's courtesy towards them, having yet attempted in any way to thrust their society upon him. But to-night, as he had half expected, the captain had already a companion. Mrs. Watson, with a very becoming wrap around her head, and a cigarette in her mouth, was walking by his side, chatting gaily most of the time, but listening also with an air of absorbed interest to the personal experiences which her questions provoked. Every now and then, as they passed Mr. Sabin, sometimes walking, sometimes gazing with an absorbed air at the distant chaos of sea and sky, she flashed a glance of invitation upon him, which he as often ignored. Once she half stopped and asked him some slight question, but he answered it briefly standing on one side, and the captain hurried her on. It was a stroke of ill-fortune, he thought to himself, the coming of these two people. He had had a clear start and a fair field; now he was suddenly face to face with a danger, the full extent of which it was hard to estimate. For he could scarcely doubt but that their coming was on his account. They had played their parts well, but they were secret agents of the German police. He smoked his cigar leisurely, the object every few minutes of many side glances and covert smiles from the delicately attired little lady, whose silken skirts, daintily raised from the ground, brushed against him every few minutes as she and her companion passed and repassed. What was their plan of action? he wondered. If it was simply to be assassination, why so elaborate an artifice? and what worse place in the world could there be for anything of the sort than the narrow confines of a small steamer? No, there was evidently something more complex on hand. Was the woman brought as a decoy? he wondered; did they really imagine him capable of being dazzled or fascinated by any woman on the earth? He smiled softly at the thought, and the sight of that smile lingering upon his lips brought her to a standstill. He heard suddenly the swish of her skirt, and her soft voice in his ear. Lower down the deck the captain's broad shoulders were disappearing, as he passed on the way to the engineers' room for his nightly visit of inspection.

"You have not made a single effort to rescue me," she said reproachfully; "you are most unkind."

Mr. Sabin lifted his cap, and removed the cigar from his teeth.

"My dear lady," he said, "I have been suffering the pangs of the neglected, but how dared I break in upon so confidential a *tête-à-tête?*"

"You have little of the courage of your nation, then," she answered laughing, "for I gave you many opportunities. But you have been engrossed with your thoughts, and they succeeded at least where I failed—you were distinctly smiling when I came upon you."

"It was a premonition," he began, but she raised a little white hand, flashing with rings, to his lips, and he was silent.

"Please don't think it necessary to talk nonsense to me all the time," she begged. "Come! I am tired—I want to sit down. Don't you want to take my chair down by the side of the boat there? I like to watch the lights on the water, and you may talk to me—if you like."

"Your husband," he remarked a moment or two later, as he arranged her cushions, "does not care for the evening air?"

"It is sufficient for him," she answered quietly, "that I prefer it. He will not leave the smoking-room until the lights are put out."

"In an ordinary way," he remarked, "that must be dull for you."

"In an ordinary way, and every way," she answered in a low tone, "I am always dull. But, after all, I must not weary a stranger with my woes. Tell me about yourself, Mr. Sabin. Are you going to America on pleasure, or have you business there?"

A faint smile flickered across Mr. Sabin's face. He watched the white ash trembling upon his cigar for a moment before he spoke.

"I can scarcely be said to be going to America on pleasure," he answered, "nor have I any business there. Let us agree that I am going because it is the one country in the world of any importance which I have never visited."

"You have been a great traveller, then," she murmured, looking up at him with innocent, wide-open eyes. "You look as though you have been everywhere. Won't you tell me about some of the odd places you have visited?"

"With pleasure," he answered; "but first won't you gratify a natural and very specific curiosity of mine? I am going to a country which I have never visited before. Tell me a little about it. Let us talk about America."

She stole a sudden, swift glance at her questioner. No, he did not appear to be watching her. His eyes were fixed idly upon the sheet of phosphorescent light which glittered in the steamer's track. Nevertheless, she was a little uneasy.

"America," she said, after a moment's pause, "is the one country I detest. We are only there very seldom—when Mr. Watson's business demands it. You could not seek for information from any one worse informed than I am."

"How strange!" he said softly. "You are the first unpatriotic American I have ever met."

"You should be thankful," she remarked, "that I am an exception. Isn't it pleasant to meet people who are different from other people?"

"In the present case it is delightful!"

"I wonder," she said reflectively, "in which school you studied my sex, and from what particular woman you learned the art of making those little speeches?"

"I can assure you that I am a novice," he declared.

"Then you have a wonderful future before you. You will make a courtier, Mr. Sabin."

"I shall be happy to be the humblest of attendants in the court where you are queen."

"Such proficiency," she murmured, "is the hall mark of insincerity. You are not a man to be trusted, Mr. Sabin."

"Try me," he begged.

"I will! I will tell you a secret."

"I will lock it in the furthest chamber of my inner consciousness."

"I am going to America for a purpose."

"Wonderful woman," he murmured, "to have a purpose."

"I am going to get a divorce!"

Mr. Sabin was suddenly thoughtful.

"I have always understood," he said, "that the marriage laws of America are convenient."

"They are humane. They make me thankful that I am an American."

Mr. Sabin inclined his head slightly towards the smoking-room.

"Does your unfortunate husband know?"

"He does; and he acquiesces. He has no alternative. But is that quite nice of you, Mr. Sabin, to call my husband an unfortunate man?"

"I cannot conceive," he said slowly, "greater misery than to have possessed and lost you."

She laughed gaily. Mr. Sabin permitted himself to admire that laugh. It was like the tinkling of a silver bell, and her teeth were perfect.

"You are incorrigible," she said. "I believe that if I would let you, you would make love to me."

"If I thought," he answered, "that you would never allow me to make love to you, I should feel like following this cigar." He threw it into the sea.

She sighed, and tapped her little French heel upon the deck.

"What a pity that you are like all other men."

"I will say nothing so unkind of you," he remarked. "You are unlike any other woman whom I ever met."

They listened together to the bells sounding from the quarter deck. It was eleven o'clock. The deck behind them was deserted, and a fine drizzling rain was beginning to fall. Mrs. Watson removed the rug from her knees regretfully.

"I must go," she said; "do you hear how late it is?"

"You will tell me all about America," he said, rising and drawing back her chair, "to-morrow?"

"If we can find nothing more interesting to talk about," she said, looking up at him with a sparkle in her dark eyes. "Good-night."

Her hand, very small and white, and very soft, lingered in his. At that moment an unpleasant voice sounded in their ears.

"Do you know the time, Violet? The lights are out all over the ship. I don't understand what you are doing on deck."

Mr. Watson was not pleasant to look upon. His eyes were puffy, and swollen, and he was not quite steady upon his feet. His wife looked at him in cold displeasure.

"The lights are out in the smoke-room, I suppose," she said, "or we should not have the pleasure of seeing you. Good-night, Mr. Sabin! Thank you so much for looking after me!"

Mr. Sabin bowed and walked slowly away, lighting a fresh cigarette. If it was acting, it was very admirably done.

CHAPTER XLIII

THE COMING OF THE "KAISER WILHELM"

The habit of early rising was one which Mr. Sabin had never cultivated, and breakfast was a meal which he abhorred. It was not until nearly midday on the following morning that he appeared on deck, and he had scarcely exchanged his customary greeting with the captain, before he was joined by Mr. Watson, who had obviously been on the look-out for him.

"I want, sir," the latter commenced, "to apologise to you for my conduct last night."

Mr. Sabin looked at him keenly.

"There is no necessity for anything of the sort," he said. "If any apology is owing at all, it is, I think, to your wife."

Mr. Watson shook his head vigorously.

"No, sir," he declared, "I am ashamed to say that I am not very clear as to the actual expressions I made, but Mrs. Watson has assured me that my behaviour to you was discourteous in the extreme."

"I hope you will think no more of it. I had already," Mr. Sabin said, "forgotten the circumstance. It is not of the slightest consequence."

"You are very good," Mr. Watson said softly.

"I had the pleasure," Mr. Sabin remarked, "of an interesting conversation with your wife last night. You are a very fortunate man."

"I think so indeed, sir," Mr. Watson replied modestly.

"American women," Mr. Sabin continued, looking meditatively out to sea, "are very fascinating."

"I have always found them so," Mr. Watson agreed.

"Mrs. Watson," Mr. Sabin said, "told me so much that was interesting about your wonderful country that I am looking forward to my visit more than ever."

Mr. Watson darted a keen glance at his companion. He was suddenly on his guard. For the first time he realised something of the resources of this man with whom he had to deal.

"My wife," he said, "knows really very little of her native country; she has lived nearly all her life abroad."

"So I perceived," Mr. Sabin answered. "Shall we sit down a moment, Mr. Watson? One wearies so of this incessant promenading, and there is a little matter which I fancy that you and I might discuss with advantage."

Mr. Watson obeyed in silence. This was a wonderful man with whom he had to deal. Already he felt that all the elaborate precautions of his coming had been wasted. He might be Mr. James B. Watson, the New York yacht owner and millionaire, to the captain and his seven passengers, but he was nothing of the sort to Mr. Sabin. He shrugged his shoulders, and followed him to a seat. After all silence was a safe card.

"I'm going," Mr. Sabin said, "to be very frank with you. I know, of course, who you are."

Mr. Watson shrugged his shoulders.

"Do you?" he remarked dryly.

Mr. Sabin bowed, with a faint smile at the corner of his lips.

"Certainly," he answered, "you are Mr. James B. Watson of New York, and the lady with you is your wife. Now I want to tell you a little about myself."

"Most interested, I'm sure," Mr. Watson murmured.

"My real name," Mr. Sabin said, turning a little as though to face his companion, "is Victor Duc de Souspennier. It suits me at present to travel under the name by which I was known in England and by which you are in the habit of addressing me. Mr. Watson, I'm leaving England because a certain scheme of mine, which, if successful, would have revolutionised the whole face of Europe, has by a most unfortunate chance become a failure. I have incurred thereby the resentment, perhaps I should say the just resentment, of a great nation. I am on my way to the country where I concluded I should be safest against those means of, shall I say, retribution, or vengeance, which will assuredly be used against me. Now what I want to say to you, Mr. Watson, is this—I am a rich man, and I value my life at a great deal of money. I wonder if by any chance you understand me."

Mr. Watson smiled.

"I'm curious to know," he said softly, "at what price you value yourself."

"My account in New York," Mr. Sabin said quietly, "is, I believe, something like ten thousand pounds."

"Fifty thousand dollars," Mr. Watson remarked, "is a nice little sum for one, but an awkward amount to divide."

Mr. Sabin lit a cigarette and breathed more freely. He began to see his way.

"I forgot the lady," he murmured. "The expense of cabling is not great. For the sake of argument, let us say twenty thousand."

Mr. Watson rose.

"So far as I'm concerned," he said, "it is a satisfactory sum. Forgive me if I leave you for a few minutes, I must have a little talk with Mrs. Watson."

Mr. Sabin nodded.

"We will have a cigar together after lunch," he said. "I must have my morning game of shuffleboard with the captain."

Mr. Watson went below, and Mr. Sabin played shuffleboard with his usual deadly skill.

A slight mist had settled around them by the time the game was over, and the fog-horn was blowing, the captain went on the bridge, and the engines were checked to half speed.

Mr. Sabin leaned over the side of the vessel, and gazed thoughtfully into the dense white vapour.

"I think," he said softly to himself, "that after all I'm safe."

There was perfect silence on the ship. Even the luncheon gong had not sounded, the passengers having been summoned in a whisper by the deck steward. The fog seemed to be getting denser and the sea was like glass. Suddenly there was a little commotion aft, and the captain leaning forward shouted some brief orders. The fog-horn emitted a series of spasmodic and hideous shrills, and beyond a slight drifting the steamer was almost motionless.

Mr. Sabin understood at once that somewhere, it might be close at hand, or it might be a mile away, the presence of another steamer had been detected.

The same almost ghostlike stillness continued, orders were passed backward and forward in whispers. The men walked backward and forward on tip-toe. And then suddenly, without any warning, they passed out into the clear air, the mist rolled away, the sun shone down upon them again, and the decks dried as though by magic. Cheerful voices broke in upon the chill and unnatural silence. The machinery recommenced to throb, and the passengers who had finished lunch went upon deck. Every one was attracted at once by the sight of a large white steamer about a mile on the starboard side.

Mr. Watson joined the captain, who was examining her through his glass.

"Man-of-war, isn't she?" he inquired.

The captain nodded.

"Not much doubt about that," he answered; "look at her guns. The odd part of it is, too, she is flying no flag. We shall know who she is in a minute or two, though."

Mr. Sabin descended the steps on his way to a late luncheon. As he turned the corner he came face to face with Mr. Watson, whose eyes were fixed upon the coming steamer with a very curious expression.

"Man-of-war," Mr. Sabin remarked. "You look as though you had seen her before."

Mr. Watson laughed harshly.

"I should like to see her," he remarked, "at the bottom of the sea."

Mr. Sabin looked at him in surprise.

"You know her, then?" he remarked.

"I know her," Mr. Watson answered, "too well. She is the *Kaiser Wilhelm*, and she is going to rob me of twenty thousand pounds."

CHAPTER XLIV

THE GERMANS ARE ANNOYED

Mr. Sabin ate his luncheon with unimpaired appetite and with his usual care that everything of which he partook should be so far as possible of the best. The close presence of the German man-of-war did not greatly alarm him. He had some knowledge of the laws and courtesies of maritime life, and he could not conceive by what means short of actual force he could be inveigled on board of her. Mr. Watson's last words had been a little disquieting, but he probably held an exaggerated opinion as to the powers possessed by his employers. Mr. Sabin had been in many tighter places than this, and he had sufficient belief in the country of his recent adoption to congratulate himself that it was an English boat on which he was a passenger. He proceeded to make himself agreeable to Mrs. Watson, who, in a charming costume of blue and white, and a fascinating little hat, had just come on to luncheon.

"I have been talking," he remarked, after a brief pause in their conversation, "to your husband this morning."

She looked up at him with a meaning smile upon her face.

"So he has been telling me."

"I hope," Mr. Sabin continued gently, "that your advice to him—I take it for granted that he comes to you for advice—was in my favour."

"It was very much in your favour," she answered, leaning across towards him. "I think that you knew it would be."

"I hoped at least——"

Mr. Sabin broke off suddenly in the midst of his sentence, and turning round looked out of the open port-hole. Mrs. Watson had dropped her knife and fork and was holding her hands to her ears. The saloon itself seemed to be shaken by the booming of a gun fired at close quarters.

"What is it?" she exclaimed, looking across at him with frightened eyes. "What can have happened! England is not at war with anybody, is she?"

Mr. Sabin looked up with a quiet smile from the salad which he was mixing.

"It is simply a signal from another ship," he answered. "She wants us to stop."

"What ship? Do you know anything about it? Do you know what they want?"

"Not exactly," Mr. Sabin said. "At the same time I have some idea. The ship who fired that signal is a German man-of-war, and you see we are stopping."

Of the two Mrs. Watson was certainly the most nervous. Her fingers shook so that the wine in her glass was spilt. She set her glass down and looked across at her companion.

"They will take you away," she murmured.

"I think not," Mr. Sabin answered. "I am inclined to think that I am perfectly safe. Will you try some of my salad?"

A look of admiration flashed for a moment across her face,

"You are a wonderful man," she said softly. "No salad, thanks! I am too nervous to eat. Let us go on deck!"

Mr. Sabin rose, and carefully selected a cigarette.

"I can assure you," he said, "that they are powerless to do anything except attempt to frighten Captain Ackinson. Of course they might succeed in that, but I don't think it is likely. Let us go and hear what he has to say."

Captain Ackinson was standing alone on the deck, watching the man-of-war's boat which was being rapidly pulled towards the *Calipha*. He was obviously in a bad temper. There was a black frown upon his forehead which did not altogether disappear when he turned his head and saw them approaching.

"Are we arrested, Captain?" Mr. Sabin asked. "Why couldn't they signal what they wanted?"

"Because they're blistering idiots," Captain Ackinson answered. "They blither me to stop, and I signalled back to ask their reason, and I'm dashed if they didn't put a shot across my bows. As if I hadn't lost enough time already without fooling."

"Thanks to us, I am afraid, Captain," Mrs. Watson put in.

"Well, I'm not regretting that, Mrs. Watson," the captain answered gallantly. "We got something for stopping there, but we shall get nothing decent from these confounded Germans, I am very sure. By the bye, can you speak their lingo, Mr. Sabin?"

"Yes," Mr. Sabin answered, "I can speak German. Can I be of any assistance to you?"

"You might stay with me if you will," Captain Ackinson answered, "in case they don't speak English."

Mr. Sabin remained by the captain's side, standing with his hands behind him. Mrs. Watson leaned over the rail close at hand, watching the approaching boat, and exchanging remarks with the doctor. In a few minutes the boat was alongside, and an officer in the uniform of the German Navy rose and made a stiff salute.

"Are you the captain?" he inquired, in stiff but correct English.

The captain returned his salute.

"I am Captain Ackinson, Cunard ss. *Calipha*," he answered. "What do you want with me?"

"I am Captain Von Dronestein, in command of the *Kaiser Wilhelm*, German Navy," was the reply. "I want a word or two with you in private, Captain Ackinson. Can I come on board?"

Captain Ackinson's reply was not gushing. He gave the necessary orders, however, and in a few moments Captain Von Dronestein, and a thin, dark man in the dress of a civilian, clambered to the deck. They looked at Mr. Sabin, standing by the captain's side, and exchanged glances of intelligence.

"If you will kindly permit us, Captain," the newcomer said, "we should like to speak with you in private. The matter is one of great importance."

Mr. Sabin discreetly retired. The captain turned on his heel and led the way to his cabin. He pointed briefly to the lounge against the wall and remained himself standing.

"Now, gentlemen, if you please," he said briskly, "to business. You have stopped a mail steamer in mid ocean by force, so I presume you have something of importance to say. Please say it and let me go on. I am behind time now."

The German held up his hands. "We have stopped you," he said, "it is true, but not by force. No! No!"

"I don't know what else you call it when you show me a bounding thirty guns and put a shot across my bows."

"It was a blank charge," the German began, but Captain Ackinson interrupted him.

"It was nothing of the sort!" he declared bluntly. "I was on deck and I saw the charge strike the water."

"It was then contrary to my orders," Captain Dronestein declared, "and in any case it was not intended for intimidation."

"Never mind what it was intended for. I have my own opinion about that," Captain Ackinson remarked impatiently. "Proceed if you please!"

"In the first place permit me to introduce the Baron Von Graisheim, who is attached to the Ministry for Foreign Affairs at Berlin."

Captain Ackinson's acknowledgment of the introduction was barely civil. The German continued—

"I am afraid you will not consider my errand here a particularly pleasant one, Herr Captain. I have a warrant here for the arrest of one of your passengers, whom I have to ask you to hand over to me."

"A what!" Captain Ackinson exclaimed, with a spot of deep colour stealing through the tan of his cheeks.

"A warrant," Dronestein continued, drawing an imposing looking document from his breast pocket. "If you will examine it you will perceive that it is in perfect order. It bears, in fact," he continued, pointing with reverential forefinger to a signature near the bottom of the document, "the seal of his most august Majesty, the Emperor of Germany."

Captain Ackinson glanced at the document with imperturbable face.

"What is the name of the gentleman to whom all this refers?" he inquired.

"The Duc de Souspennier!"

"The name," Captain Ackinson remarked, "is not upon my passengers' list."

"He is travelling under the alias of 'Mr. Sabin,'" Baron Von Graisheim interjected.

"And do you expect me," Captain Ackinson remarked, "to hand over the person in question to you on the authority of that document?"

"Certainly!" the two men exclaimed with one voice.

"Then I am very sorry indeed," Captain Ackinson declared, "that you should have had the temerity to stop my ship, and detain me here on such a fool's errand. We are on the high seas and under the English flag. The document you have just shown me impeaching the Duc de Souspennier for 'lèse majestie' and high treason, and all the rest of it, is not worth the paper it is written on here, nor, I should think in America. I must ask you to leave my ship at once, gentlemen, and I can promise you that my employers, the Cunard ss. Company, will bring a claim against your Government for this unwarrantable detention."

"You must, if you please, be reasonable," Captain Dronestein said. "We have force behind us, and we are determined to rescue this man at all costs."

Captain Ackinson laughed scornfully.

"I shall be interested to see what measures of force you will employ," he remarked. "You may have a tidy bill to pay as it is, for that shot you put across my bows. If you try another it may cost you the *Kaiser Wilhelm* and the whole of the German Navy. Now, if you please, I've no more time to waste."

Captain Ackinson moved towards the door. Dronestein laid his hand upon his arm.

"Captain Ackinson," he said, "do not be rash. If I have seemed too peremptory in this matter, remember that Germany as my fatherland is as dear to me as England to you, and this man whose arrest I am commissioned to effect has earned for himself the deep enmity of all patriots. Listen to me, I beg. You run not one shadow of risk in delivering this man up to my custody. He has no country with whom you might become embroiled. He is a French Royalist, who has cast himself adrift altogether from his country, and is indeed her enemy. Apart from that, his detention, trial and sentence, would be before a secret court. He would simply disappear. As for you, you need not fear but that your services will be amply recognised. Make your claims now for this detention of your steamer; fix it if you will at five or even ten thousand pounds, and I will satisfy it on the spot by a draft on the Imperial Exchequer. The man can be nothing to you. Make a great country your debtor. You will never regret it."

Captain Ackinson shook his arm free from the other's grasp, and strode out on to the deck.

"*Kaiser Wilhelm* boat alongside," he shouted, blowing his whistle. "Smith, have these gentlemen lowered at once, and pass the word to the engineer's room, full speed ahead."

He turned to the two men, who had followed him out.

"You had better get off my ship before I lose my temper," he said bluntly. "But rest assured that I shall report this attempt at intimidation and bribery to my employers, and they will without doubt lay the matter before the Government."

"But Captain Ackinson——"

"Not another word, sir."

"My dear——"

Captain Ackinson turned his back upon the two men, and with a stiff, military salute turned towards the bridge. Already the machinery was commencing to throb. Mr. Watson, who was hovering near, came up and helped them to descend. A few apparently casual remarks passed between the three men. From a little lower down Mr. Sabin and Mrs. Watson leaned over the rail and watched the visitors lowered into their boat.

"That was rather a foolish attempt," he remarked lightly; "nevertheless they seem disappointed."

She looked after them pensively.

"I wish I knew what they said to—my husband," she murmured.

"Orders for my assassination, very likely," he remarked lightly. "Did you see your husband's face when he passed us?"

She nodded, and looked behind. Mr. Watson had entered the smoke-room. She drew a little nearer to Mr. Sabin and dropped her voice almost to a whisper.

"What you have said in jest is most likely the truth. Be very careful!"

CHAPTER XLV

MR. SABIN IN DANGER

Mr. Sabin found the captain by no means inclined to talk about the visit which they had just received. He was still hurt and ruffled at the propositions which had been made to him, and annoyed at the various delays which seemed conspiring to prevent him from making a decent passage.

"I have been most confoundedly insulted by those d—— Germans," he said to Mr. Sabin, meeting him a little later in the gangway. "I don't know exactly what your position may be, but you will have to be on your guard. They have gone on to New York, and I suppose they will try and get their warrant endorsed there before we land."

"They have a warrant, then?" Mr. Sabin remarked.

"They showed me something of the sort," the captain answered scornfully. "And it is signed by the Kaiser. But, of course, here it isn't worth the paper it is written on, and America would never give you up without a special extradition treaty."

Mr. Sabin smiled. He had calculated all the chances nicely, and a volume of international law was lying at that moment in his state-room face downwards.

"I think," he said, "that I am quite safe from arrest, but at the same time, Captain, I am very sorry to be such a troublesome passenger to you."

The captain shrugged his shoulders. "Oh, it is not your fault," he said; "but I have made up my mind about one thing. I am not going to stop my ship this side of Boston Harbour for anything afloat. We have lost half a day already."

"If the Cunard Company will send me the extra coal bill," Mr. Sabin said, "I will pay it cheerfully, for I am afraid that both stoppages have been on my account."

"Bosh!" The Captain, who was moving away, stopped short. "You had nothing to do with these New Yorkers and their broken-down yacht."

Mr. Sabin finished lighting a cigarette which he had taken from his case, and, passing his arm through the captain's, drew him a little further away from the gangway.

"I'm afraid I had," he said. "As a matter of fact they are not New Yorkers, and they are not husband and wife. They are simply agents in the pay of the German secret police."

"What, spies!" the captain exclaimed.

Mr. Sabin nodded.

"Exactly!"

The captain was still incredulous. "Do you mean to tell me," he exclaimed, "that charming little woman is not an American at all?—that she is a fraud?"

"There isn't a shadow of a doubt about it," Mr. Sabin replied. "They have both tacitly admitted it. As a matter of fact I am in treaty now to buy them over. They were on the point of accepting my terms when these fellows boarded us. Whether they will do so now I cannot tell. I saw that fellow Graisheim talking to the man just before they left the vessel."

"You are safe while you are on my ship, Mr. Sabin," the captain said firmly. "I shall watch that fellow Watson closely, and if he gives me the least chance, I will have him put in irons. Confound the man and his plausible——"

They were interrupted by the deck steward, who came with a message from Mrs. Watson. She was making tea on deck—might she have the loan of the captain's table, and would they come?

The captain gave the necessary assent, but was on the point of declining the invitation. "I don't want to go near the people," he said.

"On the other hand," Mr. Sabin objected, "I do not want them to think, at present at any rate, that I have told you who they are. You had better come."

They crossed the deck to a sunny little corner behind one of the boats, where Mrs. Watson had just completed her preparation for tea.

She greeted them gaily and chatted to them while they waited for the kettle to boil, but to Mr. Sabin's observant eyes there was a remarkable change in her. Her laughter was forced and she was very pale.

Several times Mr. Sabin caught her watching him in an odd way as though she desired to attract his attention, but Mr. Watson, who for once had seemed to desert the smoking-room, remained by her side like a shadow. Mr. Sabin felt that his presence was ominous. The tea was made and handed round.

Mr. Watson sent away the deck steward, who was preparing to wait upon them, and did the honours himself. He passed the sugar to the captain and stood before Mr. Sabin with the sugar-tongs in his hand.

"Sugar?" he inquired, holding out a lump.

Mr. Sabin took sugar, and was on the point of holding out his cup. Just then he chanced to glance across to Mrs. Watson. Her eyes were dilated and she seemed to be on the point of springing from her chair. Meeting his glance she shook her head, and then bent over her hot water apparatus.

"No sugar, thanks," Mr. Sabin answered. "This tea looks too good to spoil by any additions. One of the best things I learned in Asia was to take my tea properly. Help yourself, Mr. Watson."

Mr. Watson rather clumsily dropped the piece of sugar which he had been holding out to Mr. Sabin, and the ship giving a slight lurch just at that moment, it rolled down the deck and apparently into the sea. With a little remark as to his clumsiness he resumed his seat.

Mr. Sabin looked into his tea and across to Mrs. Watson. The slightest of nods was sufficient for him. He drank it off and asked for some more.

The tea party on the whole was scarcely a success. The Captain was altogether upset and quite indisposed to be amiable towards people who had made a dupe of him. Mrs. Watson seemed to be suffering from a state of nervous excitement, and her husband was glum and silent. Mr. Sabin alone appeared to be in good spirits, and he talked continually with his customary ease and polish.

The Captain did not stay very long, and upon his departure Mr. Sabin also rose.

"Am I to have the pleasure of taking you for a little walk, Mrs. Watson?" he asked.

She looked doubtfully at the tall, glum figure by her side, and her face was almost haggard.

"I'm afraid—I think—I think—Mr. Watson has just asked me to walk with him," she said, lamely; "we must have our stroll later on."

"I shall be ready and delighted at any time," Mr. Sabin answered with a bow.

"We are going to have a moon to-night; perhaps you may be tempted to walk after dinner."

He ignored the evident restraint of both the man and the woman and strolled away. Having nothing in particular to do he went into his deck cabin to dress a little earlier than usual, and when he had emerged the dinner gong had not yet sounded.

The deck was quite deserted, and lighting a *cigarette d'appetit*, he strolled past the scene of their tea-party. A dark object under the boat attracted his attention. He stooped down and looked at it. Thomas, the ship's cat, was lying there stiff and stark, and by the side of his outstretched tongue a lump of sugar.

CHAPTER XLVI

MR. WATSON IS ASTONISHED

At dinner-time Mr. Sabin was the most silent of the little quartette who occupied the head of the table. The captain, who had discovered that notwithstanding their stoppage they had made a very fair day's run, and had just noticed a favourable change in the wind, was in a better humour, and on the whole was disposed to feel satisfied with himself for the way he had repulsed the captain of the *Kaiser Wilhelm*. He departed from his usual custom so far as to drink a glass of Mr. Sabin's champagne, having first satisfied himself as to the absence of any probability of fog. Mr. Watson, too, was making an effort to appear amiable, and his wife, though her colour seemed a trifle hectic and her laughter not altogether natural, contributed her share to the conversation. Mr. Sabin alone was curiously silent and distant. Many times he had escaped death by what seemed almost a fluke; more often than most men he had been at least in danger of losing it. But this last adventure had made a distinct and deep impression upon him. He had not seriously believed that the man Watson was prepared to go to such lengths; he recognised for the first time his extreme danger. Then as regards the woman he was genuinely puzzled. He owed her his life, he could not doubt it. She had given him the warning by which he had profited, and she had given it him behind his companion's back. He was strongly inclined to believe in her. Still, she was doubtless in fear of the man. Her whole appearance denoted it. She was still, without doubt, his tool, willing or unwilling.

They lingered longer than usual over their dessert. It was noticeable that throughout their conversation all mention of the events of the day was excluded. A casual remark of Mr. Watson's the captain had ignored. There was an obvious inclination to avoid the subject. The captain was on the *qui vive* all the time, and he promptly quashed any embarrassing remark. So far as Mrs. Watson was concerned there was certainly no fear of her exhibiting any curiosity. It was hard to believe that she was the same woman who had virtually taken the conversation into her own hands on the previous evening, and had talked to them so well and so brightly. She sat there, white and cowed, looking a great deal at Mr. Sabin with sad, far-away eyes, and seldom originating a remark. Mr. Watson, on the contrary, talked incessantly, in marked contrast to his previous silence; he drank no wine, but seemed in the best of spirits. Only once did he appear at a loss, and that was when the captain, helping himself to some nuts, turned towards Mr. Sabin and asked a question—

"I wonder, Mr. Sabin, whether you ever heard of an Indian nut called, I believe, the Fakella? They say that an oil distilled from its kernel is the most deadly poison in the world."

"I have both heard of it and seen it," Mr. Sabin answered. "In fact, I may say, that I have tasted it—on the tip of my finger."

"And yet," the captain remarked, laughing, "you are alive."

"And yet I am alive," Mr. Sabin echoed. "But there is nothing very wonderful in that. I am poison-proof."

Mr. Watson was in the act of raising a hastily filled glass to his lips when his eyes met Mr. Sabin's. He set it down hurriedly, white to the lips. He knew, then! Surely there must be something supernatural about the man. A conviction of his own absolute impotence suddenly laid hold of him. He was completely shaken. Of what use were the ordinary weapons of his kind against an antagonist such as this? He knew nothing of the silent evidence against him on deck. He could only attribute Mr. Sabin's foreknowledge of what had been planned against him to the miraculous. He stumbled to his feet, and muttering something about some cigars, left his place. Mrs. Watson rose almost immediately afterwards. As she turned to walk down the saloon she dropped her handkerchief. Mr. Sabin, who had risen while she passed out, stooped down and picked it up. She took it with a smile of thanks and whispered in his ear—

"Come on deck with me quickly; I want to speak to you."

He obeyed, turning round and making some mute sign to the captain. She walked swiftly up the stairs after a frightened glance down the corridor to their state-rooms. A fresh breeze blew in their faces as they stepped out on deck, and Mr. Sabin glanced at her bare neck and arms.

"You will be cold," he said. "Let me fetch you a wrap."

"Don't leave me," she exclaimed quickly. "Walk to the side of the steamer. Don't look behind."

Mr. Sabin obeyed. Directly she was sure that they were really beyond earshot of any one she laid her hand upon his arm.

"I am going to ask you a strange question," she said. "Don't stop to think what it means, but answer me at once. Where are you going to sleep to-night—in your state-room or in the deck cabin?"

He started a little, but answered without hesitation—

"In my deck cabin."

"Then don't," she exclaimed quickly. "Say that you are going to if you are asked, mind that. Sit up on deck, out of sight, all night, stay with the captain—anything—but don't sleep there, and whatever you may see don't be surprised, and please don't think too badly of me."

He was surprised to see that her cheeks were burning and her eyes were wet. He laid his hand tenderly upon her arm.

"I will promise that at any rate," he said.

"And you will remember what I have told you?"

"Most certainly," he promised. "Your warnings are not things to be disregarded."

She drew a quick little breath and looked nervously over her shoulders.

"I am afraid," he said kindly, "that you are not well to-day. Has that fellow been frightening or ill-using you?"

Her face was very close to his, and he fancied that he could hear her teeth chattering. She was obviously terrified.

"We must not be talking too seriously," she murmured. "He may be here at any moment. I want you to remember that there is a price set upon you and he means to earn it. He would have killed you before, but he wants to avoid detection. You had better tell the captain everything. Remember, you must be on the watch always."

"I can protect myself now that I am warned," he said, reassuringly. "I have carried my life in my hands many a time before. But you?"

She shivered.

"They tell me," she whispered, "that from Boston you can take a train right across the Continent, thousands of miles. I am going to take the very first one that starts when I land, and I am going to hide somewhere in the furthest corner of the world I can get to. To live in such fear would drive me mad, and I am not a coward. Let us walk; he will not think so much of our being together then."

"I am going to send for a wrap," he said, looking down at her thin dinner dress; "it is much too cold for you here bare-headed. We will send the steward for something."

They turned round to find a tall form at their elbows. Mr. Watson's voice, thin and satirical, broke the momentary silence.

"You are in a great hurry for fresh air, Violet. I have brought your cape; allow me to put it on."

He stooped down and threw the wrap over her shoulders. Then he drew her reluctant fingers through his arm.

"You were desiring to walk," he said. "Very well, we will walk together."

Mr. Sabin watched them disappear and, lighting a cigar, strolled off towards the captain's room. Many miles away now he could still see the green light of the German man-of-war.

CHAPTER XLVII

A CHARMED LIFE

The night was still enough, but piled-up masses of black clouds obscured a weakly moon, and there were only now and then uncertain gleams of glimmering light. There was no fog, nor any sign of any. The captain slept in his room, and on deck the steamer was utterly deserted. Only through the black darkness she still bounded on, her furnaces roaring, and the black trail of smoke leaving a long clear track behind her. It seemed as though every one were sleeping on board the steamer except those who fed her fires below and the grim, silent figure who stood in the wheelhouse.

Mr. Sabin, who, muffled up with rugs, was reclining in a deck chair, drawn up in the shadow of the long boat, was already beginning to regret that he had attached any importance at all to Mrs. Watson's warning. It wanted only an hour or so of dawn. All night long he had sat there in view of the door of his deck cabin and shivered. To sleep had been impossible, his dozing was only fitful and unrestful. His hands were thrust deep down into the pockets of his overcoat—the revolver had long ago slipped from his cold fingers. More than once he had made up his mind to abandon his watch, to enter his room, and chance what might happen. And then suddenly there came what he had been waiting for all this while—a soft footfall along the deck: some one was making their way now from the gangway to the door of his cabin.

The frown on his forehead deepened; he leaned stealthily forward watching and listening intently. Surely that was the rustling of a silken gown, that gleam of white behind the funnel was the fluttering of a woman's skirt. Suddenly he saw her distinctly. She was wearing a long white dressing-gown, and noiseless slippers of some kind. Her face was very pale and her eyes seemed fixed and dilated. Once, twice she looked nervously behind her, then she paused before the door of his cabin, hesitated for a moment, and finally passed over the threshold. Mr. Sabin, who had been about to spring forward, paused. After all perhaps he was safer where he was.

There was a full minute during which nothing happened. Mr. Sabin, who had now thoroughly regained his composure, lingered in the shadow of the boat prepared to wait upon the course of events, but a man's footstep this time fell softly upon the deck. Some one had emerged from the gangway and was crossing towards his room. Mr. Sabin peered cautiously through the twilight. It was Mr. Watson, of New York, partially dressed, with a revolver flashing in his hand. Then Mr. Sabin perceived the full wisdom of having remained where he was.

Under the shadow of the boat he drew a little nearer to the door of the cabin. There was absolute silence within. What they were doing he could not imagine, but the place was in absolute darkness. Thoroughly awake now he crouched within a few feet of the door listening intently. Once he fancied that he could hear a voice, it seemed to him that a hand was groping along the wall for the knob of the electric light. Then the door was softly opened and the woman came out. She stood for a moment leaning a little forward, listening intently ready to make her retreat immediately she was assured that the coast was clear! She was a little pale, but in a stray gleam of moonlight Mr. Sabin fancied that he caught a glimpse of a smile upon her parted lips. There was a whisper from behind her shoulder; she answered in a German monosyllable. Then, apparently satisfied that she was unobserved, she stepped out, and, flitting round the funnel, disappeared down the gangway. Mr. Sabin made no attempt to stop her or to disclose his presence. His fingers had closed now upon his revolver—he was waiting for the man. The minutes crept on—nothing happened. Then a hand softly closed the window looking out upon the deck, immediately afterwards the door was pushed open and Mr. Watson, with a handkerchief to his mouth, stepped out.

He stood perfectly still listening for a moment. Then he was on the point of stealing away, when a hand fell suddenly upon his shoulder. He was face to face with Mr. Sabin.

He started back with a slight but vehement guttural interjection. His hand stole down towards his pocket, but the shining argument in Mr. Sabin's hand was irresistible.

"Step back into that room, Mr. Watson; I want to speak to you."

He hesitated. Mr. Sabin reaching across him opened the door of the cabin. Immediately they were assailed with the fumes of a strange, sickly odour! Mr. Sabin laughed softly, but a little bitterly.

"A very old-fashioned device," he murmured. "I gave you credit for more ingenuity, my friend. Come, I have opened the window and the door you see! Let us step inside. There will be sufficient fresh air."

Mr. Watson was evidently disinclined to make the effort. He glanced covertly up the deck, and seemed to be preparing himself for a rush. Again that little argument of steel and the grim look on Mr. Sabin's face prevailed. They both crossed the threshold. The odour, though powerful, was almost nullified by the rushing of the salt wind through the open window and door which Mr. Sabin had fixed open with a catch. Reaching out his hand he pulled down a little brass hook—the room was immediately lit with the soft glare of the electric light.

Mr. Sabin, having assured himself that his companion's revolver was safely bestowed in his hip pocket and could not be reached without warning, glanced carefully around his cabin.

He looked first towards the bed and smiled. His little device, then, had succeeded. The rug which he had rolled up under the sheets into the shape of a human form was undisturbed. In the absence of a light Mr. Watson had evidently taken for granted that the man whom he had sought to destroy was really in the room. The two men suddenly exchanged glances, and Mr. Sabin smiled at the other's look of dismay.

"It was not like you," he said gently; "it was really very clumsy indeed to take for granted my presence here. I have great faith in you and your methods, my friend, but do you think that it would have been altogether wise for me to have slept here alone with unfastened door—under the circumstances?"

Mr. Watson admitted his error with a gleam in his dark eyes, which Mr. Sabin accepted as an additional warning.

"Your little device," he continued, raising an unstopped flask from the table by the side of the bed, "is otherwise excellent, and I feel that I owe you many thanks for arranging a death that should be painless. You might have made other plans which would have been not only more clumsy, but which might have caused me a considerable amount of personal inconvenience and discomfort. Your arrangements, I see, were altogether excellent. You arranged for my—er—extermination asleep or awake. If awake the little visit which your charming wife had just paid here was to have provided you at once with a motive for the crime and a distinctly mitigating circumstance. That was very ingenious. Pardon my lighting a cigarette, these fumes are a little powerful. Then if I was asleep and had not been awakened by the time you arrived—well, it was to be a drug! Supposing, my dear Mr. Watson, you do me the favour of emptying this little flask into the sea."

Mr. Watson obeyed promptly. There were several points in his favour to be gained by the destruction of this evidence of his unsuccessful attempt. As he crossed the deck holding the little bottle at arm's length from him a delicate white vapour could be distinctly seen rising from the bottle and vanishing into the air. There was a little hiss like the hiss of a snake as it touched the water, and a spot of white froth marked the place where it sank.

"Much too strong," Mr. Sabin murmured. "A sad waste of a very valuable drug, my friend. Now will you please come inside with me. We must have a little chat. But first kindly stand quite still for one moment. There is no particular reason why I should run any risk. I am going to take that revolver from your pocket and throw it overboard."

Mr Watson's first instinct was evidently one of resistance. Then suddenly he felt the cold muzzle of a revolver upon his forehead.

"If you move," Mr. Sabin said quietly, "you are a dead man. My best policy would be to kill you; I am foolish not to do it. But I hate violence. You are safe if you do as I tell you."

Mr. Watson recognised the fact that his companion was in earnest. He stood quite still and watched his revolver describe a semi-circle in the darkness and a fall with a little splash in the water. Then he followed Mr. Sabin into his cabin.

CHAPTER XLVIII

THE DOOMSCHEN

"I suppose," Mr. Sabin began, closing the door of the cabin behind him, "that I may take it—this episode—as an indication of your refusal to accept the proposals I made to you?"

Mr. Watson did not immediately reply. He had seated himself on the corner of a lounge and was leaning forward, his head resting moodily upon his hands. His sallow face was paler even than usual, and his expression was sullen. He looked, as he undoubtedly was, in an evil humour with himself and all things.

"It was not a matter of choice with me," he muttered. "Look out of your window there and you will see that even here upon the ocean I am under surveillance."

Mr. Sabin's eyes followed the man's forefinger. Far away across the ocean he could see a dim green light almost upon the horizon. It was the German man-of-war.

"That is quite true," Mr. Sabin said. "I admit that there are difficulties, but it seems to me that you have overlooked the crux of the whole matter. I have offered you enough to live on for the rest of your days, without ever returning to Europe. You know very well that you can step off this ship arm-in-arm with me when we reach Boston, even though your man-of-war be alongside the dock. They could not touch you—you could leave your—pardon me—not too honourable occupation once and for ever. America is not the country in which one would choose to live, but it has its resources—it can give you big game and charming women. I have lived there and I know. It is not Europe, but it is the next best thing. Come, you had better accept my terms!"

The man had listened without moving a muscle of his face. There was something almost pitiable in its white, sullen despair. Then his lips parted.

"Would to God I could!" he moaned. "Would to God I had the power to listen to you!"

Mr. Sabin flicked the ash off his cigarette and looked thoughtful. He stroked his grey imperial and kept his eyes on his companion.

"The extradition laws," the other interrupted savagely.

Mr. Sabin shrugged his shoulders. "By all means," he murmured. "Personally I have no interest in them; but if you would talk like a reasonable man and tell me where your difficulty lies I might be able to help you."

The man who had called himself Watson raised his head slowly. His expression remained altogether hopeless. He had the appearance of a man given wholly over to despair.

"Have you ever heard of the Doomschen?" he asked slowly.

Mr. Sabin shuddered. He became suddenly very grave. "You are not one of them?" he exclaimed.

The man bowed his head.

"I am one of those devils," he admitted.

Mr. Sabin rose to his feet and walked up and down the little room.

"Of course," he remarked, "that complicates matters, but there ought to be a way out of it. Let me think for a moment."

The man on the lounge sat still with unchanging face. In his heart he knew that there was no way out of it. The chains which bound him were such as the hand of man had no power to destroy. The arm of his master was long. It had reached him here—it would reach him to the farthermost corner of the world. Nor could Mr. Sabin for the moment see any light. The man was under perpetual sentence of death. There was no country in the world which would not give him up, if called upon to do so.

"What you have told me," Mr. Sabin said, "explains, of course to a certain extent, your present indifference to my offers. But when I first approached you in this way you certainly led me to think——"

"That was before that cursed *Kaiser Wilhelm* came up," Watson interrupted. "I had a plan—I might have made a rush for liberty at any rate!"

"But surely you would have been marked down at Boston," Mr. Sabin said.

"The only friend I have in the world," the other said slowly, "is the manager of the Government's Secret Cable Office at Berlin. He was on my side. It would have given me a chance, but now"—he looked out of the window—"it is hopeless!"

Mr. Sabin resumed his chair and lit a fresh cigarette. He had thought the matter out and began to see light.

"It is rather an awkward fix," he said, "but 'hopeless' is a word which I do not understand. As regards our present dilemma I think that I see an excellent way out of it."

A momentary ray of hope flashed across the man's face. Then he shook his head.

"It is not possible," he murmured.

Mr. Sabin smiled quietly.

"My friend," he said, "I perceive that you are a pessimist! You will find yourself in a very short time a free man with the best of your life before you. Take my advice. Whatever career you embark in do so in a more sanguine spirit. Difficulties to the man who faces them boldly lose half their strength. But to proceed. You are one of those who are called 'Doomschen.' That means, I believe, that you have committed a crime punishable by death,—that you are on parole only so long as you remain in the service of the Secret Police of your country. That is so, is it not?"

The man assented grimly. Mr. Sabin continued—

"If you were to abandon your present task and fail to offer satisfactory explanations—if you were to attempt to settle down in America, your extradition, I presume, would at once be applied for. You would be given no second chance."

"I should be shot without a moment's hesitation," Watson admitted grimly.

"Exactly; and there is, I believe, another contingency. If you should succeed in your present enterprise, which, I presume, is my extermination, you would obtain your freedom."

The man on the lounge nodded. A species of despair was upon him. This man was his master in all ways. He would be his master to the end.

"That brings us," Mr. Sabin continued, "to my proposition. I must admit that the details I have not fully thought out yet, but that is a matter of only half an hour or so. I propose that you should kill me in Boston Harbour and escape to your man-of-war. They will, of course, refuse to give you up, and on your return to Germany you will receive your freedom."

"But—but you," Watson exclaimed, bewildered, "you don't want to be killed, surely?"

"I do not intend to be—actually," Mr. Sabin explained. "Exactly how I am going to manage it I can't tell you just now, but it will be quite easy. I shall be dead to the belief of everybody on board here except the captain, and he will be our accomplice. I shall remain hidden until your *Kaiser Wilhelm* has left, and when I do land in America—it shall not be as Mr. Sabin."

Watson rose to his feet He was a transformed man. A sudden hope had brightened his face. His eyes were on fire.

"It is a wonderful scheme!" he exclaimed. "But the captain—surely he will never consent to help?"

"On the contrary," Mr. Sabin answered, "he will do it for the asking. There is not a single difficulty which we cannot easily surmount."

"There is my companion," Watson remarked; "she will have to be reckoned with."

"Leave her," Mr. Sabin said, "to me. I will undertake that she shall be on our side before many hours are passed. You had better go down to your room now. It is getting light and I want to rest."

Watson paused upon the threshold. He pointed in some embarrassment to the table by the side of the bed.

"Is it any use," he murmured in a low tone, "saying that I am sorry for this?"

"You only did—what—in a sense was your duty," Mr. Sabin answered. "I bear no malice—especially since I escaped."

Watson closed the door and Mr. Sabin glanced at the bed. For a moment or two he hesitated, although the desire for sleep had gone by. Then he stepped out on to the deck and leaned thoughtfully over the white railing. Far away eastwards there were signs already of the coming day. A soft grey twilight rested upon the sea; darker and blacker the waters seemed just then by contrast with the lightening skies. A fresh breeze was blowing. There was no living thing within sight save that faint green light where the rolling sea touched the clouds. Mr. Sabin's eyes grew fixed. A curious depression came over him in that half hour before the dawn when all emotion is quickened by that intense brooding stillness. He was passing, he felt, into perpetual exile. He who had been so intimately in touch with the large things of the world had come to that point when after all he was bound to write his life down a failure. For its great desire was no nearer consummation. He had made his grand effort and he had failed. He had been very near success. He had seen closely into the Promised Land. Perhaps it was such thoughts as these which made his non-success the more bitter, and then, with the instincts of a philosopher, he asked himself now, surrounded in fancy by the fragments of his broken dreams, whether it had been worth while. That love of the beautiful and picturesque side of his country which had been his first inspiration, which had been at the root of his passionate patriotism, seemed just then in the grey moments of his despair so weak a thing. He had sacrificed so much to it—his whole life had been moulded and shaped to that one end. There had been other ways in which he might have found happiness. Was he growing morbid, he wondered, bitterly but unresistingly, that her face should suddenly float before his eyes. In fancy he could see her coming towards him there across the still waters, the old brilliant smile upon her lips, the lovelight in her eyes, that calm disdain of all other men written so plainly on the face which should surely have been a queen's.

Mr. Sabin thought of those things which had passed, and he thought of what was to come, and a moment of bitterness crept into his life which he knew must leave its mark for ever. His head drooped into his hands and remained buried there. Thus he stood until the first ray of sunlight travelling across the water fell upon him, and he knew that morning had come. He crossed the deck, and entering his cabin closed the door.

CHAPTER XLIX

MR. SABIN IS SENTIMENTAL

Mr. Sabin found it a harder matter than he had anticipated to induce the captain to consent to the scheme he had formulated. Nevertheless, he succeeded in the end, and by lunch time the following day the whole affair was settled. There was a certain amount of risk in the affair, but, on the other hand, if successfully carried out, it set free once and for ever the two men mainly concerned in it. Mr. Sabin, who was in rather a curious mood, came out of the captain's room a little after one o'clock feeling altogether indisposed for conversation of any sort, ordered his luncheon from the deck steward, and moved his chair apart from the others into a sunny, secluded corner of the boat.

It was here that Mrs. Watson found him an hour later. He heard the rustle of silken draperies across the deck, a faint but familiar perfume suddenly floated into the salt, sunlit air. He looked around to find her bending over him, a miracle of white—cool, dainty, and elegant.

"And why this seclusion, Sir Misanthrope?"

He laughed and dragged her chair alongside of his.

"Come and sit down," he said. "I want to talk to you. I want," he added, lowering his voice, "to thank you for your warning."

They were close together now and alone, cut off from the other chairs by one of the lifeboats. She looked up at him from amongst the cushions with which her chair was hung.

"You understood," she murmured.

"Perfectly."

"You are safe now," she said. "From him at any rate. You have won him over."

"I have found a way of safety," Mr. Sabin said, "for both of us."

She leaned her head upon her delicate white fingers, and looked at him curiously.

"Your plans," she said, "are admirable; but what of me?"

Mr. Sabin regarded her with some faint indication of surprise. He was not sure what she meant. Did she expect a reward for her warning, he wondered. Her words would seem to indicate something of the sort, and yet he was not sure.

"I am afraid," he said kindly, "we have not considered you very much yet. You will go on to Boston, of course. Then I suppose you will return to Germany."

"Never," she exclaimed, with suppressed passion. "I have broken my vows. I shall never set foot in Germany again. I broke them for your sake."

Mr. Sabin looked at her thoughtfully.

"I am glad to hear you say that," he declared. "Believe me, my dear young lady, I have seen a great deal of such matters, and I can assure you that the sooner you break away from all association with this man Watson and his employers the better."

"It is all over," she murmured. "I am a free woman."

Mr. Sabin was delighted to hear it. Yet he felt that there was a certain awkwardness between them. He was this woman's debtor, and he had made no effort to discharge his debt. What did she expect from him? He looked at her through half-closed eyes, and wondered.

"If I can be of any use to you," he suggested softly, "in any fresh start you may make in life, you have only to command me."

She kept her face averted from him. There was land in sight, and she seemed much interested in it.

"What are you going to do in America?"

Mr. Sabin looked out across the sea, and he repeated her question to himself. What was he going to do in this great, strange land, whose ways were not his ways, and whose sympathies lay so far apart from his?

"I cannot tell," he murmured. "I have come here for safety. I have no country nor any friends. This is the land of my exile."

A soft, white hand touched his for a moment. He looked into her face, and saw there an emotion which surprised him.

"It is my exile too," she said. "I shall never dare to return. I have no wish to return."

"But your friends?" Mr. Sabin commenced. "Your family?"

"I have no family."

Mr. Sabin was thoughtful for several moments, then he took out his case and lit a cigarette. He watched the blue smoke floating away over the ship's side, and looked no more at the woman at his elbow.

"If you decide," he said quietly, "to settle in America, you must not allow yourself to forget that I am very much your debtor. I——"

"Your friendship," she interrupted, "I shall be very glad to have. We may perhaps help one another to feel less lonely."

Mr. Sabin gently shook his head.

"I had a friend of your sex once," he said. "I shall—forgive me—never have another."

"Is she dead?"

"If she is dead, it is I who have killed her. I sacrificed her to my ambition. We parted, and for months—for years—I scarcely thought of her, and now the day of retribution has come. I think of her, but it is in vain. Great barriers have rolled between us since those days, but she was my first friend, and she will be my only one."

There was a long silence. Mr. Sabin's eyes were fixed steadily seawards. A flood of recollections had suddenly taken possession of him. When at last he looked round, the chair by his side was vacant.

CHAPTER L

A HARBOUR TRAGEDY

The voyage of the *Calipha* came to its usual termination about ten o'clock on the following morning, when she passed Boston lights and steamed slowly down the smooth waters of the harbour. The seven passengers were all upon deck in wonderfully transformed guise. Already the steamer chairs were being tied up and piled away; the stewards, officiously anxious to render some last service, were hovering around. Mrs. Watson, in a plain tailor gown and quiet felt hat, was sitting heavily veiled apart and alone. There were no signs of either Mr. Watson or Mr. Sabin. The captain was on the bridge talking to the pilot. Scarcely a hundred yards away lay the *Kaiser Wilhelm*, white and stately, with her brass work shining like gold in the sunlight, and her decks as white as snow.

The *Calipha* was almost at a standstill, awaiting the doctor's brig, which was coming up to her on the port side. Every one was leaning over the railing watching her. Mr. Watson and Mr. Sabin, who had just come up the gangway together, turned away towards the deserted side of the boat, engaged apparently in serious conversation. Suddenly every one on deck started. A revolver shot, followed by two heavy splashes in the water, rang out clear and crisp above the clanking of chains and slighter noises. There was a moment's startled silence—every one looked at one another—then a rush for the starboard side of the steamer. Above the little torrent of minor exclamations, the captain's voice sang out like thunder.

"Lower the number one boat. Quartermaster, man a crew."

The seven passengers, two stewards, and a stray seaman arrived on the starboard side of the gangway at about the same moment. There was at first very little to be seen. A faint cloud of blue smoke was curling upwards, and there was a strong odour of gunpowder in the air. On the deck were lying a small, recently-discharged revolver and a man's white linen cap, which, from its somewhat peculiar shape, every one recognised at once as belonging to Mr. Sabin. At first sight, there was absolutely nothing else to be seen. Then, suddenly, some one pointed to a man's head about fifty yards away in the water. Every one crowded to the side to look at it. It was hard at that distance to distinguish the features, but a little murmur arose, doubtful at first, but gaining confidence. It was the head of Mr. Watson. The murmur rather grew than increased when it was seen that he was swimming, not towards the steamer, but away from it, and that he was alone. Where was Mr. Sabin?

A slight cry from behind diverted attention for a moment from the bobbing head. Mrs. Watson, who had heard the murmurs, was lying in a dead faint across a chair. One of the women moved to her side. The others resumed their watch upon events.

A boat was already lowered. Acting upon instructions from the captain, the crew combined a search for the missing man with a leisurely pursuit of the fugitive one. The first lieutenant stood up in the gunwale with a hook in his hand, looking from right to left, and the men pulled with slow, even strokes. But nowhere was there any sign of Mr. Sabin.

The man who was swimming was now almost out of sight, and the first lieutenant, who was in command of the little search party, reluctantly gave orders for the quickening of his men's stroke. But almost as the men bent to their work, a curious thing happened. The fugitive, who had been swimming at a great pace, suddenly threw up his arms and disappeared.

"He's done, by Jove!" exclaimed the lieutenant. "Row hard, you chaps. We must catch him when he rises."

But to all appearance, Mr. J. B. Watson, of New York, never rose again. The boat was rowed time after time around the spot where he had sunk, but not a trace was to be found of him. The only vessel anywhere near was the *Kaiser Wilhelm*. They rowed slowly up and hailed her.

An officer came to the railing and answered their inquiries in execrable English. No, they had not seen any one in the water. They had not picked any one up. Yes, if Herr Lieutenant pleased, he could come on board, but to make a search—no, without authority. No, it was impossible that any one could have been taken on board without his knowledge. He pointed down the steep sides of the steamship and shrugged his shoulders. It was indeed an impossible feat. The lieutenant of the *Calipha* saluted and gave the order to his men to backwater. Once more they went over the ground carefully. There was no sign of either of the men. After about three-quarters of an hour's absence, they reluctantly gave up the search and returned to the *Calipha*.

The first lieutenant was compelled to report both men drowned. The captain was in earnest conversation with an official in plain dark livery. The boat of the harbour police was already waiting below. The whole particulars of the affair were scanty enough. Mr. Sabin and Mr. Watson were seen to emerge from the gangway together, engaged in animated conversation. They had at first turned to the left, but seeing the main body of the passengers assembled there, had stepped back again and emerged on the starboard side which was quite deserted. After then, no one except the captain had even a momentary glimpse of them, and his was so brief that it could scarcely be called more than an impression. He had been attracted by a slight cry, he believed from Mr. Sabin, and had seen both men struggling together in the act of disappearing in the water. He had seen none of the details of the fight; he could not even say whether Mr. Sabin or Mr. Watson had been the aggressor, although on that subject there was only one opinion. Mrs. Watson was absolutely overcome, and unable to answer any questions, but as regards the final quarrel and struggle between the two men, it was impossible for her to have seen anything of it, as she was sitting in a steamer chair on the opposite side of the boat. There was at present absolutely no further light to be thrown upon the affair. The sergeant of police signalled for his boat and went off to make his report. The *Calipha* at half-speed steamed slowly for the dock.

Arrived there her passengers, crew and officers became the natural and recognised prey of the American press-man. The captain sternly refused to answer a single question, and in peremptory fashion ordered every stranger off his ship. But nevertheless his edict was avoided in the confusion of landing, and the Customs House effectually barred flight on the part of their victims. Somehow or other, no one exactly knew how or from what source they came, strange rumours began to float about. Who was Mr. J. B. Watson of New York, yacht owner and millionaire? No one had ever heard of him, and he did not answer in the least to the description of any known Watson. The closely veiled features of his widow were eagerly scanned—one by one the newspaper men confessed themselves baffled. No one had ever seen her before. One man, the most daring of them, ventured upon a timid question as she stepped down the gangway. She passed him by with a swift look of contempt. None of the others ventured anything of the sort—but, nevertheless, they watched her, and they made note of two things. The first was that there was no one to meet her—the second that instead of driving to a railway depôt, or wiring to any friends, she went straight to an hotel and engaged a room for the night.

The press-men took counsel together, and agreed that it was very odd. They thought it odder still when one of their number, calling at the hotel later in the day, was informed that Mrs. Watson, after engaging a room for the week, had suddenly changed her mind, and had left Boston without giving any one any idea as to her destination. They took counsel together, and they found fresh food for sensation in her flight. She was the only person who could throw any light upon the relations between the two men, and she had thought fit to virtually efface herself. They made the most of her disappearance in the thick black head-lines which headed every column in the Boston evening papers.

CHAPTER LI

THE PERSISTENCE OF FELIX

Of all unhappy men he is assuredly the most unhappy who, ambitious, patient, and doggedly persevering, has chosen the moment to make his supreme venture and having made it has reaped failure instead of success. The gambler while he lives may play again; the miser, robbed, embark once more upon his furtive task of hoarding money; even the rejected lover need not despair of some day, somewhere finding happiness, since no one heart has a monopoly of love. But to him who aspires to shape the destiny of nations, to control the varying interests of great powers and play upon the emotions of whole peoples, there is never vouchsafed more than one opportunity. And failure then does more than bring upon the schemer the execration of the world he would have controlled: it clears eyes into which he had thrown dust, awakens passions he had lulled to sleep, provokes hostility where he had made false peace, and renders for ever impossible the recombination of conditions under which alone he could, if at all, succeed. For such an one life has lost all its savour. Existence may perhaps be permitted to him, but no more. He stakes his all upon one single venture, and, win or lose, he has no second throw. Failure is absolute, and spells despair.

In such unhappy state was Mr. Sabin. More than ten days had passed since the tragedy in Boston Harbour, and now he sat alone in a private room in a small but exclusive hotel in New York. He had affected no small change in his appearance by shaving off his imperial and moustache, but a far more serviceable disguise was provided for him by the extreme pallor of his face and the listlessness of his every movement. He had made the supreme effort of his life and had failed; and failure had so changed his whole demeanour that had any of his recent companions on the *Calipha* been unexpectedly confronted with him it is doubtful if they would have recognised him.

For a brief space he had enjoyed some of the old zest of life in scheming for the freedom of his would-be murderer, in outwitting the police and press-men, and in achieving his own escape; but with all this secured, and in the safe seclusion of his room, he had leisure to look within himself and found himself the most miserable of men, utterly lonely, with failure to look back upon and nothing for which to hope.

He had dreamed of being a minister to France; he was an exile in an unsympathetic land. He had dreamed of restoring dynasties and readjusting the balance of power; he was an alien refugee in a republic where visionaries are not wanted and where opulence gives control. America held nothing for him; Europe had no place; there was not a capital in the whole continent where he could show himself and live. And his mind dwelt upon the contrast between what might have been and what was, he tasted for the first time the full bitterness of isolation and despair. To his present plight any alternative would be preferable—even death. He took the little revolver which lay near him on the table and thoughtfully turned it over and over in his hand. It was as it were a key with which he could unlock the portal to another world, where weariness was unknown, and where every desire was satisfied, or unfelt: and even if there were no other existence beyond this, extinction was not an idea that repelled him now. It would be an "accident"; so easy to come by; so little painful to endure. Should he? Should he not? Should he?

He was so engrossed in his own thoughts that he did not hear the soft knock at the door nor the servant murmuring the name of a visitor; but becoming conscious of the presence of some one in the room, he looked up suddenly to see a lady by his side.

"Is there not some mistake?" he said, rising to his feet. "I do not think I have the pleasure——"

She laughed and raised her veil.

"Does it make so much difference?" she asked lightly. "Yet, really, Mr. Sabin, you are more changed than I."

"I must apologize," he said; "golden hair is—most becoming. But sit down and tell me how you found me out and why."

She sank into the chair he brought for her and looked at him thoughtfully.

"It does not matter how I found you, since I did. Why I came is easily explained. I have had a cablegram from Mr. Watson."

"Good news, I hope," he said politely.

"I suppose it is," she answered indifferently. "At least your conspiracy seems to have been successful. It is generally believed that you are dead, and Mr. Watson has been pardoned and reinstated in all that once was his. And now he has sent me this cablegram asking me to join him in Germany and marry him."

Dejected as Mr. Sabin was he had not yet lost all his sense of humour. He found the idea excessively amusing.

"Let me be the first to congratulate you," he said, his twinkling eyes belying the grave courtesy of his voice. "It is the conventional happy end to a charming romance."

"Are you never serious?" she protested.

"Indeed, yes," he answered. "Forgive me for seeming to be flippant about so serious a matter as a proposal of marriage. I presume you will accept it."

"Am I to do so?" she asked gravely. "It was to ask your advice that I came here to-day."

"I have no hesitation in giving it," he declared. "Accept the proposal at once. It means emancipation for you—emancipation from a career of espionage which has nothing to recommend it. There cannot be two opinions on such a point: give up this unwholesome business and make this man, and yourself too, happy. You will never regret it."

"I wish I could be as sure of that," she said wistfully.

Mr. Sabin, with his training and natural power of seeing through the words to the heart of the speaker, could not misunderstand her, and he spoke with a gentle earnestness very moving.

"Believe me, my dear lady, when I say that to every one once at least in his life there comes a chance of happiness, although every one is not wise enough to take it. I had my chance, and I threw it away: there has never been an hour in my life since then that I have not regretted it. Let me help you to be wiser than I was. I am an old man now; I have played for high stakes and have had my share of winning; I have been involved in great affairs, I have played my part in the making of history. And I speak from experience; security lies in middle ways, and happiness belongs to the simple life. To what has my interest in things of high import brought me? I am an exile from my country, doomed to pass the small remainder of my days among a people whom I know not and with whom I have nothing in common.

"I have a heart and now I am paying the penalty for having treated badly the one woman who had power to touch it; so bitter a penalty that I would I could save you from the experiencing the like. You come to me for advice; then be advised by me. Leave meddling with affairs that are too high for you. Walk in those middle ways where safety is, and lead the simple life where alone happiness is. And let me part from you knowing that to one human being at least I have helped to give what alone is worth the having. Need I say any more?"

She took his hands and pressed them.

"Goodbye," she said. "I shall start for Germany to-morrow."

So Mr. Sabin was left free to return to his former melancholy mood; but it was not long before fresh interruption came. A servant brought a cablegram.

"Be sure you deliver my letter to Lenox," it ran, and the signature was "Felix."

He rolled the paper into a little ball and threw it on one side, and presently went into his dressing-room to change for dinner. As he came into the hall another servant brought him another cablegram. He opened it and read—

"Deliver my letter at once.—FELIX."

He tore the paper carefully into little pieces, and went into the dining-room for dinner. He dined leisurely and well, and lingered over his coffee, lost in meditation. He was still sitting so when a third servant brought him yet another cablegram—

"Remember your promise.—FELIX."

Then Mr. Sabin rose.

"Will you please see that my bag is packed," he said to the waiting man, "and let my account be prepared and brought to me upstairs. I shall leave by the night train."

CHAPTER LII

MRS. JAMES B. PETERSON, OF LENOX.

Mr. Sabin found himself late on the afternoon of the following day alone on the platform of a little wooden station, watching the train which had dropped him there a few minutes ago snorting away round a distant curve. Outside, the servant whom he had hired that morning in New York was busy endeavouring to arrange for a conveyance of some sort in which they might complete their journey. Mr. Sabin himself was well content to remain where he was. The primitiveness of the place itself and the magnificence of his surroundings had made a distinct and favourable impression upon him. Facing him was a chain of lofty hills whose foliage, luxuriant and brilliantly tinted, seemed almost like a long wave of rich deep colour, the country close at hand was black with pine trees, through which indeed a winding way for the railroad seemed to have been hewn. It was only a little clearing which had been made for the depôt; a few yards down, the line seemed to vanish into a tunnel of black foliage, from amongst which the red barked tree trunks stood out with the regularity of a regiment of soldiers. The clear air was fragrant with a peculiar and aromatic perfume, so sweet and wholesome that Mr. Sabin held the cigarette which he had lighted at arm's length, that he might inhale this, the most fascinating odour in the world. He was at all times sensitive to the influence of scenery and natural perfumes, and the possibility of spending the rest of his days in this country had never seemed so little obnoxious as during those few moments. Then his eyes suddenly fell upon a large white house, magnificent, but evidently newly finished, gleaming forth from an opening in the woods, and his brows contracted. His former moodiness returned.

"It is not the country," he muttered to himself, "it is the people."

His servant came back presently, with explanations for his prolonged absence.

"I am sorry, sir," he said, "but I made a mistake in taking the tickets."

Mr. Sabin merely nodded. A little time ago a mistake on the part of a servant was a thing which he would not have tolerated. But those were days which seemed to him to lie very far back in the past.

"You ought to have alighted at the last station, sir," the man continued. "Stockbridge is eleven miles from here."

"What are we going to do?" Mr. Sabin asked.

"We must drive, sir. I have hired a conveyance, but the luggage will have to come later in the day by the cars. There will only be room for your dressing-bag in the buggy."

Mr. Sabin rose to his feet.

"The drive will be pleasant," he said, "especially if it is through such country as this. I am not sure that I regret your mistake, Harrison. You will remain and bring the baggage on, I suppose?"

"It will be best, sir," the man agreed. "There is a train in about an hour."

They walked out on to the road where a one-horse buggy was waiting. The driver took no more notice of them than to terminate, in a leisurely way, his conversation with a railway porter, and unhitch the horse.

Mr. Sabin took the seat by his side, and they drove off.

It was a very beautiful road, and Mr. Sabin was quite content to lean back in his not uncomfortable seat and admire the scenery. For the most part it was of a luxuriant and broken character. There were very few signs of agriculture, save in the immediate vicinity of the large newly-built houses which they passed every now and then. At times they skirted the side of a mountain, and far below them in the valley the river Leine wound its way along like a broad silver band. Here and there the road passed through a thick forest of closely-growing pines, and Mr. Sabin, holding his cigarette away from him, leaned back and took long draughts of the rosinous, piney odour. It was soon after emerging from the last of these that they suddenly came upon a house which moved Mr. Sabin almost to enthusiasm. It lay not far back from the road, a very long two-storied white building, free from the over-ornamentation which disfigured most of the surrounding mansions. White pillars in front, after the colonial fashion, supported a long sloping veranda roof, and the smooth trimly-kept lawns stretched almost to the terrace which bordered the piazza. There were sun blinds of striped holland to the southern windows, and about the whole place there was an air of simple and elegant refinement, which Mr. Sabin found curiously attractive. He broke for the first time the silence which had reigned between him and the driver.

"Do you know," he inquired, "whose house that is?"

The man flipped his horse's ears with the whip.

"I guess so," he answered. "That is the old Peterson House. Mrs. James B. Peterson lives there now."

Mr. Sabin felt in his breast pocket, and extracted therefrom a letter. It was a coincidence undoubtedly, but the fact was indisputable. The address scrawled thereon in Felix's sprawling hand was:—

"By favour of Mr. Sabin."

"I will make a call there," Mr. Sabin said to the man. "Drive me up to the house."

The man pulled up his horse.

"What, do you know her?" he asked.

Mr. Sabin affected to be deeply interested in a distant point of the landscape. The man muttered something to himself and turned up the drive.

"You have met her abroad, maybe?" he suggested.

Mr. Sabin took absolutely no notice of the question. The man's impertinence was too small a thing to annoy him, but it prevented his asking several questions which he would like to have had answered. The man muttered something about a civil answer to a civil question not being much to expect, and pulled up his horse in front of the great entrance porch.

Mr. Sabin, calmly ignoring him, descended and stepped through the wide open door into a beautiful square hall in the centre of which was a billiard table. A servant attired in unmistakably English livery, stepped forward to meet him.

"Is Mrs. Peterson at home?" Mr. Sabin inquired.

"We expect her in a very few minutes," the man answered. "She is out riding at present. May I inquire if you are Mr. Sabin, sir?"

Mr. Sabin admitted the fact with some surprise.

The man received the intimation with respect.

"Will you kindly walk this way, your Grace," he said.

Mr. Sabin followed him into a large and delightfully furnished library. Then he looked keenly at the servant.

"You know me," he remarked.

"Monsieur Le Duc Souspennier," the man answered with a bow. "I am an Englishman, but I was in the service of the Marquis de la Merle in Paris for ten years."

"Your face," Mr. Sabin said, "was familiar to me. You look like a man to be trusted. Will you be so good as to remember that the Duc is unfortunately dead, and I am Mr. Sabin."

"Most certainly, sir," the man answered. "Is there anything which I can bring you?"

"Nothing, thank you," Mr. Sabin answered.

The man withdrew with a low bow, and Mr. Sabin stood for a few minutes turning over magazines and journals which covered a large round table, and represented the ephemeral literature of nearly every country in Europe.

"Mrs. Peterson," he remarked to himself, "must be a woman of Catholic tastes. Here is the *Le Petit Journal* inside the pages of the English *Contemporary Review*."

He was turning the magazines over with interest, when he chanced to glance through the great south window a few feet away from him. Something he saw barely a hundred yards from the little iron fence which bordered the lawns, attracted his attention. He rubbed his eyes and looked at it again. He was puzzled, and was on the point of ringing the bell when the man who had admitted him entered, bearing a tray with liqueurs and cigarettes. Mr. Sabin beckoned him over to the window.

"What is that little flag?" he asked.

"It is connected, I believe, in some way," the man answered, "with a game of which Mrs. Peterson is very fond. I believe that it indicates the locality of a small hole."

"Golf?" Mr. Sabin exclaimed.

"That is the name of the game, sir," the man answered. "I had forgotten it for the moment."

Mr. Sabin tried the window.

"I want to get out," he said.

The man opened it.

"If you are going down there, sir," he said, "I will send James Green to meet you. Mrs. Peterson is so fond of the game that she keeps a Scotchman here to look after the links and instruct her."

"This," Mr. Sabin murmured, "is the most extraordinary thing in the world."

"If you would like to see your room, sir, before you go out," the man suggested, "it is quite ready. If you will give me your keys I will have your clothes laid out."

Mr. Sabin turned about in amazement.

"What do you mean?" he exclaimed. "I have not come here to stay."

"I understood so, sir," the man answered. "Your room has been ready for three weeks."

Mr. Sabin was bewildered. Then he remembered the stories which he had heard of American hospitality, and concluded that this must be an instance of it.

"I had not the slightest intention of stopping here," he said to the man.

"Mrs. Peterson expected you to do so, sir, and we have sent your conveyance away. If it is inconvenient for you to remain now, it will be easy to send you anywhere you desire later."

"For the immediate present," Mr. Sabin said, "Mrs. Peterson not having arrived, I want to see that golf course."

"If you will permit me, sir," the man said, "I will show you the way."

They followed a winding footpath which brought them suddenly out on the border of a magnificent stretch of park-like country. Mr. Sabin, whose enthusiasms were rare, failed wholly to restrain a little exclamation of admiration. A few yards away was one of the largest and most magnificently kept putting-greens that he had ever seen in his life. By his side was a raised teeing-ground, well and solidly built. Far away down in the valley he could see the flag of the first hole just on the other side of a broad stream.

"The gentleman's a golf-player, maybe?" remarked a voice by his side, in familiar dialect. Mr. Sabin turned around to find himself confronted by a long, thin Scotchman, who had strolled out of a little shed close at hand.

"I am very fond of the game," Mr. Sabin admitted. "You appear to me to have a magnificent course here."

"It's none so bad," Mr. James Green admitted. "Maybe the gentleman would like a round."

"There is nothing in this wide world," Mr. Sabin answered truthfully, "that I should like so well. But I have no clubs or any shoes."

"Come this way, sir, come this way," was the prompt reply. "There's clubs here of all sorts such as none but Jimmy Green can make, ay, and shoes too. Mr. Wilson, will you be sending me two boys down from the house?"

In less than ten minutes Mr. Sabin was standing upon the first tee, a freshly lit cigarette in his mouth, and a new gleam of enthusiasm in his eyes. He modestly declined the honour, and Mr. Green forthwith drove a ball which he watched approvingly.

"That's no such a bad ball," he remarked.

Mr. Sabin watched the construction of his tee, and swung his club lightly. "Just a little sliced, wasn't it?" he said. "That will do, thanks." He addressed his ball with a confidence which savoured almost of carelessness, swung easily back and drove a clean, hard hit ball full seventy yards further than the professional. The man for a moment was speechless with surprise, and he gave a little gasp.

"Aye, mon," he exclaimed. "That was a fine drive. Might you be having a handicap, sir?"

"I am scratch at three clubs," Mr. Sabin answered quietly, "and plus four at one."

A gleam of delight mingled with respect at his opponent, shone in the Scotchman's face.

"Aye, but we will be having a fine game," he exclaimed. "Though I'm thinking you will down me. But it is grand good playing with a mon again."

The match was now at the fifteenth hole. Mr. Sabin, with a long and deadly putt—became four up and three to play. As the ball trickled into the hole the Scotchman drew a long breath.

"It's a fine match," he said, "and I'm properly downed. What's more, you're holding the record of the links up to this present. Fifteen holes for sixty-four is verra good—verra good indeed. There's no man in America to-day to beat it."

And then Mr. Sabin, who was on the point of making a genial reply, felt a sudden and very rare emotion stir his heart and blood, for almost in his ears there had sounded a very sweet and familiar voice, perhaps the voice above all others which he had least expected to hear again in this world.

"You have not then forgotten your golf, Mr. Sabin? What do you think of my little course?"

He turned slowly round and faced her. She was standing on the rising ground just above the putting-green, the skirt of her riding habit gathered up in her hand, her lithe, supple figure unchanged by time, the old bewitching smile still playing about her lips. She was still the most beautiful woman he had ever seen.

Mr. Sabin, with his cap in his hand, moved slowly to her side, and bowed low over the hand which she extended to him.

"This is a happiness," he murmured, "for which I had never dared to hope. Are you, too, an alien?"

She shook her head.

"This," she said, "is the land of my adoption. Perhaps you did not know that I am Mrs. Peterson?"

"I did not know it," he answered, gravely, "for I never heard of your marriage."

They turned together toward the house. Mr. Sabin was amazed to find that the possibilities of emotion were still so great with him.

"I married," she said softly, "an American, six years ago. He was the son of the minister at Vienna. I have lived here mostly ever since."

"Do you know who it was that sent me to you?"

She assented quietly.

"It was Felix."

They drew nearer the house. Mr. Sabin looked around him. "It is very beautiful here," he said.

"It is very beautiful indeed," she said, "but it is very lonely."

"Your husband?" he inquired.

"He has been dead four years."

Mr. Sabin felt a ridiculous return of that emotion which had agitated him so much on her first appearance. He only steadied his voice with an effort.

"We are both aliens," he said quietly. "Perhaps you have heard that all things have gone ill with me. I am an exile and a failure. I have come here to end my days."

She flashed a sudden brilliant smile upon him. How little she had changed.

"Did you say here?" she murmured softly.

He looked at her incredulously. Her eyes were bent upon the ground. There was something in her face which made Mr. Sabin forget the great failure of his life, his broken dreams, his everlasting exile. He whispered her name, and his voice trembled with a passion which for once was his master.

"Lucile," he cried. "It is true that you—forgive me?"

And she gave him her hand. "It is true," she whispered.

THE END.